## "I'm staying with you."

Shelly couldn't have heard him right. A man like Matt Collingsworth didn't put himself out for a prospective employee. But then she wouldn't have expected one of the richest men in Texas to be sitting across from her tonight, either.

"What did you say?" she asked.

"You shouldn't be alone until we know why someone tried to kill you today."

"And you're planning to serve as my bodyguard? That isn't necessary."

"Actually, it is. Family tradition, the cowboy code and all that. A real man never walks away from a woman in danger."

He'd walk away fast enough if he knew she was CIA and here to put him and his family away for life. She should be thanking her lucky stars for this entrée into the inner sanctum of the world she'd come to infiltrate. But only one word came to mind, and it seemed to be shouting inside her head and echoing through every cell of her body:

*Help!*

# JOANNA WAYNE

# LOADED

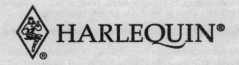

TORONTO • NEW YORK • LONDON
AMSTERDAM • PARIS • SYDNEY • HAMBURG
STOCKHOLM • ATHENS • TOKYO • MILAN • MADRID
PRAGUE • WARSAW • BUDAPEST • AUCKLAND

To all my Texas friends who so willingly share their family stories with me. To my husband for putting up with me when I'm so lost in one of my stories I forget to cook dinner or come to bed. And a special thanks to all my readers who love a cowboy tale the way I do.

ISBN-13: 978-0-373-69332-0
ISBN-10:    0-373-69332-X

LOADED

# ABOUT THE AUTHOR

Joanna Wayne was born and raised in Shreveport, Louisiana, and received her undergraduate and graduate degrees from LSU-Shreveport. She moved to New Orleans in 1984, and it was there that she attended her first writing class and joined her first professional writing organization. Her first novel, *Deep in the Bayou,* was published in 1994.

Now, dozens of published books later, Joanna has made a name for herself as being on the cutting edge of romantic suspense in both series and single-title novels. She has been on the Waldenbooks bestselling list for romance and won many industry awards. She is a popular speaker at writing organizations and local community functions and has taught creative writing at the University of New Orleans Metropolitan College.

She currently resides in a small community forty miles north of Houston, Texas, with her husband. Though she still has many family and emotional ties to Louisiana, she loves living in the Lone Star state. You may write Joanna at P.O. Box 265, Montgomery, Texas 77356.

## Books by Joanna Wayne

HARLEQUIN INTRIGUE
 795—A FATHER'S DUTY
 867—SECURITY MEASURES
 888—THE AMULET
 942—A CLANDESTINE AFFAIR
 955—MAVERICK CHRISTMAS
 975—24/7
1001—24 KARAT AMMUNITION*
1019—TEXAS GUN SMOKE*
1041—POINT BLANK PROTECTOR*
1065—LOADED*

*Four Brothers of Colts Run Cross

# CAST OF CHARACTERS

*Matt Collingsworth*—Second oldest of the Collingsworth brothers. Ranching is all he needs, until Shelly Lane turns his world upside down.

*Shelly Lane*—CIA operator. The last thing she needs is to fall for someone she's investigating.

*Langston Collingsworth*—The oldest of the Collingsworth brothers and the president of Collingsworth Oil.

*Bart and Zach Collingsworth*—Matt's other two brothers.

*Lenora Collingsworth*—Matt's mother and the CEO of Collingsworth Enterprises.

*Becky and Jaime Collingsworth*—Matt's sisters.

*David and Derrick Collingsworth*—Becky's twin sons.

*Jeremiah Collingsworth*—Matt's grandfather and Shelly's physical therapy patient.

*Juanita*—Beloved family cook.

*Ben Roberts*—CIA mole inside Collingsworth Oil.

*Melvin Rogers*—Langston's right-hand man at Collingsworth Oil and family friend.

*Billy Mack*—Neighboring rancher.

*Angelique Dubois*—Famed Houston artist.

*Brady Owens*—Shelly's supervisor.

*Leland Adams*—Cowboy who shows up at the big house with Jaime.

*Frankie Dawson*—Known for his expertise with explosives.

# Chapter One

Shelly Lane walked into the Country Café at one-forty on a Friday afternoon in the middle of June, following on the heels of Matt Collingsworth. Smells of fried chicken, cinnamon and fresh-brewed coffee greeted her. It looked like the sort of place you should seat yourself, but a short, plump woman with a knot of graying curls on top of her head was smiling and sashaying toward her.

"Hi, there," the lady said, her charming Texas drawl pulling her words into extra syllables. "You can just sit anywhere, and Jill will be around to take your order in a jiffy."

"Thanks." Shelly glanced around and noted that she was the only one eating alone. Most of the customers were family groups, though there were a few tables with just lone cowboy types. Several looked her way. Most grinned and nodded. A few waved. Colts Run Cross was a very friendly town.

Shelly located Matt—he'd joined a group of men and one super-cute young lady at a table near a window—then chose a spot where she could observe him without making it too obvious. Actually, she didn't mind him seeing her now that she was about to make contact with his mother.

The chair wobbled a bit as she slid it closer to the square

wooden table covered in a blue plaid cloth. A simple vase holding two silk daisies sat in the middle, flanked by inexpensive salt and pepper shakers and a bottle of catsup.

Her attention returned to Matt. He was far more handsome in person than in the likenesses she'd studied of him. His hair was short, dark brown and only slightly rumpled by the Western hat he'd been wearing before entering the restaurant. His jeans were worn, but clean, and though she couldn't see it now, she knew from stealthily following him about town that they showed off his lean, hard frame to perfection.

He glanced her way and smiled. A treacherous skip of her heart forced her to take a deep breath and regroup. Even the slightest attraction on her part could compromise her mission.

Jill stopped at Shelly's elbow. "The special today is fried chicken, mashed potatoes, gravy and pinto beans. That comes with corn bread or biscuits and a dish of peach cobbler and ice cream for dessert. Or you can order off the lunch menu. It's on the back."

The waitress turned the menu over and tapped the offerings with her index finger. "What would you like to drink?"

"Just tea, please, with lemon."

"Sure thing."

Jill stopped off at Matt's table, flirting shamelessly with him and his cohorts. Not that Shelly blamed her. They all had that sexy cowboy mystique about them. It was even more potent than Shelly had expected, but she knew that Matt Collingsworth was no simple cowboy. Nor was he your everyday Texas rancher.

Not only did his family own the second-largest spread in Texas, but they were sole owners of Collingsworth Enterprises, which encompassed the operations of Jack's Bluff Ranch as well as Collingsworth Oil and its related subsidiaries. Which meant they had ties to some of the most high-ranking businessmen and politicians in this country and in other key parts of the world.

The waitress arrived with the tea and Shelly ordered a grilled chicken salad, which arrived in short order. She lingered over her food, finally leaving though Matt was still engaged in a very animated conversation with the others at his table.

The sun was blinding when she stepped out the door of the small café. She fished in her handbag for her sunglasses and put them on as she crossed the street to her dark blue, nondescript sedan. She was opening the door when she spotted a black car rounding the corner, speeding toward her.

Sunlight glinted off the barrel of a revolver as it slid through the open window. Her instincts and training kicked in at the speed of light. She searched the empty streets for someone to warn, then crouched behind the car door as the sound of gunfire and bullets pinging against metal shattered the quiet afternoon.

Even if she'd had time to retrieve her weapon from the car, she wouldn't have had time to fire back. The car had roared past and she could hear the footsteps and voices of people rushing from the nearby shops, before she realized she'd been hit by a ricocheting bullet.

The keys slipped through her fingers and it felt as if a dozen wasps had all found the same spot on the back of her upper arm. Blood soaked the sleeve of her blouse. She stared; the incredulity of the situation made the facts difficult to register. This couldn't have happened. She was CIA and deep undercover. Not even her own mother knew she was in Texas.

"She's been shot," a female yelled.

But when Shelly looked up, she was staring right into the dark, piercing eyes of Matt Collingsworth. Trouble had never been more ominous—or looked so good.

## Chapter Two

*My name is Shelly Lane. I'm a physical therapist who's just arrived in Colts Run Cross and has no idea why anyone would be shooting at me.*

Shelly worked to keep the lies firmly implanted in her mind as she fought to overcome the effects of pain and unexpected vulnerability.

"Some fool fired at me from a passing car and I think a bullet ricocheted into my arm," she said, as Matt crouched down beside her.

"Is that the only place you were hit?"

"I think so."

"You're damn lucky. Your car wasn't so fortunate."

She only nodded, wondering if he was as innocent in all this as he seemed. Her experience told her to doubt him. Her instincts said differently.

"Hope this isn't your favorite blouse," Matt said, wielding a pocketknife and staring at the bloodied mess.

"No, cut away. Not the arm—just the sleeve."

"Picky, are you?" He cut away the fabric and then helped her to the sidewalk where someone had brought out a chair for her to sit on.

"The ambulance is on the way," a bystander announced.

"Who shot her?" someone else yelled.

"Some guy in a black Ford. Skidded around the corner. He's long gone now."

"Son of a bitch!"

"Probably stings like hell," Matt said, shifting so that he could get a better look. "The bullet tore into the flesh of your arm, but there are no exposed bones. A few stitches should put you back together."

He applied pressure to slow the bleeding as she dealt with the bizarre irony of having him come to her rescue. His touch was strangely heady—probably from the rush of adrenaline and the loss of blood. Still, his take-charge attitude was impressive. It was easy to understand why the ranch he comanaged with his bother Bart was so successful.

But then, organizational skills and money were exactly what was making the Collingsworths' ties to terrorists so difficult to trace. She could not let down her guard for a second.

"Who shot at you?" Matt asked.

"I have no idea."

"Do you have that many enemies?"

"I don't have any that I know of. All I know is the car came from nowhere and someone started shooting at me."

"Are you saying this was just a random drive-by?" There was no mistaking the suspicion in his voice.

She tried to move her arm so that she could see the wound.

"Probably best to keep it still," Matt said. "The ambulance will be here soon."

"I don't need an ambulance."

"Maybe not, but you have to go to the emergency room and that's as good a way as any to get there."

"Are you a doctor?"

"Nope, just a rancher. Name's Matt Collingsworth."

"Of Jack's Bluff Ranch?" She hoped there was ample surprise in her pain-laced tone.

"That's right. Have we met?"

"No, I've only been in Colts Run Cross a few days but I have an appointment with Lenora Collingsworth tomorrow at the ranch."

His eyebrows arched.

"I'm the physical therapist she hired for her father-in-law." That much was true. She'd been a physical therapist, before going back to school for a degree in criminal psychology and going to work for the CIA. Her PT background was the only reason she'd drawn this kind of major assignment so early in her career.

"Bum luck to show up in town for a new job and get shot before you even get started," Matt said.

"Do you have many drive-by shootings around here?"

"Never. This makes no sense at all."

And she could tell from his tone and expression that he liked things to make sense. She suspected he also liked being in control. He'd certainly taken over here quickly enough.

"I'll let Mom know not to expect you tomorrow—if ever. I can see how a welcome like this might convince you to turn around and go back home."

Nothing would make her willingly leave before the investigation was completed, but her supervisor was not going to like this development. If the shooting wasn't a random act of violence, then someone had to know who she was and why she was here. In that case, she'd be jerked off the assignment before she even made it to Jack's Bluff Ranch.

A siren sounded and a sheriff's squad car pulled up. A couple of uniformed lawmen jumped out, and the bystanders who had gathered around her all started talking at once.

"A bullet hit the car and…"

"No one saw the shooter, but he was in a sedan…"

"Okay, let's try to talk one at a time," one of the lawmen said. "Did anyone get the license plate number?"

"The car was a black, late-model Ford Fusion, but there was no license plate," Matt said.

"Did you see the whole thing?"

"No, I was inside the café when the shots were fired, but I raced to the window in time to get a good look at the back of the vehicle before it rounded the corner and disappeared from sight."

The lawman put up his hand to signal for quiet. "Did anyone get a look at the shooter?"

"I came running out of Flora's Antique shop when I heard the shots," an overly plump woman with heaving bosoms offered. "All I got was a glimpse of the back of the car."

The others shared similar accounts.

The lawman doing all the talking turned to Shelly. "Did you get a good look at him?"

"No. The second I saw the gun, I ducked out of the way." Which meant there were no eyewitnesses, just as the brazen shooter had no doubt intended.

"Could be some kind of gang-related initiation," one of the young cowboys who'd been sitting with Matt in the café said. "Same thing happened in New Orleans when I was there a few months back helping rebuild a church lost to Katrina."

"Well, hells bells, Charlie. This ain't New Orleans."

The ambulance arrived, and two paramedics jumped out and ran toward her. One started tending the wound that was now only oozing blood. The other commenced with a series of routine questions about the injury and about any allergies she had.

"Let's just hold on here a minute," the lawman-in-charge

interrupted. "I need the victim to answer a couple of questions before you go rushing her to the hospital, seeing as how she's not in dire need of emergency medical care."

He introduced himself as Sheriff Ed Guerra, and she told him her name.

"So, Miss Lane, do you know why anyone would be taking pot shots at you?"

"Absolutely not. I don't know anyone in Colts Run Cross except the people I've met over the last four days. They were all very friendly."

"So you just moved here?"

"I've been staying at the motel on the highway, but I came here to work for the Collingsworths. I'm a physical therapist."

The sheriff and Matt exchanged glances.

"She's supposed to work with Jeremiah," Matt said.

The sheriff nodded and nudged his cowboy hat back a bit farther. "Where are you from?"

"Atlanta."

"That's a long commute."

"I needed a change of scenery and I've always wanted to visit Texas."

"How did you hear about a job at Jack's Bluff Ranch?"

"I found the *Houston Chronicle* classifieds online and saw the Collingsworths' ad."

He nodded and scratched his clean-shaven chin. "Guess that makes sense. The rest of my questions can wait until you get that arm cleaned and stitched." He nodded to the medics. "She's all yours."

She let them load her into the ambulance. Her arm still hurt, but her biggest problem right now was finding out who had shot at her and why—before her supervisor determined she wasn't the person for this assignment.

If he found out that she'd let Matt Collingsworth get to her for even a second, he'd pull her anyway. But he needn't worry. She was focused now and would make sure that Matt's masculine sexuality and piercing eyes did not affect her again.

Her mission was to infiltrate the family and ferret out the full truth, an accomplishment that would likely destroy the Collingsworth empire and send at least some of the family members to prison for the rest of their lives.

She'd do the legwork. A judge and jury would decide the rest.

"THE PATIENT'S AWAKE NOW, Lenora. You can go in, but don't expect her to be too talkative. That pain medication is making her drowsy."

"I just want to say hello and make sure she doesn't need anything." Lenora knocked and then entered the hospital room where her would-be new employee lay beneath a pale blue blanket with an IV attached to her right arm. Her eyes were watchful as Lenora stepped to the side of the bed.

"I'm Lenora Collingsworth."

Shelly smiled and tried to push up on her elbows, giving up on the idea quickly and dropping back to the pillow. "It's nice to finally meet you, though this isn't exactly how I'd pictured the moment."

She had a nice smile and a sense of humor. She was attractive, too, with short brown hair specked with gold, and half bangs that set off her beautiful gold-green eyes.

Lenora placed her hand on the bed rail. "I can't believe this happened after I assured you that you were coming to a safe area. But in all honesty, I don't remember a single case of a random, drive-by shooting in Colts Run Cross. In parts of Houston, yes. But never in our community."

"It wasn't your fault," Shelly said. "In hindsight, I should have come straight to the ranch, but it's my first visit to Texas and I wanted to do a bit of sightseeing before I began work."

"Well, at least you got to do that. I don't want to tire you, but I wanted to let you know how sorry I am and to make certain you have everything you need."

"I appreciate that, but I don't plan to be in this bed long. The doctor stitched me back together and is giving me antibiotics and some pain medication. He says I'll be good as new soon. I'll likely leave the hospital tomorrow."

"Where will you go?"

"Back to the motel, I guess. I can't expect you to provide room and board until this arm heals and I can start work."

"Nonsense," Lenora said, relieved that Shelly wasn't planning to renege on their agreement. "You can have all the time you need to heal at the ranch. It will give you a chance to get to know Jeremiah before you start treating him. As I told you on the phone, he's a bit cantankerous since the stroke. Well, more than a bit at times, but he can be loveable when he wants to be."

"That would be great—if you're sure I won't be imposing."

"Not at all. I'll check with the hospital in the morning," Lenora said. "If the doctor releases you, I'll either pick you up myself or have someone else in the family do it, depending on their schedules. Whoever drives you to the ranch can stop off at the motel for your luggage. In the meantime, I'll have the housekeeper get your room ready."

"I have my own car, still parked on the street in front of the café."

"Matt had it towed to Hank Tanner's body shop once the sheriff and his men had finished examining it. Hank will keep it there until you have a chance to look at it and decide what you want done. No strings attached."

"So the vehicle was examined?"

"Yes, of course, dear. Ed Guerra and his department are very efficient. And don't worry about the cost of the bodywork on your vehicle. I'll cover whatever your insurance doesn't. It's the least I can do."

"I couldn't ask you to do that."

"I insist."

"Thanks. That's a very generous offer, but I'm sure the insurance will handle it. I guess all I have to do now is give my arm a little time to heal. I can't wait to actually get started."

"Just hold on to that attitude once you meet Jeremiah."

"I promise."

Lenora had a feeling that this was going to work out perfectly in spite of the troublesome start. The shooting still worried her, but she'd checked Shelly's references thoroughly. There was no reason to think this was any more than a random shooting perpetrated by some hoodlum who'd been high on drugs. It was the sheriff's job to take care of that.

The positive news was that a smart, attractive woman who was unfazed by gunfire could surely handle Jeremiah. She might even be able to stir a little romantic excitement in Matt. If any man needed a woman, it was him—not that he'd ever admit it.

Lenora found herself humming as she left the hospital. This just might turn into a very memorable summer. In fact, she was counting on it.

"SHOT AT FROM A PASSING CAR right on Main Street?" Incredulity colored Jaime's tone and lit up her eyes. "And just when I was thinking of moving into Houston to add a little excitement to my ho-hum life."

"It's not funny," Lenora said. "She could have been killed."

"Sorry, Mom. I didn't mean it that way. But you have to admit it's unusual. There has to be more to the story than that."

"Things like this happen in big cities all the time," Lenora said. "It was inevitable it would make its way out here eventually. There's no reason to believe Shelly did anything to provoke the attempt on her life."

Matt had known the topic of the shooting would come up sooner or later. In fact, he was surprised they'd made it all the way through dinner before Lenora had approached the subject.

They'd gathered on the huge screened back porch, and since it was Friday, several extended family members were still sitting around catching up on the week's happenings.

The shooting had been front and center on Matt's mind all afternoon, and the more he thought about it, the more he was convinced that the best news for them would be if Shelly Lane decided to pack her bags and move right back to Atlanta. She might be totally innocent in all of this, but the odds were that she wasn't.

"Tell me more about this woman," Langston said, after Lenora had given them the few details they knew about the gunfire incident. Langston was the oldest, the head honcho of Collingsworth Oil. He had a cabin at the ranch, but lived in Houston during the week with his pregnant wife Trish and teenage daughter Gina.

"Shelly seems really nice," Lenora said. "And mature for her age. A lot of young women would have panicked and been ready to clear out of town as fast as they could. She only wants to heal and start working with Jeremiah."

"How old is she?" Trish asked.

"Twenty-nine," Lenora said. "But she's experienced and a very competent physical therapist. I checked her credentials thoroughly before hiring her."

"Twenty-nine. Very interesting. And single, I'm guessing, since she's moving in with us." Jaime added. "And Matt's thirty-three. How convenient, not that Mom would ever play matchmaker." That brought a few laughs.

Matt groaned. His mother had managed to manipulate him into situations with half the single women in Colts Run Cross over the last few months. He hadn't taken the bait then and he wouldn't be biting this time, either, certainly not with a city girl out here for a change of scenery.

"This isn't about Matt," Lenora said. "It's about Jeremiah."

His grandfather picked that moment to join them on the porch. He propped his cane against the old wicker couch and dropped to the cushioned seat. "What about me?"

"I've hired a physical therapist," Lenora said. "She's from Georgia, but she's going to live with us and help you regain your balance and strength."

He sputtered and muttered a few curses under his breath. "If I wanted to be manhandled by a woman, I'd have remarried."

Trish walked over and sat down by Jeremiah. She had a way with the old codger, but then she pretty much had a way with everyone.

"Having a live-in therapist seems the perfect solution to me," Trish said. "You never want to go to your appointments. This way you won't have to."

"I don't go to therapy because the sessions don't do a dad-gummed bit of good. If they did, I wouldn't be hobbling around here like some useless old man, now would I?"

"You limp," Trish admitted. "But you could never be useless."

I've hired Shelly Lane," Lenora said. "If you want to get rid of that cane, you'll cooperate with her. If you're too hard-headed to work with her, then it will be your loss. She's moving in tomorrow." Lenora dusted her hands as if that were the end of the matter, but that didn't mean it was.

"Tomorrow?" Jaime questioned. "I thought this new physical therapist was in the hospital."

Lenora kicked off her black sandals and pulled a foot into the chair with her, settling it under her full black skirt. "If not tomorrow, then the next day. She's coming here to recuperate."

"Are you sure that's a good idea?" Langston questioned.

"Why wouldn't it be? She doesn't have anywhere else to go," Lenora said. "Besides, it will give her a chance to get to know Jeremiah before she starts working with him."

"Yeah, like that's an advantage," Jaime mocked.

Matt's muscles tightened. "I know you mean well, Mom, but you can't just move her onto the ranch until we have more facts about today's attack."

"What's to know?" Lenora asked. "She was just crossing the street and someone started firing at her. You were the one who told me what happened, Matt. That's why I went to the hospital to check on her."

"That's the way it looked," Matt said, "and the way Shelly told it, but at this point there's no way to know she's leveling with us. The shooter could be someone she knows."

Jeremiah swung his cane in the air, banging it into the leg of a table and sending a half-empty glass of iced tea into a wobbling dance that fortunately ended without the glass hitting the floor. "Don't know what this world's coming to, but if some sick bastard's trying to kill her, you ought to already have her out here. Can't expect a woman to take care of herself."

"Right," Jaime said, mocking him. "What would we ever do without a man to take care of us?"

"Let's get back to Shelly Lane," Langston said. "She's probably as innocent in all this as she claims, but to be on the safe side, I'd like to have Clay Markham investigate her before we move her onto Jack's Bluff. He's as competent a private detective as you'll find anywhere in Texas, and Collingsworth Oil has him on retainer."

"And I say we get Aidan Jefferies to run a police background check on her as well," Matt said. "If they both clear her, then Mom can move her in with no worries." Aidan was one of Langston's closest friends and a Houston homicide detective.

"How long are we talking about for these investigations?" Lenora asked.

"A few days at most," Langston assured her. "Actually, they'll probably know by tomorrow night if she's had any other attempts on her life or reported any type of threats. They'll definitely know if she has a police record of any kind."

"I guess I can live with that," Lenora said, "though I hate to tell her that I'm going back on my offer to move her out here tomorrow. And I don't like the idea of her going back to that motel all alone."

"Have the doctor keep her in the hospital," Matt said. "I don't know why he'd object to that, as long as we pick up the tab."

"I suppose that's an option," Lenora said. "And tomorrow's probably not the best day to have her out here, anyway, what with children from the Turnaround Program coming out for the day."

Matt groaned. "That's tomorrow?"

"Yes, and you promised to help with the horse riding,"

Lenora said, smoothing her short graying hair. "I'll give Shelly's doctor a call, but I guess I should go back into town tonight and break the news to Shelly in person."

"I'll do it," Matt said, suddenly uneasy with his mother becoming too involved with Shelly before they had an official report.

"Okay, but don't tell her the delay is because we're having her investigated. Just say I'm getting her room ready so that everything will be perfect when she arrives."

Matt shrugged. "Sorry, Mom, I'm not into sugarcoating."

"Just be nice," Lenora said. "Miss Lane's welcome to Texas has already been traumatic enough."

"I'm always nice."

"Compared to what?" Jaime asked. "A striking rattle-snake?"

"Just because I'm not a pushover for a smile and a pretty face doesn't mean I'm unsociable."

"Pretty, huh?" Jaime smiled tauntingly. "This story just keeps getting better. But I'll have to hear the rest tomorrow. I've got a date with Tommy Stevens tonight, and he should be here to pick me up any minute."

"When did you start dating him?" Trish asked. "I thought you were back with Garth."

"Not anymore. All he thinks about is running off to some new rodeo competition. Like at twenty-five, don't you think he'd have better things to do than try to stay on a stupid bull?"

Matt would have thought the guy had better things to do than date Jaime. She was as fickle as a mare at breeding time. But all she had to do was crook her finger and Garth—and half the male population of south Texas—came running. He hoped someone would shoot him if he ever got that crazy about any woman.

His cell phone rang. He checked the caller ID: sheriff's

office. He walked to the kitchen to take the call. Ten to one this had to do with Shelly Lane, and the odds were even better that it was not good news.

# Chapter Three

"What's up, Ed?" Matt asked as soon as the sheriff identified himself.

"I just talked to Emile Henley up at the Shell Station on the highway west of town. He said a stranger in a black Ford Fusion stopped for gas at his place about an hour before today's shooting."

"That's interesting. Did he think the man might have been drunk or high on something?"

"Nope, just buck-snorting arrogant according to Emile. He said he tried to make small talk when the guy came inside for cigarettes, but the man just made some comment about Colts Run Cross being a hick town and stomped away."

"Did he notice if the car had a license plate on it at the time?"

"Said he didn't notice."

"But he likely would have if the plate had been missing. The culprit probably removed it just before opening fire on Shelly Lane."

"That's what I'm thinking as well. I'd be careful if I was you about moving her onto the ranch. She seems nice enough, but truth is she might be mixed up in most anything."

"I'm in solid agreement. If it were up to me, I'd write out

a check for her time and expenses and say adios, but Mom is championing her case—as if she were the only qualified PT north of the border."

"I hear you, and your mother can be a stubborn woman at times. Can you call Miss Lane to the phone?"

"I'd have to yell awful loud. I'm out at the ranch."

"Isn't she there with you?"

"No, why would you think that?"

"I stopped by the hospital a few minutes ago to question her and the nurse said she checked herself out and told them she would be spending the night at Jack's Bluff Ranch. I figured Lenora had picked her up."

"No, Mom's been here all evening. So have I. Shelly Lane is definitely not here."

"This case is getting weirder by the minute."

"Is there something more about her past?"

"Not a lot. I ran her through the system. Everything checks out. No warrants out for her arrest. No rap sheet. Not even an outstanding parking ticket."

"So you're thinking this might have actually been a case of random violence?"

"Could be. There's been a rash of them in southeast Houston of late. We're less than an hour and a half out of the city so it's reasonable that some of the hoods down there might have connections up here. But then there was the gun."

"Are you saying you found the weapon?"

"Not the perp's, but when we were checking Miss Lane's vehicle for ballistic evidence, I found a loaded Smith & Wesson .45 in her busted-up glove compartment. It might mean nothing. Lots of women traveling alone carry high-powered pistols these days."

"But it could mean she was afraid of someone," Matt said, "someone who followed her to Texas."

"Exactly."

As far as Matt was concerned, this was beginning to look more and more like the pretty little PT had better reasons than a need for change of scenery for taking a job so far from home. And now she'd lied about where she'd be tonight.

But no matter what she'd told the nurse at the hospital, it was a sure thing she wouldn't be spending tonight, or any other night, at Jake's Bluff Ranch until he got to the bottom of this.

FORTUNATELY FOR SHELLY, Hank Tanner's Garage and Body Shop was on Birch, a quiet side street of mostly closed family-owned businesses less than a mile from the hospital. It should have been an easy twilight walk except that the temperature was still in the eighties and the humidity seemed higher still.

Perspiration wet her underarms and dripped into her eyes. Worse, her arm had stated to throb. Wiping her face with a tissue from her pocket, she crossed the street and turned the corner, thankful when she spotted the sign for the garage in the next block. Her spirits lifted more when she saw her car parked at the side of the old clapboard building.

Hopefully her weapon was still in place. The sheriff would have surely checked the damaged vehicle for ballistics evidence, but he'd have had no reason to check her locked glove compartment. But then he probably had the keys. She didn't remember giving them to anyone, but either she had or she'd dropped them when she got shot.

Stepping over a crack in the sidewalk, she cut across the corner of the parking lot, walked around the rear of an old pickup truck and got her first good look at the extent of the damage to her vehicle.

The whole side of the car was riddled with bullet holes.

She hadn't gotten a good look at the weapon, but judging from the size and number of holes, it must have been a large automatic. Her nerves grew edgy as it hit her how close she'd come to getting killed.

Attacked in broad daylight on the main street of Colts Run Cross. She could see why that might rouse both the sheriff's and Matt Collingsworth's suspicions, but what else could it be except random violence?

The only people with reason not to want her here were the Collingsworths, and it was almost inconceivable that they could have learned her identity this quickly. And even if they had, a careless, open attack like this wasn't their style.

She let her fingers slide over the damage, then walked to the passenger-side door, opened it and climbed inside. The vehicle wasn't locked, but even if it had been, entry would have been easy enough with two windows shot out.

Her spirits plunged at the first glimpse inside the glove compartment. The contents—including her weapon—were missing.

There was the possibility that Hank Tanner had her belongings inside for safekeeping, but more likely the sheriff had confiscated them. No problem there. The car and gun registrations would check out.

Still, it was amazing how vulnerable she felt without her weapon, despite the fact that she hadn't carried it on her body since arriving in Colts Run Cross. It didn't fit the PT persona and chancing someone noticing that she was carrying a weapon would constitute an unnecessary risk when there was no reason to think she was in any kind of danger.

Her cell phone vibrated—not her regular phone but the CIA one, disguised as a compact. It was her signal to call in at her earliest convenience unless she was free to take the call. She wished she could ignore it, because it was likely her supervisor and she wasn't sure she was ready to handle Brady Owens just yet. She took a deep breath and leaned against the car.

"Shelly Lane," she said, identifying herself.

"I got the word you've been shot," Brady said, without bothering with a greeting. "Are you okay?"

"Yeah, or I will be in a few days. It was only a flesh wound. Left arm. Random violence. Nothing to worry about—really."

"Any complication is reason for worry. Where are you?"

"At Hank Tanner's Garage, standing by my vehicle."

"Who's with you?"

"I'm alone. I wouldn't have answered otherwise."

"I'm just checking."

To see if the accident had somehow addled her brain and made her a risk. The Collingsworth case was Brady's baby and he'd made it clear that he wasn't comfortable with her lack of experience. She was certain he'd be even less thrilled with her now.

"I'm totally aware of the seriousness of this case, sir, but things are under control. What I meant is there's no reason the assignment shouldn't still be a go."

"That will be my decision. I haven't made it yet."

"Yes, sir."

"Have there been any new developments since you called in the report?"

"Nothing except that I've left the hospital."

"Were you released?"

"No, sir, but the wound is too insignificant to require hospitalization. I'll go back in tomorrow to have it checked."

"See that you do that. Is there anything else I should know?"

"My weapon was locked in the glove compartment of my

car at the time of the shooting incident. It's missing. I assume either the mechanic took it for safekeeping or the sheriff has it. Either way, I'm sure I'll get it back."

"Just be sure to explain it away convincingly. Do you think there is any chance the Collingsworths were behind the attack?"

"I'm all but certain they weren't. Matt Collingsworth was inside the restaurant when it occurred and was the first to come to my rescue."

"So I heard. That doesn't mean he couldn't have ordered a hit. With his money, hired guns are easy to come by."

"But we have no evidence that any of the Collingsworths have ever used a paid assassin," Shelly countered. "And Lenora Collingsworth visited me at the hospital. She seemed extremely apologetic about the shooting incident and has asked me to move to the ranch tomorrow. That would be the last thing she'd do if she knew I was with the CIA."

"It would seem that way, unless you're walking into a trap."

"They're not going to shoot me in cold blood," Shelly said. "They use money and influence—not guns—to get what they want." Shelly knew that Brady would have a difficult time denying that.

Besides, she was his best chance—maybe his only chance—to get an agent inside the family circle, and they needed that edge to push things off dead center.

They'd had a mole inside Collingsworth Oil for months. Ben Hartmann was an experienced agent and talented computer hacker, but as yet he hadn't acquired the proof to seal the case. No proof that the Collingsworths were GAS, Ben's term for suspects once they had indisputable evidence that they were *guilty as sin*.

"We've spent weeks setting this up," she argued. "Unless

there's a serious leak in our department, no one could possibly have found out why I'm really here. It would be a major setback if we called this off just because some two-bit hood with a point to prove to his fellow gang members shot up my car."

"The random violence angle is a huge assumption, Shelly. You know what I think about assumptions."

"Yes, sir." But he also knew there was always a gamble in this type of operation.

"I'd like to hear your firsthand, no-spin account of today's shooting incident."

She filled him in on the details, leaving nothing out—except for her ridiculous and very momentary attraction to Matt Collingsworth. He listened without questions until she'd finished.

Then the silence on the line seemed thick with apprehension. She knew he was rethinking everything, especially her inexperience. She didn't breathe easy until she heard the muffled clicking of his tongue against the roof of his mouth, a clear signal that he was giving in. All the agents recognized the telltale habit.

"Proceed as planned, while I have this checked into, Shelly. But watch your back and stay on high alert. Never underestimate a Collingsworth."

"That's a given."

Once the connection was broken, she stepped outside the car and looked around. It was almost completely dark now and a sliver of moon hung just over the top of a cluster of sweet gum trees on the opposite side of the street.

There were a couple of other businesses on the block—a machine shop and a tree-trimming business. Both were closed with no sign of life around the buildings, except a black cat, crouched near a trash bin, cautiously watching Shelly.

A welcome gust of wind caught an empty bag and blew it across the parking lot depositing it under Shelly's banged-up vehicle. Thankfully it was not actually her car, but one the agency had purchased specifically for this assignment.

A pickup truck turned the corner onto Birch, the beam from its headlights fanning her for an instant before returning to the street. The driver slowed, and in spite of her mental reassurances of safety, her nerves skittered nervously.

It's a small town, she told herself as the driver pulled into the parking lot a few feet away. He was probably just curious why a woman would be out here all alone. Still, she'd feel a lot safer with her weapon in hand. Today's close call had been an excellent reminder that she wasn't invincible.

The car stopped, and she got her first good luck at the driver. Her muscles clenched. This wasn't a curious passerby.

He was here to find her.

## Chapter Four

Matt slid from behind the wheel and stood by the side of his truck, his gaze fixed on Shelly. Her face and eyes were shadowed, her features blurred in the early-evening darkness. She looked pale, but her shoulders were squared and her mouth was set in hard lines as if she was determined not to let the situation get the better of her.

An unexpected protective urge surged inside him as his focus moved to her bandaged arm and then to the bullet-battered car.

"We've got to stop meeting like this," she quipped, but her attempt at humor lost its effect to the eerie screech of an owl hidden in the branches of a nearby tree.

Matt looked around, expecting to see Hank standing nearby. He didn't. The place was completely deserted except for Shelly.

"What are you doing here after hours?" he asked.

Shelly brushed her bangs to one side and propped her right hand on her hip almost defiantly. "I could ask you the same thing."

"I was looking for you," he admitted. "I tried your motel. When you weren't there, I drove here to see if Hank had heard from you."

"How did you know I'd left the hospital?"

"The sheriff called me. Apparently you told the nursing staff you were going to Jack's Bluff tonight."

She shrugged and looked backed to the car as he stepped closer. "I didn't exactly tell them that. They just surmised it and I didn't set them straight. It seemed the easiest way to walk out of the hospital without causing a major ruckus."

"Why not just wait until the doctor released you?"

"I hate hospitals and I didn't see any point in running up a big hospital bill when I didn't need to be there in the first place."

Matt scanned the quiet parking lot. "How did you get here?"

"I walked. It's not that far." She slapped at a mosquito that was buzzing around her ear. "I'm fine, Matt. And I don't hold your family responsible for any of this, if that's what you're worried about."

"I'm not worried at all." Unfortunately, that wasn't exactly true. Pretty much everything about Shelly Lane worried him—and puzzled him—especially the fact that she was standing on a deserted street alone at night after being shot at just hours ago.

He didn't trust this whole situation, wasn't at all convinced that Shelly didn't know who'd tried to kill her. Yet if she did, that would give her all the more reason not to put herself at risk like this.

He stepped between her and the car. "Are you in some kind of trouble, Shelly?"

"No. Why would you ask that? You were there when some crackpot roared in from nowhere and used my car for target practice."

"The other possibility is that he'd come to town looking for you."

"Don't be ridiculous. I don't even know anyone around this part of the country."

"Maybe someone followed you from Atlanta. Maybe a jealous boyfriend? A jilted lover?"

"The last boyfriend is engaged to be married to a fashion model. He forgot me at the first sight of my replacement—who I introduced him to, no less."

Matt doubted that any man had found Shelly that easy to forget, but he wasn't going there now. He pressed a hand on the top of the car and leaned into it. "Do you always carry a loaded gun in your glove compartment?"

She turned to look at his truck and the shotgun riding the rack behind his seat. "Obviously there's no local law against carrying weapons in a vehicle."

"Touché."

"Actually, one of my friends insisted I buy it before leaving Atlanta. She kept stressing how it wasn't safe for a woman to drive so far by herself, said I might have car trouble and get stranded in a dangerous area. Who knew the danger would be in Colts Run Cross?"

Which is what made this so difficult to buy into. He watched as the breeze teased her bangs, blowing wispy strands of hair about her forehead.

"I'm shaken, Matt. I won't deny it. My first instinct was to go running back to Atlanta. But running from random violence is like trying to get out of the path of a tornado. It can strike anywhere."

"But both are more likely in some places than others." The owl screeched again and mosquitoes were starting to treat the back of his neck like a buffet. Whatever was going on with Shelly Lane, he was pretty sure he wasn't going to get to the bottom of it tonight.

Matt rocked back on the heels of his boots. "No point in

hanging around out here," he said. "I can give you a ride back to your motel."

"Thanks."

And on the way he'd tell her that her plan to move to the ranch tomorrow had been put on hold.

They walked back to his truck in silence and he opened the door for her. He circled the vehicle, climbed behind the wheel, turned the key in the ignition and gunned the engine. The beams of his headlights illuminated the damaged side of Shelly's car as he backed from the lot.

His hands tightened on the wheel as the reality of the situation settled into a grim knot in his stomach. If the attack on her was personal, the guy wouldn't just give up because the first try didn't work. The shooter might even be a hired hit man biding his time until he could get to her again. Maybe waiting for dark, when she was alone in a motel at the edge of town.

A spray of gravel shot from the back wheels of his pickup truck as he sped away from Hank's. He couldn't take her to the ranch when no one knew for certain she was on the up and up. But he couldn't just dump her to fend for herself if she was in real danger.

So where did that leave him?

SHELLY SAT UP STRAIGHTER, staring at the neon sign identifying the rambling wooden roadhouse whose parking lot they'd just pulled into as Cutter's Bar and Grill.

"Why are you stopping here?"

"I could use a cup of coffee," Matt said.

"I don't drink coffee this late," she said.

"Then how about a beer?"

"I can't drink alcohol. I'm still feeling the effects of the pain medication they gave me at the hospital. Besides I'm not dressed for going out."

That wasn't exactly a valid argument since she had on the same jeans she'd had on at lunch today. Topping them was the crimson cami she'd had on under the bloodied blouse that Matt had cut the sleeves out of. There was a blood stain on it, but it so closely matched the color of the shirt, it looked more like fabric shading. Her attire would likely be the same as half the women in the bar.

"You look fine," Matt said, "and I could really use the coffee."

She hesitated, then pulled down the visor and checked her reflection in the small lighted mirror. "I at least have to put on some lipstick," she said, already reaching in her handbag for a tube. She'd have never gone out in D.C. looking like this, but she wasn't in the nation's capital and this wasn't a date. It was her job. This might be the perfect opportunity to start winning Matt's confidence.

Matt took her arm as they crossed the parking lot and walked through the open doorway. Shelly took in the sights and the atmosphere.

Cute cowboys in Western shirts, jeans and boots perched on worn wooden barstools and drank beer from bottles and whiskey and Tequila from shot glasses. Couples filled the dance floor, two-stepping to a slow country ballad.

Matt exchanged waves and greetings with some of the patrons as he led Shelly to the left side of the main room, away from the bar and dance floor. Couples and small groups were enjoying late dinners. Odors of fried onions and peppery spices hung heavy in the air; there was a refreshing absence of stale cigarette smoke and Shelly assumed Cutter's Bar had followed suit with many other Texas restaurants and bars and allowed smoking only outside the building.

Most of the patrons were in their early to mid twenties,

but there were some older customers as well, including a group of six women who looked to be their late fifties.

They seemed to be having the most fun of all, laughing and talking loudly. One of the older women caught Matt's eye and waved him over. The other women at the table seemed equally as delighted to see him as Shelly and Matt maneuvered through the maze of tables and mismatched chairs.

Shelly knew from her research that all the Collingsworths were not only well-liked but respected throughout this part of Texas. Watching Matt, it was easy to see why. He wore his wealth the way she might wear a pair of old jeans. Easy. Comfortably. Free of even the slightest pretension.

"This table looks like solid trouble," Matt said, leaning over to kiss the cheek of the one who'd initially spotted him. "What are you gorgeous hens doing out without the roosters?"

"They're all over in Austin at a cattle auction, so we decided to hit the town."

"Look out, cowboys," Matt said.

"Land sakes, we don't want them," one woman said.

"Right," another agreed. "We just got rid of our own. We're just here to eat someone else's cooking."

"And have company that doesn't moo."

They all laughed again and Matt introduced Shelly to the rancher's wives. She felt an unexpected twinge of guilt that they accepted her so readily when she was here under false pretenses. But how could these women, or anyone else in this town possibly know the traitorous paths that the Collingsworths had followed?

Make that had *allegedly* followed, but the evidence against them was overwhelming—just not indisputable as yet.

Matt spoke and waved to several more people before they finally stopped at a table near the back, where it was only slightly quieter. He held her chair for her, then took the seat opposite hers. She was keenly aware that in a bar full of sexy cowboys, he still stood out.

It wasn't his looks that set him apart, though he certainly held his own in that department. It was his self-confidence, Shelly decided. He was a man who knew who he was and what he was about.

A waitress sashayed over, and true to his word, Matt ordered a black coffee.

"If you're hungry, they have great burgers here," he said. "Good chicken-fried steaks, too."

Shelly had learned quickly that battered and fried steak— as big as the plate and covered in thick cream gravy—was a staple of every restaurant in this part of Texas. She'd tried it, and loved it. Then promptly gave it up before she gained too much weight to fit into the new jeans she'd purchased for this assignment.

"I can bring you a menu," the waitress said. "Kitchen's open until midnight."

"Thanks, but I won't need one. The burger sounds good."

"With cheese, jalapenos, onion rings?"

"Just cheese. And a glass of iced tea, unsweetened."

Shelly wasn't hungry, though she'd barely touched her dinner at the hospital. But picking at food would be less awkward than having nothing to do but stare at Matt, while he bombarded her with questions that she'd be forced to answer with rehearsed lies.

She was certain that's what this coffee date was about. He was obviously suspicious of the day's events and determined to check her out. That convinced her even more that neither he nor his family had any idea who she really was. All she had to do was play this cool and she'd soon be living inside the gates of Jack's Bluff Ranch.

"Don't you drink beer?" she asked when the waitress walked away.

"Occasionally. Mostly I'm a whiskey man, but I had a drink after dinner and I figure that's enough. I have an early day tomorrow"

"It's Saturday."

"Cows don't know that. Besides, I'm helping out with one of Mom's do-gooder events tomorrow."

"What does that entail?"

"This is her Turnaround Project where she brings a group of inner-city preteens out to get a feel for ranch life. They're kids who've been in trouble in school and sometimes with the law. Behaviorally something or other."

"Behaviorally challenged?"

"That's it. Or as Jeremiah says, undisciplined brats. They usually come in with huge chips on their shoulders, but by the time they leave, most are strutting around and grinning like rodeo champs."

"Sounds interesting."

"For the most part." The waitress returned with Matt's coffee and Shelly's tea. "Tell me about you," he said, once the waitress walked away.

"What do you want to know?"

"Guess we should start with the basics."

"Name, rank and serial number?"

"I was thinking more along the line of why a woman from the big city is looking to work in Colts Run Cross?"

"A thirst for adventure, though today's excitement wasn't exactly what I had in mind."

"Were you giving private, live-in care in Atlanta?"

"No, I worked for a rehab center." She told him something about the setting and the work, all verifiable if he checked.

"I take it you're not married," Matt said.

"No. I came close once. It didn't work out. What about you?" she asked, though she knew he was single.

"Never came close."

"That's hard to believe."

"Why?"

He stared at her with his steely gray, almost brooding eyes, and a tingle that felt far too much like anticipation zinged along her nerve endings. This was completely unlike her—and too dangerous and unprofessional for words.

She forced herself to picture Matt with huge warts on his nose and thick bushy eyebrows that jutted out like porcupine quills.

"It's just that most men have either been married or had a close call or two by the time they reach your age," she said, going for an easy nonchalance.

He smiled, and the warts vanished. "I have a few more years before Medicare kicks in."

She blushed in spite of herself. "I didn't mean that the way it came out."

"It's okay. The truth is, I'm not the marrying kind."

"Tell me about Jeremiah," Shelly said, hoping to get the conversation on safer ground. "Your mother indicated he can be a bit difficult at times."

"She said that, did she? Let's just say that dealing with my grandfather on a daily basis will make this afternoon's trouble seem like a bad dream."

She grimaced. "That bad, huh?"

Matt worried the handle of his mug. "Before the stroke, my grandfather was the CEO of Collingsworth Enterprises and went into his Houston office five days a week. The only concession he'd made to aging was that he'd hired a driver a few years back to fight the traffic for him while he read the morning paper and made phone calls.

"Now he refuses to set foot in the building. He claims he's not interested, but we all know that he just doesn't want to go back there and have his former employees see him hobbling around and relying on the cane."

Jeremiah's stroke had caused a few problems for the CIA, as well. As CEO and with a reputation for being a hard-edge and aggressive businessman, he'd been the focus of their initial investigation. They'd suspected that he might be totally responsible for the terrorist funding in exchange for favorable business deals and that the rest of the family might not even be aware of his illegal dealings.

But when he'd suffered the stroke and disappeared from the picture, the illegal and traitorous activities had actually surged, making it obvious that at least one other member of the family was in on the illegal scheme, perhaps even Lenora Collingsworth who'd replaced Jeremiah as CEO.

"So lots of luck with the old codger," Matt said.

"Thanks. I have a feeling I'll need it."

The waitress returned and placed the burger in front of Shelly. The mammoth toasted bun spilled over with leafy green lettuce and thick slices of the bright red, home-grown tomatoes Shelly had gotten used to since arriving in Colts Run Cross.

Not surprisingly, her appetite sprang to life. Halfway through the burger, she let her gaze scan the row of men and women seated at the bar. A tall, lanky man on the end was staring back at her.

He was in his late twenties, she'd guess, with light brown hair that crawled into his shirt collar. No visible tattoos, but his nose had a slight crook to it as if it had been broken and not reset properly. Still, he was cute enough in a rugged sort of way.

When their gazes locked, he tipped his beer in her direction as if they might have met before. He was probably just one of the locals she'd crossed paths with over the past few days. Still, a wary tremble of foreboding slithered up her spine. She couldn't afford to have someone from her distant past show up and recognize her as shy little Ann Clark from Biloxi, Mississippi.

But he'd seemingly forgotten her now and was flirting with a young woman who'd just sidled in beside him at the bar. Shelly pushed the rest of the burger away. "Do you mind if we go now, Matt? My arm is starting to throb a bit."

"No problem." He motioned to the waitress for their check.

"Do you know what time Lenora is picking me up tomorrow?" Shelly asked. "I'd like to be packed and ready to go when she arrives."

Matt propped his elbows on the table and leaned in closer. "I'm afraid there's been a slight change in plans."

Her guard went up. "What kind of change?"

"I'm going to give this to you straight, Shelly. My brothers and I aren't totally convinced you've been on the up and up with us."

Acid trickled and burned along the lining of her stomach. If she handled this wrong, the whole assignment could go up in smoke. "I'm not sure what you're getting at."

"Just that the kind of random violence we saw today has been previously unheard of in Colts Run Cross."

"So you think that he had to be targeting me?"

"That makes more sense."

"Sorry to disappoint you, Matt, but I don't have those kind of enemies. And if I did know who'd shot at me, why on earth would I lie about it?"

"You tell me."

She feigned an indignant expression and straightened her

back and shoulders. "What difference does it make what I say if you think I'm a liar?"

"I'm not saying you're lying. Having you checked out by a private investigator is just a reasonable precaution. It's not personal."

"Really? It sounds extremely personal to me." But it was not a problem for her. *You go for it, Matt Collingsworth. Check all you want. The CIA has me covered.*

"In all likelihood, we're only talking a couple of days here," Matt said. "I'll cover your expenses at the motel or, if you'd prefer, I can drive you into Houston and book you a room in a more luxurious hotel."

Why not? Money was no object for the Collingsworths.

"The motel's fine. I can wait around there until you decide if I pass muster," she said, "as long as it doesn't take too long." She stood to go, grabbing her handbag from the back of her chair and slinging it over her shoulder.

"There is one more thing," Matt said.

"Let me guess. You want me to stay handcuffed to the bed in the motel until you're sure I'm not luring evil into your quaint little Texas town."

He smiled again, a kind of taunting, half smile that tightened her chest. Not attraction, she told herself. She had that totally under control.

"Handcuffs sound interesting," Matt said, "but I was thinking of something a little less dramatic."

"Such as?"

"Until we know why someone tried to kill you today, I don't think you should stay alone."

"Do you have a better idea?"

"Yeah. I'm staying with you."

She couldn't have heard him right. A man like Matt Collingsworth didn't put himself out for a prospective employee whom he suspected might be a blatant liar. But then she wouldn't have expected one of the richest men in Texas to be sitting across from her tonight in a Texas roadhouse, either.

"What did you say?" she asked.

"On the off chance that the guy who shot you today was looking to kill you specifically, you shouldn't be alone tonight."

"And you're planning to serve as my bodyguard?"

"Why not? I've never gone up against a killer before, but I've handled some bulls that were looking to leave my kidneys scattered over the rodeo ring."

"That isn't necessary."

"Actually, it is. Family tradition, the cowboy code and all that. A real man never walks away from a woman in danger, even one with a loaded Smith & Wesson in her possession."

He'd walk away fast enough if he knew she was CIA— here to put him and his family away for life. But he didn't know, and for now, it would apparently be only her and Matt in a slightly shady motel on the edge of town. Breathing the same stale air stirred by the whirring ceiling fan and overworked air conditioner. Perhaps close enough she'd hear the rustle of sheets when he shifted positions.

She should be thanking her lucky stars for this entrée into the inner sanctum of the world she'd come to infiltrate. But only one word came to mind and it seemed to be shouting inside her head and echoing through every cell of her body.

*Help!*

# Chapter Five

Shelly stepped onto the white mat and stared at herself in the foggy bathroom mirror. Water dripped from her hair and drops of moisture glistened on her freshly scrubbed skin. The bathroom in the motel was small, steamy now and barely big enough to accommodate her and her bag of toiletries.

Taking one of the fluffy white towels from the rack, she wound it around her head turban style, catching the short strands of hair so that the trickle of water no longer sluiced down the back of her neck. She reached for another towel to buff her naked body, but stopped as her fingers brushed the slightly damp bandage on her left arm. Wet, in spite of her efforts to keep that arm extended out of the water's reach.

She'd started her mission with a costly mistake, albeit one she'd had no control over. However, thinking back on the shooting incident now, she doubted Brady saw it that way. He hadn't chewed her out or removed her from the case yet, but when anything went wrong, he tended to blame the agent in charge. Screwups of any kind were not tolerated in his department.

But the plan was working. She was in control and even coming to terms with the sensual reactions Matt inspired. He possessed a masculine virility that personified the cowboy charm to perfection. She doubted there was a woman alive who wouldn't feel some sort of stirring in her soul when suddenly thrust up close and personal with him.

Add that to the fact that she'd been so busy learning the ropes at the agency, she hadn't been intimate with a man in months. She thought back. Make that a year and two months unless you counted those kisses with her senior-year boyfriend at her ten-year high school reunion last year. They'd been about as exciting as downing a spoonful of cough syrup.

Shelly finished drying and then slathered her skin with a slick coat of scented lotion. Moisturizer for her face came next, and there was no missing the paleness that made her skin look almost translucent in the glare of the overhead light. The wound and the loss of blood took a little more out of her than she'd wanted to admit, but a good night's sleep and she'd be just fine.

She pulled on the oversize nightshirt, turned out the light and padded to the bed. Fortunately, there had been lots of empty rooms at the motel and Matt had taken the one adjoining hers. The door that separated them was, at his insistence, open a crack. He'd double checked the locks on her door that opened directly to the parking lot and the ones on her small-paned window.

There was a soft tap on the adjoining door just as she slid beneath the covers. She yanked on the sheet, tucking the top folds of the smooth cotton beneath her armpits. "Come in."

Matt stepped inside, shirtless, his hair damp from the shower, his feet bare. His jeans rode his hips, the button at the waist was undone.

Her resolve to stay unmoved dissolved in a flash of heat. She turned to study the faded roses on the spread she'd pushed to the foot of the bed earlier.

Matt stepped even closer. "Are you too tired to talk a minute?"

"I'm exhausted, but I can probably stay awake for a sentence or two."

He leaned against the rough-hewn pine headboard. "I just had a call from Sheriff Guerra."

She let her hopes rise a little. "Have they apprehended the shooter?"

"Afraid not."

"Has he found out if anyone around here owns a car like the one my attacker was driving?"

"No. All they know is that a man in a black sedan bought gas in a local station less than a half hour before the attack on you. The owner was working at the station at the time and he took the man to be just passing through."

"When did you find that out?"

"Earlier this evening," he admitted.

"Why didn't you mention it before now?"

"Guess I forgot."

He hadn't forgotten. He didn't trust her. But he was here, protecting her though he owed her nothing. Could a man like that be guilty of selling out to the enemy? Or did he just have the misfortune to be born into a family that put money above moral decency and respect for innocent lives?

This was getting her nowhere. "What is it you wanted to talk about, Matt?"

"They haven't found the man who attacked you, but they may have found the car he was driving."

"When?"

"I'm not sure, but I just got the news. A wrangler from Gill Collin's ranch called in a report that he'd found a burning car. It was in a wooded area just past their south pasture. Ed Guerra called me as soon as he arrived on the scene and verified the report."

The name Gill Collin didn't register. She doubted it should

have. She took a deep breath and exhaled slowly. "Was there anyone in the car? Was it deliberately set on fire?"

"No one was in the car, but the sheriff is assuming at this point that the fire was deliberately set. The good news is the car wasn't burned to the point they couldn't recognize the VIN or that it was a black Ford Fusion. The sheriff ran a check on it. The car was reported as stolen from a grocery store in Conroe about an hour before the attack on you."

"So we're no closer to identifying the man who tried to kill me."

"Not unless you can come up with someone who might want you dead."

The Collingsworths would be the obvious first guess, yet she didn't think they were behind it. There were others with reason to hate her, but they were all behind bars and had been for months. People like the Maitlin brothers whom she'd helped send to prison for arms dealing.

Then there was Arthur Cox. He'd been involved with smuggling illegal aliens into the country, including one responsible for a failed bomb attack on an overseas military base.

Both Cox and the Maitlin brothers had sworn revenge, but she'd merely assisted in the investigations leading to their arrest. If they'd gone after anyone, it would have been the senior investigator, and that hadn't happened.

More importantly, no one knew she was here. Shelly Lane was a physical therapist from Atlanta with viable credentials and a fake background that was beyond suspicion. All she had to do now was convince Matt she was authentic.

"If the man was trying to kill me, Matt, then he had me confused with someone else. No one has a reason to hate me that much. I lead a quiet life."

Matt shifted, moving so near that she felt the pressure of

his thigh against her leg through the sheet. "I want to help you, Shelly, but I can't unless you level with me."

"I have leveled with you. I have no idea why anyone shot at me." She had to stay in control, had to think clearly and not let this get out of hand.

Matt's hand slid along the sheet until his fingertips touched hers. His touch was disconcerting, but nothing like the compelling heat of his eyes as he stared into hers. "You can trust me, you know. I have no stake in this, except to see that you don't get killed on my watch."

But *she* had a tremendous stake in this, and her job was all about digging into his secrets, not the other way around.

"If you need me, I'm just steps away, Shelly. All you have to do is call my name."

"You're surely not planning to stay awake waiting on some deranged killer to show up," she said.

"I'm a light sleeper. Now get some rest. We'll talk more in the morning."

She was exhausted, but when she closed her eyes and kicked back the covers, her knee settled in the warm spot left by Matt's body. She cringed and curled into a ball, hating that she found Matt attractive, but knowing that she'd do what she came to Texas to do—no matter what stunts her hormones pulled.

MATT WOKE FROM A RESTLESS sleep and stared at the shadows that crept about his walls and ceiling. If forced to explain his actions tonight, he'd be hard-pressed to come up with a good reason for assuming responsibility for the protection of a woman he'd just met and didn't totally trust.

Sure, there was an element of truth in his statement about family tradition and a real man always protecting a woman, but he could have called the sheriff and hired an off-duty deputy to stand guard over Shelly tonight. He'd considered doing just that, but when it came time to make the call, he couldn't turn the task over to anyone else. Far more disturbing were the urges that had rolled through him when he'd been sitting beside her on the bed.

He'd played it cool—at least he'd given it his best shot. For sure, he hadn't done anything irrevocably stupid like kissing her, but he'd come close. The possibility of danger and being with a woman in a dingy motel room was a lethal combination.

Giving up on sleep for the time being, he kicked out from under the bleached white sheet and threw his legs over the side of the bed. He took a bathroom break, then grabbed his jeans from the chair where he'd slung them and wiggled into them. He could use a breath of fresh air. Not that air ever seemed as fresh or as fragrant to him anywhere as it did on Jack's Bluff Ranch.

He was yanking up the zipper when he saw the shadow of a man move past his window. Maybe just a restless guest like himself, but caution kicked in and Matt grabbed the pistol from his beside table.

He eased the door open and stepped outside just in time to see a tall, thin man wearing a baseball cap lean over and start fiddling with the lock on Shelly's door.

The wind caught Matt's open door, slamming it shut and alerting the would-be intruder that he was there. The man glanced his way for less than a heartbeat before he took off running across the parking lot. Matt raced after him, his bare feet digging painfully into the uneven gravel and sending pebbles skittering in all directions.

He'd almost caught up with him when he heard a motorbike sputter then roar to life. As he turned toward the sound, something hit him square in the forehead. The pain was blinding and slowed him down just long enough for the man to jump on the back of the now-speeding bike.

Matt took aim with the pistol but there was no way he could get off a clean shot at the back tire with the driver weaving from one side of the road to the other. In seconds, they'd disappeared beyond the tree line.

He could jump in his truck and try to follow, but with their head start and the acres of wooded land they could cut through on their motorbike, there would be little chance he could catch them. A couple of motel lights came on, the illumination slanting through as guests peeked from behind cracked blinds. One man stepped outside in his underwear.

"Is that you making that ruckus?"

"Nope, I was just out for a smoke when a couple of guys on a Harley sped through the parking lot."

"So what happened to your head?"

Matt reached to the spot that felt as if someone had cracked it open with a two-by-four. A sticky pool of blood squished between his fingertips. "Guess a rock flying off his tire caught me." A major lie. The rock had definitely been hurled by a man with muscle and great aim.

The man's next comment wasn't fit for mixed company, but it pretty much summed up Matt's feelings about the bikers as well. That was the least disturbing facet of all of this. The most distressing was that one of the men had been at Shelly's door and who knows what he might have done if Matt hadn't been here.

His insides felt scratchy and gritty, the way they had that time he'd been stuck in that West Texas sandstorm. He stopped at Shelly's room and tried the knob of her door. The lock still held and her room was still dark. The meds and her state of exhaustion had probably let her sleep through everything.

Once inside his own space, he took a deep breath only to be struck by the suffocating sensation that the walls were closing in around him. He tiptoed to the door that separated his room from Shelly's and opened it enough that he could assure himself she was still sleeping soundly and safely.

Moonlight splayed across her bed, caressing her delicate features and painting silver threads along the column of her neck. Her eyes were closed, her breath even and gentle, as if she were in the deep throes of a pleasant dream.

She wasn't his responsibility, he reminded himself. He was a rancher, not a sheriff. He liked life uncomplicated and stress-free.

Still, there was something about Shelly Lane that burrowed inside him and made him feel hungry for something he couldn't even name. He didn't like the feeling at all.

MATT EXPLAINED THE SITUATION to Shelly over morning coffee he'd made in his motel room's pot. He'd probably had worse, but he couldn't remember when. She didn't complain about the coffee and seemed rather unfazed by his account of last night's adventure.

"I called the sheriff's department after I got back in my room," he continued after another gulp of the lukewarm brew. "The clerk took the information and said she'd pass it along to the deputies on duty in that area. Her inference was that they'd then be on the lookout for the two bikers. It was clear, however, that she didn't consider the incident emergency caliber."

"I can see her point," Shelly said. "The man didn't break into my room. He was just standing by my door. And you didn't have a rock thrown at you, until you started chasing the guy's friend across the parking lot." She sipped her coffee. "No guns were fired. No crime was committed. Thus, not emergency status."

"Apparently the sheriff's clerk thinks like you do. So does the motel manager for that matter. He said the guy was probably looking for someone, most likely a girlfriend he thought was running around with some other guy. Claims it's happened before, which says a lot for the quality of guests he gets at the motel."

"Well, if you're the only bed for hire in town you're bound to get some by-the-hour customers."

He knew she was right. That didn't change his mind about what he'd decided in the sleepless hours just before sunrise. "I need you to go into Houston with me today."

She stared at him over the rim of her cup. "For what purpose?"

"I have an artist friend there who's got a real talent for drawing faces from a description."

"You mean a police sketch artist?"

"No, she's better at it than any sketch artist the police can afford. She doesn't like becoming involved with criminal cases, but if she's available, she'll do it as a favor to me."

"I don't see how my seeing her would help. I didn't get a good look at the shooter."

"No, but if the shooter and the unidentified jerk who bought gas from Emile Henley are the same man, Emile can describe him. I just need you to see if the resulting sketch reminds you of anyone you know or have seen before."

"Don't you have duties with the behaviorally challenged?"

"I'll find a replacement. So, are you up for the trip?"

"If it will help us identify the lunatic who fired at me and destroyed a stolen car, how can I refuse?"

His sentiments exactly. As soon as they had an arrest and a full report on Shelly, he could go back to his life. In the meantime he'd just have to work doubly hard to keep his libido under control.

Shelly was in the front seat of Matt's truck traveling toward the service station to pick up Emile for the drive into Houston. Nothing was going according to plan, including the biker incident, but she had to concentrate on the positive.

She might not be on the ranch yet, but she was definitely getting closer.

"Tell me more about this artist," she said as Matt turned onto another two-lane highway. "Is she anyone I might have heard of?"

"Possibly. Her name's Angelique Dubois. I'm not much of an art critic, but she's regarded highly by the local art community."

"Not *the* Angelique Dubois who does the charcoals of nudes."

"That's the one. You sound as if you're familiar with her work."

She caught herself before she admitted that she'd gone to a showing of Angelique's drawings in the D.C. area just a few months ago. It didn't fit her Atlanta physical therapist's image. "I read an article about her on the Internet. I can't believe you got someone of her professional stature to do a police sketch for a low-profile crime."

"I called in a favor."

"How do you know her?" she asked.

"I met her when Mom dragged me to a charity event at a gallery that was showing her work. Actually, it was probably one of Mom's setups. Her primary goal in life lately seems to be to marry me off. Well, that and getting Jeremiah steady on his feet and out of the house more."

"Did the setup work?"

"Better than most. Angelique and I dated a few times."

"But you're not dating now?" Just making conversation,

she told herself, but she tensed involuntarily as she waited for his response.

"No. She didn't particularly warm up to ranch life and I took to her world even less. We stayed friends, though, and I sent a rich buyer her way last month, a ranching friend from Australia."

The Collingsworths had rich friends in every corner of the globe, and Shelly was about to make her first step into that world of wealth, influence, social contacts and even art.

She needed to apprise Brady of her current status at her first opportunity. He'd be wary when she told him about the unexplained bikers, but he'd have to see that she was making too much headway to pull her off the case now.

Matt turned on his CD player and a jazzy instrumental blared from the truck's speakers. She would have expected him to listen to country, though she wasn't sure why. He hadn't fallen into any of the other wealthy Texas rancher stereotypical slots she might have assigned him.

Shelly shifted, so that she could study the angles and strong features of his profile as they talked. "Is ranching as romantic as it seems in books?"

"All depends on which books you read and which day you're on the ranch."

Matt nudged his white straw Stetson away from his forehead, and thick, dark locks of hair crept from beneath the brim, skimming the angry wound from last night's rock injury. Not his only scar, though. There was an almost invisible one running along his left temple.

His jaw was chiseled, his nose classic, his chest broad. Even his scent was masculine, a hint of spice and seductive musk. Her pulse quickened. Not what she needed to be thinking about.

"What's a typical day like for you?" she asked, hoping conversation would keep more sensual thoughts at bay.

Matt kept his left hand on the wheel, but snaked his arm across the space between them, resting his right hand near her shoulder. "The day starts at sunrise when I step out on my porch and get that first invigorating whiff of fresh air. Birds serenade me from the trees around the house and there's a good chance I'll spy deer drinking from the pond. Might even see a fish jump and see a family of ducks out for a morning swim.

"After a few minutes, I'll amble back inside and start a pot of real coffee—not like what we drank this morning—while I go over the day's agenda in my mind."

"No calendar of activities or a secretary to keep you on task."

"I have a calendar. I seldom need to refer to it. We have a staff to handle reports and finances, but they work out of the headquarters building near the wranglers' bunkhouse. Bart and I both spend as little time in there as we can. Fortunately, we have people for the paperwork who need little supervision and don't mind being cooped up for several hours a day."

"Then what kind of duties are on your agenda?"

"A colt about to be born. Branding that needs to be done. Decisions to make about what types of cattle to increase and which to cut back on. Auctions to attend. New equipment to check out. Wranglers to oversee."

He retuned his right hand to the wheel. "I guess that sounds corny to a city girl."

"Not at all," she murmured. It sounded earthy and real, far removed from the world of crime and national security she dealt with every day. "Do you have much involvement with Collingsworth Oil?" she asked.

"Almost none."

"But it is a family business, isn't it?"

"It is, but we all do what makes us happy. We're lucky that

way. My brother Bart and I run the ranch. My brother Langston is president of the oil company and my youngest brother Zach is going into law enforcement when he gets back from his honeymoon."

"How did Langston end up with so much control of the oil business?"

"He likes it. So did Jeremiah when he was on top of his mental game. The rest of us don't, although Mom is doing a bang-up job of CEO of Collingsworth Enterprises since Jeremiah had to step down from the position. I think she's growing tired of it though and is ready to return to her charities and grandmothering."

"But you must at least go to board meetings for the oil company?"

"The annual meeting, but only because Langston insists that we all know the financial status of the business." He turned toward her. "Why are you so interested in Collingsworth Oil?"

She pulled down the visor and checked her lipstick, giving her a reason to avoid eye contact with Matt. "This kind of life is all new to me. Besides, listening to you helps keep my mind off my wounded arm and battered car."

"I'll take care of the car. You'll have to rely on the doc for your arm. When do you need to get it checked again?"

"Today, but it can wait until after we visit with Angelique."

Matt nodded, then slowed the car and pulled into a three-pump service station accompanied by what looked to be a country mini-mart.

A man in faded jeans and a black T-shirt waved to them from the open doorway of the store.

"I need to use the facilities," she said, realizing that this might be her only opportunity to make a quick phone call to Brady.

"Okay, I'll wait here. Bathrooms are inside to your left, past the drink machines."

She threw her handbag over her shoulder and hopped down from the truck. Emile was giving last-minute instructions to the young man who was apparently going to watch the station while they made the trip into Houston. Once inside the bathroom, she used the CIA phone to make a call to Brady's private, non-traceable line, hoping for decent reception. He answered on the second ring.

"Good news and bad," she said.

"Hit me with it—the bad first."

She told him about the visit of the moonlight biker before explaining that Matt had taken on her protection as his personal responsibility. "He's concerned because he thinks someone is trying to kill me, proof positive that he has no clue that I'm with the CIA."

"There's no such thing as that kind of proof in this business. Don't take anything for granted, Shelly."

"Absolutely not." But Matt wouldn't be doing all this if he thought she was here to investigate his family. He'd just fire her, and that would be that.

"I'd feel better if I was certain the attack was random and the biker visit was unrelated."

"I'm Shelly Lane, a physical therapist from Atlanta. No one has a reason to kill me. If it wasn't random, the perp has me mixed up with someone else. He'll realize that soon enough. But most likely it's some weird gang-related activity."

"That's possible. Gang-related violence has been up in Houston ever since so many of the druggies fled New Orleans after Katrina."

"I'm already making headway with Matt Collingsworth, Brady. It would be a shame to get pulled off the case before I have a chance to try my skills with the rest of the family."

"You don't have anything on Matt yet."

"That's the point. I don't think he's involved in the workings of the oil company. Indications are that he's all rancher, all the time."

"I hate to burst that bubble of self-confidence, but there's new evidence to the contrary."

She leaned against the stained sink, pretty sure she did not want to hear what was going to come next.

# Chapter Six

"Agents picked up a man last night in Brownsville, Texas, who is known to have ties with terrorist organizations in the Middle East. The CIA's been watching him for a while, but couldn't get the goods on him until he was caught smuggling illegal aliens across the Mexican border. At least two of the men he brought into the country were from Middle Eastern countries and had ties with the Taliban."

"How is that related to Matt Collingsworth?"

"When he was arrested, he had Matt's name and phone number on him. He claimed not to know any of the Collingsworths, but said he'd been given Matt's name as someone who hired illegals."

"That's possible, I guess, but Lenora Collingsworth certainly checked my credentials thoroughly and is having me further investigated now."

"More reason to suspect that Matt's dealings with the man involved more than he claimed. At this point, we have to assume that any family member might be involved in illegal activities and those who aren't might still have information that can lead us to arrests and convictions."

And there was even an outside chance—way outside at this point—that none of the evidence they had against any of the Collingsworth family would check out. Brady knew it, but would not want to hear that from her. She broke the connection and went to rejoin Matt.

He looked the same, but she saw him differently than she had mere minutes ago. Then, she'd let him slide into the role of protector, let herself start relaxing in his presence and experience twinges of attraction deep inside her psyche.

Now, Matt Collingsworth was just one more important piece of the criminal puzzle she had to solve. There was no room for mistakes in judgment. No room for mistakes of any kind.

ANGELIQUE DUBOIS MET THEM at the door of her quaint turn-of-the-century house in Houston's Heights district, wearing a pair of extremely skinny jeans and a flowing teal blouse. She was absolutely gorgeous. Take that back. The word didn't do her justice. She was positively ethereal, like a goddess floating on a sea of off-white carpet.

Her black hair was straight and sleek and hung nearly to her waist. Her olive complexion was flawless. Her skin was bronzed with a natural glow that required no makeup though there was a glimmer of gloss on her full lips and a smidgen of berry-colored liner at the base of her long, thick lashes.

Her eyes were the real kicker—intense, the color of polished onyx. And they were staring up at Matt with the kind of overt hunger that Shelly might have reserved for a pair of Manolo Blahniks about to go on the half-price sale rack.

Emile shuffled his feet and stared at his grease-stained hands and dirty nails, as if noticing them for the first time, as Matt took care of introductions. Finally, he offered his right hand to Angelique.

She shook his quickly and turned to Shelly. "I'm sorry that

your welcome to Texas was so traumatic. Matt said you narrowly missed being killed yesterday."

"But luckily I got off with barely a scratch," she said, patting the bandage on her arm. "I really appreciate your willingness to lend your expertise in finding my attacker."

"Matt asked for my help," Angelique said as if that were explanation enough. "Can I get you something to drink? Hot tea or there's chilled champagne if you'd prefer a mimosa. And, yes, there's coffee, Matt. I knew you'd want that."

"Great. You know what I think of champagne."

"Lacks the proper kick and should be reserved for momentous occasions and boring toasts. I think that's how you put it," she said, laughing.

"Close enough. Who else wants coffee?"

Shelly and Emile put in their orders for black and unsweetened. Matt and Angelique went to fetch the brew while Shelly took in the ambiance. The furnishings were comfortable and reminiscent of the same period as the house, but accessorized with a mixture of jewel-toned colors that mimicked brilliant sunrises and Caribbean seas.

Shelves and tables were adorned with unique sculptures, books and small, framed photographs in black-and-white. An unframed charcoal canvas of a shapely young woman strategically draped in what appeared to be the folds of a curtain she'd pulled away from a window hung over the mantle.

"Is that your work?" Shelly asked, when Angelique returned carrying a silver tray laden with thinly sliced sweet breads and pastries.

"Yes. Do you like it?"

"It's intriguing," she said. "I love the way the shadows and shadings give it that fantasized feel. Forgive my layman's terms for describing what's probably a very sophisticated artistic method."

"No need to apologize. Vocabulary is unimportant. The artist's purpose is to portray an image that can touch the soul."

"Beautifully put."

"I'd love to paint you," Angelique said. "Your face is a fascinating blend of strength and vulnerability, and your body is lissome and sensual."

Shelly's face burned at the thought of nude modeling, not to mention the fact that she'd never thought of her body as lissome or sensual. When she looked up and realized Matt had returned and also heard the comment, the blush burned even deeper into her cheeks.

"Thanks," Shelly said, "but I'm uncomfortable enough having my photograph taken with my clothes *on.*"

"If you change your mind, you know where to find me. Now, I guess we should get started on the sketch. Emile, you sit on the sofa next to me and try to picture the man just as he looked when he walked into your store."

"I can try."

"It will be easier than you think. Just close your eyes and relive the moment in your mind. When the image is intact, open your eyes and start describing him. I'll interrupt with questions as you talk and you should speak up when my sketch veers from the way you see him."

"I only saw the man for a few minutes."

"But you probably noticed more than you think you did. The mind captures images we're not aware of seeing." Angelique picked up the sketch pad and pencil she'd left lying on the coffee table. She settled on the far end of the Queen Anne sofa. Emile sat next to her. Shelly took her coffee to the loveseat opposite them, afraid after she did that Matt would likely take that as an invitation to join her there. He grabbed one of the pastries and a napkin, then did just that.

This time, Shelly managed to keep his nearness from overriding her professional judgment. The possibility that she might recognize the man Angelique was about to sketch had her on edge for very good reasons. If it turned out to be someone she knew, it would mean she was the target of a planned hit. In that case, not only would she be in danger of being ambushed and shot at again, but it would mean her cover was indisputably blown.

Emile began to describe the man, speaking slowly and awkwardly at first, but he gained momentum quickly as the sketch started to take shape.

"His chin was square."

"Like this?" Angelique said, making the adjustment.

"Yeah, that's more like it, and his brows were thicker with some hairs shooting out all whichaway, like a porcupine's."

Angelique changed the drawing until Emile was satisfied with the brows and the hair. "What about the mouth?"

"He had big lips, blotchy, you know, like he'd had cold sores recently."

Angelique went through the same process with the mouth, changing the lines until Emile nodded.

"That's starting to look like him," he said.

"Tell me about his eyes."

"Oh, boy. A man never looks at another man's eyes."

"Let's give it a try anyway."

"Kind of mean-looking."

"Check this shape," she said. Her perfectly manicured fingers seemed to move effortlessly across the pad.

Emile frowned. "Try making them narrower, and with the lids down, like they weren't open all the way."

She made the adjustments. The sketch was definitely not of the man Shelly had noticed staring at her at Cutter's Bar last night. It was even possible that the sketch didn't resemble the man in the black Ford at all. That had happened more than once with the sketch agents they'd used at the agency and they had access to people trained in transferring verbal descriptions to the blank page.

Angelique kept at the task, making minute modifications until Emile finally broke into a broad grin.

"I don't know how you did it from my rambling, but that's him to a T. You're amazing."

"I just drew what you said." Angelique tore the sketch from the pad and handed the drawing to Matt. "I hope this helps."

He scooted closer to Shelly and held it so that she could study it with him. His arm brushed hers and awareness zinged through her, in spite of the gravity of the situation. This whole attraction bit was starting to become extremely annoying. She forced her total concentration on the sketch.

"I've never see him around Colts Run Cross," Matt said.

"Just like I told you yesterday," Emile said, appearing far more relaxed, now that he was off the hook. "I don't think he's from around here."

"What's the verdict, Shelly?" Matt laid a hand on her arm. "Do you know him?"

She shook her head. "I've never seen him before."

"You're sure?" Suspicion haunted his voice and his eyes.

"I'm sure."

"Then I guess we'll just turn this sketch over to Sheriff Guerra and let him get it out to law-enforcement personnel across the state. The quicker this guy is arrested, the less likely he'll attack someone else, randomly or otherwise."

Angelique walked them to the door, stopping after she opened it to straighten Matt's shirt collar, though it wasn't crooked. Her delicate hand lingered on his chest, a seductive gesture that didn't go unnoticed by Shelly, but seemed to fly right past Matt. His only interest appeared to be in getting the sketch into the sheriff's hands.

Or maybe it was to just deliver her back to the motel and get on with his life. Either way, they made a quick exit. The drive back to Colts Run Cross was an hour and a half of awkward silence, except for occasional bursts of conversation between Matt and Emile.

Her entrée into the Collingsworth household might be about to run into a dead end.

MATT PACED THE HOSPITAL waiting room, while the young doctor on Saturday call examined the wound and then had the nursing staff change the bandage.

Matt's cell phone rang. He grabbed it, hoping it was the sheriff telling him the sketch had produced an identification. Probably way too soon for that now, though. They'd dropped off the sketch less than a half hour ago and picked up Shelly's gun while they were there. She'd handled the weapon like a pro, not like a woman who'd just bought a gun for a long road trip.

The caller ID said Langston. "I thought you were replacing me," Matt said. "Why aren't you saddling horses for the visiting inner-city brood?"

"As usual, Mom has twice the volunteers she needs so I slipped away to take care of some business. Are you still with Shelly Lane?"

"Yeah. Angelique completed the sketch, but Shelly says the likeness doesn't resemble anyone she knows."

"That would fit with the news from Clay Markham? So far our physical therapist checks out perfectly. And Aidan talked with a fellow detective who works for the Atlanta Police Department."

"Always nice to have friends in high places."

"And sometimes in low places. Aidan has both. He says

Shelly has never reported any safety concerns to the police, nor is there a record of her having ever made a 911 call. From all indications, she's a model citizen with no reported stalkers or danger in her background."

"Are you saying I should just bring her to the ranch as Mom's wanted all along?"

"I don't see any real problem with it, but you're with Shelly. You decide."

Making the call *should* be a simple task. Shelly insisted that no one had reason to kill her. The cops and private investigators had no evidence that she was in any kind of trouble or mixed up in any way with killers.

But Matt had always had a sixth sense with cattle. He knew from looking in a cow's eyes when her pregnancy was going sour. He knew if a calf or foal was unhealthy, almost before it's feet touched the ground. Shelly wasn't livestock, but all his instincts yelled that she was in danger.

Not that he knew a damn thing about women, except that the status quo usually flew out the window when a woman like Shelly stepped onto the scene. And he liked his status quo. He was still dealing with that fact, when Shelly and the doctor joined him in the waiting room.

"You'll have your hands full with this one, Mr. Collingsworth."

"Are there complications?"

"Not with the injury, but Shelly does not follow doctor's orders. She skipped out without being released last night and today she's telling me how to do my job."

It was clear he was joking, probably flirting with Shelly. Maybe he'd be willing to take her home with him? Then Matt's life could get back to normal.

"You look as if you took a blow yourself?" the doctor said, stepping closer for a better look at the cut on Matt's forehead.

"It's nothing a little time and a smear of antibiotic cream won't take care of. What's the verdict with Shelly's wound?" Matt asked, almost hoping the doctor wanted her back in the hospital. That would eliminate his having to make any decision on what to do with her tonight. But from the size of the much smaller bandage on her arm now, he'd guess that wasn't going to happen.

"I prescribed an ointment to be used twice a day, in the morning and at night before changing the bandage. Keeping the wound clean is very important, so she should keep it bandaged until Tuesday. I should see her in seven days. We'll remove the stitches then."

"I could probably remove the stitches myself," Shelly said, "since I don't have a car at my disposal."

The doctor looked to Matt. "It would be better if she had that done in the office. That way we can make certain the wound is healing appropriately."

"I'll see that she comes in," Matt said. It didn't hit him until after he'd blurted out the words that they sounded as if he and Shelly were a couple and he would still be taking care of her a week from now.

That, coupled with the plan taking form in his mind, rattled him to the point that he almost dropped the keys when he went to unlock his truck. The plan wasn't to his liking, but he didn't see much else he could do, unless he wanted to spend another sleepless night in the motel.

"You really don't need to babysit me any longer, Matt," she said, as if reading his confusing thoughts. "Just drop me off at the motel. I'll be fine. And if a drunk biker comes calling in the middle of the night, I have my gun that the sheriff returned."

"The gun you admitted you don't know how to use."

"What's to know? You just aim and pull the trigger. I've seen it done in a thousand movies."

He backed out of the parking lot and turned right, toward the motel. He couldn't believe he was about to say what was bucking around in his mind and fighting its way to his tongue.

"We'll stop off at the motel and pick up your things."

Shelly's brows arched and the golden flecks in her eyes sparkled like fire. His insides felt vaguely the way they had when he'd been kicked in the gut by a snorting bull, all shaky and queasy. But he had to do what he had to do.

"I think it best you stay with me tonight," he said.

"You mean stay at the ranch?"

"Yes, but at my house." His small, rustic, cozy cabin that he was used to living in alone. "Just until tomorrow," he said, before she got the wrong idea, like the one that was messing with his libido right now.

"Is this your mother's idea or yours?"

"Mine."

"Because you still don't trust me to live with your family?"

He couldn't deny the truth of that, but admitting it would only make things worse. "Because the investigation isn't finished."

The sparks in her eyes seemed to be shooting at him now. "Then I'll wait until it is."

She had a lot of nerve being angry with him after he'd spent the past twenty-four hours trying to make sure she was safe. He had a good mind to dump her at that motel and go home to his nice, comfortable bed alone.

Nice thought, but he could no more walk away and leave her unprotected than he could have decided to stop breathing. He wouldn't even try to understand why he'd let her get to him this way. She just had.

The problem was that those nagging doubts of suspicion

wouldn't die. And he wasn't willing to move her into the big house until he felt certain she wasn't into anything that would bring trouble or danger to his family.

"It's your call, but we'd both be more comfortable than at the motel. You'd have a modern bathroom and an air conditioner that doesn't buck and whistle all night. And we could join the family for brunch in the morning," he said, hoping that would sway her. "You can meet Jeremiah."

Shelly cocked her head and shot Matt a dubious look. "Does this house of yours have two bedrooms?"

"Actually it has three. And if you're worried that I plan to take advantage of you, forget it. When I take a woman to bed, it's because she wants to be there."

She stretched her feet in front of her and pushed against the back of the seat, the movement accentuating her perky breasts.

"Okay, Matt Collingsworth, on those grounds, I accept your invitation to stay with you tonight."

He swallowed hard, glad he'd won the argument, but worried at the same time. He'd keep his word, but he had a feeling this might well be a night for a cold shower.

## Chapter Seven

Shelly had seen pictures of the ranch, had even driven by it when she'd first arrived in Texas, but that hadn't quite prepared her for this. A lump formed in her throat as the reality and significance of the moment hit home.

She was about to be on-site, undercover and officially on a case that, if successful, might save thousands of innocent lives. Who knew what reprehensible and deadly acts might be committed using money funneled to terrorists through Collingsworth Oil? All for the purpose of making even more money for a family who were already worth billions.

Her sense of responsibility swelled as Matt punched in a code and the gates swung open. But she couldn't let Matt discern those feelings. She had to stay firmly planted in her role of a Georgia girl who knew nothing much about the Collingsworths or the ranch.

"Nice gate, but I always pictured cowboys climbing down from a battered pickup and unlatching a rusty latch."

"Sorry to disappoint you. But if it's any consolation, the automated gate opener is new, part of the added security after a year of dealing with lunatics."

Her interest piqued. She knew something of the problems his new sisters-in-law had experienced, but it would be nice to hear Matt's version of them. "Then you've had other trouble?"

"Long stories for winter nights by the fire. But all the endings were happy."

"After the way everyone reacted to the attack on me," she continued, "I would have thought there was no crime in this part of Texas."

"Crime is everywhere these days, but we don't get the kind of drug and gang-related crimes they get in big cities or along the border. Unfortunately, the Collingsworth brothers do have a knack for getting linked with women in jeopardy."

"Do tell. More of the cowboy code at work?"

"You could say that. Our neighbor Billy Mack calls it the Lenora Do-gooder Curse. Mom's constantly quoting from the Bible parable about how to whom much is given, much is required. Guess she has that so drilled into our brains that, when we see someone who needs help, we feel compelled to rush to the rescue."

"That explains her having the inner-city kids out for a day of ranch life? Does she do that often?"

"Every other Saturday during the summer months. We all pitch in, wranglers included, but she has lots of volunteers from neighboring ranches as well."

"How many kids are we talking about?"

"No more than twelve at a time, all between the ages of eleven and fourteen. Mom insists that each kid have their own adult mentor for the day. Mostly that's for safety reasons, but also because she says that, for some of them, it's the only time they have an adult's full attention—unless they're with a cop or a judge."

"Cops and judges. So you're talking about kids with serious problems?"

"Sometimes."

"How does she decide which kids to include?"

"Her friend Carolyn Kenny does it for her. She's a juvenile court judge in Houston."

Shelly knew the Collingsworth family were major financial backers of several charitable organizations, but this was more than just a donation. They brought these kids into their world and gave them individual attention. Billionaires out riding horses with delinquents. It wasn't what she'd expected to find.

Shelly tried to reconcile what she'd seen firsthand of the Collingsworths, especially Matt, with what the CIA believed to be true about them. It refused to gel.

That didn't change her reason for being here or her motive for worming her way into their lives. "Your mother sounds amazing. You have a lot to live up to."

"Tell me about it. I respect what Mom does, but I'm not that good with people myself. Give me horses and cows any day. If they turn on you, it's because you gave them a reason."

They continued down a smooth blacktop road surrounded by acres and acres of a pastoral countryside that epitomized tranquility and the American West. She wasn't sure exactly what she'd expected the ranch to be like, but so far, it seemed the setting for a romance novel. Green and open and inviting.

"Those are longhorns in the pasture to your left," Matt said, slowing for her to get a better look.

A half dozen cattle were clustered near the fence and Shelly turned to peer out the window for her first up-close view of the huge animals with their vicious-looking horns. One looked up as if knowing it were on display; it seemed proud to show off its armor.

"How long are those horns?"

"For a steer they can measure up to a hundred and twenty

inches tip to tip. Cows and bulls have shorter horns, but a seventy to eighty inch tip range isn't uncommon. The ones you're looking at now are cows."

"Is your herd primarily Texas longhorns?"

"No. They make up only about a fourth of our herd at the present time, but I keep adding more. Hook 'em horns."

"Should I know what that means?"

He slapped the butt of his hand against his temple as if she'd offended him. "Longhorns are the University of Texas mascot. Hook 'em horns is the school battle cry."

"And I take it you graduated from UT."

"Yep. And proud of it."

"How many types of cattle do you raise?"

"Six, though our main beef-producing stock is Santa Gertrudis. They do well in hot, humid environments. But we're constantly researching genetic improvements within our herds."

Matt swerved to miss a turtle that was lumbering across the road.

"He's huge," she said.

Matt grinned. "Haven't you noticed? Everything's bigger and better in Texas."

Whether he meant it to or not, the comment concocted a sensual image that sent a traitorous tingle of responsiveness dancing along her nerve endings. "So I've heard," she said, hating that she could feel the heat settling in her cheeks.

They drove in silence, as the road meandered away from fenced pasture land into a wooded area where towering pines intermingled with sweet gum, oak and birch.

A baby deer with a smooth spotted coat and long spindly legs stepped into a clearing near the edge of the road. Matt slowed to a stop a few yards away. Amazingly, the fawn stood still, head high, looking right at them. Shelly stared back until the fawn turned away and disappeared back into the cover of trees and brush.

"He was beautiful," Shelly said. "And he didn't even seem wary of us."

"Because we don't allow hunting on the ranch. Does make regular visits to the pond behind my house. They're so tame, they'll wonder right up to me. But then I spoil them a bit by putting out corn for them during the winter."

Ranch life was becoming more enticing by the moment. So was the rancher sitting next to Shelly—and therein lay the problem. Matt might seem too good to be true, but he was a suspect in her investigation.

She held on to that thought, until he rounded yet another curve in the road and a massive, rambling house came into view. The wooden structure was painted white with dark green shutters. Huge clay pots of blooming begonias and hanging baskets of bougainvillea provided a riot of summer color to the wide front porch.

The whole effect was picture-book Southern ranch right down to the swing that was currently occupied by a beautiful dark-haired woman who looked as if she might be ready to deliver a baby at any moment.

"That's the big house," Matt said.

"It's incredibly…" She struggled for a word to describe the sensations the house stirred.

"It's home," Matt said, putting it into the one word that said it all. "My brothers and I all have our own places, but the big house is still the center of all the family activities. You'll see that for yourself tomorrow morning. Family Sunday brunch is a long-standing tradition."

The woman in the porch swing looked up and waved as they passed. Matt waved back.

"Is that one of your sisters-in-law?"

"That's Langston's wife, Trish. You'll love her. Everyone does. She's expecting a baby boy within the next few weeks."

Trish was having a baby with a man Shelly was here to help send to jail. The information that helped seal the deal might even come from Trish during a casual conversation with the new physical therapist. It could just be a comment in passing that Shelly would gather for the CIA—a piece to the complex puzzle that would lead to conviction.

The irony of it bothered Shelly, but she couldn't let herself get caught up in guilt when she was only doing her job. Her gaze moved away from the house, to the stables off to the left. A half dozen magnificent horses lazed in a fenced area just beyond that.

"Do you ride?" Matt asked.

"A little." But only because she'd had lessons in preparation for this assignment. "I've never been around horses much and I find them a bit intimidating."

"We have some gentle mares that will break you in easy— if you stay."

It was clear he had not fully accepted that possibility yet. They reached open pastureland again and the ranch seemed to stretch for miles, mostly flat. "Where is the bluff?"

"Bluff?"

"Jack's Bluff."

"Oh, that." A smile claimed his mouth. "Different kind of bluff. My great, great grandfather who'd arrived in America penniless, won the original ranch in a game of poker. His winning hand was a pair of jacks, hence Jack's Bluff."

"He won all of this in a card game?"

"No, he won a patch of land that for the most part hadn't been cleared. He and succeeding generations of Collingsworths made the ranch and the oil company what it is today. You'll have to get Mom to tell you the story of how it all came about. It always sounds a lot more romantic when she explains it."

A tale of rags to riches. A family determined to forge ahead and find wealth in the rough and tumble world of Texas. That would take courage, ambition and possibly a willingness to bend all the rules. Maybe that was also a part of the Collingsworth heritage.

The truck bumped along, the woods growing deeper, the road to Matt's cabin more narrow and not as smoothly paved as the road to the big house had been. "That's it," Matt said, as his cabin came into view.

Shelly loved it at once. Where the big house had been large and rambling, Matt's cabin put her in mind of Goldilocks and the three bears. The house was stone and wood, interesting but non-assuming. It fit so well in its environment that it almost seemed an extension of nature's beauty.

Matt stopped and killed the truck's engine. "Welcome to my little corner of the ranch."

His private space. And he was about to usher her inside. A traitorous anticipation danced along her nerve endings and she feared it had nothing to do with the real reason she was here. She couldn't let herself start thinking of Matt as a man. He was a suspect. And she was here to find evidence that could send him to prison for a long, long time.

EVERYTHING WAS PERFECT. Nothing was right.

Matt knew who he was and where he belonged. It was as clear as the shine on his boots. Shelly had been in the same boat, just as sure, just as confident—until he'd stepped into her life. Now she vacillated between resolute dedication to her job and feeling as if she were setting up the pope for a prison term.

The CIA had valid evidence, collected over a period of months, all of it pointing to the Collingsworths—Matt included—as being guilty of funding terrorism. The latest evidence suggested that they might even be actively involved in smuggling dangerous illegals into the country.

So why was it that Shelly was finding it so difficult to believe Matt could be guilty? Surely she wasn't swayed by the singular fact that she found him attractive. She wasn't that shallow or nearly that unprofessional. Yet he did get to her on a sensual level.

She walked to the window of Matt's guest room and watched the setting sun. The room was comfortable, the queen-size iron bed covered in a beautiful quilt that looked as if it might have been handed down for generations.

A rustic, antique desk topped with a brass lamp and supplied with writing essentials sat against one wall. A forty-five inch television hung on the opposite wall, in dramatic contrast with the pine boot bench that sat below it. A mixture of old and new, of ranch tradition and modern technology. The same kind of contrast that personified Matt's personality.

He not only looked the part, but played the role of simple cowboy to perfection while talking of genetic improvements and socializing with seductive, esteemed artists.

But neither his self-assurance nor his complexity were what had her cocooning in the guest room for the last two hours. Nor was it the need for rest as she'd told Matt. The quandary was that the attraction she felt toward him had magnified since arriving on the ranch.

If she couldn't work her way past it soon, she'd have no ethical choice except to walk away from the assignment. Brady would view that as failure of the worst kind. The other agents would agree. And the last thing Shelly needed in her life was failure. She was a solid career woman. The CIA was her life.

She turned at a light knock at her door, then crossed the room and opened it.

Matt had changed into a short-sleeve knit shirt and a pair of khaki shorts. No boots. In fact, no shoes. But even without the western attire, he reeked of virility.

"Are you hungry? Potatoes are baking, the salad's made and steaks are ready for the grill."

"I could have helped."

"You can have kitchen cleanup duty."

"Deal. I'll be with you in a minute."

"Take your time. I'll decant the wine. My selection's not that great but I have a couple of cabernets or a pinot noir that I bought on a trip to Napa. I've been saving it for a special occasion."

"Then you shouldn't waste it."

"I wouldn't be. Cooking dinner for a woman happens rarely enough with me for it to classify as an occasion."

"Then I vote for the pinot." And for a night where nothing heated up but the grill, a significant breakthrough in the case would be nice, too.

She brushed some gloss on her lips, bronzed her cheeks and checked her reflection in the mirror one last time. She'd slipped into a pair of white shorts that did nice things for her tanned legs, and an azure cotton shirt that was gathered at the neckline, skimming her breasts before falling loose to her waist. Her white, strappy sandals buckled at the ankle.

Not too sexy. Not too dowdy. Low-key worked best for an undercover agent.

Satisfied with her appearance, she joined Matt in the kitchen where he was pouring wine into glasses. He handed her one and lifted his for a toast. "To a quick arrest of the suspect," he said, "and a fast recovery for you."

She touched her glass to his, then sipped the wine before settling on a leather and wood barstool.

"The potatoes need another thirty minutes. What do you

say we take our wine down to the pond until it's time to grill the filets?"

She nodded, then turned to a collection of snapshots that were clustered on the wall of the breakfast nook.

"Angelique helped me put that display together," Matt said. "She's big into black-and-white pictures and she thought I had too many bare walls."

Cooking dinner for women might be a rare occurrence, but she'd bet he'd cooked for Angelique. But somehow she couldn't see the sultry artist settling for the guest room.

Jealousy reared its ugly head. Shelly pulled her lips taut and ignored it, turning her attention back to the snapshots. They were mostly of Matt and his brothers; all were faces she recognized from her research.

"Is that you in the football uniform?"

"Yep. Quarterback for the Colts Run Cross Cougars, circa twenty years in the past. I was in the seventh grade."

Even then he'd been cute. The man with his arm around Matt wasn't half bad, either. "Who's that with you?"

"My dad. That was taken in the fall. He was killed the next spring. It was the last picture the two of us were in together."

"How was he killed?"

"He was a helicopter pilot with the Air National Guard. His chopper went down during routine training maneuvers. The only explanation we ever got was that there was an equipment failure. One day he was the center of all our lives. The next day he was dead."

"That must have been hard on all of you."

"Yeah, but especially on Mom, I think. She had six kids to take care of. My youngest brother and sister are twins and they hadn't even started first grade."

"She must have been furious with the government when he died so needlessly."

"Mom? Furious with the government? I don't think that ever entered her mind. As far as she's concerned, Dad is a hero who died serving his country."

"Do you think that way, too?"

"Yeah." He answered quickly, as if he'd given this a lot of thought before tonight. "I don't agree with every politician who runs his mouth off to get a few votes, but I believe in America. I believe in freedom and in doing whatever it takes to preserve it. I know that may sound corny."

"It doesn't sound corny at all."

Nor did it sound like a man who'd sell out to the enemy. Dichotomous thoughts flooded her mind, hitting with such intensity they left her dizzy. Couldn't Matt just once do or say something to make her job easier?

"Are you sure you feel like walking down to the pond?"

"I feel fine."

"You just looked a little pale there for a minute."

"Must be the wine on an empty stomach."

They both knew she was lying since she'd only had a sip, but he let the subject drop. He held the back door open for her, then walked beside her down a worn path that trailed from his back door to a pond bordered by towering pines.

"Mornings and dusk are the best times of day on the ranch," he said. "It's when the daytime, dusk and nocturnal creatures cross paths. The clearings around the pond come alive with activity."

Somehow the thought of being surrounded by wild animals, even small ones, didn't seem as appealing to her as it apparently did to Matt. "We're not taking snakes, I hope."

"You can't live in Texas without seeing an occasional snake."

"Then make sure they know I'm just visiting."

A tree frog chorus began a high-pitched serenade. A bull

frog filled in with alto chords. And a couple of jays squawked at them from a distance. They had almost reached the pond, when she spotted the heron. It swooped to the bank and balanced perfectly on one strawlike leg.

She was still staring at it in awe when the first of Matt's nightly parade of deer appeared at the edge of a shadowed clearing. This time it was a magnificent buck with impressive antlers and soulful eyes.

Shelly held her breath so long it burned in her lungs. She didn't want to make any move that would frighten him away. She needn't have worried. The buck looked right at her, then walked to the edge of the pond and drank from the clear blue water. Three graceful does joined him a few moments later.

"No wonder you love it here, cowboy."

Matt responded with an arm around her shoulder. She turned and met his gaze. A bad move. The moment of awe she'd been experiencing was swallowed up by an ache that seemed to hit every cell of her being at once.

Matt was too alive, too masculine, *too near.* His lips touched hers—just a brush, as if he were testing the waters.

She sank into his kiss and the sweet, salty taste of his lips was like an elixir for the soul. She wanted to drown in his kiss, to hold him so tight she could feel every twinge of his muscles and sink her fingertips in smooth flesh of his broad shoulders.

She'd never wanted anything more, but—

It was all wrong. Very, very wrong. She yanked away so fast she stumbled backward.

Matt caught and steadied her. "I'm sorry, Shelly. I didn't mean for that to happen. It…"

He was fumbling for words. She was struggling just to keep from throwing herself back into his arms. "It's okay, Matt," she said, her voice strained from the breath-stealing kiss. "You just surprised me. That's all."

He nodded, but his gaze stayed locked with hers. Whatever she was feeling, she had to get over it fast. She positively could not let him kiss her again. Not because Brady would care as long as it got useful information. But because she refused to want Matt in that way.

Matt pushed his hands into the front pockets of his shorts. "I overstepped the boundaries," he said. "You can relax. I promise I won't touch you again."

Good, because she wasn't crazy about having her will-power put to the test again.

# Chapter Eight

"Grandma, Derrick kicked me under the table."

"Did not." The boy's denial was accompanied by a mischievous smirk.

"Did, too."

"Don't kick your brother, Derrick."

"Pass that sausage gravy down this way before you set it down, Bart."

"This bisque is absolutely to die for, Lenora. You'll have to teach me to make it."

"I'll be happy to, but I warn you—it doesn't always turn out this well. It all depends on the quality of the shrimp."

"And thanks for putting the seafood crepes on the menu. I've been craving them all week."

"Langston told me, and we have to keep our mom-to-be happy."

"Are there more biscuits in the warmer?"

"Yes, I'll get them," Lenora said.

"Let me," Matt said, already pushing back from the table.

Matt had promised that Shelly's first Collingsworth Sunday brunch would be a treat, but she hadn't been prepared for anything quite so elaborate or delicious. Nor had she expected to be so totally welcomed into the family. It wasn't that they'd made a production over having her join them at the massive dining room table. Quite the contrary.

Once the introductions had been made, they'd just accepted her as one of their family. Their large, boisterous, hungry family. The only surprise was Jeremiah. From all the talk she'd expected him to react negatively to her. Instead he'd given a sly wink as they'd bowed their heads for the blessing. Almost as if they were coconspirators in a private scam.

That had been the end of their bonding, though. Before the amen had cleared Langston's mouth, Jeremiah had dived into his meal with gusto. All else was forgotten for him. The rest of the family spent as much time chatting as eating.

Matt's sister Becky complained that her estranged husband wanted to keep the boys an extra week that summer. His unmarried sister Jaime raved over a dress she'd found on sale at the Galleria.

Langston's pregnant wife, Trish, described the newest addition to the nursery—a musical mobile of prancing horses that Langston's office staff had given them. Bart's wife Jaclyn, hung on Trish's every word. Shelly suspected she was eager to have a child of her own.

Shelly made herself the designated listener. It was her job. She reminded herself of that with every breath.

Just because the Collingsworths exuded bountiful love and warmth within their family circle didn't mean that they hadn't crossed the lines of morality and legality when it came to their business dealings.

Just because Matt could send desire zinging though her didn't mean he wasn't guilty of treacherous acts in the name of greed. Just because his kiss had haunted her dreams last night didn't mean she couldn't keep him at a distance and see this assignment through.

And why was she even thinking about him now?

She turned her attention to Melvin Rogers. He'd been introduced as a family friend, but she knew from the conversation that he worked for Langston. He was young, early thirties, Shelly guessed. His sandy-blond hair was cut stylishly short. He was nice-looking, but lacked that enigmatic cowboy appeal the Collingsworth men wore so well. He was more West Coast suave, though even that didn't quite ring true.

Too bad she wasn't sitting close enough to him to question him about his duties with Collingsworth Oil; that would have to wait for a more opportune time. Showing too much interest in the business at this point could work against her.

"Looks as if you're going to be in good hands, Jeremiah. I'd hire me a physical therapist just to improve the scenery around my place if I could get one as pretty as Shelly."

Billy Mack, the outspoken, slightly past middle-age man they'd introduced as a neighbor, made the statement. Eerily everyone grew quiet. The gazes moved from her to Jeremiah as if they were watching a tennis match.

"What the hell are you talking about? *Physical therapist.* I'm through with all that."

"I told you I'd hired a physical therapist," Lenora said. "I thought you realized that it was Shelly."

"And I told you I don't need some woman haranguing me about exercise. I'm too damn old for that. Now pass me the salsa so I can liven up these eggs." He banged his cane on the floor to emphasize his point. Derrick nudged his twin brother and they both snickered, appreciating that there was some excitement at the table.

Lenora wiped the corner of her mouth with her napkin. "I'm sorry, Shelly. But just ignore Jeremiah's outburst and enjoy your brunch. And don't worry. He'll come around. He just doesn't take to change very easily these days."

"I understand. I'll take it slow with him, give him time to get to know me and vice versa."

Thank God for Jeremiah. Thank god for any lifeline to keep her from totally drowning in the warm, loving dynamics of this family.

Right now, her real past was no longer her past. The mother who'd never had time to fit Shelly in between her constant stream of relationships was no longer her mother. Shelly had a new reality—one created for her by the agency.

Fake name, fake past, fake memories. Unfortunately, her emotions still belonged to her real past. Matt and his family were playing havoc with those.

The rest of the meal passed with no more outbursts from Jeremiah, and the adults, were lingering over coffee when Matt's cell phone rang. He excused himself to take the call and returned a few minutes later, all smiles.

"That was Ed Guerra," he said. "A cop from New Orleans recognized the shooter from the sketch that was sent out to all the law-enforcement personnel in Louisiana and Texas. The guy's got an arrest record thicker than a bound volume of all the Harry Potter novels, and he's been spending a lot of time in Houston of late."

"Like we need more criminals in Texas," Langston said. "Did the sheriff give you a name?"

"Frankie Dawson. He deals drugs and makes explosives. I'm not sure how the two go together, but the cop from New Orleans says he's got a reputation for planting bombs under the houses of people he considers his enemies."

"Sounds like a real charmer." Bart set his cup on the table. "Has there been an arrest?"

"No, but the sheriff is convinced this was a case of mistaken identity."

"What makes him so sure?"

"It's the guy's modis operandi. He has a temper and when someone crosses him, he goes after them. Usually it's about drugs, but not always."

A muscle tightened in Langston's jaw as he leaned over and put an arm around the back of his wife's chair. "Aidan deals with that sort of senseless violence all the time in the drug-infested areas of Houston, but I didn't think something like that could happen in Colts Run Cross."

"It's sick," Lenora said. "Shelly could have been killed by this thug. Any of us could have been, if we'd been in his path."

"Let's just hope he's arrested soon," Trish said, "and that he stays in jail."

Lenora placed her hands flat on the table and straightened her back as if taking a stand. "That settles it, Shelly. You did nothing to provoke the shooter and there's no reason for you not to move into Zack's old suite in the big house. Now who's got an argument with that?"

No one spoke up.

"You'll have privacy and the full run of the ranch," Lenora continued. "Unless you've changed your mind about wanting to live and work here. I wouldn't blame you if you have, but I'm hoping you'll stay."

"I wouldn't dream of running out on you before my job is done." Finally she could say something that was true.

AFTER THREE DAYS AND NIGHTS of living in the big house, surrounded by Collingsworths, Shelly felt as if she'd known them all her life. Odd as that may seem, since her life had been nothing like this.

They were relaxed and easy, yet never dull. Everyone was totally involved in their jobs or their passions—apparently even Matt. She'd only seen him once since he'd dropped off her and her luggage on Sunday night.

Shelly was certain he was still upset that she'd jerked away from his kiss. Not that she blamed him. And not that she could react differently, if she had it to do all over again. She was on solid ground now, fitting in with the family, chatting with whoever happened to be around. She could do nothing to jeopardize that progress.

The only first-week goal she hadn't accomplished was to gather some grain of information the agency could use. No luck there. But she had finally gotten Jeremiah to agree to *talking* to her about therapy. One small step toward her getting to keep both feet firmly planted inside the Collingsworth compound.

The sun was barely over the horizon, and the house was quiet except for the ticking of the grandfather clock in the downstairs hallway as she started down the staircase. She'd tossed and turned all night, never able to fall into a deep sleep and finally deciding to give it up and go for a brisk walk.

Her CIA phone vibrated in her pocket before she hit the bottom step. She hadn't talked to anyone in her office since she'd reported her status early Monday morning and a call this early in the morning could mean trouble. She ducked out the back door and took a worn path to a spreading oak tree near the riding arena. She climbed up and perched on top of the fence, locking her heels on the second rung before returning the call.

It was Brady who answered, and even though it was an hour later in D.C., she knew he seldom started work this early.

"Quick response," he said, always a man of few words. "Are you still on the ranch?"

"I am, but I'm outside and apparently am the only one stirring at this ungodly hour."

"Can't sleep, huh?"

"You got it," she answered, yawning into the words.

"How's it going?"

"Nothing to report. I've met all the family except the younger brother Zach who's honeymooning in Hawaii, but I'm not getting any guilty vibes and little talk of business."

"I told you they'd project a good image."

"It's a little more than that. They're patriotism seems to be a lot more than lip service. They talk about duty and honor openly. They don't just practice philanthropy, either. They live it."

"It can still be an act."

"Sure, but why go out of their way to impress a lowly physical therapist?"

"You make a good point. But they're filthy rich. They had to step on a few toes to get where they are. You stamp enough toes and cross enough lines, the morals issues get blurry. And you've seen the evidence we have on them. There's way too much smoke for there not be a raging fire somewhere."

"I concede that someone in the organization may be guilty, maybe even one of the Collingsworths, but not all of them. Take Becky Ridgely."

"That's the daughter married to the pro football player?"

"Right. She's a full-time mother with almost no connection to the business end of things. And there's Jaime. She works at the oil company, but only three days week. And she hadn't worked there long. And Matt's into ranching—not oil."

"It was his name that was found on an illegal alien a few nights ago."

"Anyone could have given the man Matt's name. Finding it on him doesn't automatically make Matt guilty."

"Doesn't make him innocent, either. That's the second time you've mentioned him. You're not falling for Matt Collingsworth, are you?"

"Of course not. I barely know him. I'm telling you my gut instincts. That's all I have to go on as yet. But I did meet someone I think you should check out."

"Who's that?"

"Melvin Rogers. He works with Langston Collingsworth at the oil company."

"Will do, but Ben hasn't mentioned him and Ben's getting in pretty tight with some of the management team. That gets me to the real reason I called. Ben thinks another large transfer of funds is about to occur."

Brady had the utmost faith in Ben and had been ecstatic when he'd landed a position inside the Houston office of Collingsworth Oil. Shelly saw him as an arrogant blowhard, but then so were more than a few of their most successful agents.

"Is this speculation or does Ben have proof?"

"He intercepted correspondence from a foreign bank verifying that they are ready to make the requested transfer at a moment's notice. The money will be paid in cash to someone in Saudi Arabia who was identified only by a series of numbers."

A one-time code name that would be almost impossible to trace. Her stomach rolled sickeningly, the fact that the news bothered her made her sicker yet. Why couldn't she fully accept that at least one of the Collingsworths was likely padding the pocketbooks of some of the world's most evil men?

"Keep your eyes and ears open every second, Shelly. There's not a lot of time to work your way into their confidence before this goes down. Don't miss an opportunity to get close and personal with any of the family members. If we get the chance to turn this into an arrest, we'll want every scrap of evidence we can lay our hands on."

"Right."

"Keep me posted."

"You, too, sir."

"Busy day. Gotta cut and run."

And he did. She dropped the compact-shaped phone back in the velvet pouch with her lipstick and pushed it deep into the front pocket of her jeans. As long no one saw her talking on it, it was doubtful anyone would take it for a phone.

"Hi, there."

She jumped at the sound of Matt's voice. She hadn't heard him approach. She'd have to be more careful in the future, keep a closer vigil when she was on the phone with head-quarters. She took a deep breath to still her nerves.

"Good morning, Matt."

"How's the arm?"

"Pain's gone, except for a twinge every now and then, when I bump it or move it the wrong way."

"Good, and how's it going with my teddy bear of a grandpa?"

"Not as well, but we're meeting after lunch to *talk* about the possibility of his giving me and my methods a try."

"That's progress."

"You're up and out early, or is this the typical ranching starting hour?"

"Actually I've been up most of the night. One of our mares foaled during the wee hours of the morning and there were complications."

"Is everything okay?"

"Both mother and baby are doing fine. The equine vet just left. I don't have to call him often, but this birth had me worried."

"It must be a valuable horse if you had to miss sleep yourself with all the wranglers you have."

"It's not a matter of monetary value. I'm the rancher.

When there's trouble with my animals, I take responsibility. I like it that way and think it's probably why I never got into the oil business. Nursing cold, black crude doesn't offer the same type of gratification as watching a calf or foal take that first wobbly step."

Shelly studied Matt in the soft glimmer of the sun's early-morning rays. She could see fatigue in the slight stoop to his shoulders and in the wrinkles at the corners of his gunmetal gray eyes. Mostly she saw his strength. Taut muscles. Sun-bronzed skin. Tough as steel, yet caring enough to be there for a horse in need of care.

He'd be a fantastic lover.

The thought ambushed her, then took over her senses so fast, it left her reeling. Vivid images pressed into her mind. His arms around her, his hands and fingers imprinting into her back, his legs tangling with hers.

"Would you like to see the new foal?"

"Yes," she answered quickly, thankful that if he'd noticed her flushed state, he hadn't mentioned it.

He put a hand on the small of her back and walked beside her until they'd cleared the stable doors and entered the soft filtered light inside.

He spoke to the horses as they made their way to the rear of the building, calling each by name and stopping occasionally to scratch a nose poked in his direction.

"You're good with them," she said.

"Not nearly as good as my sister-in-law Kali, but I like to think I connect with them."

"So you're not just a cowman?"

"I'm a man of many talents."

There was no mistaking the sensual teasing tone of the comment. So maybe he had noticed how flustered she'd become and sensed it had to do with him.

"There he is," Matt said. "Sakima."

"He's so little."

"Probably didn't feel that tiny to his mother when she was pushing him out."

"Is Sakima an Indian word?"

"Yes, it means king, or so I've heard. I don't know which tribe the word stems from, though."

"Sakima, I like it. And it fits him. He already looks regal."

"Lying in the hay by his mother's feet?"

"Well, he's just a prince now."

She leaned against the door of the stall as Matt checked out the newborn. The mother stared at him nonchalantly as if she knew her baby was in good hands.

Shelly felt as if she'd entered another world, galaxies removed from the world where she normally lived on the vicious edge between crime and punishment.

The sun was higher in the sky when they left the stable and the heat dug in between her shoulder blades and stroked her cheeks. She didn't see how a person could ever get used to South Texas summers. "I should get back to the house and let you get to work," she said.

"Yeah." But he didn't turn to walk away. And neither did she.

"I hope you're not still upset with me about the other night."

"I thought you were upset with me."

"No. I was wrong," he said. "It won't happen again. Scout's honor. The next time we kiss—if there is a next time—you'll have to ask for it."

If he didn't move his hand and step away soon, she'd start begging now. But only because her mind refused to believe he could be guilty of aiding the enemy. She couldn't possibly have this kind of attraction for someone who would fund cruel, heartless killers.

"C'mon," he said. "I'll walk you back to the house. Juanita's likely got coffee brewed and breakfast cooking by now."

Matt wanted her to go with him. He'd made that clear, but he wouldn't want her around for a second if he realized she was here to help rip his family apart and send one or more of them to prison.

She'd wanted this assignment so badly she'd practically begged for it. Now she wished anyone was here but her. Still, she'd do her job. This was a battle the good guys had to win.

AS MATT HAD SUSPECTED, Juanita was already busy in the kitchen when he and Shelly made it back to the big house. He and his brothers had a hell of a time talking his mom into hiring a cook. But she'd quit complaining and started singing Juanita's praises long ago.

Shelly had taken her coffee back to her room instead of having it with him. Just as well. Matt had too much to do before the morning got away from him; he couldn't dawdle over breakfast. He'd grabbed coffee and a hot tortilla that Juanita had stuffed with bacon, eggs and a dash of salsa before heading out.

He was pumped, though after the night he'd had he should be dragging. He had been before he'd spotted Shelly—with her cute little bottom perched on top of the fence.

Running into her had affected him like a double shot of espresso. Every part of him had come instantly to life—especially parts that had no business springing into action with a woman who'd pulled away from his kiss the other night.

The kiss was his mistake, but he hadn't had a woman get to him like this since his first year in college when Betty Estes had taught him the kind of tricks he'd never learned in Boy

Scouts. Then, it had been mostly physical. Hell, it had probably been all physical, but at eighteen, what else was there?

He wasn't eighteen now. He was pushing thirty-four, had dated lots of women, made love to his share and had managed to walk away from all of them without losing a night's sleep. He wasn't proud of the fact that he never became emotionally involved. It was just the way it was— or the way it had been up until last Friday.

He hadn't had a decent night's sleep since he'd met Shelly, and his appetite was none too great, either. Worse part was that she wouldn't clear out of his mind. He'd try to think of feed production; she'd dance all over the numbers. Even last night, when he should have had nothing but foaling on his mind, he'd thought about how close she'd come to losing her life.

She got to him on a dozen different levels and in ways he hadn't began to comprehend. Part of it was probably the whole woman-in-jeopardy scenario. He felt compelled to protect her, whether she wanted to be protected or not. Her mix of vulnerability and spunk was a more powerful aphrodisiac than any perfume on the market.

Not that Shelly didn't smell great. Normally he was pretty much desensitized to odors. A steady dose of manure and cow droppings could do that for you. But Shelly smelled like spring. Fresh. Clean.

And he was letting this get out of hand. Shelly was temporary. He barely knew her. And he didn't have time for a lot of mushy relationship business.

Still, there was something about her. And regardless of what the sheriff had said, he couldn't quite push past the suspicion that she might still be in danger. Reason enough to keep his eye on her for a while even if she didn't seem to want his company.

"IT WAS A SIMPLE TASK. YOU screwed up. And you know how I feel about mistakes."

"The random violence angle was your idea. I carried it off just like you said. The car has more holes in it than a rapper's jeans. There's no way she should have walked away from it alive."

"Alive? She's barely hurt. I want her dead. Now."

"She's just a friggin' physical therapist. What's so important about knocking her off?"

"That's not your concern. I give the orders. You take them. It's called 'money rules.' You have one week, or the deal is off."

Sweat pooled under his armpits and dampened the front of his shirt in spite of the fact that the air conditioner in his Houston apartment was clunking along at full power. He needed that money. He could clear out of the country with it, leave his enemies behind and live like a king in Mexico on what he'd get for this job. But a week…

"I need more time. She's living at Jack's Bluff. I can't just storm the place and take her out. They have security and gun-wielding wranglers everywhere."

"One week. Work fast. You're not the only one whose time is running out."

## Chapter Nine

Jeremiah hobbled into the first-floor study exactly twenty-two minutes past their scheduled meeting time. She knew he had neither forgotten the appointment nor become confused about the meeting time. She'd found him in the front yard talking to Billy Mack about five minutes before they were supposed to meet and reminded him.

He swung his cane as he sat down, banging it against the leg of a bookcase before propping it against his chair. "A pretty young woman like you ought to have better things to do with her time than waste it talking to an old codger like me."

"I'm getting paid for my time and I certainly hope it won't be a waste."

"You could have saved yourself a trip to Texas if my daughter-in-law wasn't always trying to do my thinking for me. I may not get around like a young whippersnapper, but I'm not senile."

"Glad to hear that," Shelly said. "I don't treat senility, but I'm a very competent physical therapist. I'm pretty sure I can help you—if you're willing to put forth some effort."

Jeremiah checked his watch as if he had another appointment, then frowned as if he were late for it. "I'm over a year post-stroke and not stupid. I know the odds of seeing any kind of improvement at this point are slim to none."

"Actually, recent research has proved that certain exercises used routinely can lead to substantial improvements in balance and range of motion." Fortunately, she'd done her homework. "I can show you articles on that if you'd like."

"Keep your articles." He picked up his cane and pointed it toward the window. "You see that big oak tree out there?"

She nodded, wondering where he was going with this.

"I planted it the year my only child was born."

He had to be talking about Lenora's late husband. That would make the tree approximately six decades old. She'd known that Randolph was the only heir to the Collingsworth fortune before he'd fathered his own large brood.

"I built this house, too," Jeremiah continued, "with my own hands and little help from anyone else."

"You did a great job. It's still in marvelous shape." She still had no idea what point he was trying to make, or if he had one.

"I made Collingsworth Oil what it is today, too."

Now, they might be getting somewhere.

Jeremiah scratched a pale, wrinkled cheek, then nudged his brass-rimmed glasses up the thin bridge of his nose. "Sure my son improved the bottom line. So has Langston, but I set the wheels in motion. I made deals they'd never think of, took risks they'd never dare."

His mouth started to twitch and he stared into space, finally letting a smile reach his lips. At first she thought he'd lost his train of thought—a not so uncommon trait for men his age even if they haven't suffered a stroke—but when he spoke again, she knew he was merely reliving a time when he'd felt far more potent than he did today.

The smile disappeared and his expression became drawn.

"I was worth something to my family back then. Now I'm just a liability. And my huffing and sweating and taking on a hundred more aches in these worn-out joints just so they can feel like they tried to rehabilitate me isn't going to change the fact that I'm old. So take your theories and your exercises and go back to Atlanta."

In spite of his bluster, he was clearly depressed over the changes since the stroke and quite likely afraid of failure if he went back into therapy. He had probably never shown weakness nor felt this powerless in his life.

Her heart went out to him. She wished that it didn't. Sympathizing with him made trying to wheedle information so much more difficult. But she had no choice, especially now that she knew his mental functioning was more stable than first impressions had suggested.

He'd been CEO of Collingsworth Enterprises until the stroke, and knowing what she did of his personality, she suspected he'd run things the way he saw fit, whether or not Langston agreed. Admittedly, he took risks and made deals they wouldn't have considered.

Yet he was out of the office and apparently uninvolved with company operations and the money continued to exchange hands—and at an escalated rate.

Jeremiah leaned forward, using his cane for support. "Go home, or stay here on the ranch if you like. It doesn't make two cents' worth of difference to me. Just don't badger me about therapy. It's not going to happen."

"It's your call," she said. There was no reason to antagonize him, when her purpose was to get close. "I'd love to hear more about your work with Collingsworth Enterprises, though. Big deals. Risk taking. It sounds as if you've had an exciting life."

He studied her, likely judging whether or not she was

serious or merely humoring him. He must have decided in her favor, since he leaned back in his chair and let go of the cane.

"The oil business is not what people think it is. Those complainers always screaming about the price of gasoline don't know the half of what we go through to keep their big cars running."

"They should probably talk to you," she said.

"Dart tootin' they should. It's not the *Beverly Hillbillies,* you know. You don't just walk out in your backyard and find oil. You gotta spend money and go hunting for it."

"You must have to make deals with all kinds of people."

He nodded. "Especially today. The world's changing. The balance of power is steadily shifting." His hands knotted into bony fists and his voice rose. "And now we got the CIA breathing down our neck." He was practically screaming now. "The CIA doesn't have jack squat—"

"What's going on here?"

The interruption startled Shelly. She looked up to see Matt's brother Bart standing in the doorway—his eyes narrowed, yet piercing.

He glared at Jeremiah. "What's the problem?"

"I'm educating Shelly about the oil business," Jeremiah said.

"I'm sure Shelly's not interested in the inner workings of the company. Besides, you know our rule. What goes on at Collingsworth Oil stays at Collingsworth Oil."

"I thought that was Vegas," Shelly joked, trying to ease the tension that had walked in with Bart. No such luck.

"Is the therapy session over?" Bart asked.

"Never got started," Jeremiah said. "Never going to."

"In that case, how about taking a ride over to Tom Greer's with me. He's cutting his operations back since his wife was hurt in that car wreck in February, and he's got some hay-baling equipment he wants to sell."

"Since when do you want my opinion on equipment?"

"I don't. I'd just like your company and you and Tom always find things to talk about."

Shelly didn't buy it. What he wanted was to keep Jeremiah from saying more about the CIA. It was just her luck that Bart would show up at that precise moment. Her would-be patient had been in the mood to talk. She'd see that she found time alone with Jeremiah again, hopefully before the day was over.

Jeremiah departed with Bart, leaving her to ponder a half dozen possibilities she couldn't back up with facts. Maybe Jeremiah had been the one to initially secure oil deals by contributing to terrorist causes. But who had taken over where he left off? Langston? Lenora? Or was it as Brady believed—an accepted practice of Collingsworth Enterprises with multiple family members savvy and going along with the practice?

But then Brady only knew the family by reputation. He hadn't eaten with them, slept in their houses. Hadn't kissed Matt Collingsworth.

Her lips tingled at the memory, followed by a crush of longing that swept through every inch of her. She gathered her resolve.

This case was far too important, and if she stepped down from the case, there was no way the agency could just slide another agent into her spot; she was the only agent who was a licensed physical therapist.

Yet the memory of the kiss clung to her lips and her mind as if she'd been bewitched.

THE BIG HOUSE WAS exceptionally quiet for the rest of the afternoon. Lenora and Jaime were at their jobs in downtown

Houston. Becky had taken her young sons and the two boisterous lab puppies—one of which belonged to the honeymooning couple—to visit friends at a neighboring ranch.
Matt was nowhere to be seen, and even Juanita had finished
dinner preparations and gone back to her own house for a
few hours downtime.

Apparently her schedule was flexible. She showed up in
the mornings, put breakfast on the table and stayed busy in
the kitchen all morning. Lunch was on the table at twelve and
eaten by whoever showed up. The participants varied, but
usually included Becky and her sons, a wrangler named Joe
Bob who was practically family and totally charming, and
sometimes Bart and Jaclyn.

Shelly had shown up every day, hoping to glean some
tidbit of useful information. That had been a bust, though
she'd loved talking to Bart's wife, Jaclyn, and found her
open and interesting.

Becky was more difficult to relate to. She was friendly,
but nowhere near as outgoing as her younger sister Jaime.
She never talked about herself or her estranged husband.
The boys, however, talked about their dad almost constantly.
It was clear they missed him and couldn't wait for their
summer visit with him in July.

Shelly picked up one of the family albums from the book-
shelf in the family room and dropped to the sofa to peruse
the snapshots. She skimmed the first few pages, mostly
images of a much younger Lenora and a very handsome man
who must have been her late husband, Randolph. These must
have been taken right after their marriage—or before. Lenora
didn't appear to be much past her teens when the pictures
were taken.

Shelly turned the next page and a loose snapshot slipped
from the folds and fell into her lap. There was writing on the

back and Shelly checked that out even before looking at the photo.

*I love you more than life itself, Randolph Collingsworth, and I can't wait to marry you and bear your children. Your world will be my world. Hugs and a million kisses, Lenora.*

Lenora had been so young, yet she'd followed her heart. It had worked for her. She was one of the lucky ones.

Shelly's mother had fared much worse. She'd chosen the wrong man—over and over again. A half dozen stepfathers and more "uncles" than Shelly cared to remember had taken up residence in their house. Shelly had even liked a few of them. No matter. None ever stayed for long.

Restless now and haunted by memories she preferred to leave cloaked in shadows, Shelly retuned the album to the shelf and walked toward the back door, swinging through it for a reviving breath of fresh air.

She'd made it to the bottom step before an uneasy feeling sent a shiver up her spine. Apprehension and training cued her senses, and she scanned the area looking for movement and listening for any errant sounds. A slight breeze rustled the leaves in the nearby oak trees and ruffled her short hair. A crow cawed. Another answered.

Nothing amiss, but the flesh around her freshly dressed wound prickled, a reminder of the bullets that had fallen all around her mere days ago.

A car engine sounded in the distance, coming steadily nearer. A shaky breath burst from her lungs. She wouldn't be alone much longer. The relief that accompanied that thought both surprised and disturbed her. Even temporary timidity in a CIA agent was unacceptable.

The car pulled up in the driveway and Jaime jumped out as soon as the engine died. She waved to Shelly, while a tall man dressed in cowboy attire climbed from the passenger seat. Shelly recognized him instantly as the young cowboy who'd been staring at her in Cutter's Bar the other night.

Jaime hung on his arm as they crossed the drive and joined Shelly at the back door. "This is Leland Adams," she said, draping herself over his shoulder and holding on to his arm as if he might try to escape. "Leland, meet Shelly, my grandfather's new physical therapist."

He showed no signs of recognizing her and she decided it was best not to point out that he'd been casually flirting with her in the bar.

"Leland's new in town," Jaime said.

So he had likely been looking for a woman to hook up with the other night. She wasn't sure how Jaime had connected with him so quickly, but she could have met him before then or else last night when she'd gone out with friends.

A lonesome cowboy would notice Jaime at once. She was what the hip magazines would classify as a super hottie. Great looks, a sparkling personality and dressed to entice.

"I'm going to give Leland a quick tour of the house and then we're driving out to the lake to catch dinner and a sunset—if there's one to catch. The weather forecast predicted a line of thunderstorms heading this way."

Shelly glanced out the window. There was no sign of rain, but she knew from her research that Houston weather was unpredictable, something about the nearness to the Gulf of Mexico.

"Tell Mom I'll be home early, since I have to work tomorrow." Jaime accompanied the word *work* with a gagging expression.

"Spoken like a true heiress," Leland said.

Obviously he was not so new to these parts that he didn't know of her family's wealth. But then the Collingsworth name ranked right up there with the Bush name in Texas prominence.

Leland was the stranger. Shelly considered warning Jaime to be careful, but she didn't want to come across like an alarmist. In all likelihood, Leland was just a cute cowboy out for a good time.

"Sounds like a fun evening," Shelly said. "But you'd best take good care of her, Leland. I'd hate to have her four brothers take you to task." If Leland was even half smart, that should be enough to keep him from trying anything with Jaime she didn't want.

He grinned and raked his fingers through his scraggly hair. "I'll be a perfect gentleman."

It struck Shelly again how odd it was for her to feel protective of a member of the family she was investigating on extremely serious charges.

But, thus far, nothing about this assignment was textbook. Her goal was to blend into the family so seamlessly that they forgot she was around and talked freely in front of her. She'd expected that to require major effort on her part. Instead, the effort was in not becoming so much a part of the family that she couldn't see them objectively.

Leland stopped and turned as he started to follow Jaime up the stairs. Shelly felt his stare boring into her just as she had the other night at Cutter's Bar. A second later, he looked away and took the stairs two at a time, easily catching up with Jaime before she reached the landing. He must have whispered something funny to her as he did, because their laughter echoed through the house.

Restless, Shelly exited via the back door and strode off at a brisk pace. She was almost at the stable before she realized she'd unconsciously gone in that direction. The image of Matt flashed into her thoughts, his hair mussed and his chin whiskered from the sleepless night he'd spent bringing a reluctant colt into the world.

Her knees seemed to liquefy as the image solidified and seared its way into every corner of her mind. Just hormones, she told herself, and her body's way of protesting the fact that it had been denied physical satisfaction for so long.

Forcing her feet to keep going, she pushed through the door of the stable. Afternoon sun poured through the high windows, painting bright stripes of gold across the walls and the few horses that remained in their stalls. A cinnamon-colored steed whinnied and stuck his head over the stall door as if entreating her to pay him a visit or take him for a ride.

She stopped at his stall and hesitantly reached to scratch his nose the way she'd seen Matt do it this morning. He balked and backed away, pawing at the straw and sending it flying beneath his firm belly. Shelly jerked her hand away and backed up so fast she stumbled against the opposite stall.

So she was jittery around horses. Big deal. She faced killers, didn't she?

The stable door squeaked open. She steadied her breath and turned to see Matt and Bart step inside, their bodies haloed in a bright beam of sunlight.

"Langston can handle it," Matt said.

"He's been saying that for months, but the CIA shows no sign of letting this go."

Shelly shrunk against the wall, thankful the rays of sun fell to the right of her, leaving her in the shadows. Hands at her side, she stood perfectly still, hoping the steed wouldn't give her away. Miraculously, the horse ignored her, his head turned as if he, too, was eavesdropping on the conversation.

"They don't have anything," Matt said. "If they did, they'd be making arrests, not rattling cages."

Shelly's heart slammed hard against her chest. Did this mean Matt was in on the payoffs?

Bart knocked away a spider that had dropped from the ceiling on a silky thread and landed right in front of his nose. "The feds wouldn't be spending this much time on the investigation, if this wasn't more than a fishing trip."

"Langston says it's under control," Matt reiterated. "And he's too shrewd a businessman to be leaving anything to chance."

"He's got a pregnant wife ready to deliver within the month. That's his focus right now."

"Can't blame him for that."

"I'm not blaming. I'm just concerned, that's all. We can't afford…"

The steed picked that moment to shake his head and snort loudly, drowning the last of Bart's sentence. The men swung their attention in her direction. Shelly gave up the shadows and stepped into the middle of the aisle that separated the rows of stalls, waving and smiling as if she hadn't heard a word of their conversation.

Matt started toward her. "Couldn't stay away from Sakima, could you?"

"Not a chance. He's so adorable."

"I didn't see you standing there," Bart said. "Why didn't you say something when we came in?"

"You were having a conversation. I didn't want to interrupt."

"Conversation's over," Matt said. "Let's check out the new foal."

"You two go ahead," Bart said. "I'll come back later with Jaclyn. She loves the young colts and I've promised her a sunset ride anyway—if the rain holds off."

Matt chatted casually as he checked out the newborn and

the mother—talking as much to the horses as to her. His tone was calming, and the bond between him and the animals couldn't have been more evident if it had been tangible.

She was as mesmerized by him as she was of the mare and colt. But instead of putting her at ease, his presence created currents of crackling electricity that zinged through her senses.

He finished with the horses and walked back to where she was standing. He trailed a finger down the length of her arm, and the innocuous touch felt like fire on her skin. Finally she looked up. His face was inches from hers, his lips taunting her, daring her not to remember how they'd felt pressed against hers.

"Let's go for a ride."

"A horseback ride?" Her voice was breathy, her heart-beat erratic.

"Why not? There's plenty of time before dinner, and I promise I'll fix you up with the gentlest mare on the ranch. We can take the wooded trails. It will give you a chance to see some of the undeveloped land you can't get to by car."

She and Matt—alone in the woods, with this wild hunger for him raging inside her. Did she dare risk it? Was he fighting the same insane passion, or was all the heat and sensual tension radiating from her?

Not that it mattered. Some agents had no doubt used sex to weaken a suspect's resistance. She couldn't. Nor could she put her own heart on the line when there was no chance this could work. She had little faith in love under the best of circumstances. This was the worst.

Even if Matt was as innocent as she wanted so desperately to believe, he'd hate her once he'd found out she'd tricked her way onto Jack's Bluff Ranch for the express purpose of bringing his family down.

"It's okay to say no, if you don't want to go ride with me," he said.

"No, I'd like to go horseback riding," she said, forcing herself to do the job she'd come to do. "As long as we take it slow. Remember, I'm a city slicker."

"We'll go as slowly as you like, and I'll be right by your side. I'll go saddle up a couple of horses and meet you outside the stable in about ten minutes."

She managed a nod, waiting until he was out of sight to fall back against one of the support columns that separated the stalls. For the last few years, she'd feared she'd never fall into anything that even resembled love again.

What a time to find out she'd been wrong!

"LANGSTON, THIS IS BART. Do you have a minute?"

"Yeah, I'm just finishing up here at the office and about to leave for home."

"Are thinks okay with Trish?"

"Perfect. She went to her gynecologist this afternoon. He thinks it will be a couple more weeks before she goes into labor. She's antsy, but feeling good. What's up with you?"

"Shelly Lane."

"What about her? Mom says she's a perfect fit for the family and she's confident Jeremiah will warm up to her in no time."

"I know. The rest of the family has no qualms at all with her. Even Jaclyn is fond of her."

"But not you?"

"She worries me."

"Anything specific?"

"I walked in on her and Jeremiah this afternoon and she had him talking about the oil company's problems with the CIA. Then this afternoon, Matt and I ran into her in the stables. She had to have heard and seen us but she didn't say a word until we spotted her."

"C'mon, you surely don't think she's a spy for the CIA?"

"It's possible. What's more likely is that she's trying to get something on us that she can use in a blackmail scheme. She wouldn't be the first to try some kind of scam to get money out of the family."

"You're getting a little paranoid. She's here because Mom hired her."

"I just don't want any trouble. We already have enough."

"Are you suggesting we try to pressure Mom into firing her?"

"No. But I think you should make sure the private investigator leaves no alley unexplored where her background's concerned."

"I'll see that he gets that message. And thanks for the heads-up though I'm surprised to be hearing this from you. Matt's usually the suspicious brother."

"Not this time. He lit up like neon when he noticed her in the horse barn. I think he's finally met a woman who fires his engine."

"And you want to get rid of her. Mom would die if she knew that."

They both laughed, but Bart was certain Langston would follow up with the private investigator. Only now, he was almost sorry he'd said anything.

Matt liked her. That should have been good enough for Bart.

MATT STOOD BESIDE THE TWO saddled horses, their reins in one of his hands. He reached the other out to Shelly. She quivered as she took it, her nerves on edge and not just from the size of the horses.

Her CIA phone vibrated. She ignored it. Brady would have to wait. It was time to ride.

# Chapter Ten

The two horses walked side by side along the swiftly running creek. It was swollen from the May rains, but would likely be bone dry by the end of August.

Normally, Matt would have soaked up the scenery, noticed every new growth of underbrush, checked for deer tracks to see if the herd numbers were up or down, and enjoyed the scurry of squirrels and the plodding of the turtles along the muddy banks.

All he could see today was Shelly.

She'd monopolized his thoughts from the moment he'd met her, though he'd tried to convince himself it was caution that had sent him back to town to check on her that first night. That had been a crock, a protective facade he'd pulled over his eyes to keep from acknowledging the way she got to him.

The timing for this couldn't be worse. This was his busiest time on the ranch. He had a million things he should be focusing on. Langston was worried that the troubles with the CIA were coming to a head, and anything that affected any member of the Collingsworth family affected them all.

It had always been that way, especially between him and his brothers. They might fight with each other, but go against one of them and you went against them all.

Even worse than the timing issues, Shelly was the wrong woman. The ranch was his life. She was a city girl, here on a Texas adventure. But the day-to-day reality of ranch life didn't provide the kind of excitement most women envisioned when they thought about cowboys.

He wasn't all that exciting, either, and he was smart enough to know it. He might have the money to live the life of the rich and famous, but he had no desire to jet set or to be a staple of the *Houston Chronicle*'s society section. Ranching was his life.

"I never thought I'd say it about a horse ride, but that wasn't half bad," Shelly said, "except when I spotted that snake wiggling its way through the pine straw."

"A king snake. They're harmless." The rattler she hadn't seen wasn't, but there was no need to point that out when he was drowning in the most seductive smile he'd ever seen.

Bad timing. Wrong woman. So why the hell did just being near her get his blood and juices pumping this way?

"Are there snakes in the creek?"

"It's Texas. Snakes are everywhere."

"Not inside the big house?"

"No, only the brave would take on two rambunctious boys and Jaime."

"That is not true, Matt Collingsworth and you know it. You adore your nephews and Jaime is—"

"Jaime is Jaime. We'll leave it at that."

"I like her. I like the whole family."

"Even Jeremiah?"

"He's growing on me. I think at least some of the bluster comes from his being afraid of all the changes that happened so quickly. Growing old slowly is bad enough, but when a stroke steals so much from you in the blink of an eye, it's difficult to adjust."

"I know. He's a pretty terrific guy when you think about it. He had to be father to all of us after my dad died. He had that drill-sergeant personality even then, teaching us about honor and responsibility.

"I can still hear his lectures ringing in my ears. 'A man is only as good as his word.' That was a favorite line of his. I probably heard that at least once a day growing up. It worked, though. I *am* as good as my word."

"And did your brothers buy into his philosophy?"

"Yeah. I'd have to say they did. We're all very different, but if one of my brothers tells you something, you can be sure it's damn straight. What about you? Do you have brothers? Sisters?"

"No. I'm an only child."

"Spoiled, I guess."

"Rotten."

"That explains that strange smell."

She stuck her tongue out at him. The kidding backfired; he imagined her tongue tangling with his own. He'd vowed that if they kissed again, she'd have to ask for it. Who'd known that promise would be so difficult to keep?

Still, it was probably for the best. Fat chance he'd ever be satisfied with just a kiss, when desire was bucking around inside him like a mad bull.

Shelly looked upward. The wind caught her hair and blew wispy strands of it into her face. His hands itched to reach across the distance between them and tuck it behind her ears. His fingertips would brush her cheeks, might even trail to the curve of her neck. His mouth went dry.

"I think I felt a raindrop," she said.

He pulled his attention to the weather long enough to check the sky. He'd meant to keep an eye on it, but his attention had been captured by more exciting things. A raindrop plopped on his nose, followed by a few more, though the moisture was barely a mist at this point.

"Main storm's to the west of us and moving that way," he said. "We won't get the brunt of it, but it's probably best to go to my place and wait it out. It's nearby."

The words had spilled out of his mouth so fast, he had to wonder if the idea hadn't been skirting the edges of his subconscious before he said them, maybe the reason he'd brought her in this direction.

Moisture glistened on the cleft of Shelly's breasts, just above her blue cotton T-shirt. The tightening in his groins was almost painful. His apprehension level surged.

"Or we can just start back to the big house," he offered. "We'll get wet, but nothing that a few towels and a change of clothes can't remedy." And nothing would happen there that either of them might regret.

She hesitated, but only for a moment. "Your place."

He'd almost swear there was a hint of anticipation in the tone. More likely, he was reading into it what he wanted to hear. But he'd keep his promise. The first move would have to be hers.

THE RAIN WAS STILL FALLING steadily when they reached Matt's rustic home on the edge of the woods. It dripped from Shelly's hair, the cool wetness meandering down her forehead and the back of her neck.

Matt climbed off his horse first, and then walked over to give her a hand dismounting. She slid her feet from the stirrups and he caught her at the waist, pulling her from the saddle and into the circle of his arms.

Matt's hands tightened around her waist, his thumbs digging into her flesh, searing through her shirt. The air ⁺ween them grew steamy, and she was aware of the quick intake of his breath when his gaze fixed on the distinct outline of her pebbled nipples thrusting against the wet shirt.

His thumbs inched higher burying into the soft mound of flesh and pushing her breasts upward. She had a crazy urge to lift the shirt, raise it over her arms and fling it into the rain. Instead she crossed her arms over her chest.

"I'll secure the horses out back," he said, releasing her suddenly and pulling away. "The door's unlocked. Make yourself at home."

She raced to the porch as a streak of jagged lightning lit the gray sky. The rain might last longer than they'd thought— minutes or hours that she'd be alone with Matt, stranded inside his cozy cottage with electrical currents firing between them that were far more dangerous than the storm.

*Get close* was the name of the game, she reminded herself, but not so close that disentangling herself would jeopardize her mission—or shatter her heart.

Once inside, she slipped out of her shoes and padded to the bathroom for a couple of towels. She used one to dry her dripping hair and face and took the other to the back door for Matt.

She was dabbing at the back of her neck when she heard the stomp of his boots just outside the door. "Tell me I can't pick great weather for a ride," he teased as he swung the door open and joined her inside.

He pulled off his hat and placed it on a shelf near the back door with a couple of other western hats, all well-worn. Locks of his thick hair fell over his forehead. Impulsively, she reached to push them back then caught herself and pulled her hands back to her side.

A smile touched his wet lips, and though he didn't say anything, she knew he realized what she'd done and knew exactly why she'd pulled her hand away. His knowing she was fighting her feelings, like a young woman afraid of losing her virginity to a virile cowboy, made this all the worse.

She tossed him the dry towel.

"Thanks." He blotted his face, but never took his eyes off her. "I like the view," he said, grinning and for the first time openly flirting with her, "but you might want to get out of those wet clothes."

The ridiculous blush crept to her flesh again. "A good idea. Do you have a shirt I can borrow?"

"Better than that. I have a robe. I'll put your wet clothes in the dryer."

Getting out of the wet clothes made perfect sense, but the thought of being naked beneath a robe that had hugged Matt's body and likely even retained the soapy, musky scent of him was risky at best.

But Matt didn't wait for an answer. He disappeared down the hall and returned a minute later with a cotton robe still encased in plastic.

"You don't have to give me a new one."

"It's the only one I have," he said, placing it in her hands. "A Christmas gift from Becky who thinks I lack the rudiments of civilized living out here."

"Christmas was months ago."

"The Christmas I received that was years ago. A man living alone doesn't have much use to be covered up when he gets out of the shower."

Another image she didn't need. She took the robe and whispered a hurried thanks before she returned to the bathroom. Locking the door behind her, she leaned against it a few seconds, regrouping and taking deep breaths to still the sensual turmoil.

No man had ever affected her the way Matt did, and she

was still mystified as to exactly what it was about him that got to her. His virility? His rugged good looks? The way his mouth had felt on hers? Or was it the way he'd taken over as her protector from the moment they met?

Probably all that and more, and still she had to let it lie. She had a job to do and she'd do it. It was the way it had to be. She only prayed that all her instincts were right and that Matt was as innocent as she believed him to be. If she was wrong about that, she may as well turn in her resignation today.

The snap on her wet jeans was difficult to maneuver and by the time she'd undone it and the equally reticent zipper, she felt a little more in control. Pushing them past her hips, she let them fall to the floor and then kicked them past her feet.

Unfortunately, the uneasiness returned when she slipped her fingers beneath the elastic waist of her panties. Some of her friends back in D.C. routinely went without underwear. Shelly never did, and the realization that she was about to be doing just that in Matt's house sent heated spikes from her brain right to the core of her being.

She hesitated, then wiggled her panties over her hips and kicked them off. After all, the robe was not transparent. Determinedly, she yanked the wet shirt over her head and reached behind to unclasp her bra. The straps slid over her shoulders and arms and she let the lacy garment fall to the floor with the rest of the wet clothes.

Grabbing the robe, she ripped off the plastic and shook the garment loose. She shoved her arms into the sleeves and pulled it tight. It hung from her shoulders like a sheet, touching her almost nowhere except the shoulders. She yanked on the ties, bunching the fabric at the waist.

Her mirror image taunted her. Very attractive. Kind of like

a pregnant rag doll. That should take care of any sexual urges Matt might have. She gathered her wet clothes, realizing as she balled the panties and bra that there was no way she was handing them to him.

He'd said to make herself at home. Surely that included using the dryer without his supervision. She found the laundry room just off the garage. It was as neat and clean as the rest of the house. Apparently Matt did not like clutter. Yet another trait she could live with.

*Live with.* Her insides rocked insanely. How had that thought crossed her mind? At best she was here to ruin his family's reputation. At worst—well she didn't even want to go there.

She threw the clothes into the dryer and went to find Matt. He was in the kitchen, but unfortunately he hadn't been nearly as accommodating in his choice of attire. His dry jeans rode low on the waist. His clean, white western shirt was open with the tail of it hanging loose. The spattering of dark hairs on his chest seemed to be inviting her fingers to curl around them.

His bare feet slapped against the tile floor as he stepped toward her. "Cocktail hour. The choices for fancy drinks are limited, but I have the basics on hand. Scotch, whiskey, gin and tequila. I can fix you a margarita if you like, or there's wine. I'm not much of a connoisseur, but Jaime stocks the wine closet at home and she makes sure I have few choice bottles on hand."

"Right, so you don't embarrass yourself with lady visitors."

"I could probably count them on one hand. Haven't we already had this conversation?"

"You said you'd never come close to getting married. We didn't discuss numbers." And she had no business doing it now. But the question was out there, and she had no inclination to call it back.

"Then we should probably set the matter straight." Matt set two highball glasses on the counter and turned to face her. "I date, Shelly, actually more than I want, since my mother has decided I need a wife. I don't have sex indiscriminately, and I haven't had unprotected sex since my last semi-long-term relationship. That was two years ago."

"I didn't mean to give you the third degree."

"It's okay. I like things out in the open. I told you, I'm an uncomplicated kind of guy."

"What are you having?" She neatly changed the subject.

"Vodka and tonic."

"I'll have that, too. Easy on the vodka."

"Afraid I'll get you drunk and have my way with you?"

"That might complicate your life."

"It just might."

When the drinks were ready, they returned to the den, with its floor-to-ceiling windows that looked out on the pond and the forested area to the right. Raindrops danced on the windows intermingling with late afternoon shadows. Shelly settled in the upholstered chair nearest the window and pulled her bare feet into the chair with her, tucking them under the robe.

Matt took the sofa. "What made you become a physical therapist?"

Answers to any questions about her background had all been scripted and rehearsed. They were nothing near the truth. Oddly, she'd like to speak honestly with Matt. But she couldn't tell him about how she'd been perfectly happy as a physical therapist until 9/11 had made her rethink her career goals. She'd watched the towers fall on television and knew then that she had to do something more for her country. The CIA had been her choice.

Instead, she went to the memorized script. "The mother of one of my best high school friends was a physical therapist. She loved her work and just hearing her talk about it made me want to give it a try. And it got my dad off my case to become an attorney like him. After reading John Grisham's books, I *knew* I didn't want to be a lawyer. Too many slimy clients."

"I can understand that. Do your parents live in Atlanta?"

"They did. Dad retired last year and they moved to Florida. They live on what I only half-jokingly refer to as reservation for retired people. They call it paradise."

"I plan to retire right here. Well, actually I don't plan to retire at all. Hopefully, I'll stay busy until they bury me beneath Jack's Bluff earth." He swirled his drink in the glass. "Most people spend a lifetime looking for their niche. I was born into mine."

"Seems all you're missing is someone special to share it with." A stupid thing to say, especially when she knew that life as he knew it was likely to disintegrate in days—maybe hours. Yet she found herself waiting for his reply, as if it mattered more than anything she could have asked.

"If I found the right person, I'd marry her in a heartbeat."

"But you haven't found her yet?" The husky vibration in her voice gave too much away. Echoed the emotions riding much too close to the surface, emotions she shouldn't be having.

"I didn't say that. I'm not sure how I'd know, unless the woman I was attracted to reciprocated a little. Maybe by not turning away every time the heat and passion started to build between us."

His attraction for her was on the table now, heady, more intoxicating than the drink. A hunger shot threw her, raw and so fervent it hurt. She ached to cross the room and fit herself into his arms. Longed to feel her body pressed against his, to hear his heart beating in time with hers.

Instead, she struggled with a response.

She was so lost in the moment that she didn't hear the approaching car until she saw Matt's gaze dart to the window. She followed suit in time to see Sheriff Guerra step out of his squad car.

Matt opened the door while the sheriff was still stamping up the steps. "What brings you out in the rain?"

"I was looking for Shelly Lane. She wasn't at the big house, so I thought I'd try your place."

"Lucky guess." Matt tilted his head in her direction.

A knowing smile crossed the sheriff's face as he looked from her to Matt and back to her again.

"We were horseback riding and got caught in the rain," Matt said. "Shelly's clothes are in the dryer."

His smile widened. "Darn rain can sure mess up a good afternoon."

Matt ignored the comment. "Do you have news for Shelly?"

"Yep. A couple of state troopers found Frankie Dawson this morning up near Lufkin."

*Her shooter.* Shelly stood and tried in vain to smooth the bunched fabric. "Did they make an arrest?"

"Little late for that. He was slouched over the steering wheel of a stolen sedan with two bullets in his brain. Likely never lived long enough to know what hit him."

"A gang-related hit?"

"More'n likely. Violence begets violence. The rule of the streets. But I guess we can close your case. Just thought you'd like to know that you don't have to worry about him anymore."

"Thanks."

"Would have been nicer to have answers," Matt said. "We still don't know for certain that Shelly was a random victim."

"And now you probably never will, but it sure looks that way to me. Guess I'll get back to town. Can I give you a ride back to the house, Shelly, or do you want to wait out the rain?"

She hesitated. Surprisingly, Matt didn't. He was already buttoning his shirt and he looked all business now. "How about giving both of us a ride to the big house? That way I can pick up my truck. I'll get Jim Bob to trailer the horses back."

Confusion clouded her mind and chilled her heart. She was falling hard for the protective cowboy. She had to call Brady and tell him she couldn't do this any longer. Time and opportunity were running out.

BILLY MACK CLIMBED THE steps to the front porch of the Collingsworth house and sauntered over to the swing where Lenora nursed a tall glass of iced tea. "You were awful late getting home tonight."

Lenora planted her feet and stilled the swing so that her neighbor could sink down beside her. "Were you watching for me?"

"Yep. Can't have my widow-lady neighbor coming in at all hours. People will talk."

"Only if you go gossiping to them," she teased. "Besides, it's only ten past seven." Billy Mack had been her neighbor since the day she married Randolph and moved to Jack's Bluff. She and his wife had been best friends, crying and laughing together as they raised their kids.

Now it was she and Billy Mack who were left. He spent increasingly more time hanging around her ranch, even flirted occasionally. She didn't mind. He was lonesome. But both of them knew her heart would never belong to anyone but Randolph.

"Did you see a dozen fender benders?" Billy Mack asked.

"At least. You'd think Houstonites would be used to rain, but the concept of slowing down for wet streets never seems to catch on."

"Does the rain have you down, Lenora, or is that CIA business still playing havoc with your spirits?"

"Men are supposed to get less attentive to women's feelings as they grow older. How is it nothing gets past you?"

"You're not that difficult to read. When you're happy as a hog in a mud hole, you're smiling. When your face is long enough to eat oats out of a butter churn, you got something troublesome on your mind."

"I am troubled," she admitted. "Mostly for Langston. He's taking the brunt of the CIA investigation when he should be concentrating on nothing but the birth of his son."

"So they haven't given up with those absurd allegations?"

"No, and they're beyond absurd. Langston runs a tight ship and he would never do anything traitorous. He's loves his country and he's moral and upright. They should be able to see that, but they don't."

"Is Melvin still in charge of getting to the bottom of the charges that company money's gone to terrorist leaders?"

"Yes, and he says all the business dealings have been squeaky clean."

Billy Mack spread his hands on his thighs, letting his blunt, weathered fingers stretch along the denim of his worn overalls. "Maybe Langston should hire someone outside the company to take on that task."

"Who would know more about the operations than Melvin? He's Langston's right-hand man."

"It's just a thought," Billy Mack said. "I know you all think of him as family, but he's not, you know."

Lenora stopped the swing again, shifting so she could look Billy Mack in the eye. "What's that supposed to mean?"

"What I said. He's just not family. That's all."

"He's *almost* family. And Langston has hired an outside accounting firm to go over the most minute detail of every money exchange made over the past year. He expects to get that report back soon."

"Good. I always knew that boy had something in his head besides nits."

They both looked up as a car came down the side road and turned in the drive. Ed Guerra waved from behind the wheel, but didn't get out. Matt and Shelly did and were joined quickly by two excited black lab puppies.

Shelly stopped and scooped Chideaux up in her arms. That one belonged to Zach's wife Kali, but was staying with them while Zach and Kali were on their honeymoon. Blackie belonged to David and Derrick and much preferred to run and bark than be held. He was busily circling Matt's heels now.

"What was the sheriff doing out here?" Lenora asked as Matt and Shelly joined them.

Matt squatted on the top step and tangled with Blackie while he filled them in on the details about Frankie Dawson's murder.

"I hate to hear any of this," Lenora said. "It's a sorry welcome to Texas we've given you, Shelly."

Shelly nuzzled Chideaux beneath her chin. "It wasn't your fault. We have crime in Atlanta, too."

"I still hate that you were hit with the worst of our great state as soon as you arrived. But I just had an idea. I've coerced Matt into going with me to the black-tie art auction for Children's Hospital Saturday night. Why don't you join us? It will be fun."

Shelly turned to Matt, but Chideaux had joined Blackie in the game of tussle and Matt kept his attention focused on the dogs.

"Tell her you want her to join us," Lenora encouraged.

Matt still didn't look up. "It's up to her."

Matt's hardheadedness could be annoying at times, and Shelly was such a nice lady.

"I really don't have anything to wear," Shelly said.

"You and Jaime are practically the same size, and she has a closet full of formals. I'm sure you could find one you like, and I know she'd be glad for you to borrow a dress."

"I wouldn't want to impose…"

"Nonsense. I'll talk to Jaime when she comes in."

"Which reminds me, I'm supposed to tell you she went to dinner with a friend and will be late," Shelly said.

"If she's too late tonight, you can pick out a dress tomorrow."

"Okay, Mrs. Collingsworth, if Jaime doesn't mind and we find one that fits, count me in."

Still no comment from Matt. Lenora was starting to get tired of throwing perfectly suitable women at him only to have him ignore them. Actually, they probably weren't all perfectly suitable, but she didn't see what he could possibly have against getting to know Shelly better. She was not only pretty, but personable and smart.

Shelly excused herself and went inside.

"It wouldn't hurt you to be a bit more attentive when there's a gorgeous woman around, Matt Collingsworth."

Matt smiled, kissed her on the cheek and took the steps two at a time. "Good night, Cupid, er, Mom."

"You should listen to me," she called after him.

"I think you can let up with the matchmaking," Billy Mack said as Matt drove off in his own truck.

"I just want Matt to be happy and to find someone to share his life with the way his brothers have. You know how important that is, Billy Mack. We lost our loves too soon, but imagine if we'd never had them."

"Don't even want to try." He reached over and lay his hand on top of hers. "But I'd say Matt's got some powerful heart-bustin' feelings for Shelly bucking around inside him right now."

"Do you really think so?"

"Sure as shooting. Open your eyes. You'll see it."

Lenora let the comment sink it. She wasn't certain Billy Mack was right this time, but he frequently was. And after all, she'd had a good feeling about Matt and Shelly from the first time she'd met the new physical therapist in that hospital room.

"Don't go cooking up plans," Billy Mack said. "They're adults. They'll take care of things on their own."

Easy for him to say, but she knew Matt. He'd need a push. Luckily, a plan was already forming in her mind. She couldn't do a thing about the CIA, but this she could manage.

*Chapter Eleven*

Trish squirmed beside Langston in the king-size bed. He reached over and spread his hand on her swollen belly and felt the solid kicks. His son was growing inside the woman he loved.

He'd heard the word joy used all his life. Now he knew what it meant—a heart so full that it sometimes felt like it might rise like a helium balloon and float to the heavens. His might have done just that were it not for the problems with the CIA weighing it down.

Trish thrashed in her sleep then jerked and started inching away from him. He watched her in the silver of the moonlight streaming through the window. She was always beautiful—always would be in his eyes—but he literally couldn't keep his eyes off her since she'd become pregnant. He'd missed this with his daughter. He wanted to treasure every second of the beginnings of his son's life.

"Little fellow keeping you awake?" he asked

"I think he's playing football with my kidneys." She eased her legs over the side of the bed. "I've got to go to the bathroom again."

"Can I get you something? Warm milk? Cheese crackers and fudge?"

"You're never going to let me live that down, are you?"

"Probably not."

During the first trimester she'd had this unreasonable craving for cheese crackers and fudge. The first time it had hit had been in San Francisco where she'd gone with him to a conference. He'd left their hotel room at two in the morning to go in search of the snack.

Crazy thing was, he hadn't minded at all. If she'd decided she needed a couple of stars and a planet or two to go with it, he'd have done his best to get that for her, too.

When she came back to bed, he made a place for her in his arms.

"I'm sorry I woke you," she said. "Maybe I should start sleeping in the guest room until the baby's born."

He buried his face in the soft flesh where her neck met her shoulder. "Does that mean the honeymoon's over?"

"It means the breadwinner needs his rest."

"You didn't wake me," he admitted. "I was as restless as you."

"It's the CIA investigation, isn't it?"

"Yeah."

"You know their allegations are false, Langston. If they had evidence, they'd be prosecuting. You've said that yourself a hundred times over the last few months. They don't have evidence—because there isn't any."

"I may have been overly optimistic." He felt her tense and wished he didn't have to tell her this, not now with the baby due so soon. He'd been fretting about it all night, and had finally acknowledged that the truth would be the only way he could break the worst of the news to her.

"Is there something I don't know?"

"I told you I'd hired an accounting firm to analyze our financial expenditures to the minutest detail."

"And there's no reason to think they'll discover anything your own accountants haven't."

He pulled her closer. "Only they did. Over six million dollars that was allocated to purchase equipment from overseas suppliers over the past two years has vanished. The equipment was reportedly delivered, but in actuality was never even ordered. There is no paper trail for where that money actually went."

"So you think it might have gone to a terrorist organization?"

"I don't know where in the hell it went, but I plan to find out." Here came the really hard part. "I'm going to have to make a trip to our Middle East facilities, Trish."

"When?"

"I have reservations for a Tuesday flight."

"But the baby is due within the next two weeks."

"I hope to be back in a week."

"But what if the baby's early? You wouldn't be here. Oh, Langston, you can't miss the delivery. You've talked of being there and seeing your son take his first breath since the moment I told you I was pregnant."

"I know." But better to miss the first breath than miss his son's whole life while he sat in a prison cell. "I think Collingsworth Oil has been set up, Trish. I don't know why or by whom, but someone—or some group—has orchestrated a brilliant plan to put us under and send me—and possibly other members of the family—to prison. I can't let that happen."

"You can't take this on yourself. Every member of the family is an equal owner of Collingsworth Enterprises."

"The oil business is my baby. I'll let them know what's going on, but I have to take full responsibility for this."

"But you'll be able to straighten this out. I mean, there is no chance they can arrest you, is there?"

"No, of course not," he lied.

"I'm afraid, Langston."

"Don't be, sweetheart." He was afraid enough for both of them.

IT WAS AFTER TEN BEFORE Shelly had an opportunity to return Brady's call. Her suite, a spacious bedroom and cozy sitting room, had formerly been Zach's quarters. The only other room in this wing was the game-and-billiards area and it was empty now.

She didn't know if her supervisor would answer or have the call transferred to someone working night shift at headquarters. Brady answered on the first ring.

"State your name and business."

Her pulse quickened. Shifting to this high level of security could not be good. "It's Shelly," she said, adding her private code word though she knew he'd recognize her voice. "Are their new developments in the Collingsworth investigation?"

"The money is expected to be transferred on Monday. We've got it covered. There's a good chance Langston Collingsworth will be under arrest by Monday evening. He's being followed now in case he tries to leave the country. Arrest of other family members will likely follow shortly, with CEO Lenora Collingsworth second in line."

The walls of the room started closing in on Shelly, and she held to the back of the loveseat to keep from sinking to the floor. "Are you certain the Collingsworths are actually behind this?"

"Everything looks that way. Langston Collingsworth is the one name that's stayed constant as we've progressed up the evidence level. But the names of all his brothers are playing prominently in the latest deal."

Her head begin to spin. There had to be a mistake. "I'm

inside the family situation," she said. "I find it virtually impossible to believe M—" She stopped herself. "I can't believe anyone in the family is guilty."

"They've been misleading people for a long time, Shelly. Playing their good-old-boy rancher and philanthropy cards without a miscue. It sounds as if they may have even gotten to you."

"No." At least she didn't think so. She was almost certain she hadn't been misled. If she was right… Her mind changed gears and was off and running in another direction. "The evidence could have been planted. This could be a setup."

"Not likely, considering that the investigation has been going on for over a year."

"But you do admit it's possible."

"The person setting them up would have to have a lot of power in the company. And motivation."

Still it was possible. "What do you want me to do now?"

"Stay on the assignment. I'll pull you off just before we make the arrest. In the meantime, don't miss any opportunity to gather information. Get back to me immediately with anything that could possibly affect our actions."

"I can do that."

"And, Shelly, be careful."

She could do that, too. She wasn't sure that she would. Now more than ever, she needed any scrap of info she could glean. And she'd go to any extreme to get it.

She was convinced that Matt wasn't involved in this in any way, but suppose she was wrong. Suppose her attraction to Matt had colored her every thought since she'd met him. Suppose he and all his brothers were GAS, guilty as sin. She sank to the loveseat, her mind a foggy blur of fears and possibilities. She couldn't pull out now, not with things racing toward culmination.

A light knock at the door jerked her to attention. "I'm coming." Her voice sounded as if it were being muffled by gauze. She took deep breaths as she crossed the room and opened the door to find Jaime dancing to a song she was plugged into via headphone.

"Oh, good. You're still up. I was afraid I might wake you." She pulled off the headphones. "Mom said you needed a dress to wear to a black-tie gala Saturday night."

"If you're sure you don't mind my raiding your closet."

"Not only do I not mind, I have several slinky, seductive numbers in mind."

"Not too slinky."

"There's no such thing."

"I'll need a sleeve to cover my bandage."

"Or a glittery stole. I have several. Come on back to my room. We'll play dress up."

Shelly wasn't up to playing anything, but she didn't dare turn down an opportunity to pick up a tidbit of new information. No matter what she believed—or wanted to believe—they were almost down to the wire and anything she learned could be valuable.

"Your date ended early," Shelly said as she and Jaime headed to Jaime's room.

"Leland is a dud. He's one of those jerks who just wants to hook up with someone with money. I run into more of those than I can count. Always have. It's the worst part of being from a rich family. The best part, of course, is the dresses. Wait until you get a look inside my closet."

"How did you figure him out so quickly?"

"All the questions. Like how big the ranch was, how much we were worth, that sort of thing. He even asked about you."

"What about me?"

"Who you were, what you were doing here and why. That

sort of thing. Like I said he was on the money make. He would have likely called you if he thought you were loaded. He still might."

"Hopefully not. I can see why dealing with guys like him would be a pain, but growing up rich must have had some advantages."

"Are you kidding? I didn't have a clue we were rich when I was young. My allowance wasn't even as big as some of the other girls in the class. Not only that, but I also had to work for mine, plus give some to the church.

"And believe me, there was no designer-label anything back then. As far as Mom is concerned, quality is not determined by price tag." Jaime mimicked her mother with that last phrase.

"She seems extremely generous now."

"She's generous to a fault, but she's also a stickler for responsibility. Which explains why she's unhappy that I haven't found my niche in life and settled down with a man or a career yet."

"You're working at Collingsworth Oil."

"Hopefully not for long and only to get her off my back. I've tried the corporate life. It's not me."

"I always thought big business might be interesting. Do you get to hobnob with the movers and shakers when you're in the office?"

"Yes, but that's not all it's cracked up to be. The movers and shakers don't have great moves. Give me a cowboy any day."

Shelly could definitely identify with that, though she wouldn't have understood it mere days ago. Jaime bounded ahead of her and was already pulling ball gowns from a walk-in closet the size of most people's bedrooms when Shelly caught up.

Jaime held up a blue silk that looked like something a starlet might choose for the Academy Awards. "Try this one on. You'd have the guys falling out."

Shelly ran her fingers along the low-cut bodice. "The guys wouldn't be the only things falling out."

"I have two-sided tape to keep the puppies in."

Shelly looked down to her size 34D puppies and shook her head. "Let's go for something cut a bit higher."

"Party pooper." Jaime pulled out several more before she came up with an emerald-green silk dress that made Shelly's mouth water.

"Let me try that one on."

Jaime kept rummaging through the closet while Shelly slipped out of her clothes and into the dress that hugged her bodice, waist and hips before flaring a bit to the hem. There was still plenty of cleavage showing, but no danger of a wardrobe malfunction. The most daring element was the slit that revealed lots of thigh.

Jaime returned with a beaded wrap to accessorize the dress and hide her bandage. She draped it over the bedpost and stopped to stare at Shelly. "Wow! You look fantastic. That dress was made for you."

"I love it," Shelly admitted, "but the slit may be cut a tad too high."

"For church, maybe. Not for an artsy affair. And I have just the jewelry to go with it." Jaime went to a wall safe hidden behind what appeared to be an electrical box in the closet. In seconds, she'd opened it and produced a diamond-and-emerald pendant and a pair of dangling emerald earrings. The trio was probably worth more than a year's pay for Shelly.

Shelly shook her head. "They're beautiful, but much too expensive. I absolutely can't wear them."

"You have to." Jaime circled her neck with the pendant and fastened the clasp. "They look terrific with the dress and your eyes. Just look at you. You'll have Matt panting so hard he won't be able to drive."

The mention of Matt brought the full weight of the investigation crashing down on Shelly again. The dress started to bind like ropes and she had to fight the urge to rip it from her body and run from the room.

"Shoes," Jaime said, oblivious to the change in Shelly. "What size do you wear?"

"Seven, but I can wear something I have."

"Not unless you have the perfect pair. I can't let you mess up that gorgeous dress with anything less. Becky's a size seven and she has a gorgeous pair of silver sandals I talked her into buying at the last Neiman Marcus sale. I doubt she's even worn them yet."

"I can't ask her to—"

"I'll do it for you, but she won't mind if you wear them. We share everything but men in this family. I'll even share that. You can have Leland."

"Now you're being much too generous."

A half hour later, her arms laden with her attire for Saturday night, Shelly dragged herself back to the guest suite.

With all her heart, she hoped Brady was wrong about the Collingsworths' guilt. But was he right about her? Had her feelings for Matt and her bonding with the rest of the family made it impossible for her to see the bigger picture? Or were the Collingsworths truly the most amazing and close-knit family she'd ever been around?

All she knew right now was that she'd never felt as if she belonged anywhere the way she felt here on Jack's Bluff Ranch. She knew it was only an illusion, one that could never last. Matt might be enthralled with her now, but he'd tire of her soon enough. Men moved on when relationships grew stale.

Shelly had witnessed that over and over again, with friends as well as her mom, though her mother held the I've-been-dumped prize. Not to mention that Matt would hate her when the full truth came out.

She opened her door and dropped the beautiful emerald dress on the bed. She'd wear it for Matt two nights from now. And then if things went according to Brady's educated predictions, she'd be on the team that sealed the deal against Matt's family.

There was no surer way to nip a relationship in the bud.

"FINE. I'LL FIND ANOTHER driver, but don't come whining to me the next time you're looking for a job you old reprobate."

Shelly had just poured her third cup of coffee of the morning when she heard Jeremiah's loud and very angry voice. She turned to the see him hobbling down the staircase, dressed in a suit and tie instead of his usual chinos and cotton shirt. His cane was in one hand, his cell phone in the other. Not the safest way for a man with his lack of balance to descend, but also not the time to point that out, unless she wanted to chance the cane flying in her direction.

"Can't get decent help anymore. Dadgummed idiots leave you high and dry without a never-you-mind about it," he sputtered to himself. He stopped when he noticed Shelly staring at him. "No, I'm not doing any exercises this morning," he snarled, taking the stairs even faster. "I got business to take care of."

"So that's why you're looking so dapper this morning."

He straightened his tie with a bony hand and stretched his thin, corded neck. "I have to go into town. That damned

CIA—paid for with my tax dollars by the way—has got nothing better to do than torment God-fearing, patriotic Americans."

"Are you meeting with the CIA?" Brady hadn't mentioned that.

"I plan to set them straight, as soon as I find out exactly what the Sam Hill's going on." He reached the bottom step and lifted his cane to point it in her direction. "They've got my grandsons buffaloed, but they don't scare me."

"Does that mean you're going into the office today?"

"I don't see any other way to get to the bottom of this."

A rather drastic move on his part; Lenora had told her he hadn't gone back since his stroke. Obviously, he had some mental grasp of the seriousness of the situation. She wondered if the rest of the family was fully clued in as well.

Sleep had been a long time in overtaking her troubled mind last night, and she'd had lots of time to rethink everything she'd seen and heard since first meeting Matt Collingsworth only a week ago. The crime and the family refused to meld in any scenario she concocted, leaving her more convinced than ever that they were being framed.

"Do you drive, Shirley?"

"It's Shelly." The stress was obviously affecting his short-term memory. "And I'm an excellent driver." Stunned that the opportunity to visit the height of the action might be about to fall in her hands, she wasn't about to blow it. "I'd be happy to drive you into Collingsworth Oil today, if you have a vehicle I can use."

"We can take my Lincoln. Not that I couldn't drive it myself if it came to that, but my license expired and I don't aim to have one of those smart-alecky Houston cops haranguing me."

"I'll drive. Give me fifteen minutes to change clothes."

"Make it ten."

"Yes, sir."

This would not only give her extended time alone with Jeremiah, but also give her a firsthand look at the business setting of the CIA investigation. She didn't know what she was looking for exactly, but it was imperative that she find it today!

THE EXECUTIVE OFFICES of Collingsworth Oil encompassed the eighteenth floor of an older and very stately skyscraper in downtown Houston. Shelly knew this from CIA research, but seeing it in person gave her a much better feel for the setup.

Her first impression was that Houston professional women were more sophisticated than she'd expected. After encountering two stylishly dressed young women in the elevator, Shelly was thankful she'd changed into the more chic of the two business suits she'd brought to Texas with her.

"I'll get that," Jeremiah said when she started to push though the double glass doors to the reception area.

She stood back and waited. He might be all brag and bluster when it came to conversation, but like the rest of the Collingsworth men, he was also a gentleman.

"Mr. Jeremiah," the receptionist called, obviously pleased to see him. "No one told me you were coming in." She rushed over and embraced him warmly.

"Don't go blubbery on me." His voice grew husky, and though the hug was quick and perfunctory, Shelly could tell his return after so long an absence had a bigger emotional impact on him than he would ever admit.

The receptionist turned her gaze to Shelly as if expecting some kind of introduction. Shelly extended her hand. "I'm Shelly Lane, Mr. Collingsworth's physical therapist and occasional driver."

"Nice to meet you." Her attention reverted back to Jeremiah. "Is Langston expecting you or are you here to see our illustrious CEO?"

"I'm here to see both of them. And, no, they're not expecting me."

"I'll let their secretaries know you're here."

"Don't bother. I'll announce myself."

"I'm not sure that's a good idea."

"Didn't ask you." His bluster was back. He started toward a closed door. "Come along, Shelly. You can wait in the lounge while I take care of business. The coffee's decent, or it used to be."

Shelly took a quick look around the reception area. The furnishings were in subdued earthy tones and rich woods and fabrics that embodied the family's ranching heritage.

Jeremiah looked straight ahead, his pace slow but steady. He didn't stop until they'd almost reached the end of the long hallway. "This is Langston's office," he said, stopping in front of a closed door. And that's my office." He nodded toward an open door just past them marked CEO, Lenora Collingsworth. "At least it was my office before this." He shook his cane as if it were the cause instead of the effect of his problem.

"It's nice you had Lenora to step in for you."

"It probably saved a lot of jockeying for power among my grandsons."

"But Bart and Matt don't seem that interested in the oil business."

"The CEO has final say at Collingsworth Enterprises. That's the oil company *and* the ranch. And while the boys are one for all when it comes to trouble, they don't like taking orders from each other."

"So Lenora basically took over to keep peace in the family."

"You could say that."

"I guess you must have given her a lot of help and advice."

"Nope. I wasn't doing a lot of helping with anything those first few months after the stroke. Luckily, my daughter-in-law didn't need much assistance. She just stepped in and took over. Made a lot of changes that probably needed to be made, though she tends to go overboard with handing out benefits."

"What kind of changes?" Shelly tried to sound only casually interested in the operations of the business.

"Better health benefits, more lenient family leave program. She's even got a fully-staffed nursery on the seventeenth floor so that new mothers can be close to their babies after they return to work."

"She's an amazing woman."

"Won't argue that, but they've got things in a hell of a mess without me."

"You mean because of the CIA investigation?"

He narrowed his eyes. "How'd you know about that?"

"You told me."

"Right. 'Course I did. I know that."

A slightly overweight middle-age woman with graying hair stepped out of Langston's office. Her pale gray suit was accented with a bright teal scarf that lit up her eyes. Her two-inch pumps looked expensive, but sensible. Her smile looked strained.

"It *is* you," she said, walking toward them. "I heard you were here and I had to see it for myself." She slipped an arm around Jeremiah's waist as if they were old friends. "You look terrific."

"Still a charming liar, I see." He turned to Shelly. "This is Langston's executive secretary, Lynette Hastings. And this is Shelly Lane." He stepped around them as they exchanged handshakes and moved toward the door she'd just exited. "Is Langston around?"

"He is, but he's about to start a very important meeting and I doubt he'll be free for a couple of hours."

"Did he tell you to say that?"

She was saved from answering by the arrival of Lenora. In lieu of a greeting, Jeremiah pointed his cane at her accusingly. "Why didn't you tell me there was a family meeting this morning?"

"I didn't want you to worry. How did you find out about it?"

"I was looking for Matt. Jim Bob said he and Bart had both gone into Houston for some kind of emergency meeting. I can still add two and two and come up with four."

The newly discovered possibility that Matt might appear at any moment upped Shelly's pulse, but only until the gravity of situation hit home again. Anxiety had pulled Lenora's usual smile into taut lines and painted dark circles under her eyes.

Lenora laid a hand on Jeremiah's forearm. "You're the rightful head of this family, and I should have told you about the meeting. Bart and Matt are already here. We should join them."

"Langston said Jeremiah should—"

Lenora put up her hand to interrupt Lynette. "It's okay. I'll handle Langston. Jeremiah's in this as deeply as the rest of us."

Shelly tried not to read too much into that last comment.

"You can wait in my office, Shelly," Lenora said, finally including her in the conversation. "It's more comfortable than the lounge. Martha can get you coffee and if you want something to eat, she can order it from the first-floor deli. Oh, and there are several daily newspapers on the bookcase behind my desk. Feel free to peruse them."

"Thanks."

That was Lenora. Hospitable, even when her heart was in anguish. Which would make them hate Shelly all the more when they found out she was an integral part of the team out to prove them guilty and end life as they knew it.

She sucked in a shaky breath as Jeremiah and Lenora entered Langston's reception area with Lynette close on their heels. If the evidence against the Collingsworths was false, there had to be a way to prove it.

If they were being framed, there had to be a way to prove that as well. It would have to be someone with decision-making power. Someone right here inside Collingsworth Oil. Perhaps someone sitting at a desk behind one of these closed doors. Someone with motivation to aid the terrorists or to destroy the Collingsworths. Maybe both.

The only flaw to that theory was that Ben Hartmann had been on the inside for almost six months now and according to Brady, was not picking up the same vibes that she was. Ben didn't have a sliver of a doubt that the current allegations were dead on.

In spite of Lenora's invitation to wait in her office, Shelly walked right past the open door and started back down the hall, checking the names on the offices as she went. Four vice presidents. She recognized all the names, though the only one of the four she'd actually met was Melvin Rogers. That was only because he'd shown up at the Collingsworth Sunday brunch.

She stopped outside Melvin's door. She'd love to snoop in his files, but even if he were in the big family conclave, his secretary would be in the outer office. She'd also love a chance to chat privately with Ben, but she didn't dare risk asking anyone where to find him.

A woman in a straight black skirt and tailored white blouse walked past with a tall man who appeared in his mid-thirties.

They were deep in conversation and barely noticed her as they passed. A second later, a gorgeous young woman who looked more like a super model than an oil-company employee stepped out of Melvin's office, pulling the door shut behind her.

His secretary? Good chance. Shelly hesitated only a second before she opened the door to Melvin's office and stepped inside.

As she'd hoped, the outer office was empty. Tense, her nerves on edge, she knocked lightly on the door past the secretary's neatly ordered desk.

She waited for Melvin's voice. When it didn't come, she turned the knob, pushed the door open and stepped inside. Leaving the door open a crack so that she could hear when the secretary returned, she crossed to the four large wooden file cabinets that were set along the side wall. She tried each one. The first three were locked. The fourth wasn't.

Without a clue as to what she was searching for, she opened the top drawer and scanned the files. Each was labeled with what appeared to be the name of a specific project.

Choosing one at random, she pulled a folder titled Drilling Project Twelve: Risk Analysis. There were pages of maps inside followed by various charts. A page slipped from the folder and she bent to pick it up.

At the sound of voices in the outer office, she shoved the file back in place and closed the cabinet door. The voices were louder now. She was almost certain that one belonged to Ben Hartmann, though she hadn't expected to run into him in the executive wing. The other might belong to Melvin.

A second later, the door opened. Definitely Melvin, looking as if he were about to strangle her or perhaps toss her from the window of the eighteenth floor. Ben looked

downright shocked. Their gazes met and she could see the
irritation burning in his eyes.

Melvin stepped toward her. "I'm sure there must be a
very logical reason for your being in my private office, Miss
Lane. For the life of me, I can't imagine what it could be.
Care to set me straight?"

# Chapter Twelve

Shelly tried to think of a clever comeback explanation to Melvin's rude insinuation. None came to mind, and Ben's glare wasn't helping. He needn't worry. She wasn't stupid enough to say or do anything to blow his cover or her own.

"I drove Jeremiah into the office this morning," she said, thinking fast. "I thought if you weren't busy, we might be able to grab a cup of coffee while I waited for him. Seems as if everyone else is in a meeting."

Melvin's eyes lost some of their fire.

"I guess I shouldn't have just walked in," she continued, "but Lenora told me to make myself at home around the offices, so I thought I'd give you a minute and see if you or your secretary returned."

Shelly was sure that wasn't exactly what Lenora had meant, but she could tell by the change in Melvin's expression that he was buying it. Vanity had him believing she'd like his company. She would, but not for the reasons he was thinking. Ben had moved over near the window and appeared to be studying the Houston skyline with avid interest.

Melvin leaned his backside against his desk. "How did you talk Jeremiah into coming into the office?"

"It was his idea. I just filled in when he couldn't readily find a driver."

"I'm sure he appreciated that. He gave up driving in Houston traffic several years ago, after losing a lane change battle with an SUV. I don't think Langston was expecting him today, though. Did he say why he wanted to come in?"

"Nothing that made sense."

Melvin nodded. "He's flirting with senility these days. That stroke did a number on him."

Ben stepped away from the window and toward the door. "You two seem to have things to talk about. Why don't I come back later? You can give me a call when you want to finish discussing that project?"

Melvin nodded. "Good plan. I'll take my lovely visitor to coffee and I'll get back with you before lunch. In the meantime, just keep what we were talking about under your hat."

"That's a given."

She'd interrupted Ben's opportunity for one-on-one time with one of the company's upper echelon. No wonder he'd looked irritated to see her. The phone on Melvin's desk jangled as Ben started to make his exit.

"My private line," Melvin said. "I'll need to take that."

"I'll wait in the hallway," Shelly offered.

Melvin motioned to them to close the door behind them as he took the call. Ben followed her past the secretary's desk, but grabbed her wrist before she reached the hallway.

"What the hell are you doing?" He mouthed the words. She had no trouble reading his lips.

"My job," she mouthed back.

He pulled a business card from his pocket and used a pen from the desk to scribble something on the back of it before pressing it into her hand. The secretary picked that exact minute to show up.

Shelly pocketed the card. Ben managed to unclench his mouth enough to smile at the woman and murmur good morning before striding away.

Melvin joined Shelly a few minutes later and suggested they take the elevator to the deli as the coffee was better there as was their chance of finding a table quiet enough where they could talk.

She blew off Ben's irritation. He was on the premises all the time. He'd had months to get close to Melvin. This might be her only opportunity to have a private chat with him, and it could be important.

Melvin knew the business. He also knew the family, was practically one of them. If he wanted, he could no doubt clue her in on any number of personal and business matters.

TEN MINUTES LATER, SITTING across from him at a table for two and sipping a latte, her optimism took a nosedive. So far, Melvin had failed to take any of the bait she'd offered. Most important, he'd avoided even her not-so-subtle attempts to steer the conversation to the CIA investigation.

She stirred another sprinkle of sweetener into her coffee. "How long have you been with Collingsworth Oil?"

"A few years."

"I'm impressed."

"By what?"

"You've moved up pretty high on the corporate ladder to have only been with the company a few years. So what's your secret to success? Wait, don't tell me. Let me guess. You're a Collingsworth relative?"

His eyes narrowed and he frowned as if she'd accused him of having bad breath. An odd reaction for someone who'd been accepted so fully into the business and the family circle.

"Rest assured, I'm *not* family."

"Judging from the way you fit in at brunch last week, they must think of you that way."

"I'm accepted, but I'm not to the manor born. There's always a difference. Not that I'm complaining. Just stating a fact."

But there was an edge to his voice. She wondered if he sensed the investigation was building to a crescendo. "What's it like working for Langston?" she asked, still hoping for some inside information to back up her theory.

"Probably calmer than working for Jeremiah. That is who you work for, isn't it?"

"I was hired by Lenora."

"That's interesting. I thought maybe Matt had hired you, seeing as how the two of you hit it off so quickly."

That felt a lot like a jab, though he was smiling when he said it. "Matt's been helpful," she said, resentful that he'd put her on the defensive. "But then, so has the rest of the family."

"I heard the man who shot you was murdered. Guess he didn't realize there are two rules around here that no one breaks."

"What would those be?"

"You don't mess with Texas and you don't cross the Collingsworths or their women."

She didn't like his insinuation that she belonged to Matt or the way he made it sound as if the Collingsworths had something to do with Frankie Dawson's murder. In fact, she didn't like Melvin, and she liked him less by the second. It was almost as if he knew she was with the CIA. But that was impossible. The only way he could know was if he'd heard it from Ben.

"Apparently the CIA doesn't know those rules, either," she said, deciding to take his remark and push it a bit further. "Jeremiah says they're investigating Collingsworth Oil."

Melvin propped his elbows on the table and leaned

closer, capturing her gaze with a penetrating stare. "You wouldn't be trying to squeeze information out of me, would you?"

"No. It's just that I find it extremely difficult to believe the Collingsworths guilty of anything the CIA would investigate. They seem so honest and forthright."

"I agree." He finished his coffee. "I hate to drink and run, but I've got to get back to work."

She took one last sip of her latte and then pushed back from the table. "Someone could be framing the Collingsworths." She threw it out as if the thought had just occurred to her.

"I guess anything's possible." He put a hand to the small of her back as they exited the deli. "But I wouldn't worry about that too much if I were you, Shelly. In fact, I wouldn't worry too much about anything."

"Why?"

"Life's too short."

There was no reason she had to ride up the elevator with Melvin, so she said goodbye at the deli and went to the restroom to read Ben's note. It, too, was short and to the point.

*Back off. GAS.*

GAS. Guilty as sin. Meaning he must have obtained the conclusive evidence they'd been searching for. Maybe from Melvin?

She walked out of the building and crossed the street, stopping in the shade near the corner so the traffic would drown out her voice. Using her regular cell phone so as not to attract questioning stares, she put in a call to headquarters.

She needed facts, and she needed them now.

SHELLY HAD HOPED MATT MIGHT meet up with her and Jeremiah after the meeting and that they would ride back to the ranch together. Instead, Jeremiah had been waiting for her in Lenora's office. Apparently the family confabulation was ongoing; Jeremiah, however, seemed eager to go.

At his suggestion, they stopped for lunch at a small and very crowded Italian restaurant near the office.

The hostess, a middle-aged woman with a puffy eyes and overpermed hair, was all smiles when she saw him. "Mr. Collingsworth, I kept wondering when you'd be back to see us."

"I see you're still packing them in like sardines."

"Business is good." She glanced around the restaurant. "I'm afraid your usual table is not available, but I can still sit you in the side room." She turned to Shelly. "Mr. Collingsworth thinks Houston businessmen talk too loudly when they eat."

"What I said was, 'You need better acoustics,'" he reminded her. "Sounds like a school cafeteria in here."

"Very noisy," she agreed. "But nowhere else can you get my food. My mother's recipes. All fresh ingredients." She put a thumb and two fingers to her mouth to indicate it was delicious.

"Okay, quit your bragging and give us the quietest table you have."

"For two?"

"Of course, for two. Do you see anyone else?"

Jeremiah's abrupt manner didn't faze the hostess and apparent owner who just shook a finger at him. "You haven't changed a bit. I thought someone else might be joining you."

"Not today."

She led them through another door, and just as she'd promised, it was much quieter. There were no large groups of people, and since it was further from the kitchen, the banging and clattering was stifled. She offered them a table by the window. "Is this okay?"

"No, but we'll take it. Ought to get a free dessert since you gave my table away."

"Ought to charge you double for staying away so long."

She placed the menus on the table as he settled into his chair. "But in honor of your return, the drinks are on the house. The usual?"

He nodded. "With a double shot of scotch."

She turned to Shelly. "And for you?"

"Iced tea. I'm driving."

"You can take this back with you," Jeremiah said, handing the woman his menu. "I'll take the spaghetti and meatballs and a small Italian salad."

"Always your favorites," she said.

"I'll have the same," Shelly said, hoping she could manage enough appetite to force down a few bites. If she'd had more time with the Collingsworths before all this came to a head, she might have a better feel for the situation. As it was, she had only first impressions and her instincts to go on. Based on that, she could not accept the GAS verdict.

The drinks came quickly and the salads weren't far behind. Jeremiah tore into his as if forking lettuce were an Olympic event or at least a catharsis for his obvious frustration.

She let him finish most of his drink, hoping it would mellow him a bit, before approaching the subject of the morning's meeting. She ran her index finger along the side of her iced tea glass, collecting condensation. "Did the meeting at Collingsworth Oil ease your mind?"

He waited so long to answer that she wondered if he hadn't heard or had just decided to ignore her. Finally, he swung his leg around so that it was completely under the table and he was facing her. "It's more serious than I thought—the most ludicrous allegations I've ever heard!"

"Then the CIA really is targeting the company?" Her deceitfulness ground inside her like jagged glass.

"It's more like they're targeting the family, myself included. Even Lenora. They think we've been tossing money to terrorists in exchange for special favors on oil deals."

"What are they basing that on?"

"They claim they have evidence and that arrests are imminent. They're either bluffing or badly mistaken. My grandsons and my daughter-in-law wouldn't turn over one red cent to terrorists if their lives depended on it. The Collingsworth blood that runs through their veins would never let them." Anguish edged his voice and made his words shaky.

She'd never been more certain a man was telling the truth.

"That's enough talk of business," he said, when the waitress appeared with their overflowing plates.

She let the subject drop, though it was still claiming all of her attention. Evidence proved that money had gone from the accounts of Collingsworth Oil into the hands of the terrorists. If none of the Collingsworths were behind it, then someone else was. The options as she saw them were simple. Guilty. Or framed.

Ben Hartmann was convinced of the former. She was just as convinced of the latter, but there was zero evidence to back up her theory.

They ate in silence, until Jeremiah's plate was almost empty and she'd actually made a small dent in her serving.

Jeremiah dipped the end of a slice of garlic bread into his sauce. "Where were you when I was waiting for you in Lenora's office?"

"I ran into Melvin Rogers. We had a cup of coffee together in the deli."

He nodded but didn't comment.

"Your family seems very fond of him."

Jeremiah finished his sauce-soaked bread, but he was staring out the window now, almost as if he'd drifted to someplace else in his mind and forgotten she was there. When he finally spoke, his voice had a melancholy sadness about it that squeezed at her heart. "I'm glad she's not here to see this."

"Glad who's not here?"

"My wife. Corrine was a good woman. She had to be a saint to have put up with me. But then, she loved our son Randolph so much that nothing else ever mattered. Sometimes I think God called her home early just so she wouldn't have to face the heartbreak when Randolph's helicopter went down."

"How long has she been dead?"

"Almost thirty-two years now. She died with cancer right after Becky was born. Lenora said she held on long enough to hold her first granddaughter in her arms."

"You must have loved her very much."

"Still do."

Shelly tried to imagine that kind of love, a commitment that went years beyond the grave and still lived in his heart. "You were lucky to find each other."

"Damn lucky." He scratched his chin and then raked his fingers through his thinning hair. "Met her at a church social and I knew the minute she walked into the room that I was going to marry her. I felt like someone had hot-wired me and was sending enough current through me to light up the room. Sounds corny, but that's how it was."

The same way her insides grew hot and awareness zinged through her nerve endings when Matt was around. The way she melted at his touch and hungered to feel his lips on hers again. The way he monopolized her thoughts and had created that bittersweet ache in her heart.

"Have you ever been in love, Shelly?"

The answer stuck in her throat. Until she came to Colts Run Cross and Jack's Bluff Ranch, she hadn't even believed in love.

All she knew of relationships were the kind her mother had been in repeatedly. Four marriages. Four divorces. Countless failed affairs. And the liaison her mother was in right now was already on the downward spiral. Not that she and her mother talked often.

Jeremiah propped his elbows on the table and buried his head in his hands for long seconds before looking up and meeting her gaze. "If you ever love someone, Shelly, don't ever betray them."

"Betrayal must be difficult to forgive," she offered, thinking of how many times her mother had been betrayed, most of all by Shelly's father who'd simply disappeared when he'd found out she was pregnant; he'd never come back into their lives. His betrayal had haunted Shelly most of her life—until she'd finally hardened her heart against it and moved on.

"I don't know how difficult it is to forgive someone else, but it's dang near impossible to forgive yourself."

He'd been there. She saw in the heartrending depths of his eyes. He'd betrayed Corrine at some point and then she'd died and left him to live with the loss, and the pain of what he'd done. She reached across the table and laid her hands on his. He jerked his away as if the touch confirmed his vulnerability.

Betrayal was a death sentence to a relationship. No matter how felt about Matt, there was nowhere for them to go. She was undercover CIA—in his home and in his life under false pretenses. He'd taken her under his wing and offered protection.

Her job was to destroy him and his family.

There was no greater betrayal than that.

THE ENTIRE FAMILY, except for Zach and his new wife, were on hand for Friday night family dinner at the big house. Shelly had been amazed that the mood at the table barely reflected the problems they were dealing with. Shelly knew that was due to a major effort by everyone involved not to pull the others down.

It was also helped by everyone's excitement over a phone call from Zach and Kali saying they had cut their honeymoon short by a few days and that they'd be home tomorrow. David and Derrick had been especially thrilled over the announcement, because they'd been promised surprises from the returning couple.

At eight years of age, the twins had no conception that there could be problems that the adults in their lives couldn't handle. Shelly was pretty sure that Langston's teenage daughter Gina was also unaware of what they were up against. His wife, Trish, however, was the one exception. Anxiety haunted her dark eyes.

"Whose turn is it to do cleanup chores?" Bart asked after they'd lingered over coffee and dessert until long past the time Lenora had told Juanita to take the rest of the night off.

"I'll take care of it," Shelly offered. No sacrifice on her part; she'd feel much more comfortable alone in the kitchen than sitting as the lone traitor in the midst of the family. She'd expected a phone call from Brady all afternoon telling her to make some reasonable excuse for leaving and to get the hell out of Dodge.

He hadn't called. Nor had she. Leaving would be the same as giving up, and she wasn't ready to do that. Her mind was still wrapped around the idea that someone was framing them. But who had the capacity to do it and who hated them that much? And why? Without motivation, she had no argument to take to Brady.

"I'll help," Jaime said.

Matt stood from his seat at the opposite end of the table from Shelly and Jaime and started gathering the tableware. "What, no date on a Friday night?"

"As a matter of fact, I *don't* have a date tonight."

"Why didn't someone tell me the world was coming to an end?" Bart teased, then grimaced, as he no doubt realized how close he'd come to a truth that had nothing to do with Jaime.

"But I have two dates tomorrow, if that eases your mind."

"Better rest up for that," Matt said. "I'll help Shelly with cleanup."

Shelly's heart beat erratically at the prospect of being alone with Matt. She'd struggled all through dinner to keep her eyes from locking with his, had been afraid that he'd see the desire burning inside her. Afraid that he'd realize how hard she was falling for him.

She wanted nothing more than to go back to his house with him tonight and throw herself into his arms. She hungered for his kiss. Ached to press her body against his, to explore all the planes and angles of his hard body.

She wanted to make love with him, wanted it so desperately that she could feel the molten juices of desire pooling in the core of her being. But she couldn't, as long as the lies about her identity stood between them.

Everyone helped clear the table, but then wandered away, leaving only Matt and Shelly and a need that crushed into her chest with such force she had to hold onto the counter for a few seconds to get her bearings.

"I'll rinse and load the dishwasher," she said, knowing she needed to get busy and stay that way every second they were together. "You can put the leftovers away."

"Is that your best offer?"

"Try *only* offer, cowboy."

"Then I guess I'd better grab it." He reached around her for the leftover peas. "You were brave to drive my grandfather into Houston today."

"It went well. We had lunch and he talked a bit. And I had coffee with Melvin while Jeremiah was in the meeting with you."

"How did that go?"

"A little strained."

"He's under the gun with the rest of us with this CIA business. But no reason to bother you with any of this. Did you find a dress to wear tomorrow night?"

"I did."

A very sexy and elegant dress that would make her feel like a princess instead of the rat she felt like now. She slid a plate under the faucet at a bad angle and water splashed onto the front of her shirt. A few drops made it all the way to her face.

Matt picked up a dishtowel and blotted the drops from her cheek. Their gazes met for a second and her heart started beating so loudly she was certain he must hear it.

The towel dropped from his fingers and he slid both hands behind her head, his thumbs trailing her earlobes. "I'm trying to keep my promise," he whispered, his tone teasing though his voice was hoarse with emotion. "But I'm going crazy waiting on you to ask for a kiss."

That made two of them.

"Ouuu! Mushy stuff," David squealed as he rushed to the counter and grabbed a peanut-butter cookie from the few left on the serving plate.

"Kissy, kissy," Derrick chimed in, running right behind him to grab the last of the treats, followed by Blackie who merely barked his disapproval.

Shelly sucked in a shaky breath and leaned away from Matt to put the plate into the dishwasher. One more second and she might have been in Matt's arms, in spite of her good intentions.

She couldn't keep flirting with temptation and expect nothing to happen. Yet she couldn't leave as long as there was a chance she could clear him and his family. Damned if she did. More damned if she didn't.

Bart joined them in the kitchen just as she placed the last spoon on the dishwasher rack. He'd come to refill his coffee mug, but since the pot was empty, he decided on a beer. He offered them both one as well. Shelly took hers and escaped out the back door for a long walk, leaving the brothers to discuss whatever was on their minds.

Leaving her to wish she really were Shelly Lane, physical therapist, free to ask Matt for that kiss.

# Chapter Thirteen

Lenora watched as Billy Mack got out of his new red pickup and sauntered toward the front porch of the big house. She wasn't surprised to see him, even though twilight was about to fade to full darkness.

She rearranged her skirt, but kept her right foot tucked beneath it. She was too weary to stand and welcome him like a legitimate guest. Not that he was one. During the years since their respective spouses had died, they'd depended on each other too much to stand on ceremony. Besides, Chideaux was nestled comfortably in her lap.

"Using Kali's dog to practice up for the new grandbaby?" he teased as he dropped onto the swing beside her.

"I don't need practice. My arms have been ready for another grandchild ever since David and Derrick grew too big for me to hold and cuddle. But I think Chideaux misses Kali and Zach."

"As do you," he said. "And don't go denying you aren't ready for your youngest son to come home."

"More than ready. Did you hear that he called today? They're flying in late tomorrow. They'll be here for Sunday brunch. I'm making all his favorite breakfast foods, a home-coming celebration of sorts."

"Glad to see you're hanging in there so well with the CIA problems kicking at you like a mad dog."

"I'm not," she admitted. "I'm just doing a good job of pretending. I have to think this too will pass. I know none of my sons have done anything wrong. They're too much like their dad."

"Yep. Good genes from you and Randolph. How could they miss?"

"And there is one bright spot, other than that we'll soon have a little one to spoil rotten."

"Let's hear it. I could use some good news."

"You were right. Matt and Shelly Lane have really hit it off."

Billy Mack's eyebrows arched. "Did he tell you that?"

"He didn't have to. I see it in their eyes when they're together."

"Don't push too much. You know how scared Matt's always been of the L word."

"Only because he's never been in love before. The real thing doesn't come around that often."

"Shhh." She nodded toward the worn path that circled the house. "There's Shelly. I was hoping she was with Matt, but she must have gone for a walk alone."

"Walking instead of spooning. I know that disappoints you."

"You're showing your age, Billy Mack. Young people don't spoon anymore, at least not the way you meant it."

"They still do it. They just call it something different."

Shelly joined them on the porch and Billy Mack jumped up to give her his seat.

"You stay right where you are," she said. "I'll take the top step so that I can stretch out." Instead, she leaned against the support post and hugged her knees to her chest.

"I don't know if I thanked you properly for driving Jeremiah into town today," Lenora said. "I know that's above and beyond your job description and you're not even officially on duty yet."

"I didn't mind. It gave us a chance to talk. I think he may be warming up to me."

"I'm sure he is. Melvin said the two of you had coffee as well."

"We did."

"He's a nice guy. We all lucked out when Jeremiah brought him into the business and into the family."

Billy Mack nodded in agreement. "For a cantankerous old fart, he has a lot of friends. Melvin was the son of somebody from his past."

"Did Jeremiah talk much about our problems with the CIA?" Lenora asked.

"Some. Mostly he talked about his late wife. He was in a very melancholy mood."

Lenora leaned back and let her mind unleash old memories. "Corrine was the love of his life."

"He said it was love at first sight."

"I'm sure it was, though you wouldn't have always known that by the way he bellowed when things didn't go his way. But we saw a different side of him when she was diagnosed with cancer."

"It's never easy for a man to watch the woman he loves suffer," Billy Mack said. "But Jeremiah took it as hard as any man I've ever seen. I remember that his wife had a private nurse who lived here in the big house. Jeremiah fired her a month before Corrine died, said he wanted to take care of his wife himself. He hardly left her side after that."

"You remember that better than I do," Lenora admitted.

"You'd been storked, and you already had three little ones to care for."

"You have a good memory."

"Yep. Remember things that happened decades ago. Starting to have trouble with what happened yesterday. I remember that nurse was a looker, though. What was her name? Helen, Ellen, Louella, something like that. Anyway, she was mighty riled when Jeremiah up and fired her."

"Jeremiah did right by Corrine and that's all that matters. Love that goes against the odds. It's the heritage of Jack's Bluff."

"And here we go again," Billy Mack said. He reached over and patted Lenora's hand. "I've heard the legend of Jack's Bluff before and I hear a beer in the kitchen calling my name."

Shelly stretched her legs in front of her and toed her way out of her tennis shoes as if she planned to sit awhile. "Matt mentioned there was a story behind the ranch's name, and he said you told it better than anyone."

"Does that mean you want to hear it?"

"I'd love to."

A DOZEN FIREFLIES danced in the growing darkness and the shrill chorus of a thousand tree frogs wafted through the night air. Shelly stared at Lenora and imagined her sitting in that same swing on hundreds of nights like this while her children grew up around her.

Such roots, a continuance that spanned generations. Tonight their lives were full of anxiety and chaos, and still the family had all gathered at the big house like it was the center of their universe. But what would happen when the arrest warrant was issued and at least one of them was handcuffed and carried off to jail?

The thought pulled at her heart like ribbons of steel. Still, she wanted to hear Lenora's story.

"I'll give you the short version," Lenora said, "or we'll never get to bed tonight. Jeremiah's great-grandfather, Calvin Collingsworth, was a commoner in England who fell in love with a woman betrothed to royalty."

Lenora slowed the movement of the swing and smiled. "Betrothed, don't you love that word? It has such a romantic flavor. Nonetheless, the betrothal was not a match made in heaven as the woman fell madly in love with Calvin."

"Sounds like a fairy tale. No wonder you love telling it."

"All except this part where the fairy tale lovers got caught and Calvin went to prison. I'm not sure what happened to his beloved at that point, but when Calvin broke out of prison a few months later, he went back for her and they set sail for America."

"What year was that?" Shelly asked, firmly caught up in the story.

"Eighteen ninety. When ships were not the luxury cruisers they are today. They survived the storm-tossed crossing and landed penniless in the land of opportunity. Calvin decided to make his luck at the gambling tables and won a ranch while playing poker one night in a rough-and-tumble Mississippi River town. He won on a bluff, holding just a pair of Jacks."

"Thus, Jack's Bluff," Shelly said. "Luck was definitely a lady to him."

"Except the ranch wasn't what it is today. It was just a few acres of uncleared land. Most of his neighbors were raising cotton, but Calvin began raising cattle and buying up every scrap of adjoining land that he could. Then in 1920, oil was discovered on the land, and the rest is history. But it's not the oil that makes Jack's Bluff magical. It was that Calvin followed his heart. Just like everyone in the family has from that day to this. Like I did, when I married Randolph."

Lenora's voiced choked on the last sentence, the first indication of how difficult things were for her right now.

"I can see how true love can make a real difference in a person's life," Shelly said, her own feelings for Matt riding much too close to the surface.

"It makes all the difference, Shelly. When you find it, fight for it. Never let it go."

That wasn't an option for Shelly, not now, not even if Matt felt the same way about her as she did about him. But she was going to fight to the bitter end to see that justice was done, even though she was convinced it meant switching sides in the middle of the battle.

Not that she didn't love the agency and all that it stood for. She did. But this time they were wrong.

Chideaux woke up and started to wiggle. Lenora set him on the porch. He stretched and wandered over to Shelly.

Lenora slowed the creaking swing. "Care to join me in the kitchen for a cup of hot tea?"

"Thanks, but I have a few personal things to take care of in my room." Things like trying to make sense of the few facts she possessed, so that she had at least a chance of convincing Brady Owens to hold off on pressing formal charges. It was a long shot at best.

Sort of like winning a ranch with nothing but a pair of Jacks.

"MELVIN ROGERS WAS HIRED on at the management level, even though he'd had no higher level management experience."

"That's interesting," Shelly said, making notes as she listened to Maddie Gatlin's research findings. "But not surprising, now that I've been around the Collingsworths. I can see them going out on a limb and giving a friend's son a chance, if they thought he had potential."

"And he was heavy on potential. A court-ordered psychiatry report when he was thirteen said his intelligence was near genius level. But then it also said he had aggressive tendencies."

"What prompted the court order?"

"Melvin made threats against some boys in his seventh-grade class."

"What kind of threats?"

"He told them he was going to blow up their houses while they were asleep. The court decided it was an idle threat and let him off, as long as he attended counseling sessions for three months."

"What other problems has he had?"

"That's all the bad I could find. On the positive side, he graduated from UT with a double degree in computer science and mathematics."

"So he finally put his intelligence to work. Maybe that's why Jeremiah decided he had potential."

Shelly had been on the phone with Maddie for the past half hour. Maddie had dug up everything she could find on Melvin, but there was nothing to suggest he had reason to frame the Collingsworths.

On the contrary, he had everything to gain by their continued success. He was a vice-president and treated like family. It didn't get much better than that.

"I don't know what you're trying to prove, Shelly, but I think you're hitting a dead end on the Melvin Rogers track."

"You could be right."

"I heard the case was all but closed anyway, that they already have enough evidence to arrest the four Collingsworth brothers."

The air rushed from Shelly's lungs, leaving a horrid burning sensation in her throat. "Are you sure?"

"I heard it from Cates. He's usually pretty reliable."

"But you heard they were arresting all four brothers?"

"That's the story I got."

This was not the development Shelly wanted to hear. "I'll try to get Brady. I need to know exactly what's going on."

"I suspect he's ready to pull you and Ben Hartmann out of there. Oh, but there was one other thing. You asked about Melvin's parents."

"Right. Were you able to find out anything about them?"

"His mother was named Ellie, maiden name, Mellinger. His father was Gabe Rogers. She divorced him when Melvin was twelve years old."

"About the time Melvin was making threats in school. Did she remarry?"

"No, she went back to school to brush up on her nursing skills and went to work at a hospital in Dallas, Texas. That's where she and Gabe had lived for most of their married life. She died six years ago."

"Supposedly one of his parents was a friend of Jeremiah's. I'm not sure which." Shelly thanked Maddie and put in the call to Brady. She got his answering machine and left him a message that she needed to talk to him ASAP. He was probably home with his family, celebrating the upcoming arrests that he'd been dying to make for over a year.

Brady returned her call an hour later. She grew nauseous as he talked, and her stomach retched to the point she could barely stay on the line.

"Ben finally hacked into the right files," Brady explained. "It's all there. Records of money transfers that exactly match the information we'd gotten from our double agents."

"Did you determine which individual actually made the transfers?"

"No, but every member of the family over twenty-one

owns equal parts of the company. That means every member of the family will face charges."

"There has to be some mistake. I've lived with these people, Brady. I know that they are not capable of such an act."

"You've lived with them exactly one week, and not the best week of your life. The mistake was mine in leaving you on assignment after you were shot at last week. A trauma like that can throw off even an experienced agent's judgment."

And he considered her extremely inexperienced. "My judgment wasn't affected," she insisted.

"Then you weren't ready for the case to begin with. I know you don't want to hear this right now, Shelly, but you may not be cut out to be an undercover agent. That's not to say you can't find your niche with the agency."

That was the least of her worries at this point. "Can't you even consider my theory that someone faked the evidence against Collingsworth Oil? Think of the bad press the agency will be in for if you wrongly arrest four members of a family with this kind of clout. They dine with presidents. Their philanthropy in the Houston area is infamous."

"You're out of line, Shelly. I want you off the ranch tomorrow and back in the D.C. office on Monday morning for a debriefing. Tell the Collingsworths you have a family emergency and make whatever flight arrangements you need to make. Put it all on your expense account."

She swayed as the room began to spin. The wheels were in motion; nothing she could say or do could stop Brady's team from running over this family—who she knew was innocent—and smashing them into the dirt.

She should leave the ranch now, spare herself the agony of facing Matt and Lenora and their friends at the benefit tonight. But she wouldn't give up until she had to. She had twenty-four hours left to stop this travesty before Matt and his brothers went to jail.

SHELLY STOOD OVER HER BED, dressed only in a pair of silky thongs as she considered the irony of the situation. She was going to the gala with Matt, wearing Jaime's ball gown and Becky's silver sandals. She'd look great. She'd feel like Judas.

She wasn't even sure why she was going. Her nobler self insisted it was because there was a chance she'd learn some vital piece of information that might help the Collingsworth's defense. Her earthier self knew that it was at least in part because she wanted this one night with Matt before the attraction he felt for her turned to loathing.

She raised her arms and, careful not to muss her makeup, let the emerald silk ball gown slide over her head and down her body. A tingle danced along her spine as the fabric brushed her nipples and embraced her hips.

She'd slipped her right foot into one of the sexy sandals when someone knocked on her door. No doubt Jaime, coming to see if she passed scrutiny.

Shelly pushed her left foot into the other shoe and reached for the borrowed necklace. "Come in," she called, "but close your eyes until I'm fully ready to wow you."

The door opened. It wasn't Jaime. It was Matt. In a black tux and looking so handsome that it literally hurt to look at him. Her mouth went dry and her stomach rolled like the Atlantic Ocean in a hurricane.

"Wow!" he whispered.

A blush heated her cheeks. "I thought you were Jamie."

"The wow still stands. Need some help with that?"

She nodded and held it in place as he stepped behind her and took the necklace from her trembling fingers. Once the clasp was fastened, he put his hands on her shoulders and turned her around to face him. "You're stunning, Shelly."

"It's the dress."

"It's you."

She'd never thought of what it would be like to have someone ravage her body, but she hungered for it now. Tonight would test her mettle, as it had never been tested before. Her only hope of not ending up in his arms was to make certain they were never alone.

"We should go downstairs and meet your mother," she said."

"There's been a slight change of plans. Mom has a raging headache and she's begged off. I'm afraid you're stuck with me for the entire evening."

He leaned closer so that his lips were only inches from hers. Whatever existed between had become a tangible entity that sucked the oxygen from the room and left her mind and emotions so conflicted she could barely function.

If things were only different. If there were a way to start all over again with him. But there wasn't. They'd already passed the point of no return.

She'd hold on for one more night. Tomorrow she'd walk away from him and Jack's Bluff. End it between them, before they ever had a chance to begin.

# Chapter Fourteen

The trip into Houston had been by limousine. Matt explained that he refused to drink and drive and he'd need at least a couple of shots of whiskey to get through any affair where the main topic of conversation wasn't football or cattle. Under other circumstances, riding with him in the back of a luxurious chauffeured vehicle would have been pure thrill. Tonight it had been awkward and strained.

But once they'd stepped inside the magnificent art gallery that was hosting the benefit, it was impossible not to get caught up in the glitter and glam. The front foyer with its dazzling crystal chandelier dangling from the three-story ceiling was the focal point of the affair. Beneath it, a pianist played show tunes on a grand piano atop a revolving stage.

Champagne fountains flowed freely, and exquisite morsels that titillated her taste buds were passed around on silver trays. More impressive yet was the constant parade of designer gowns worn by women of every size and age. Not to mention the diamonds that dangled from their ears and necks and dipped into their cleavage. The men weren't bad, either, all in black tie attire and flaunting their importance and charisma. The crème de la crème of Houston society.

Matt fit in every bit as well as he had in Cutter's Bar and

Grill. His charm defied setting, and though he might prefer talking about football or cattle, so far he'd held his own discussing whatever topic had arisen.

They were chatting with the mayor and his wife, when Melvin Rogers arrived on the scene. Shelly did a double take when she saw who'd walked in with him. None other than her CIA cohort Ben Hartmann. Ben had apparently become a lot more infused in the mainstream of Collingsworth Oil than she'd realized.

Angelique spotted them from across the room and came over to join them. She gushed over Matt, air-kissed the mayor and his wife and finally turned her attention to Shelly. "What a pleasant surprise to run into you here."

"Thanks. It's nice to see you as well. I should also thank you for the sketch. It was extremely accurate."

"Best of all, it produced results," Matt added.

"I'm glad I could help. Have you had a chance to view the art and make your silent bids?" she asked, directing the question to the four of them.

"I bid on your painting," the mayor's wife said. "And on that sculpture by Michael Allen. I have lots of competition for both."

"Push it higher," Angelique said, smiling and waving at someone else who'd caught her eye. "It's all for a good cause."

"Right," the mayor agreed. "The Children's Hospital does tremendous work."

"I guess Shelly and I should view the offerings," Matt said. "I have orders from Mom that I'm to come home with a bright and cheerful painting to hang in the nursery of her soon-to-be-born grandson."

That brought new questions about Matt's family, and it was minutes later before he finally steered her away from the foyer and toward a winding staircase.

"Are you sure this is the right way to the auction?"

"No, but it's the right way to the second-floor balcony. I need more air and less people."

"I thought you were having a good time."

"I like people, just not all crowded into one room."

"Did you see Melvin when he came in?" she asked.

"I caught a glimpse of him. I'm sure we'll run into him again later. We won't have to stay late, though. I only promised Mom we'd make an appearance. The Children's Hospital is one of her pet projects."

"She obviously loves children."

"Does she ever! That's why she's so worried about my not being married as yet. She's afraid she'll miss out on a grandchild."

A sign propped on the bottom step said the second floor rooms were not open to the public that evening. Matt guided her past the sign and to the top of the second floor. The balcony opened off a circular room to their right.

The quietness of the night and the beauty of the star-studded sky wrapped around them the second they stepped from the confines of the building. She vacillated between fear and hope that he'd make a sexual advance.

He didn't. Instead he walked to the railing and leaned against it, staring into space.

She stayed a step behind him. "Is something wrong?"

"Pretty much everything."

"Does this have to do with the meeting you had at Collingsworth Oil today?"

"Exactly. I know Jeremiah told you something of the problems with the CIA. I think you should know the rest."

"You don't have to explain your private life to me."

"I know that, but I'd like you to hear my side of the story before you get a twisted version from the news media."

So he knew the warrants were imminent. That made sense. Brady would have had the field agents tighten the noose in hopes of a full confession. Guilt and regret balled in her chest, squeezing her heart until it felt like it might fly into a million jagged fragments.

"The CIA believes our family has committed a heinous crime," Matt continued.

She listened while he explained what she already knew, hating that she was forced to remain in her covert role while he bared his soul. But she'd taken an oath. She couldn't dishonor that as long as she still worked for the CIA.

"The CIA is insisting we cooperate with them, but their view of cooperation is that we admit fault. We can't do that. Not one of us would ever stoop to dealing with terrorists, no matter what they offered in return. But it looks as if someone inside the company may have done just that."

She hadn't expected that admission from him. "What makes you think that?"

"Large sums of money are missing from the company's foreign bank accounts."

"Why do you have foreign bank accounts?"

"Sometimes it makes it easier to do business in the global market."

"How long have you known about the missing money?"

"Since yesterday. Langston hired a private accounting firm that specializes in fraud and they discovered it. As yet we don't know exactly how the transactions were made or who they went to, but it certainly leaves the possibility open that the CIA's allegations are valid, even if they're looking at the wrong suspects."

"What will you do?"

"Keep fighting the charges. Hire attorneys. Make bail if that's an option."

His shoulders drooped beneath the weight of the issues. She stepped closer and he reached out to her, tugging her into the crook of his arm. She relaxed against him, knowing only that she couldn't turn away when he needed her.

"I'm pretty sure we're being framed," he said. "It's the only rational explanation."

"What's the motivation?" she asked, voicing the question that haunted her.

"That's the conundrum. Anytime you have wealth or influence in economic circles, you make enemies. But this would have to be someone on the inside, someone who could finagle the records and cover up so well that the company's accountants never picked it up. Someone we trust."

Someone like Melvin Rogers. Not that she had any real reason to suspect him, other than her instincts and the fact that he rubbed her the wrong way. "Do you have any idea who might be behind this?"

"No one we can all agree on. And we don't want to make unfounded accusations."

"You need to look for motivation. That's the key."

"You sound like Langston's homicide-detective friend."

"It's my *CSI* addiction," she lied.

But motivation was the key, and she couldn't possibly see how destroying the Collingsworths would do anything for Melvin except shut down the gold mine he'd lucked into.

Matt's cell phone jangled and he pulled it from his pocket, checking the digital readout for caller ID. "I need to take this," he said.

She nodded and backed away. "I'll wait inside."

She found a spot at the top of the stairs where she had a good view of the party going on below. She spotted Ben almost immediately. He'd hooked up with Angelique and was obviously enjoying himself. He'd definitely adjusted well to the lifestyle his undercover job provided. But then, who was she to talk when she was here with Matt Collingsworth?

She watched until Angelique was approached by a distinguished-looking gentleman and Ben wandered off by himself. Leaving her post, she hurried down the stairs hoping to catch up with him before he joined a new group of people.

She had a few questions for him that she'd like to ask in person. And this was the one place she could get by with that. She walked off in the direction he'd disappeared. No sign of him in the first viewing gallery, so she meandered the hallway, peeking into each room.

When she'd reached the end of the central hallway without spotting him, she decided to go back to the stairs and wait for Matt before she became separated from him as well. She'd started in that direction when she heard her name called. She spun around to find Melvin only steps away.

"We meet again," he said, a taunting jeer that set her nerves on edge.

"Yes, I saw you when you came in with a friend."

"Ben's not exactly a friend." He stepped closer and leaned into her space. "But then you'd know that, wouldn't you?"

"I don't know what you're talking about."

"Don't be coy, Shelly. We need to talk—alone."

"What about?"

"The reason you're really in Texas."

*He knew.* And if he did, the information had to have come from Ben. Anger shot through her. Had Ben let it slip accidentally, or could he have been sucked into some bizarre scheme? She had to find out what Melvin knew.

"There's an empty room upstairs," she said, wondering how they'd avoid running into Matt before she had a chance to find out what was going on.

"There's one much closer. At the end of the hallway."

Possibilities bombarded her mind as she followed him down a second hallway, one with dimmer lights and no doors but one opening off it. She grew instantly wary, "We'll talk upstairs or nowhere," she said. "Your call."

"Right. My call."

She turned as a needle plunged into her arm and a painful sting hit her bloodstream. Trying to break free, she swung her elbows, trying to pound him in his chest, but the drug he'd shot into her had already drained her strength and affected her agility.

She moved in slow motion, stretching her neck to search for someone to call to. But the narrow hallway they'd taken had veered from the main section of the gallery. There was no one in sight.

She tried to scream. Melvin's hand covered her mouth. And then he shoved her through the doorway and into a dark alley. She heard the screech of a cat and the engine of a car idling mere feet from where they were standing.

"Nice broad," someone said in a voice that seemed to be coming from under water. She struggled to focus, but the alley was fading in and out and getting blurrier by the second.

"No mistakes," Melvin said. "Follow my orders to the letter."

"Don't worry. You're not dealing with a dope like Frankie. Short of blowing someone up, he never got it right."

"Just get the job done or you'll end up like him."

Her limbs had gone numb, but she knew she was being dragged down the shadowed alley. Her head banged against something hard. She felt herself falling. She never felt herself stop.

MATT FINISHED HIS CALL and went in search of Shelly. He hadn't meant to talk so long, but that had been Zach. He'd just landed at the airport and wanted a full report on the latest developments.

Matt was ready to head back to the ranch. He planned to do that as soon as he found Shelly. He'd ask Angelique to choose a picture and make sure he won the bid. That would satisfy his mother without his being stuck here all night.

He ran into the mayor's wife at the foot of the stairs. "Have you seen Shelly?"

"Yes. Heading that way." She nodded to the narrow hallway to the left of the auction area.

"Was she by herself?"

"No, she was with a young man. They were walking quickly. I thought she might be looking for you. She seems very nice, Matt."

Yeah. Real nice. And she'd vanished.

Unexpected dread tied knots in his ragged nerves as he hurried in the direction the mayor's wife had indicated. He was likely overreacting, but it had only been a week since Frankie Dawson had tried to kill her. Then someone had murdered him.

Nothing made sense these days. So how could anyone know for certain the violence against Shelly had been random? He'd been to enough functions at this galley that he knew that the door at the end of this hallway opened into an alley. He ran the last few yards and pushed through the door.

No one was there. Only one silver sandal. One that Shelly had been wearing. His heart slammed into his chest as a wave of adrenaline rushed his bloodstream. He scanned the alley in time to see a car rounding the corner at breakneck speed.

Déjà vu. Only this time Shelly was most likely in the escaping car. By the time he ran to the front of the building and located his limo, the abductor's car would be long gone.

A truck turned the corner nearest him and rumbled to a stop. The painted sign on the side said Maurice's Catering. It should have read Heaven Sent.

Matt raced to the car, opened the door and yanked the man from behind the wheel. "Sorry, but a woman's been abducted."

The man stumbled away from the car as Matt jumped in and gunned the engine. He never looked back. Somehow he had to find that car. He had to find Shelly—before it was too late.

Miraculously, he spotted what he thought was the abductor's vehicle two blocks in front of him, speeding through a yellow light. Matt swerved in front of another car and pressed the accelerator to the floorboard, slowing just enough at the red light to make sure he didn't crash before speeding though the intersection.

The car turned at the next corner. Matt made the same turn. He was catching up. And this was familiar territory, only a block from Collingsworth Oil. A new fear collided with the terror already building inside him.

Was there some way her abduction could be connected to the problems with the CIA? Surely not.

A pedestrian stepped off the curb in front of Matt. He barely saw the man in time to throw on his brakes and skid around him. As he did, the catering truck shaved the side of a car parked on the street, slowing him down even more. When he reached the corner, the car he'd been following had disappeared.

His spirits plunged. He couldn't give up, but he was driving blindly now with no clue which way the car had gone. The Interstate was only a few blocks to the east. If the driver had taken it, Matt wouldn't have a chance in hell of locating the car by himself.

He grabbed his cell phone and punched Langston's number. His brothers could always be counted on in a crunch. Only, this time, even they might not be able to help. Still, it was worth a try.

SHELLY OPENED HER EYES. Images and shadows swam in a blurry soup in front of her. She felt sick. Her arm throbbed. Her head felt as if it had been used for a basketball. The rest of her was numb.

She drifted in and out of the fog until her mind began to clear in haphazard spurts of memory. Her and Matt standing on a balcony. Following Ben. Talking to Melvin. Jaime's friend, the cowboy from Cutter's Bar and Grill.

Her stomach retched as the pieces began to slide into place. Melvin had led her into a trap. Ben had to have told him who she was. He and Ben were in this together. But why? What could they possibly gain by abducting her?

Ransom money from Matt? Had both of them been seduced by the Collingsworth's wealth? Could they have wanted it badly enough to sink to this?

Burning sensations prickled her body as sensitivity begin to return to her arms and legs. She was being half carried, half dragged by someone with strong hands and muscular arms. Leland. He'd been waiting for her in the alley.

Her vision improved to the point she could tell they were in a darkened hallway with only a glimmer of light. She tried to move her hands and finally realized her wrists and her ankles were bound.

Her feet banged against something hard and then she was dropped to the floor. A light came on, the glare burning her eyes and temporarily blinding her.

When her pupils adjusted, she looked up and into the sneering face of Leland Adams. She scanned the area around her, shocked to find that they were in Lenora Collingsworth's office. Pictures of Lenora's family stared down at her from the tall bookcases.

Shelly's gaze fastened on one of Matt and a new resolve pushed strength into her drug-weakened muscles.

"You won't get away with this, Leland." Her tongue was thick, but her mind had gained a semblance of clarity. "Matt won't pay a ransom for my return. I'm just a lowly family employee."

"A ransom?" He laughed as if this was all a joke. "Honey, you aren't going to live long enough for me to collect a payoff. You're seconds away from eating a bullet. I'd think you'd taste it by now."

The metallic taste of fear clogged her throat. "Why here, Leland? Why bring me to Collingsworth Oil? Why not kill me in the alleyway where Melvin dumped me?"

"I just follow orders, sweetie."

"Melvin's orders."

"What do you care? You're dead no matter who's picking up my tab. But don't worry, I don't plan to leave you here. We're just planting murder evidence."

Evidence to make it look like the Collingsworths had killed her and disposed of the body. As soon as Brady discovered that she was missing, he'd see that they were the first people investigated. Her blood and other evidence of the murder would be found in the hallway and in Lenora's office.

Melvin had thought of everything. The final crush in destroying the Collingsworths. The only remaining question was *why* he hated them so much.

She worked frantically to free her hands, her only chance to fight back. Leland pulled a pistol from his waist and pointed it at her head.

Her blood ran cold, but she refused to go down without a

struggle. *The mind was a powerful weapon in itself. Keep the attacker talking. Make him doubt himself.* Strategies she'd learned in her training program fixed themselves in her mind.

"How much is Melvin paying you to kill me?"

"Enough."

"And then he'll kill you, just like 'he killed Frankie Dawson."

"Shut up, you bitch."

But she had his attention. His right hand was still holding the pistol, but his finger had eased away from the trigger.

"He killed Frankie because he screwed up the job. I won't."

"He killed Frankie because he couldn't risk his squealing on him one day. He'll kill you for the same reason. No real risk to himself in doing it. Killing riffraff off the street is easy. No one ever gets arrested for that. No one really cares."

"He won't be worried about me. I'll be long gone, living like a friggin' millionaire in Mexico."

But sweat had popped out on his brow and was wetting his underarms. Good signs that she was pushing the right buttons.

"You could be as wealthy as you want, Leland. All you have to do is call Matt Collingsworth right now and ask him for ransom. A million or two is nothing to him. His family has billions."

"You already said he wouldn't pay a ransom, you crazy bitch."

"You have nothing to lose by trying."

A nervous tic attacked the muscles in his face, and he put one hand up to try and stop the twitching. His trigger finger was none too steady, either, but it was back in position. She had to do something fast or she'd never live to walk out of this room.

She didn't want to die. Not this way. Not now. Not before

she'd had a chance to have a family of her own. She'd never been sure she wanted that until now when she felt the possibility slipping away. Or maybe it was Matt who'd changed her view on life.

"Make the call, Leland. I can give you the number. Name your price and see if the Collingsworths will come up with it."

A clanking sound seemed to come from inside the walls or possibly from down the hall.

Leland backed against the desk. "What was that?"

"Probably the cleaning crew," she said. "If you shoot me and run, they'll see you and then they'll find my body and know you killed me," she murmured, grasping at anything that could keep her alive.

"No, the cleaning crew doesn't show up until after midnight. I got lots of time left."

"Sometimes they get here early."

"No, Melvin said midnight for certain, and Melvin doesn't make mistakes."

The noise sounded again, louder this time, as if it were right there in the room with them. Leland started freaking out, the frenzied twitch jerking his face into bizarre contortions. He muttered a string of vile curses and pointed the gun at a spot right between her eyes.

She worked frantically to free her hands. The tape held. But she couldn't just lie here and let him kill her. She stiffened and strained her muscles. But Leland's hand had steadied again and a wild glaze covered his eyes.

There would be no reasoning with him now. She would die before she ever really had a chance to live.

"I love you, Matt," she whispered. She hadn't even been thinking the words, but when her subconscious planted them on her lips, she knew that they were true.

# Chapter Fifteen

Gunfire exploded in Matt's head, tearing through his skull like jagged shrapnel. He rushed through the unlocked doors of Collingsworth Oil like a bull out of the chute. Not even slowing to flick a light switch, he raced down the hallway, toward the sound of gunfire and the lone glow at the end of the hall.

Agony rocked through him, hurling questions at him. The same questions that hadn't let up since he'd found Shelly's second shoe near the elevator of the building's parking garage.

Why Shelly? Why here? Why the hell had he wasted time calling for help instead of coming here the second he'd lost sight of the car?

He half expected to crash head-on into whoever had fired the shot, but caution never entered his mind. All he could think of was getting to Shelly.

The light was on in Lenora's office, highlighting the blood splatters on the open door. A guttural cry started deep inside Matt's soul and ripped through his body before echoing around him. He couldn't lose Shelly like this.

He was panting as he thrust into the room. His first glimpse was of a man he'd never see before, writhing in pain and holding one hand over his blood-soaked stomach.

"Matt, you came."

The voice went straight to his heart. His gaze found Shelly. A live, breathing Shelly, curled into a ball beside the massive wood file cabinet. Safe, for now.

But when he looked back to the man, he was no longer clutching his stomach. His bloodied fingers clasped a pistol.

"Make one move, and I'll kill her."

"The hell you will."

Fury erupted inside Matt, and in one swift movement, he kicked the gun from the man's hand and sent it flying to the far corner of the office.

The man spit out a grating groan and his body went limp.

Matt bent over him and checked the pulse in his neck. There was none.

But Matt's own heart was pounding as he crossed the room and wrapped his arms around Shelly, cuddling her in his arms for a second before slicing through the tape that bound her.

"This is all my fault. I should never have left you alone. Some protector I turned out to be."

"You saved my life. I thought he was already dead. I would have never seen the gun."

Matt tried to make sense of the scene. "Who shot him?"

"I rolled into him. He stumbled and dropped the gun. When he tried to catch it, it went off. He was already shaking from a noise in the hall."

"It's the air-conditioning system. Mom complains about it all the time."

"How did you find me, Matt? How did you know to come here?"

His mother would call it a miracle. Jaime would say it was fate. Trish would say it was meant to be. "Instinct," he said. "And your shoes."

She smiled and leaned her head against his shoulder. He wanted to say a million things to her, but all he could do was hold her.

He didn't know how long they sat that way, clinging to each other without saying a word. Either seconds or minutes later, the quiet was broken by the arrival of a half dozen Houston cops. Langston's homicide friend Aidan Jefferies was in the lead.

"Hell of a mess you've made here, Matt." Aidan turned to the body. "Is he dead?"

"Yeah."

"Care to explain what happened?"

Shelly pulled away from Matt. "The man abducted me, but I didn't shoot him—"

"Too bad," Aidan interrupted. "The city might have given you a medal. This guy is wanted for a dozen or more murders in the New Orleans and Houston areas and those are just the ones we know about."

"Then you know him?"

"He's legend. Known as the Popper because he'll pop anybody for a night's drinking money. Also known as Twitch because all his past trips on LSD come back to haunt him. He has as many aliases as Matt here has bulls."

"Melvin Rogers paid him to kill me."

The muscles in Aidan's face pulled into taut lines. "Do you have proof of that?"

"Melvin drugged me himself and then handed me into Leland's hands."

"I'll need a full statement from you, but give me a second to call in a request for the crime scene unit. And, Matt, give Langston a call on his cell phone. He's on his way down here now. The rest of your brothers are likely with him. Never seen brothers stick together like you guys do. Tell them to bring hot coffee—lots of it—and donuts. I got a feeling this is going to be a long night."

Bring it on, Matt thought. He could handle anything now that Shelly was safe.

IT WAS TWO IN THE MORNING when Zach dropped Shelly and Matt off at Matt's place. There had been no mention of her going back to the big house.

He'd said he'd never do anything she didn't want him to do, but as good as she'd felt in his arms tonight, he had to believe she wanted him, too. Maybe not with the same hunger he was feeling right now. He could understand that.

She'd been through a lot over the past few hours. If all she wanted him to do was hold her, he could live with that. What he couldn't handle was falling asleep tonight without her in his bed and in his arms.

He opened the front door and held it while she stepped inside. Her silhouette was outlined in the moonlight and shadows. His sister Becky always said the house lacked a woman's touch. What it had really lacked was Shelly.

Odd that he could be so certain of that in one short week, after years of wondering if he was cut out to be in any long-term relationship. But there wasn't a doubt in his mind. He loved her on a dozen levels, all of them begging for release right now.

"What a night," Shelly said. "And to think it had started out with you telling me I looked stunning."

"You still do." He fit a hand on the back of her neck and let his fingers tangle in her hair. Even that felt good.

"I've ruined Jaime's designer dress and lost both of Becky's expensive silver high-heeled sandals." She put her hand to her neck and caressed the pendant. "I still have the necklace, though."

He wondered if she thought any of that really mattered. "Dresses and shoes can be replaced."

She pulled away from him. "I still don't get it about Melvin. Why would he go to such lengths to hurt your family?"

Matt's frustration swelled. "We went over all of that with the police. The answers will come when we have all the facts."

"He'll be arrested as soon as—"

"Can we please just let it go for tonight, Shelly?"

"I think I'm afraid to."

"You don't have to be afraid anymore. You just have to let the police handle it from here on. Melvin is out of your life, out of all our lives."

"It's not Melvin that frightens me." Her voice was raspy. "It's you. It's us. It's..."

She sounded tormented and that hurt. Was she reading his mind and sensing that it was all he could do not to take her right here and now? She must think he was a heartless monster to want her like this after what she'd had to deal with.

"I'm not going to lie to you, Shelly. I went through hell and back when I found that sandal in the alley and figured you had to have been abducted. Then when I heard that shot, I nearly went berserk. I'm crazy about you and I've never wanted to make love to a woman the way I want you right now."

"Because you don't—"

"Please. Just let me finish and then you can tell me what a jerk I am. I want you so badly it hurts, but I meant what I said the other night. I won't kiss you or undress you or push myself on you in any way until you're ready. So it's all up to you. If you want me, you'll have to let me know."

"Matt."

Her voice was tentative, as if she were about to tell him something that she knew he didn't want to hear.

"It won't change anything if you turn me down, Shelly. I'll still be here in the morning and I'll want you all over again. I won't be closing any doors."

The ripped satin dress made tantalizing swishing whispers as she stepped toward him. Her eyes—deep, forest green pools that he was drowning in—bore into his.

"I want you, Matt. I've wanted you since the day we met." She stretched to her tiptoes and touched her lips to his. The need inside him erupted in a rush of passion. He quit thinking and let his body take over. A man's way, but it was the only way he knew.

THE KISS DEEPENED AND Shelly melted into the thrill of it, her body pressing against Matt's. She'd tried to hold back, knowing she had no right to take his love. But once he'd said how much he wanted her, her resolve was swallowed by her raging, wanton desire.

Tomorrow, she'd be strong. Tomorrow, she'd face the reality of her deception and confess everything to Matt and his family.

Tonight, she needed Matt so much she couldn't bear to turn away. Tonight she'd find sweet fulfillment in his arms.

Matt's tongue invaded her mouth, tasting and tangling and claiming her breath. The kiss undid her, opened her up like a surgeon's scalpel and released emotions that had been locked away all her life.

She whimpered when his mouth left hers, but only because his lips were sweetly tormenting as they seared a path down the column of her neck to the swell of her breasts.

"The dress has to go," he whispered.

He unzipped it with one hand while the other cupped and gently squeezed her left breast. The dress slipped to the floor as Matt fit his lips around her peaked nipple. The feel of his tongue circling her areola had the effect of an exotic aphrodisiac, creating a pooling moistness between her thighs.

She thrust her body against him, and he lifted her from the floor, then let her body ride down his, pressing hard against his erection while a thousand sensations exploded inside her.

And then he lifted her in his arms, carried her to the bedroom and lay her on top of the snow-white quilt.

"Just let me look at you," he whispered as he fit his hands beneath the waistband of her silky thong panties and pulled them over her hips and down her legs.

He stretched out beside her, rising on one elbow so he could watch her reactions as he trailed the fingers of his right hand around her breasts and down the smooth flesh of her stomach. He traced it again, this time letting his fingers slide between her thighs and his thumbs skim the opening to her most intimate crevice.

But she wanted more. She wanted to see and feel him, all of him, without the black tuxedo slacks that he'd looked so devilishly handsome in when the night had first started. She needed to memorize every plane and angle of his face and body so that she could pull them up in a million dreams.

"Your turn to lay back and my turn to undress you," she murmured.

"A man lives for moments like this."

"So does a woman." She hadn't before, but only because she'd never imagined anything could feel this way. She undid the button and zipper and fit her hands beneath the waistband of his trousers and boxers. He made it easy for her, lifting his hips so that the pants would slide past them. She yanked the pants and boxers from his feet and tossed them to the floor.

They were both naked now, lying side by side, the peaks of her nipples brushing his chest. He fit his leg between her thighs, opening her so that the could dip his finger inside her. She ran hot at the gentle thrusts, bathing his finger in her hot juices.

"I can't wait much longer."

She fit her hand around his erection. It was long and hard and pulsing with need. "You don't have to wait. I'm more than ready."

"Should I use protection or are you on the pill?"

"Protection."

He reached in the drawer of the bedside table and pulled out what he needed. "Don't get the wrong idea," he said. "The ones I had were laced with cobwebs. These were optimistically bought with you in mind."

"I didn't ask." But she *had* wondered. The nature of a woman.

Seconds later he raised over her, and this time she spread her legs on her own. He pushed inside her, a quick thrust that set her on fire. She buried her face in the smooth flesh of his shoulder as he thrust over and over, his momentum a growing crescendo.

She'd needed this so badly. Needed Matt with all his strength and all his virility. Needed him now so much her fingers were digging into his back as she thrust against him. She wanted nothing to separate them, not even air. This had to last a lifetime.

Matt thrust again and she cried out as they reached orgasm together, the thrill of it stealing her breath. They held on tight, clinging until the afterglow had taken full hold of them.

"I love you, Shelly. And don't say it back. Not until you're ready. But I've never felt like saying that to a woman before, and I needed to get it out before it exploded inside me."

Tears burned the backs of her eyes. She should have told him the truth. She should have never let things go this far. Should have never let him say 'I love you.'"

"We need to talk, Matt."

"No. I don't want to hear what's causing that strain in your voice. Not tonight."

He was right. They shouldn't tarnish this moment. The bitter truth could wait until morning. She cuddled back in his arms and closed her eyes, though she knew she wouldn't sleep.

"I love you, too, Matt. More than you'll ever know. No matter what happens, remember that."

"WE HAVE TO TALK."

Matt reached for Shelly and pulled her back in his arms. "Didn't anyone ever tell you those are the four words a man dreads hearing most from his woman?"

But he couldn't begin to understand the dread that had settled in her heart. He'd said he loved her. Love was supposed to conquer all. It did in songs and movies. It never had in her mother's life. Maybe that's why Shelly had so little faith that it could work this time in hers.

She pulled away from him and slid her legs over the side of the bed. She was wearing his robe. He was still naked, the bulge beneath the sheet making it obvious he was ready to make love again. She tried to convince herself that he still would be when she was finished.

"This isn't easy for me, Matt, but I have to get it out."

"I don't want to—"

"I'm not who you think I am. I'm not Shelly Lane." There she'd blurted it out and there was no way around it now.

He pushed up on his elbows. "What are you talking about?"

"I'm an undercover agent for the CIA."

He winced as if she'd slapped him. "Keep talking."

She did, but nothing came out right. "The allegations affected national security, Matt. And the evidence was overwhelming. I was doing what my job called for. We've stopped any number of terrorist attacks by gathering this type of information. We've saved lives."

He didn't say a word, but after five minutes of listening to her futile attempts to redeem herself, he turned his back on her and scooted off the other side of the bed.

"I haven't given the CIA anything to use against you," she insisted, desperate now to make him understand. "In fact, I've stressed to my supervisor that none of you could possibly be guilty. After last night's incident, the agency will have to see that I'm right and that Melvin was behind all of this."

He grabbed a pair of jeans from the closet and yanked them on.

"Say something, Matt. Anything. Just don't clam up on me like this."

"What is there to say?" He pulled on a pair of socks from the top dresser drawer. "I don't even know who you are."

"You said that you loved me."

He sat back down on the bed just long enough to shove his feet into a pair of boots. "The keys are in the truck. You can go to the house and pack your things while the family's at church. Be off the ranch before they get back."

"If that's how you want it."

"Feel free to take the truck into town or to the airport. Hell, just take the truck. Payment for your physical-therapy services." He turned and walked away without looking back.

Shelly wrapped her arms around her chest as if that could hold her together. Her heart felt as it someone had squeezed it to mush and left it to rot inside her chest. She'd known all along it would come to this, had told herself that falling in love with Matt could never work—that it would end up tearing her apart.

But how could she not have loved Matt Collingsworth?

SHELLY PLACED THE CALL TO Brady Owens and explained about Melvin and the abduction. He was shocked and admitted that he hadn't heard a word from Ben Hartmann. Not surprising, since Ben was likely still asleep at ten o'clock on Sunday morning.

Brady was convinced that Ben would never have revealed her identity. She didn't see any other way Melvin could have found out who she was. But the most important development was that Brady would call off the arrests and start his investigation over based on the new information.

All in a day's work for the CIA.

"I owe you an apology," Brady said once the bulk of the conversation was concluded. "You were dead on with everything, even your suspicions about Melvin Rogers. I dare say there's more to that than we've uncovered."

"I agree, though I can't even imagine why he'd hate a family who did so much for him."

"Money, a woman or revenge. It always boils down to one of those."

"He didn't keep the money for himself," Shelly said. "That rules out greed."

"So if there's not a woman, that leaves revenge. At any rate, I'd still like to see you in the office Monday morning for a debriefing. And I plan to recommend you for a promotion."

"There's a problem with that."

"The debriefing?"

"No, sir. I can make that. Then I plan to tender my resignation."

"This wouldn't have anything to do with Matt Collingsworth, would it?"

"No, sir." Because Matt Collingsworth was having nothing to do with her. "I just don't think I'm cut out for this line of work."

"What will you do?"

"I'd like to spend some time with my mother and see if we can reconnect." She hadn't fully decided that until the words came out of her mouth, but it was what she wanted to do.

They might never have the perfect mother-daughter relationship, certainly nothing like Lenora had with her children, but she was still Shelly's mother. Shelly should make a stab at understanding her.

"I don't suppose there's anything I can say to change your mind about leaving?"

"No, sir."

"We made a mistake, but we're not the bad guys, Shelly."

"I know. Keeping America safe is one of the most important careers going. It's just not for me."

"We'll talk more Monday."

They'd talk, but her mind was made up. She'd found something here on Jack's Bluff that she wanted and it had nothing to do with the wealth or the prestige. It was family—and love. She'd never get a chance to have that with Matt, but if she was lucky, she'd find it with someone else some day.

That is if she ever got over loving Matt.

THE COLLINGSWORTHS had it all—wealth, influence, family. They did as they pleased, used whomever they pleased, rewarded people only if it suited their purposes. No one knew that better than Melvin Rogers.

Jeremiah Collingsworth had used his mother and then thrown her out as if she were trash under his feet. He'd been all too willing to break his marriage vows while his wife lay dying, but it had been Melvin's mother who'd paid. Melvin might never have known it had he not found and read her diary after she died.

Jeremiah could have married Melvin's mother after his own wife died. Then she'd have never turned to the cruel bastard who'd fathered Melvin. Neither her life nor Melvin's would have been the living hell with him it had become. Melvin would have been Jeremiah's son just as his mother had died believing. He'd be a flesh and blood Collingsworth and not the friend who could sit at the table but never share the name.

Not that it would matter now. Even after he'd worked out everything to the most minute detail, the CIA wouldn't play into his hands. Too bad, especially after he'd figured out so quickly who Ben Hartmann was and had fed him information that would have insured the Collingsworths conviction.

He'd even learned from bugging Ben's apartment that Shelly Lane was CIA. If Frankie Dawson had done what he'd been paid to do, they would have never reached this point. She'd have been dead before she had a chance to be seduced by Matt and the rest of the Collingsworths.

Nonetheless, the Collingsworth dynasty was about to come to an end. Melvin's revenge would be sweet. And deadly. And soon.

No one could stop him now.

SHELLY HAD WAITED UNTIL she was certain everyone had left for church before driving back to the big house for her things.

The thought of facing any of the family with the truth when her heart was in shambles was more than she could deal with. Luckily, no one had skipped the worship service this morning. They had too much to be thankful for.

The traditional Sunday brunch would be a major celebration. Zach and Kali were home from their honeymoon and they were all well on their way to having proof that Melvin had framed them.

The only thing they were losing was a physical therapist who Jeremiah didn't want anyway. And once they'd talked to Matt, they'd feel the same loathing for her that he did.

Luckily she'd managed to get tickets for a four o'clock flight from Houston to Dulles. An airport service was sending a car to the gates of Jack's Bluff Ranch. She'd wait there, parked in Matt's truck, out of sight in case her transportation didn't arrive before they returned.

She trudged down the steps from her former guest suite, lugging her two suitcases. Her handbag and carrying case were slung over her left shoulder. The muscles in her wounded right arm were acting out today, a painful reminder of last night's rough and tumble treatment. The least of her present concerns.

She looked back at the house only once as she drove away. She didn't need reminders. The memories of the house and the Collingsworth family were firmly planted in her mind.

Choosing a protected spot just off the road and beneath a cluster of pine trees, she parked the truck and waited. And waited. And waited. At ten before twelve, she called the car service. They'd been held up behind a six-car pileup on Interstate 45, but they were moving now and should be there shortly.

The Collingsworth convoy began driving in at twelve. No one noticed Matt's truck or her. At twelve-forty, her ride had still not arrived. The family would be gathered at the huge dining room table by now.

One of the brothers would say grace. Maybe Matt. Jeremiah would be banging his cane for someone to pass the biscuits. Lenora would be bustling around making sure the serving dishes were full. The twins would be plotting mischief. Trish would be eating for two.

*Put it behind you, ex-CIA lady, before you start boohoo- ing all over your travel clothes.*

Two blasts of a honk snapped her back to her senses. Her ride had arrived. She climbed out of the truck and was strug- gling with her bags when a motorbike flew down the ranch road, skidding to a stop at the gate.

Melvin Rogers. She stared in shock. This should have been the last place he'd show up. He surely knew by now that she'd lived through his paid attempt on her life.

There was no sign he saw her while he waited for the gate to open, but she got a good look at him. He was in ratty jeans and an old T-shirt, unquestionably not Collingsworth Sunday-brunch attire.

The gate opened and he swerved through it, passing her waiting ride and roaring away. She picked up her bags and hurried toward the gate. But even as she stepped across the rattling cattle gate, she couldn't shake Melvin from her mind.

What could have possibly drawn him back here when he knew everyone was gathered and that he was a wanted man.

Revenge.

Brady's word came back to haunt her. But revenge for what? It wasn't as if he were a bastard brother or the black sheep of the family. He was just a guy Jeremiah had brought into the fold and given a great job to.

The driver stored her bags and opened the door for her. "Is it just you?"

"Just me," she said.

"Where to?"

"IAH."

"What time's your flight?"

"Not for hours."

"Good thing you gave yourself plenty of time or you'd never have made it. There was a hell of a wreck on I-45. Gas tank on an eighteen-wheeler caught fire in the crash, and before the fireman could get it put out, the whole truck blew like a fire in a fireworks plant. I'm sure it's still smoking. You'll be able to see it when we go by on the other side of the interstate."

Explosions everywhere. Frankie Dawson, known for his explosive prowess. Hired to get rid of her. And Melvin, kicked out of school for threatening to blow the houses of his friends. For revenge? For not being included when he thought he should have been?

Oh, God. That was it. Melvin was almost family, but not quite, because Jeremiah had an indiscretion that he'd never forgiven himself for. With the nurse he'd fired, leaving him to take care of his ailing wife on his own. But the nurse wasn't Ellen, or Helen or Helene. It was Ellie. Ellie Mellinger Rogers.

Melvin's plan to frame the Collingsworth family hadn't worked, but he had an ace in the hole. He'd come back to the ranch this morning to blow them to smithereens.

He was going to prison anyway. He had to know that. He had nothing more to lose and this was his last chance for revenge.

"Turn around. Take me back to the ranch."

The driver looked at her image through his rearview mirror. "What'd you forget?"

"Nothing, but hurry. As fast as you can."

"You sound as if this is life or death."

"It could be." She tried to get Matt on his cell phone. It rang, but he didn't answer. Neither did the phone at the big house. They always let the answering machine pick up during meals.

"Should I wait?" The driver asked as she jumped out of the car.

"No." She used Matt's code to open the gate and raced toward his truck.

"What about your luggage?" the driver called after her.

"Toss it out. I'll get it later." She jumped in the truck, started the engine and yanked the gearshift into Reverse.

Bombing the house was unbelievably bizarre, but it made sense in a crazy way. Melvin's devastating and unrequitedly evil attempts to destroy the Collingsworths. His familiarity with explosives and the people who could provide them. His returning to the house today when he was likely bucking for the top of the Texas most-wanted list.

Matt's family would think she was insane. Maybe she was, but if she was right about this, the big house at Jack's Bluff was on the verge of exploding with all the family inside.

The ultimate revenge of a brilliant madman.

Panic roared through her veins as she pushed the truck to its limits, almost turning it over at the last sharp turn. She threw on the brakes practically at the front steps and jumped from the truck. She started yelling the second she pushed through the front door.

"Everybody out of the house! Now! I'll explain later, but you have to hurry. Please, hurry!"

Langston was the first to reach her. "What is it, Shelly?"

"I just saw Melvin speeding away from the ranch. I think he may have planted a bomb. I think the house may be about to explode."

To her surprise, he took her words at face value. He raced back to the dining room with her a step behind.

"There's an emergency," he said, his voice calmer than hers had been, though his tone left no room for argument. "Everyone clear out of the house at once. Stay together and head for the stable. Now!"

Trish grabbed her daughter's arm. "Let's go, Gina. Do what Daddy says." But Trish was eight months pregnant and moving too slowly. Langston picked her up as if she weighed nothing and carried her out of the house. Gina, Becky and the twins followed.

Shelly scanned the room. "Where's Matt?"

"He didn't show up for brunch," Lenora said, fear pummeling her voice as she herded her family out of danger. "We thought he was with you."

Jeremiah started banging his cane. "What's the dadburn commotion about?"

"A fire drill, Grandpa. Now stop your bellowing." Bart scooped the old man out of his chair, threw him over his shoulder and carried him out. Jaclyn was right by his side.

Zach grabbed his mother's arm and the hand of his new bride and ran with them from the house. Jaime linked hands with Shelly. No one stopped to ask questions. No one panicked. They all just cleared the house and ran.

Jaime and Shelly were almost to the stable when David started yelling. "Blackie! Blackie! You gotta come with us, Blackie!"

Becky tried to calm him, but his cries become louder and more frantic. "Lemme go! Lemme go. I gotta save my dog."

Blackie was still near the house, barking at a squirrel that was staring him down from the trunk of an oak tree.

And then Derrick, who had been standing quietly beside his mother, started running back toward the house.

"I'll get him, David. I'll get Blackie for you."

Langston, Bart and Zack all started after him, but Shelly was closest. She reached him first, but not before he had the squirming, barking puppy in hand.

They were almost home free when the bomb blew, shaking the earth and sending fire and wood shooting skyward. She pushed Derrick to the ground and fell on top of him, covering him with her body while Blackie licked her face and hell rained down on her back.

# Chapter Sixteen

Matt had been walking for hours, tramping through pastures and wooded areas with no thought for where he was heading. His head was splitting, the pain worse than the day he'd been kicked in the head by that bull over in San Antonio. He'd learned his lesson that day, had given up rodeo competition for good.

Hopefully he'd learned a lesson with Shelly as well. A man might as well take advice from a fool as listen to his heart. He'd suspected from the very first that she was not what she seemed. So why hadn't he stood by his convictions instead of believing every word that had come from her lying mouth?

He couldn't hate her for doing her job. He...

He couldn't hate her at all. That was the problem. He'd believed what he wanted to believe. And last night, when they'd returned to the ranch, it had been him who didn't want to hear what she had to say. He just wanted Shelly.

Heaven help him. He still did.

He looked around to get his bearings. Not surprisingly, he'd ended up near the big house. Stopping at the base of a towering pine, he pushed up his sleeve and checked his watch. Almost one. The family would be having brunch.

He couldn't have forced down a bite of food on a bet. Not until he made up his mind what to do about Shelly. He stepped into a clearing then stopped dead still as the sound of an explosion rattled his brain and shook the ground. He looked up and saw a giant ball of fire leap into the sky above the big house.

His heart flew to his throat and he started running. He didn't stop until he reached the cluster of his family and spotted Shelly being led toward the stable by Langston and Bart. Her face was covered in soot, her blouse torn.

Derrick saw Matt first and ran toward him. "Shelly saved Blackie, Uncle Matt."

"She saved all of us," Langston said. "I'm not sure what will be left of the house, though."

Lenora latched on to Langston's arm and leaned against his shoulder. "Houses can be rebuilt, son. People are all that matter. And we're all alive because of Shelly."

Matt wanted to hear every detail of her bravery, but there would be time for that later. Years and years of time, he hoped. But right now, he just wanted to hold her close until his heart could get used to having love around.

# Epilogue

*Five months later*

The first hint of fall was in the air when Lenora slipped out the back door of her newly restored house and walked swiftly toward the oldest oak tree. She stood there for long seconds, staring at Randolph's tombstone before she finally dropped to the grass. She leaned against the trunk of the tree, curling her legs beneath her full denim skirt.

"The rehearsal and dinner are this evening," she said, talking to him the way she always did. As if he could still hear her voice. As if he needed these visits as much as she did.

"By this time tomorrow, all our sons will be married. I was afraid I might never see this day for Matt, but Shelly took care of that.

"Well, Shelly's not her real name, but she decided it fit, and she loves the way it sounds when Matt says it. She absolutely adores him.

"They're getting married here at the ranch. I wish you could see the house now that all the damaged areas have been rebuilt. I hate to admit it around your father. You know how Jeremiah likes to brag about the house he built. But I love my new kitchen. I have the neatest new appliances. The range practically does all the work. And that dishwasher can clean the dirtiest of pots without anyone having to rinse them first.

"And your sons have proved themselves quite the woodworkers, too. They built a new dining table that looks so much like the old one, you'd hardly know it was new. And the laughter is just as loud when we all gather around it.

"We're getting to be a rather large group now that Langston and Trish have their marvelous baby boy. And did I tell you that Bart's wife Jaclyn is expecting? She positively glows. And Bart is strutting around like the proudest rooster in the pen."

A butterfly landed on Lenora's skirt. She watched it until it flew away, marveling that something that exquisite could have come from a caterpillar. But ugly things had a way of becoming beautiful. Take all that trouble with the CIA. If it hadn't been for that, Matt would never have found the love of his life.

"Melvin's out on bail until his trial," she said, "but your sons and even Jeremiah are certain he's going to prison. It was revenge, just as Shelly said. Not because he was Jeremiah's son as she'd thought at first, but because he wasn't.

"You said something strange was going on when your father fired Corrine's nurse. Well, when the hubbub about Melvin came out, Jeremiah finally came clean with me. Apparently he'd come home drunk one night and he and the nurse did the deed. She'd gotten pregnant shortly after that. She was already in another relationship so she never bothered to find out for sure whose baby she was carrying."

Lenora heard the approach of a vehicle and looked toward the road. It was only Billy Mack's pickup truck, but the first of the real guests would be arriving soon. She needed to get back to the house and change into the dress Jaime had helped her pick out for the occasion.

"To make a long story short, Melvin's mother left notes in her diary that made him think he was Jeremiah's son. Jeremiah thought he could be right, but insisted on a blood test. Turned out he's not Jeremiah's son, but your father hired him anyway.

"No one knows for sure what went wrong at that point, but the word leaking from his defense attorney's office is that Melvin was furious that Jeremiah used his mother and then kicked her out instead of marrying her when Corrine died.

"Billy Mack says it's more likely Melvin was just angry that he missed out on being a Collingsworth by bad luck. And you might like to know that he didn't transfer everything he stole to terrorists, either. He socked a couple of million dollars away in a Swiss bank account in his name."

She rose and brushed bits of leaves and grass from her skirt. "That's about it, except that I'm still a bit worried about our daughter Becky. Those boys of hers need their father and she's just too hardheaded to accept that football is so important to him.

"If you were here, you'd know what to say to her. I don't anymore. And then there's Jaime. I don't see marriage in sight for her, though she does a super job of enjoying life. She's just—well, she's Jaime."

Lenora started to walk away, then stopped and looked back at the lonesome grave. There was nothing to see, though you'd think that part of her heart should be spilled around it somewhere. "I miss you, Randolph. I always will. But then you always knew how much I loved you."

THE BLUE DRESS SHELLY had chosen for the party tonight was laid out on the bed. The black boots Matt had given her for her birthday were ready and waiting. It was her night, hers and Matt's. The last night they'd spend before they became man and wife.

Matt stepped behind her and slipped his arms around her waist. "The party's going to start without us if you don't get dressed."

"I can live with that."

"After your mother flew here just for the occasion. I don't think you'd dare cancel out on her."

"She spent all day talking about her latest breakup. I'm not sure that counts as a visit to share my wedding celebration."

"It's a start."

"Maybe." But Shelly doubted it. She'd tried to connect with her mother, but the relationship wouldn't take. Everybody didn't have the kind of wonderful, caring mother Matt did. That was life. She was learning to accept it.

"My hesitance to go to the party has nothing to do with my mother."

"Is it my family?"

"Heavens no. I love them all. They're the family I always wanted and never had."

"Then it must be me. Cold feet about saying I do tomorrow?"

"Nothing about me is ever cold when you're around, Matt Collingsworth."

"Then what is it?"

She pulled away. She doubted she could say this in a way he'd understand. "I love our life just the way it is. I love the way you kiss me as if you can't get enough of me. I love the way you can't keep your hands off me when we're together. I love the way we make love like there's no tomorrow, and then minutes later, you're ready to do it again."

He pulled her back in his arms. "So what's the problem?"

"I know things will change over time, but I don't think I can bear it if we lose the hunger and passion."

"How could I ever not be hungry for you when I've waited for you all my life?"

He kissed her lips and the thrill of him ran through her like liquid fire. It always did. "But what about later, Matt? What will happen when I no longer excite you?"

"You'll always excite me, even when we're old and gray and so feeble we have to help each other to the bed."

He was half teasing. She wasn't. "Do you promise, Matt?"

"I promise." He tilted her chin so that she had to meet his gaze. "You're not your mother, Shelly. I'm not like the men she's chosen to be with. I've only loved one woman in my life. That's you. And I'll be around to love you 'til death do us part. I wouldn't make a vow I don't plan to keep."

"I guess I did let my issues with my mother creep into the back of my thoughts. A lifetime of not trusting love is hard to get past."

"I'm always going to love you."

"How can you be so sure?"

"Because I know me and I know you. And I know our love is real. Forever and always. We can't miss. Ask my mom. She'll tell you it's the legend of Jack's Bluff."

"She did tell me, but what about Becky? She split up with her husband."

"For now, but she still loves him. They'll find a way to make it work. But just for the record, we're not them, either. You have to trust me, Shelly. You have to trust yourself and trust our love."

"I do trust you. It's just that—"

"No, you either trust me or you don't. Do you believe I love you?"

"Yes." The answer was honest. "But forever is such a long time."

"And I was just thinking it's not nearly long enough."

He kissed her again, and she let the sweet promise of his love wash through her. Forever and always. With Matt. In this place they both loved. Surrounded by family. Held tight by roots of the past and challenges of the future. How could she ask for more than that?

She reached for the blue dress. "Party time."

"Are you sure you're ready, Shelly?"

"I'm positive, Matt Collingsworth."

\* \* \* \* \*

*Look for Becky's story soon!*
*MIRACLE AT COLTS RUN CROSS*
*November 2008.*

*The editors at Harlequin Blaze have never been afraid to push the limits—tempting readers with the forbidden, whetting their appetites with a wide variety of story lines. But now we're breaking the final barrier—the time barrier.*

*In July, watch for BOUND TO PLEASE by fan favorite Hope Tarr, Harlequin Blaze's first ever historical romance—a story that's truly Blaze-worthy in every sense.*

*Here's a sneak peek...*

Brianna stretched out beside Ewan, languid as a cat, and promptly fell asleep. Midday sunshine streamed into the chamber, bathing her lovely, long-limbed body in golden light, the sea-scented breeze wafting inside to dry the damp red-gold tendrils curling about her flushed face. Propping himself up on one elbow, Ewan slid his gaze over her. She looked beautiful and whole, satisfied and sated, and altogether happier than he had so far seen her. A slight smile curved her beautiful lips as though she must be in the midst of a lovely dream. She'd molded her lush, lovely body to his and laid her head in the curve of his shoulder and settled in to sleep beside him. For the longest while he lay there turned toward her, content to watch her sleep, at near perfect peace.

Not wholly perfect, for she had yet to answer his marriage proposal. Still, she wanted to make a baby with him, and Ewan no longer viewed her plan as the travesty he once had.

He wanted children—sons to carry on after him, though a bonny little daughter with flame-colored hair would be nice, too. But he also wanted more than to simply plant his seed and be on his way. He wanted to lie beside Brianna night upon night as she increased, rub soothing unguents into the swell of her belly, knead the ache from her back and make slow, gentle love to her. He wanted to hold his newly born child in his arms and look down into Brianna's tired but radiant face and blot the perspiration from her brow and be a husband to her in every way.

He gave her a gentle nudge. "Brie?"

"Hmmm?"

She rolled onto her side and he captured her against his chest. One arm wrapped about her waist, he bent to her ear and asked, "Do you think we might have just made a baby?"

Her eyes remained closed, but he felt her tense against him. "I don't know. We'll have to wait and see."

He stroked his hand over the flat plane of her belly. "You're so small and tight it's hard to imagine you increasing."

"All women increase no matter how large or small they start out. I may not grow big as a croft, but I'll be big enough, though I have hopes I may not waddle like a duck, at least not too badly."

The reference to his fair-day teasing was not lost on him. He grinned. "Brianna MacLeod grown so large she must sit still for once in her life. I'll need the proof of my own eyes to believe it."

Despite their banter, he felt his spirits dip. Assuming they were so blessed, he wouldn't have the chance to see her thus. By then he would be long gone, restored to his clan according to the sad bargain they'd struck. He opened his mouth to ask her to marry him again and then clamped it closed, not wanting to spoil the moment, but the unspoken words weighed like a millstone on his heart.

The damnable bargain they'd struck was proving to be a devil's pact indeed.

\* \* \* \* \*

*Will these two star-crossed lovers find their*
*sexily-ever-after?*
*Find out in BOUND TO PLEASE by Hope Tarr,*
*available in July*
*wherever Harlequin® Blaze™ books are sold.*

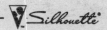

# SPECIAL EDITION™

Little did hotel-chain CFO Tom Holloway
realize that his new executive assistant
spelled trouble. But even though
single mom Shelly Winston was planted
by Holloway's worst enemy to take him
down, Shelly was no dupe—she had
a mind of her own and an eye for
her handsome boss.

**Look for**

# IN BED
# WITH THE BOSS

by *USA TODAY* bestselling author
## *CHRISTINE RIMMER*

*Available July
wherever you buy books.*

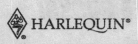

# MADE IN TEXAS

It's the happiest day of Hannah Callahan's life
when she brings her new daughter home to Texas.
And Joe Daugherty would make a perfect father
to complete their unconventional family. But the
world-hopping writer never stays in one place
long enough. Can Joe trust in love enough to
finally get the family he's always wanted?

## LOOK FOR
# Hannah's Baby
## BY
# CATHY GILLEN THACKER

*Available July*
*wherever you buy books.*

## LOVE, HOME & HAPPINESS

# REQUEST YOUR FREE BOOKS!

## 2 FREE NOVELS
## PLUS 2
## FREE GIFTS!

HARLEQUIN®

# INTRIGUE®

## Breathtaking Romantic Suspense

**YES!** Please send me 2 FREE Harlequin Intrigue® novels and my 2 FREE gifts (gifts are worth about $10). After receiving them, if I don't wish to receive any more books, I can return the shipping statement marked "cancel." If I don't cancel, I will receive 6 brand-new novels every month and be billed just $4.24 per book in the U.S. or $4.99 per book in Canada, plus 25¢ shipping and handling per book and applicable taxes, if any*. That's a savings of close to 15% off the cover price! I understand that accepting the 2 free books and gifts places me under no obligation to buy anything. I can always return a shipment and cancel at any time. Even if I never buy another book from Harlequin, the two free books and gifts are mine to keep forever.

182 HDN EEZ7  382 HDN EEZK

| | | |
|---|---|---|
| Name | (PLEASE PRINT) | |
| Address | | Apt. # |
| City | State/Prov. | Zip/Postal Code |

Signature (if under 18, a parent or guardian must sign)

Mail to the **Harlequin Reader Service:**
**IN U.S.A.:** P.O. Box 1867, Buffalo, NY 14240-1867
**IN CANADA:** P.O. Box 609, Fort Erie, Ontario L2A 5X3

Not valid to current subscribers of Harlequin Intrigue books.

**Want to try two free books from another line?**
**Call 1-800-873-8635 or visit www.morefreebooks.com.**

* Terms and prices subject to change without notice. N.Y. residents add applicable sales tax. Canadian residents will be charged applicable provincial taxes and GST. Offer not valid in Quebec. This offer is limited to one order per household. All orders subject to approval. Credit or debit balances in a customer's account(s) may be offset by any other outstanding balance owed by or to the customer. Please allow 4 to 6 weeks for delivery. Offer available while quantities last.

**Your Privacy:** Harlequin is committed to protecting your privacy. Our Privacy Policy is available online at www.eHarlequin.com or upon request from the Reader Service. From time to time we make our lists of customers available to reputable third parties who may have a product or service of interest to you. If you would prefer we not share your name and address, please check here. ☐

HI08R

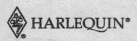

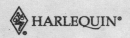

HARLEQUIN®

# INTRIGUE

## COMING NEXT MONTH

### #1071 IDENTITY UNKNOWN by Debra Webb
*Colby Agency*

Sande Williams woke up in the morgue—left for dead, her identity stolen. Only Colby agent Patrick O'Brien can set Sande's life straight, but at what cost does their partnership come?

### #1072 SOLDIER CAGED by Rebecca York
*43 Light Street*

Kept under surveillence in a secret, military bunker, Jonah Baker is a damaged war hero looking for a way out. Sophia Rhodes may be the one doctor he can bend to his will, but their escape is only the first step in stopping this dangerous charade.

### #1073 ARMED AND DEVASTATING by Julie Miller
*The Precinct: Brotherhood of the Badge*

Det. Atticus Kincaid knows more about solving crimes than charming ladies. But he'll do whatever it takes—even turn quiet Brooke Hansford into an irresistible investigator—to solve a very personal murder case, no matter the family secrets it unearths.

### #1074 IN THE MANOR WITH THE MILLIONAIRE
by Cassie Miles
*The Curse of Raven's Cliff*

Madeline Douglas always had dreams of living in the big house. But taking up residence in historic Beacon Manor is the stuff of nightmares, which only the powerful and handsome Blake Monroe can help to overcome.

### #1075 QUESTIONING THE HEIRESS by Delores Fossen
*The Silver Star of Texas: Cantara Hills Investigation*

With three murder victims among her social circle, Caroline Stallings isn't getting invited to many San Antonio events. Texas Ranger Egan Caldwell is the one man returning her calls, only he's spearheading an investigation that may uncover a shared dark past.

### #1076 THE LAWMAN'S SECRET SON by Alice Sharpe
*Skye Brother Babies*

Brady Skye was a disgraced cop working tirelessly to win back his reputation. But only the son he never knew he had can help him piece together his life—and reunite him with his first love, Lara Kirk—before someone takes an eye for an eye.

HICNM0608

## "You're Safe Here."

"Are you sure?" she asked, looking up, her face streaked with tears.

His eyes looking down at her were as dark and violent as the storm. She felt the burning pressure of his body against hers. She tried to drag her gaze from his, but lacked the willpower. His eyes burned into her very depths, igniting flames that licked through her body. A soft moan tore from her throat as his lips claimed hers. Her mouth was on fire, then her entire body.

The kiss was as violent and primitive as the thunder and the rain. Suddenly, she realized she might be safe from the storm, but there was a different kind of danger threatening her.

---

**PATTI BECKMAN**
and her husband, Charles, traveled to south Florida to research the romance and politics of the Everglades. Back in Corpus Christi, her hometown, she wove her tale, recapturing the splendor and richness of the area.

Dear Reader,

Silhouette Special Editions are an exciting new line of contemporary romances from Silhouette Books. Special Editions are written specifically for our readers who want a story with heightened romantic tension.

Special Editions have all the elements you've enjoyed in Silhouette Romances and *more*. These stories concentrate on romance in a longer, more realistic and sophisticated way, and they feature greater sensual detail.

I hope you enjoy this book and all the wonderful romances from Silhouette.

Karen Solem
Editor-in-Chief
Silhouette Books

# PATTI BECKMAN
## Storm Over the Everglades

*Silhouette Special Edition*
Published by Silhouette Books New York
**America's Publisher of Contemporary Romance**

SILHOUETTE BOOKS, a Division of Simon & Schuster, Inc.
1230 Avenue of the Americas, New York, N.Y. 10020

Copyright © 1984 by Charles and Patti Boeckman, Inc.

Distributed by Pocket Books

ISBN: 0-671-53669-9

First Silhouette Books printing June, 1984

10 9 8 7 6 5 4 3 2 1

Map by Ray Lundgren

America's Publisher of Contemporary Romance

Printed in the U.S.A.

**Books by Patti Beckman**

Silhouette Romance

*Captive Heart* #8
*The Beachcomber* #37
*Louisiana Lady* #54
*Angry Lover* #72
*Love's Treacherous Journey* #96
*Spotlight to Fame* #124
*Daring Encounter* #154
*Mermaid's Touch* #179
*Forbidden Affair* #227
*Time for Us* #273

Silhouette Special Edition

*Bitter Victory* #13
*Tender Deception* #61
*Enchanted Surrender* #85
*Thunder at Dawn* #109
*Storm over the Everglades* #169

# Storm Over the Everglades

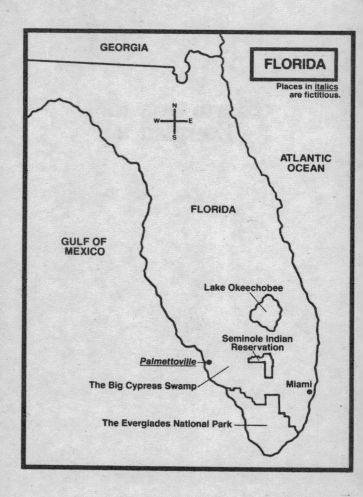

GEORGIA

FLORIDA

Places in _italics_
are fictitious.

N
W E
S

ATLANTIC
OCEAN

FLORIDA

GULF OF
MEXICO

Lake Okeechobee

Seminole Indian
Reservation

_Palmettoville_

The Big Cypress Swamp

Miami

The Everglades National Park

# Chapter One

"I assume you are Miss Lindi MacTavish."

The deep masculine voice almost caused Lindi to spill her coffee. She turned in surprise, shocked to discover that she was impaled by the smoldering, dark-eyed gaze of the man who towered over her.

It was not a friendly gaze. In the confusion of the moment, she was not certain how to describe the man's expression—dark, brooding . . . almost angry.

That first encounter with Travis Machado in the crowded Miami airport was one Lindi was destined to remember for the rest of her life.

In the storm of emotions that had torn her life apart in the past twenty-four hours, this strange man represented a fresh onslaught. She stared at him in a confused effort to place him in some logical frame of reference, but he fit none of the familiar stereotypes she could call to mind.

9

A childhood rhyme flitted through her tumultuous thoughts: doctor, lawyer, Indian chief . . .

No, he was none of those. But then she had second thoughts. Perhaps in another time, another setting, he might have been an Indian chief. He had the tall, proud, almost haughty bearing; the coal black eyes; the luxurious mane of dark hair; and the swarthy, weather-beaten complexion of a man accustomed to a rugged outdoor existence. The clothes he wore— form-fitting tan jeans with razor-sharp creases, wide belt with a large, ornate silver buckle hugging a trim waist, Western boots, blue sport shirt straining against powerful shoulders—seemed mere concessions to the civilized world. His cheekbones were high, his jaw stubborn and firm. His dark mustache— worn in Burt Reynolds style, heavy and drooping slightly at the corners—added to the slightly malevolent macho image he projected, as did the faint scar along his left jaw line.

Trapped by the power of his glaring stare, Lindi shuddered involuntarily. It was as if the overwhelming events of the past chaotic hours had been leading up to this moment.

A long-distance telephone call to her small East Side New York apartment less than twenty-four hours before had shattered the routine of her life. Engrossed in the page of copy she was editing at her desk, she had picked up the phone and answered absently. Suddenly her attention was riveted.

The voice she heard was that of her brother's wife, Frances MacTavish. Her sister-in-law was sobbing and barely coherent. "Frances, what is it?" Lindi asked, her throat constricting.

"It's Roy," Frances choked out. "He's—he's been in an accident."

For a moment, Lindi's breathing stopped. Then she swallowed hard and forced herself to draw a long, deep breath. She was familiar with the stories of identical twins who appeared to be in tune with one another though separated by great distances, one sensing, somehow, a climactic occurrence in the life of the other. She had never had that extrasensory rapport with her twin Roy, perhaps because they were fraternal rather than identical twins, but they had always had a close, loving relationship. With their parents and grandparents gone, Roy was her only family. Her heart lurched with fright. "Frances, he . . . he isn't—"

"He's alive," Frances replied brokenly, allaying Lindi's worst fear. "But Lindi, he's terribly hurt—"

Roy's wife was gaining control of herself and was beginning to speak more coherently. "It was a hit-and-run driver. Roy had left the newspaper office and must have been crossing that side street north of the building. One of the men in the office glanced out of the window and saw it happen. The car came speeding around the corner, hit Roy, and just kept right on going. No one was able to get the license number. They called an ambulance and then got hold of me, and I rushed right over to the hospital. Roy is in the intensive care unit. Our doctor has tried to reassure me, but they really don't know how serious it is yet."

Tears trickled down Lindi's face. She felt overcome by a wave of grief and impotence. She wanted desperately to reach out to comfort Frances and to be at her twin brother's side, but more than a thousand miles separated them. "Frances, I'll get the first plane down there."

"Oh, Lindi, I hate to disrupt your work this way. But I—I just had to call you . . ."

"Well, of course you did! Now, Frances, I don't know how soon I can get a seat on a plane. This is the tourist season, you know. It may be tonight or the morning before I can get down there. I want you to promise to call me again as soon as you find out any more about Roy's condition."

"Yes, I promise."

Their brief conversation ended, Lindi sat immobilized, staring at the telephone for several long moments, unable to function. A great deal had to be done before she could leave, but she was temporarily numbed by shock.

Then something soft and warm nuzzling her leg aroused her. She looked down at a black-and-white floppy-eared dog of scrambled lineage. "Oh, Elmer," she said in a choked voice, reaching down to rub the mutt's ears. Then she burst into tears. Blindly, she lifted her pet onto her lap. She held the warm body close as the tears ran down her cheeks. Elmer emitted a sympathetic whimper and attempted, dog fashion, to console her with a slurping lick.

Somehow the companionship of the dumb animal comforted her. She squared her shoulders, reached for a facial tissue from a green box almost buried amidst the pile of papers on her desk, and resolutely went about attending to the monumental task of putting her affairs in order.

"First things first," she muttered. She saved the copy on the screen of her word processor by transferring it to a floppy disk. Then she switched off the computer. Next she phoned the airport and was told that the earliest possible reservation she could get was on an early flight the next morning. Last, she began listing business matters that had to be resolved.

Five years earlier, after she had received her college

degree, she had gone to work for a Madison Avenue public relations firm. Three years later, she had resigned to realize her ambition to be her own boss. Since then she'd had her financial ups and downs as a free-lance writer and editor. Between article sales to magazines, editing jobs for book publishers, and speech writing, she managed to pay her half of the rent on a small but comfortable East Side apartment that also served as her office and also eat on a fairly regular basis.

Now she was thankful for the freedom her career gave her to drop everything and fly to her brother's side.

"Of course, it also gives me the freedom to make no money at all," she muttered grimly. But forget that, she had a little money put aside for an emergency, and she'd be able to pick up the loose threads of her business when she returned.

First she broke the news to the congressman whose campaign speech she was working on. He was not overjoyed. "Lindi, this is an important speech! I have to have it."

"I know, and I'm sorry, Senator. But my brother is in the hospital and I have to fly to Florida. I have the speech two-thirds finished. I can get somebody else to wrap it up. Sid Levine is an excellent writer. He and I often work together on projects like this. I'll see that he has the polished speech in your hands no later than tomorrow morning."

"Well, all right," the congressman grumbled. "But it had better be good."

"Guaranteed to get you elected," Lindi said aloud and to herself thought, Unfortunately for the taxpayers.

Next, she called a publisher to say she would not be

able to edit the manuscript that had been delivered to her that morning. She got an extension on a deadline for an article she had promised a woman's magazine and then wrote out checks to cover several pressing bills and put them in envelopes. Then she began packing.

Elmer was underfoot wherever she went, disturbed as his canine intuition kept telling him that dramatic events were about to disrupt the calm routine of his existence.

By then it was evening. A key turning in the lock of the apartment door announced the arrival of Lindi's roommate, Cimi Layne. The tall young woman paused at the bedroom doorway, staring at the open suitcase and clothes scattered across the bed. "What in heaven's name is going on here?"

Lindi sat on the edge of the bed, feeling weak and on the verge of tears again. "Cimi, it's my brother Roy. He's—he's been in an accident—" She swallowed hard, but the tears started anyway, burning her eyes.

"Oh, my God," Cimi gasped. She crossed the room in two long-legged strides, joining Lindi as she sat on the bed. Lindi's blurring veil of tears created a misty vision of her glamorous roommate. They held hands as Lindi told Cimi about the phone call she'd had earlier that day. "Frances, that's my brother's wife, said Roy is in the intensive care unit. He was run down by some hit-and-run driver. They don't know who. They don't know yet how seriously he's injured. I'm expecting another call from her to give me some more details. It's the height of the tourist season so the earliest flight I can get out of here is early tomorrow morning . . ."

Lindi paused, aware that she was running her

sentences together in a slightly incoherent manner. "I'm sorry, Cimi. I'm not making a whole lot of sense. But I've been going in circles all day trying to get everything in order so I can leave."

"And probably haven't eaten a bite all day," Cimi muttered.

"I guess not," Lindi admitted, realizing that fact for the first time. "Maybe that's why I feel kind of shaky."

"I wouldn't be surprised. Come on."

Cimi took her hand and led her forcibly into the tiny kitchen, sat her in a chair, and then went about warming a bowl of homemade soup.

Elmer danced around her feet, attempting to call attention to his hunger pangs.

Lindi watched the tall, raven-haired woman move expertly from the stove to the drainboard. She often thought that Cimi Layne in action in the kitchen was one of life's great incongruities. Cimi was the showgirl type, long-legged, slim-waisted. She had enormous black eyes in an exquisite, symmetrical face. Her complexion was as smooth as the best porcelain. She could have been stereotyped as a rich man's plaything, wrapped in mink, stepping out of a Rolls Royce. To see a creature so generously endowed by nature at work in the kitchen was an anomaly that Lindi could never quite reconcile. Cimi was an excellent cook, attended church regularly, didn't drink or smoke. Somehow, Lindi thought, Cimi's looks and character didn't synchronize. Looks like hers should lead to sin. To complete the paradox, for the past year Cimi had been playing the part of a femme fatale in a daily soap opera, a part that suited her looks but was totally at odds with her real character. They often joked about it.

"Where does your brother live?" Cimi asked, placing the bowl of steaming soup before Lindi.

"In a little town on the west coast of Florida, Palmettoville. I'm sure you've never heard of it. It's one of the few isolated places that haven't been overcrowded and overdeveloped. Roy's the publisher of a small-town newspaper, *The Clarion*. Our grandfather started the paper there. Roy inherited it from him."

"Don't just look at the soup. Eat it," Cimi commanded.

Lindi obeyed. It was delicious, as was anything Cimi prepared.

"Try a hunk of this homemade bread. You can dunk it in the soup. You look as though you need some nourishment."

Then Cimi poured some dry dog food into a bowl and placed it on the floor. "This is for you, my friend," she told Elmer, who emitted a short bark of appreciation and then happily crunched his way through the meal.

The nourishing soup warmed and strengthened Lindi's drained body. "Roy and Frances have six-year-old boys, twins." Lindi sighed. "How are they going to manage with Roy laid up in the hospital? He just barely makes a living out of that small newspaper."

"Well, don't worry yourself sick over the situation until you get down there. It may not be all that bad. Now, can I help you with your packing?"

They were completing the task when the phone rang. It was Lindi's sister-in-law again. She sounded tired but less frantic now. "They've moved Roy from the intensive care unit to a private room, so I guess that's a good sign, at least. They have a special nurse with him tonight. He's conscious, but he's groggy from all the pain medicine he's been getting. The doctors still can't tell me a whole lot about his condition. It will be tomorrow before they have results from all the tests they're doing."

"I'll be there in the morning," Lindi promised. "The best flight connection I could get is to Miami. I'll rent a car there."

"Oh, I'd hate for you to do that. Maybe I can drive over to get you. What time does your plane land?"

"At eight tomorrow morning. But Frances, I'm not going to have you drive all that distance to get me. You need to stay with Roy."

"Well, maybe I can get somebody from the newspaper to drive over there . . ."

"Just don't worry about it. How are the kids?"

"All right. They're staying with friends tonight. We haven't told them yet how seriously their father is hurt."

They talked a few minutes longer, then ended the conversation.

Cimi made a pot of tea and they sat on Lindi's bed talking. Sleep seemed out of the question. "I have no business keeping you up like this," Lindi told her roommate with a twinge of guilt.

"No problem. I don't have to be at the studio tomorrow until after lunch. I can sleep in. Tell me about your brother. Does he have red hair like you?"

"Yes." Lindi nodded. "And you should see his twin boys; same red hair, same freckles."

"Twins and red hair. Sure runs in your family, don't they?"

"The MacTavishes had strong genes, I guess." Lindi nodded. "You should have seen our grandfather, Eli MacTavish, the one who started *The Clarion*.

He had a shock of blazing red hair and fierce eyebrows that jutted out over his gold-rimmed glasses. He still spoke with a Scottish brogue, rolling his *r*'s. It wouldn't have taken much imagination to visualize him in kilts, blowing his horn across the highlands to assemble his people to battle a feuding clan."

Cimi chuckled at the image. "Must have been a rather awe-inspiring gentleman."

"I suppose. He was gruff, but I was never afraid of him. Roy and I grew up in Connecticut, you know. It was always the greatest treat of our lives to spend vacation time down in Florida with Grandfather. He treated me like a princess. When Roy and I weren't playing on the beach, we spent our time hanging around Grandfather's newspaper office. I can still see him in his ink-smeared apron, ink all over his fingers, mumbling to himself as he puttered around his printing machinery. He was a giant of a man, well over six feet tall. Some of his editorials were as fierce as he looked. They just about had the paper smoking as it rolled off the press. They kept the town pretty well stirred up. Half the town wanted to tar and feather Grandfather; the other half loved him. But he didn't care whose toes he stepped on. He wasn't afraid of the Devil himself."

"So that's where your brother got his newspaper fever."

"Well, we both did in a way, I suppose. After our parents died, Roy and I stayed in Florida with Grandfather Eli. He saw us through our teenage years and college. When Roy finished college, he went back to help Grandfather run the paper and became the publisher when Grandfather died. My writing career took a different turn, but if it hadn't been for Grandfather's influence I guess I might have become a schoolteacher or archaeologist or heaven knows what. Grandfather instilled in me a great respect and fascination for the written word."

The two of them checked the things Lindi had packed, to be certain she wasn't leaving some vital article behind. Lindi wrote a short list of calls for Cimi to make for her, people she hadn't been able to reach that afternoon. When Elmer gave her hand a lick, she exclaimed, "Good heavens, in all the excitement, I forgot all about you! Cimi, I hate to impose even more on you, but would you mind terribly looking after this mutt until I get back?"

"Of course not," Cimi said, rubbing Elmer's black-and-white ears. "I consider him one of our roommates anyway. We get along fine, don't we, old fellow?"

Elmer agreed with a slurp on the back of her hand.

Lindi had only a few hours of fitful sleep riddled with bad dreams that night. She was in a cab headed for the airport long before dawn.

The flight was soothing. In the airplane she existed in a controlled environment—soft music, controlled air, controlled lights, pleasant stewardesses. She dozed most of the way, catching up on her sleep.

When she arrived in Miami, she left the plane, walking down the long tube jokingly called the "people-eater." Security doors clanged shut behind her as she stepped out into a brightly lighted area. Suddenly she was thrust back into a world of noise and commotion. She blinked, her eyes adjusting to the glare. Children were running all over the place. Voices assailed her ears. She heard mostly Spanish. For a moment, she had the unsettling feeling that she had taken the wrong plane and had landed in South America.

She saw that she was in a long area with seating on

either side. Down the center was a wide corridor, crowded with pedestrian traffic, that led to the main terminal. There were giant picture windows through which she could see the planes as they approached the terminal. It was a view of the back-door operation of the airport, the loading and fueling of the planes, the men in the yellow slicker jackets who did the maintenance and drove the big yellow trucks.

Lindi walked down the concourse past the seating areas for the different loading gates. She made a right-hand turn and found herself in the heart of the airport, an open lobby with rows of seats, potted plants, an information desk, and a magazine stand that included a snack bar.

She needed a cup of coffee before attempting to tackle the matter of securing her luggage and renting a car. She took a seat at the snack counter and gave her order to a plump waitress who addressed others at the counter in a rapid and continuous flow of Spanish.

Lindi stared in surprise at the miniature cup that was placed before her. She thought it could not possibly contain more than a few tablespoons of thick, black liquid. But the waitress had moved to the far end of the counter where members of the airport crew were lounging over snacks, cheerfully rattling rapid-fire Cuban Spanish.

Unable to catch the waitress's eye, Lindi resigned herself to the morning demitasse. She took a healthy swallow. Instantly she was thrown into a spluttering, gasping seizure. Tears streamed down her cheeks. She became the amusing center of attention at the counter. Laughter and good-natured comments were offered by the crew, all in a language she didn't understand.

The waitress came to her rescue with a glass of

water. "Señorita, that is Cuban coffee," the plump matron admonished. "Very thick. Very strong. You drink slow. Sip. Not drink fast like American coffee. You know?"

"Don't you have American coffee?" Lindi gasped, after she had recovered from her strangling spell.

"Not in the Miami airport," the waitress smiled. "See, we have many Cuban delicacies, guava pastries, mango pie. You try?"

Lindi sampled a guava pastry. It was delicious, a cross between peach and nectarine, very sweet. And she made a second attempt to drink the coffee, this time treating it with much more respect.

It was at this point that the deep voice of Travis Machado had spoken her name, startling her.

Now she gazed at this man who commanded her attention with such overpowering presence. She became aware of the impact of the moment as if a great force had suddenly slammed into her life, turning its direction irrevocably and forever toward a new destiny. It was a disturbing, almost frightening, experience, something she sensed rather than felt.

Lindi moistened her lips, which had gone strangely dry. With a conscious effort, she drew her eyes from the hypnotic gaze that was so disturbing. She answered harshly, a sharp edge of defensiveness in a voice that was not altogether steady. "Yes, I'm Lindi MacTavish. And just who the devil are you? And how do you know me? I've never seen you before in my life."

The man with the strange, dark, angry eyes said, "My name is Travis Machado. Your sister-in-law asked me to pick you up here and bring you back to Palmettoville."

# Chapter Two

Lindi took a moment to adjust to an entirely new set of reactions to this strange, tall man who stood towering over her. The reservations and suspicions that had engulfed her suddenly dissolved, a mingling of relief and curiosity taking their place. She became somewhat flustered and self-conscious. "Well, how do you do, Mr. Machado. I—I didn't know . . . I mean, Frances didn't tell me to expect you." Then, in a rush, she asked, "How is my brother?"

Machado shrugged. "Doing all right I suppose, under the circumstances. They've moved him to a private room."

"Yes, Frances told me that last night. Have they been able to tell how badly he's injured?"

"Well, I really can't answer that. Mrs. MacTavish hadn't seen the doctors yet when I spoke to her this morning."

You're certainly not the most talkative man I've

ever met, Lindi thought with a touch of impatience. There was a moment of strained silence during which they simply looked at each other. The icy reserve that surrounded Travis Machado like a cold mantle made her uncomfortable and, for some irrational reason, angry. Was he irritated at her because he'd had to drive all the way to Miami to get her? If so, why had he volunteered to do so?

The MacTavishes, contrary to the stereotyped image of Scottish people, were not taciturn. Lindi liked to talk with people she encountered. She made a fresh effort to loosen up Travis Machado. "How on earth did you recognize me, Mr. Machado? We've never met before."

"It wasn't difficult. There are not that many red-headed women in the Miami airport."

Was there just a hint of amusement in his dark eyes, or did she imagine it?

"I suppose that's true. So far about all I've encountered are Latin types. But still, you could have been mistaken. I'm sure there could have been another woman with red hair. You seemed quite certain when you spoke to me."

His gaze had momentarily strayed from her hair to her face and she felt her cheeks grow warm. With a sudden stab of anger, she wondered if he was glancing at her freckles, which she had considered a curse since adolescence. Then his look trailed further down her body, straying over the curves of her firm, high bosom that strained against the light blouse she was wearing, to her belted waist, and then to the outline of her thighs revealed by her tightly drawn skirt as she sat on the counter stool with her legs crossed. Her cheeks grew warmer and her resentment deepened. She didn't mind a male look of approval, but neither did she appreciate having inventory taken of her anatomy in such a slow, searching manner, as if she were on a slave block.

"Well," he finally said, "there is a strong family resemblance between you and Roy, of course."

"Naturally," she said coldly. "We're twins."

"I know."

She waited for him to elaborate, but he left it at that, irritating her further. Obviously she was going to have to drag every shred of information she wanted out of this man. After the strain she had been under and the sleepless night, she wasn't sure she was up to the effort. "You've known Roy and Frances quite a while?"

He merely shrugged.

"I suppose you must be good friends of theirs to offer to drive all the way over here to pick me up."

His only reply was a brief nod. Then he said, "Shouldn't we pick up your luggage?"

It was a direct and, she thought, rather curt way of ending the conversation. "Yes," she said shortly, gathering up her purse and overnight bag.

They left the snack counter, walked about ten feet, turned right, and took an escalator that moved them underground to the baggage area. Lindi, striding impatiently ahead of Travis Machado, approached the great metal conveyer turntable stacked with luggage. She waited as it turned until she was able to seize her two large bags. No sooner did she have them in her possession than a pair of powerful, sun-tanned hands took them from her grasp. In so doing Machado's fingers brushed hers. The contact startled her. She felt as if she had touched an electrical outlet that gave her a shock. For a second she was very close to the tall man, so near she could feel his body heat. His male scent filled her nostrils. The closeness aroused a response that unnerved her. Her thoughts were chaotic. Her knees felt weak. Her face burned.

She stepped away from him as if she'd accidentally moved too close to a hot stove. Wide eyed, she glanced at him, then away, her heart hammering. What kind of insane chemistry had begun to work inside her?

She was quite aware that a total stranger of the opposite sex could arouse a sudden and violent attraction in a normal, healthy person. One might catch a fleeting glimpse of a person on the street, on a movie screen, or in a crowd and feel an instant animal arousal, a kind of primitive sexual flash fever. A civilized person recognized such moments for what they were and quickly dismissed them from conscious thought.

But why this man? Why this moment? She was furious with herself. Travis Machado had shown absolutely no friendliness. He had been cold, brusque. Obviously, driving to Miami to get her had been done out of some kind of sense of obligation or duty to her brother. Why Frances had asked him to meet her, Lindi couldn't imagine. Perhaps because no one else was available.

In any case, for her suddenly to be engulfed by a wave of physical attraction for this taciturn man with his strange, dark, angry eyes had to be a case of temporary insanity. She soothed her humiliation by telling herself her irrational behavior had been brought on by the stress and nervous tension of the past hours.

Refusing to look at him anymore, she surrendered her baggage ticket stub to a security guard who checked it against her ticket and waved them on.

They walked several hundred yards to the parking garage. Machado led the way to the self-service elevator and touched the button that took them to the second level. There he directed her to his vehicle. Somehow she wasn't surprised to find it was a rusty pickup truck.

He tossed her luggage unceremoniously onto the truck bed and unlocked the truck doors. She wondered why he had bothered locking the vehicle. Who in their right mind would want to steal it?

She climbed into the passenger side and tried to find a place on the torn vinyl seat that wouldn't snag her hose.

The vintage truck made a grinding sound as Machado turned on the starter, then came to life with a clattering roar. Eventually it settled down to a rumble, and the broad-shouldered man pushed in the clutch and moved the floor shift lever into position. The truck shuddered, then backed out of the parking space. Lindi felt her vision drawn magnetically to the strong, brown hands gripping the steering wheel, and again that electrical tingle raced through her nervous system and down her spine. Cheeks flushing, she looked away.

They drove from the parking garage to an underground area where acrid exhaust fumes stung Lindi's nostrils and paused at a booth where Machado surrendered his parking ticket together with a sum of money. Then, at last, they were out in the bright Miami sunshine. Although it was early March and Lindi had left two feet of snow turning to icy mush only a few hours ago, now she rolled down a window to enjoy the semitropical morning breeze.

"I was surprised at how Spanish Miami has become," Lindi said. "When I got off the plane, I thought for a moment they'd made a mistake and put me on a plane to South America.''

He nodded. ''Much of Miami has become a Cuban colony. Eighth Street on the map of Miami has been changed to Calle de Ocho.''

From the Miami airport, they exited to the right on Le Jeune Road, then went west on Route 836 for about a mile, turned south on Route 826 for nearly five miles, and exited on West Eighth Street, which became the Tamiami Trail, the highway across the lower Florida peninsula that would take them through the Everglades to the west coast.

Lindi was becoming accustomed to the silence between them; it was no longer strained. Travis appeared engrossed in the business of driving, paying her no further attention. A sensation of relaxation, a brief respite from the tension of the past hours, stole over Lindi. She determined to push worry about her brother out of her mind for the time being. One's nervous system could stand just so much strain, and there was absolutely nothing she could do until they arrived at the hospital in Palmettoville.

The battered old truck purred with the mechanical contentment that comes from an engine used to loving care. The broad shoulders of Travis Machado almost touched hers in the confines of the small cab, the strength of his hands on the steering wheel giving Lindi a feeling of security. Machado projected a sense of being able to cope with any situation that might arise on this drive through the swampy wilderness of the Everglades.

From time to time, Lindi stole a glance at the rugged profile of this unusual man, curiosity about him nagging her. He stirred her imagination as no other man she had ever met. His guarded privacy invited speculation. She allowed her imagination to roam. She tried to picture him working at various kinds of jobs and professions: a merchant, used-car salesman, druggist, delivery man. None of them fit. Then she tried mechanic, fire fighter, commercial fisherman: they seemed more in character. There was about him an aura of the outdoors, of physical action.

Then her imagination took another tack, straying to conjecture about his personal life. A picture of wife and children took form in her fantasy: his wife appeared as a lusty, attractive woman with laughing, flirting eyes and a provocative swing to her hips.

That image somehow made her uncomfortable. With a determined effort, she turned her attention from the mystery of Travis Machado to a different kind of mystery, the desolate wilderness through which they were driving, the Everglades, called by some a river of grass. Fifty miles wide, it stretched more than a hundred miles down the lower peninsula of Florida from the great inland Lake Okeechobee to the Gulf of Mexico. Childhood memories conjured up visions of the fierce, cutting, saw-toothed grass, of giant cypress trees six hundred years old lost in the uncharted backwaters of dark swamps, of alligators and small green tree snakes and the flash of pink feathers of the roseate spoonbills, their silly flat bills looking like a joke of nature. She saw again narrow creeks winding through the saw grass, creeks that could lure unwary boaters made soft by civilization into a confusing maze of pathways where they would be lost forever among the mangroves and floating islands.

Lindi shivered. She remembered childhood nightmares in which dead tree limbs dripping moss became the arms of drowning giants clutching at the sky as they were sucked into the mist-shrouded swamps, while vultures became specters out of a dark underworld the Indians believed existed.

The Everglades could defeat time, make civilization a dream. She could visualize those early inhabitants, the real citizens, the rightful owners of the wilderness, the ancient Calusas and later the Seminoles. In her mind she could visualize the primitive people, their brown bodies greased with fish oil to repel swarms of sandflies and mosquitoes, living in their thatched-roof dwellings, the *chikee*, in harmony with the life and seasons of the swamps. She saw them gathering on beaches for tribal feasts, taking their food from the lush tropical growths of cabbage palm hearts, elderberries, wild grapes, and the black berries of the palmetto. She pictured the fish and oysters and the deer felled by arrows whose sharp tips were fashioned from chipped shells.

She could imagine the scream of a panther, the rustling swish of the wings of a wood stork, the splash of an armor-plated alligator. It was a steaming, prehistoric setting out of the dawn of creation. All that was lacking were the saber-toothed tiger and the giant mammoths who had left their bones in the silt eons before.

Lindi drew a breath, returning to the present with an effort, conscious again of the reality of the bright sunlight, the truck, the flash of cars whizzing by them.

This highway they were on, the Tamiami Trail, cut straight across the lower peninsula of Florida through the wasteland of grass. It came out of the earth and sky behind her and plunged into the horizon ahead. Above them, a few silver puffballs of clouds drifting on high currents of the gulf airstream contrasted with the royal blue sky. Businessmen, impatient with the distance between Miami on the east coast and Fort Myers on the west, saw nothing but the road as they drove along, while tourists in motor homes and campers gawked at the wilderness surrounding them. Between cars, the eternal silence of the Everglades descended like a curtain, shutting out civilization.

Lindi remembered the vivid stories her grandfather had told of the building of this road. He had been a young man when the staggering job of laying a road across the desolate acres of muck and swamps was begun in 1916. It was finally completed twelve years later, in 1927. He told her of the wrenching battle between man and nature, how when it was started, no one really knew how to build a road through the water and saw grass. The highest point of land was a scant twelve feet above sea level. During the rainy season, it was all under water. In the dry season, great fires turned the sea of dry and brittle grass into a raging inferno.

The builders found there was only one way to do it—blast down to the limestone, every foot of the way, and fill rock in to the surface, building instead of a mere road a great coast-to-coast causeway of limestone.

Her grandfather had worked on the road gang one summer, fighting his way through the saw grass with a machete, waist deep in water, burned by the sun and tormented by mosquitoes, constantly threatened by deadly rattlesnakes and water moccasins. They built crude log roads over which rumbled oxcarts loaded down with dynamite. Men drowned, were bitten by snakes, blown up by the dynamite, and crushed under sinking dredges, but the road was built by man's stubborn triumph over nature, and now they were traveling over it, taking it for granted.

"Roy and I spent summers with our grandfather in Palmettoville when we were growing up," Lindi suddenly said aloud. "He took us on nature trails into the Everglades and named some of the plants and birds. The ones I remember most are the beautiful roseate spoonbills and some kind of long-legged storks."

"Probably the black-and-white wood ibis," Machado said. Dark eyes flashed from the road to the wilderness for a second, and Lindi caught the glimpse of a strange, intense glow in them. For an instant her fantasy of the primitive people laughing and dancing in a tribal celebration around a great smoking campfire flashed through her mind. She thought Travis Machado fit more easily into that framework than into any civilized category in which she had tried to place him.

"Do you know much about the Everglades?" she asked.

"A little," he replied in his noncommittal manner as he turned his attention back to the road, once again the twentieth-century man engrossed in the business of directing a metallic monster over a trail of concrete.

To fill in the silence, Lindi continued. "My ancestors were settlers here when Florida was still pretty much frontier country. My great-grandfather migrated from Scotland and lived out his life on the Florida coast, I suspect spending most of his time treating malaria and typhoid. His son, my grandfather Eli MacTavish, was the founder of *The Clarion* newspaper my brother now operates in Palmettoville. He saw it all firsthand, the big Florida land boom and bust of the 1920s, the growth of cities, the roads through the Everglades. My grandfather was a big man with a bristling red beard and fierce eyebrows. He lived to be ninety-five, loud and robust until the day he died."

She laughed fondly, remembering the huge man who could sound so gruff and write such vitriolic editorials and yet be so gentle with her. "I always thought of him as something right out of Sir Walter Scott's *Lady of the Lake,* the leader of a highland clan—kilts, bagpipe, and all."

For the second time that day, she thought a shadow of a wry smile flashed across Machado's lips, gone before she could be sure it had been there. "Would he have been Roderick Dhu or James Fitz-James?"

Lindi stared at her companion, momentarily too surprised to reply. All the stereotyped images she had been trying to fit Travis into broke apart. She hadn't expected such familiarity with literature from him. Was he a schoolteacher? No, that didn't seem possible.

"You surprise me," she confessed aloud. "Not many people are that familiar with a writer like Sir Walter Scott."

"I read a book now and then," her companion answered. "It just so happens that Scott's epic poem is one I like."

Looking at him, she decided that yes, he seemed the type who would like to read tales about men who were larger than life, who fought great battles and set off on heroic quests.

She saw familiar landmarks that told her they were approaching Palmettoville. She mused aloud, "I wonder if the town has changed any since the last time I visited Roy and his family."

"You won't find many changes," he murmured. "Same waterfront section with the clutter of boats, the fishermen sitting around on the docks swapping stories while they mind their nets, the same narrow streets, cinder-block houses, banana trees in the yards, sandy soil.''

"How about that huge old banyan tree in the middle of the street near the post office? If they've cut that down I'll cry.''

"Save your tears. They'd sooner chop down City Hall.''

"Good! Roy and I played hide-and-seek in the roots of that old tree when we were children. I'm sure it's older than the town itself . . .''

She realized she was babbling because of nervous tension as they were approaching the hospital. Her hands felt cold, her throat tight.

Soon Travis Machado was steering his truck into the parking lot of the medical complex. The modern facility had been built since the last time Lindi had visited Palmettoville. It was a sprawling cluster of white buildings surrounded by a grassy lawn and the familiar tropical plants—bougainvillea profuse with great clusters of scarlet floral bracts, broad-leafed banana trees and elephant ear plants, stately royal palms outlined against the cloudless sky.

"I'll let you off at the entrance and bring your luggage in after I find a parking place,'' Machado said.

Lindi thought it was the most civil thing he'd said to her since he had picked her up at the Miami airport.

She strode into the building. Automatic glass doors swished closed behind her. Her shoes whispered softly on gleaming white vinyl. At the information desk she obtained her brother's room number. A self-service elevator took her to the third floor. Butterflies gathered in her stomach as she walked down a long hallway, impatiently searching out the room numbers. She turned a corner and saw a familiar figure stepping out of a room, closing the door quietly behind her.

"Frances!" Lindi exclaimed.

The slender, dark-haired woman turned. Her black eyes seemed enormous. Her pale face reflected the strain she had been under these past hours.

Lindi's heels beat a rapid tattoo. Then she and her sister-in-law were in each other's arms. Frances was crying softly.

Lindi felt a stab of cold fright. "Frances—"

Her brother's wife shook her head. "Don't pay any attention to me, Lindi. I'm just worn out. Roy isn't going to die."

"Thank God for that," Lindi said fervently.

Frances took her hand and led her to a small alcove at the end of the hall where there was a small waiting area. They huddled close together on a couch. Frances pushed strands of her hair back, groped in her purse with nervous movements, and found a crumpled package of cigarettes. She lit one, her hands trembling, and drew in a deep lungful of smoke. "I talked with the doctor about half an hour ago. He's seen the x-ray films and lab reports. It—it looks pretty bad, Lindi—"

She broke into sobs. Fighting back her own tears, Lindi patted Frances's arm mutely, not knowing what to say or how to comfort her. She felt a dark pit of dread inside her.

Frances drew a breath, struggling to regain control of her voice. "Both his legs are broken, and some ribs. A lot of bruises, that sort of thing. All that will heal in time. But there was damage to his spine. They won't be able to tell for some time how permanent it is. At this point they—they don't know for sure if he'll ever walk again."

# Chapter Three

Lindi felt a crushing wave of grief. For a second an album of family pictures flashed across her mind: memories of the two of them riding their bikes, playing ball, scrambling up trees, diving into waves on the beach. She had been a tomboy, trying to keep up with her active twin brother. The thought of Roy being confined to a wheelchair was more than she could bear.

"Will they let me see Roy?" she asked.

"They gave him a shot to make him more comfortable. The nurse said he'd probably sleep most of the day."

"You look as though you could do with some sleep yourself, Frances."

"I guess I must look like death warmed over," Frances admitted, self-consciously touching her cheek.

"Well, you needn't apologize. Did you lie down at all last night?"

"Not really. I dozed in a chair a little . . ."

"Why don't we take you home so you can get some rest. If Roy's going to sleep most of the day there isn't anything we can do here. You won't help Roy by collapsing from exhaustion. We can come back later this afternoon."

Her sister-in-law sighed and nodded. She seemed too numbed to function on her own. Lindi took her hand and gently led her down the hallway. They paused at Roy's door. Lindi entered the room, standing quietly beside the bed for a moment. Through a haze of tears, she gazed at her twin brother's bruised face. He appeared to be resting easily, the white hospital bed sheet rising and falling with his steady, rhythmic breathing.

Lindi touched his hand, a choking wave of emotion filling her throat. Then she turned and walked blindly from the room. A surge of anger mingled with her grief. What kind of monster could have run her brother down like that and then fled without offering any help?

She and Frances rode the elevator to the lobby.

Her sister-in-law asked, "Travis found you at the airport with no trouble?"

"Yes." She felt an odd, prickling sensation at the mention of the dark-eyed, brooding man who had driven her here from the airport.

"I was so worried that he might miss you somehow and you'd have to rent a car."

"No; he zeroed right in on me. I guess my red hair was a beacon." She paused. A multitude of questions about Travis Machado were clamoring to be asked. "Is—is he a friend of Roy's?"

"He works for the paper. He's the managing editor."

Lindi froze in her tracks, staring at her sister-in-law with wide-eyed surprise. "Well, he sure is an odd one! I talked about Roy and *The Clarion* and about Grandfather Eli being the founder of the paper all the way home, and not once did Mr. Machado say a word about being the editor!"

Frances managed a tired smile. "Yes—Travis is a bit unusual. He's something of a mystery to all of us. But he's a good newspaperman."

Lindi's first shock was washed away by a wave of anger. Why had Travis Machado deliberately let her ramble on about *The Clarion*, not saying a word about being the managing editor? Just to let her make an idiot of herself? He had probably been sitting back in that cold, remote reserve of his, enjoying a big joke at her expense.

She couldn't remember when she had encountered a man who both fascinated and infuriated her so much!

"He let me off at the door and said he was going to bring my bags in," Lindi muttered. "What the devil do you suppose he did with them?"

"Let's ask at the information desk. He probably gave them to the receptionist."

That proved to be the case. Lindi's suitcases had been placed behind the information desk for safe-keeping. The two of them carried the bags out to the parking lot where Frances's vintage station wagon had been parked all night.

Frances unlocked the battered old car. Lindi deposited the suitcases in the rear. "Better let me drive."

"Thanks," her brother's wife said gratefully. "I guess I didn't realize how tired I am."

Lindi pushed a toy spaceship out of the way and slid into the seat behind the steering wheel. The back seat was cluttered with a stack of papers, a basketball, a catcher's mitt, a baseball bat, and a swimming mask with snorkel. The car smelled of chocolate, old hamburgers, dog, and rust.

"Forgive the mess." Frances sighed. "As you can see, I've been carting the twins around. I got in the car one morning last week and Tim's pet lizard climbed up my leg. Nearly gave me heart failure. They keep promising to clean up this disaster area, but they get sidetracked."

"Gee, I'm eager to see them. It's been over a year since the last time I visited you. They must have grown a foot."

"At least. And twice as noisy, if that's possible. But they're just normal, healthy boys, for which I'm grateful."

"When you called last night you said they were staying with friends?"

"Yes, Grace and Bill Todd, a couple who live next door. They have a boy the twins' age. They're in the first grade together. This morning Grace took them to school." Suddenly Frances covered her face with trembling fingers. "My God," she choked. "It keeps hitting me. What if Roy has to spend the rest of his life in a wheelchair? He won't be able to play ball with the boys, take them fishing, teach them to ride bikes. . . ."

Lindi tried to remain calm for Frances's sake. She knew how much Roy adored his sons, how he liked to romp with them and join in their games. She made a fierce effort to keep her feelings hidden. "Frances, it's not going to be that way. We must have faith that

Roy's going to be all right. Modern medicine can do miracles."

Her words sounded hollow in her ears, but her sister-in-law seemed to take heart from them. Her sobbing quieted, and she regained her composure.

Lindi turned the key in the ignition. The old engine wheezed reluctantly to life. The wagon's squeaking springs complained as she eased it out of the parking lot and into the flow of traffic.

"I'm not too familiar with this part of town. This area is all new out here. There's a new shopping center and a bunch of buildings that weren't here the last time I was in Palmettoville."

"Yes—it's the beginning of a land boom, I'm afraid," Frances said.

"Oh, dear. Don't tell me this quiet, lovely little town is about to turn into another overcrowded resort area."

"That's exactly what is about to happen," Frances said grimly. "Only, it's a lot worse than you can imagine. If a certain element has its way, in three years you won't know this town."

"When did all this happen?"

"It started about a year ago. Roy saw it coming. He began writing editorials about it last year. He's been fighting a one-man war against them. But they're gaining too much power . . ."

" 'They?' Who's 'they'?"

"A group of outside developers. And some local people too—bankers and businessmen who care more about profit than about their friends and neighbors who live here!"

Lindi heard an edge of bitter anger sharpen her sister-in-law's voice. "They'll stop at nothing. And that's why Roy is in the hospital—" Her voice broke.

Lindi's startled gaze darted momentarily from the road to the other woman's face. The grief and worry that had been filling Frances's eyes had been replaced with bright, hard fury.

"Back up a minute." Lindi gasped with bewilderment. "Are you telling me Roy was deliberately run over?"

"It's very possible." Frances nodded grimly. "There's a power struggle going on in this quiet little town, Lindi, with big money involved, and Roy is on the wrong side of the fence. He has your grandfather's talent for writing editorials that tell the truth no matter who he makes mad."

"Have you talked to the police about this?" she gasped.

"Oh, they're investigating the accident, of course, and took a statement from me. But what can they do? Nobody got a clear look at the car that hit Roy. There were no witnesses on that side street. Some of our people at *The Clarion* caught a glimpse out of the window of the car as it sped away, but nobody was able to see the license number. That's what makes it seem so deliberate—as if the hit-and-run driver had picked that time and place, knowing the side street is usually deserted that time of day, just waiting for Roy to step out of the building—"

Lindi felt stunned. Slowly she shook her head. "This is more than I can grasp. I'm beginning to feel as if I've walked into some kind of nightmare. Maybe you'd better fill me in on some more details."

"It's complicated, Lindi. There's a lot of intrigue involving small-town politics, out-of-town money, ambition, and greed. I'd rather wait until Roy can talk to you about it. He knows exactly what's going on behind the face of this quaint little fishing village better than I do. He can fill you in on the whole unbelievable, corrupt mess.''

Lindi drove in a daze, turning down familiar streets lined with palm trees. Now they were driving down the main street of the coastal village. Here nothing had changed. It was the same quiet small town Lindi remembered from her childhood. It seemed isolated from the other crowded areas, somehow hidden from the tourists, the condominiums, the retirement developments of the rest of the state. On the east, the big cypress swamp of the Everglades reached almost to the city limits. On the western fringe of the city was the waterfront, the rickety piers, the fishing boats, the watery lanes of the gulf winding between ten thousand miniature islands of tangled mangrove jungles.

On a corner of the main street was the square building, dazzling white in the Florida sunshine, bearing the familiar sign, *The Clarion*. Parked in front of the newspaper office was Travis Machado's battered pickup truck. When Lindi saw it, she felt her heart give a peculiar lurch. An image of the tall man with the strange, dark, angry eyes awakened a mixture of churning emotions. She felt resentful because of his manner toward her this morning, yet there was a mystery about him that was fascinating.

When they drove past the newspaper office, Frances averted her eyes as if unable to bear the sight of the narrow street beside the building where her husband had been struck down.

A few blocks more and they turned onto the waterfront area. Here they drove near the docks, where fishing boats of all descriptions, from small outboards to diesel-powered shrimpers, swayed and bumped softly against their moorings in the wash of the gentle morning surf. The pungent odor of fish, brine, and tar tinged the air. Sea birds circled and squawked above, diving at any sight of a possible food morsel. Tin-roofed sheds bore signs advertising diesel engine repair, bait, and boat and fishing supplies. A marine engine roared into life; then the boat left a wake behind its churning propeller as it wound its way through the channels between the mangrove islands.

At least nothing here had changed, Lindi thought gratefully.

After they had circled past the waterfront area, the winding street took them into a modest residential area, and Lindi pulled into the driveway of a pink stucco house on a corner.

"Those kids!" Frances exclaimed. "They've left their bikes in the driveway again!"

She got out, opened the garage door, and wheeled the bicycles inside while Lindi removed her bags from the rear of the station wagon. Then Frances unlocked the front door.

"Please forgive the mess," she said, picking up one of the twins' jackets from near the front door.

Lindi could see no reason for her sister-in-law to apologize. Frances was an immaculate housekeeper. Lindi thought that compared to her cluttered New York apartment, this house could be a model for a magazine. It was a modest three-bedroom home, neatly but inexpensively furnished. Lindi could see her sister-in-law's handiwork all about her. Frances had sewn the drapes and recovered a second-hand living room set in matching fabric. The colors she had chosen, yellows mingled with traces of earthy browns, brought the sunshine and outdoors into the room. Healthy house plants, framed prints, and bookshelves had transformed what could have been a depressingly plain house into an appealing, cheerful home. Obviously Roy and Frances were barely able to make ends meet on the earnings of the small-town newspaper, but Frances had the talent to make the most of their income.

Lindi remembered how her roommate Cimi had quickly taken steps to help ease her distraught state the night before. Now Lindi thought she could do the same for her sister-in-law.

"Why don't you relax in a warm tub for a bit while I make some hot tea and a snack, Frances? Then you can take a nap while the house is quiet before the twins get home from school."

"That sounds good." Frances nodded numbly. "Want me to show you where things are in the kitchen?"

"I've been in your kitchen before. If I need any help, I'll yell."

"All right then."

Lindi brewed tea, scrambled eggs, fried bacon, and toasted bread. She was scooping the eggs from the pan onto a platter when Frances rejoined her, tying the sash of a blue robe as she entered the kitchen. "That sure smells good."

"You probably haven't eaten a thing since yesterday."

"I had several cups of coffee last night. That's all."

Lindi served her sister-in-law a platter of scrambled eggs and bacon at the breakfast table, which was situated in an alcove just off the kitchen area. When they took their seats at the table they were surrounded by windows that gave a view of the fenced-in backyard, which contained a lush tropical growth of banana trees, avocado trees, and brilliant red bougainvillea.

"Speaking of coffee, I had quite an experience at

the lunch counter of the Miami airport this morning. I ordered a cup and got some of that potent Cuban brew.''

"Oh, yes. It's very thick and strong, isn't it?"

"That's putting it mildly! A spoon would stand up in it. I took a big swallow and it just about removed my tonsils!''

Mentioning the Miami airport brought Travis Machado once again to mind. Lindi would have preferred to forget the irritating man, but he persisted in dogging her thoughts. Trying to sound casual as she toyed with her coffee cup, Lindi asked, "How long has Travis Machado been managing editor at *The Clarion?*"

"Oh, he drifted into town about a year ago, riding in on a motorcycle. He walked into *The Clarion*, told Roy he was a newspaperman, and asked for a job. At the time, Roy was swamped with the printing end of the business and really needed someone to help run the paper. Travis had with him a glowing letter of recommendation from a big daily up in Mobile where he'd been the assistant city editor. Roy checked out the letter and proceeded to hire Travis on the spot.''

"You said something about Travis being something of a mystery—"

"Well, yes. He's a very private person. We don't know a whole lot about his past except for some stories he's told about knocking around the world on tramp steamers when he was in his early twenties. Then he decided he wanted to write, so he got a job on a newspaper. He worked his way up from copy boy to the assistant city editor of a large paper, so he certainly knows the newspaper business. He could get a good job on almost any big paper in the country.

And yet he chose to come to this out-o
and accept a job on a small weekly
enough for him to live on. No one ca
but he seems happy enough at what
says he's working on a novel in his spa
that's why he chose this kind of life-sty
an old houseboat he fixed up down c
front."

"Well he does sound . . . unusual,"
mured, finding the subject of Travis Mac
intriguing than she cared to admit to herse
suppose he's part Indian? He gave me tha
sion."

"We've wondered about that. Some people
are convinced he's part Seminole. He speak
language, you know. And he's completely at ho
the Everglades. He has a swamp buggy and
disappears all weekend in the 'Glades. A pe
who didn't know that territory like an Ind
would get hopelessly lost and probably eaten by
alligator."

Lindi shivered at the thought. "Grandfather Eli
took Roy and me on some trails along the outer fringe
of the big cypress swamp, but he warned us never to
go any further. He told some hair-raising stories
about hunters and fishermen who wandered into that
swampy jungle and were never heard from again."

"Those stories were probably true. Civilization has
made a lot of inroads in the 'Glades, but there's still a
lot of that mysterious wilderness that only the Indians
know."

Lindi felt a compelling desire to explore further the
subject of Travis Machado. The more she learned
about him, the greater a fascinating mystery he became. But she reminded herself that this was not the

to get into a long discussion with her sister-in-
Frances was emotionally and physically exhaust-
She needed rest.

Now it's off to bed with you," Lindi exclaimed.

Lindi was feeling the strain of the past twenty-four
urs herself. After Frances retired to her bedroom,
ndi cleaned up the breakfast dishes, unpacked her
gs in the spare bedroom, kicked off her shoes, and
retched out on the bed. She stared at the ceiling, her
houghts churning with concern for her twin brother.
he remembered what Frances had said about the
ruthless developers who threatened the peaceful village and her brother's life. Had her sister-in-law been
so distraught by Roy's injury that she was exaggerat-
ing? What exactly was going on behind the scenes in
this isolated coastal fishing village that seemed so
sleepy and contented on the surface?

And then, almost hypnotically, her thoughts were
drawn to the dark-eyed Travis Machado, who had so
mysteriously drifted into this town. Just as he persistently intruded into her thoughts, so had he also
thrust himself into her life, a situation that she found
disturbing and not altogether to her liking.

She drifted off to sleep, dreaming fitfully of a tall,
threatening figure emerging from the dawn mists of
the Everglades, scooping her up in powerful arms to
carry her off into the darkness.

The high-pitched voices of children awakened her
with a start, and she realized at once that the twins
were home. She swung her legs off the bed and
hurried into the bathroom where she splashed water
on her face. She ran a comb through her hair and
made hasty repairs to her makeup. She took two small
packages from her suitcase and walked out of the

spare bedroom and down the hall to the front of the house.

Frances was already up and dressed. The twins were with her on the couch, both of them talking ninety miles an hour at the same time, telling about their day in school. When Lindi entered the room, two freckled faces with blue eyes and snub noses turned in her direction. The chattering halted in midsentence. "Kids, you remember your Aunt Lindi," Frances said. "She's come to visit us while Daddy is in the hospital."

There was a moment of shyness, which dissipated almost as suddenly as it had begun when their eyes fell on the packages under Lindi's arm. Fortunately, she'd had two model airplanes tucked away in her apartment closet, awaiting their birthday.

"Guess what I brought you," she grinned.

They were all immediately on friendly terms. "Hi, Aunt Lindi," either Tim or Jon said. She still couldn't tell them apart.

"What's in the packages?" the other one asked.

"That's for me to know and you to find out," Lindi said teasingly. "How about a hug for your old aunt first?"

She knelt to meet them on their level, and the two husky youngsters swarmed over her. Then she sat on the floor with them while they demolished the wrappings on the packages. "Hey, neat!" one of them cried. "A Phantom Jet fighter!" He ran around the room, holding the plane in flying position.

The other, holding an identical model said, "Gee, thanks, Aunt Lindi." Then, his blue eyes looking straight up at hers, he said, "Daddy got hurt. A car ran over him."

Then she knew this one was Tim. He was the polite, serious one, she remembered. "Yes, Tim, I know."

Tim got up to fly his plane, intercepting his brother. "You didn't tell Aunt Lindi 'Thank you' for the plane," he said accusingly.

"Oh, yeah," Jon said absently. "Thanks." Then he dashed out the front screen door, making his plane do a loop on the way.

"I guess that's about as much as one can expect in the way of good manners from a six-year-old." Frances sighed.

"You look a bit more rested," Lindi said, joining her sister-in-law on the couch.

"Yes, thanks to you, Lindi. I guess I was on the ragged edge. But I had a good long nap. Now I'm going to feed the twins some hamburgers and cart them off to the neighbors, and we can go back to the hospital."

By then it was midafternoon. Lindi took a quick shower and changed into a cool, casual print dress while Frances made hamburgers for them all.

On the way to the hospital, Lindi stopped at a florist's and bought some flowers for Roy. When they arrived at the hospital and entered Roy's room, Lindi felt a choking wave of love for her twin brother. He turned his head painfully and his eyes lighted when he saw them. "Frances . . . Lindi!" he whispered.

"Hi," Lindi managed before the tears started. Then she was hugging her brother.

He patted her awkwardly, his movements slow and obviously causing him pain.

Lindi dried her eyes, seeing him more clearly now. His eyes reflected the pain and trauma he'd suffered, but he was fully awake.

Frances kissed him. "How are you feeling, honey?"

"I don't think I'd want to go jogging," he said weakly.

"Having much pain?"

"Only when I breathe," he said, managing a shaky grin.

"You must be better if you can joke about it," Lindi said.

"Well, they've got some great pills here. The nurse gave me one when I woke up. She said if I start hurting, she had another pill waiting. So I guess I can't feel too sorry for myself." Then he asked Lindi, "When did you get here, Sis?"

"I arrived in Miami early this morning."

"Oh, yeah. Travis went to pick you up."

"You knew about that?"

"Yes. I talked with Travis this morning before he went to get you. Then they gave me some kind of shot and whamo! I was in dreamland."

They talked for a few more minutes; then Lindi could see Roy was getting tired. She and Frances kissed him and left the room.

Each day that week when Lindi went to the hospital, she could see Roy growing stronger. By the end of the week, he was sitting propped up in bed.

On Saturday, Travis Machado came by to give Lindi a ride to the hospital. It was decided that Frances would stay home with the twins that morning while Lindi visited Roy. In the afternoon, Lindi would play baby-sitter so that Frances could go to the hospital.

Lindi felt a strange tension growing as she went to the door to meet Travis. The moment his hooded, dark-eyed gaze fell on her, her emotions began churning.

"Good morning," she stammered, furious at herself for feeling so painfully self-conscious. It was a state she hadn't experienced since her first adolescent crushes.

Travis nodded, his gaze sweeping over her in a searching manner that both excited and angered her.

She pushed open the screen door and joined him on the front porch. She was dimly aware of the high-pitched voices of the twins playing in the house, the sounds of birds in the trees and traffic in the street. All sensations of sight and sound became a faint, jumbled background to the intense focus of her attention—the man before her.

Nervously, she wiped her palms on her slacks. "It—it's very considerate of you to give me a ride to the hospital . . ."

He acknowledged her thanks with a cool bow of his head. "It's nothing. I want to go by to see Roy anyway."

Her reaction to him intensified. He appeared determined to treat her in a chilly, unfriendly manner. Why?

And yet, she thought, as they walked to his waiting pickup truck, she sensed his male awareness of her. It was impossible to unlock the secrets hidden in the dark pools of his eyes. They were like the black depths of a rain forest at midnight. On the other hand, they smoldered like coals burning in the jungle darkness as they surveyed the lines of her body.

On the way to the hospital, she was acutely aware of him as she had never been of another human being. She stole glances at his rugged profile, tracing the lines of his high brow, strong jaw, drooping dark mustache, and strong, cleft chin. Her curiosity about him verged on the painful. It prompted an impulsive attempt to dispel some of the aura of mystery about him.

With a boldness that surprised her, she said, "I guess I made a bit of a fool of myself on the ride from Miami, telling you all about *The Clarion*. Why didn't you tell me you are the editor? Were you having a laugh at my expense?"

"No. You didn't ask me."

"That's hardly an answer," she said, her frustration putting an edge in her voice. Then, with growing boldness, she said, "Frances tells me you had a very responsible position as city editor of a large daily newspaper. You must know quite a bit about the newspaper business."

"A little," he said shortly.

"Don't you find it boring, working on a small-town weekly?"

"No, not at all."

She refused to give up so easily. "I find it odd that someone with your experience would want to settle in a small town way out here in the boonies. Do you have relatives here?"

He took his eyes off the road for a second to give her a scathing look. "I live where I chose to live, just as you chose to live in New York."

His momentary distraction sent the truck's front wheels bouncing into a hole in the back street they were on. The resulting jostle threw her shoulder against his. The contact of their bodies sent a flash of tingling warmth through her.

Travis growled an epithet under his breath. She inferred from the dark look on his face that if she kept quiet, he might not wreck his truck.

She said no more during the remainder of the drive to the hospital. But their brief conversation had only intensified her curiosity about this strange, brooding man. Where did he come from? What was he doing here? Why was he so secretive about his private life?

Perhaps if he were someone else she would simply shrug it all off. Travis Machado, however, was not a man who could be easily dismissed. This was the second time she had been with him, and sparks were flying as if struck from steel touching a grindstone. She could feel the intensity of his brooding anger like a palpable force in the air. He both infuriated and fascinated her.

She walked into the hospital beside him, feeling small beside his powerful, broad-shouldered physique. He walked lightly for such a large, strong man. She could picture him more at home stalking wild game in the jungle swamps of the Everglades than striding across the tile floor of a modern building. That recalled to her mind the conjecture about his relationship with the Indians of the Everglades. Was he part Seminole?

They found Roy with pillows behind his head and shoulders, looking alert and in relatively good spirits. When Roy and Travis shook hands, Lindi looked at their faces and saw the respect and liking the two men had for each other.

After chatting for awhile, Machado said, "I'm glad you're improving, Roy. Now I have to be leaving. Give you and your sister a chance to visit." He glanced at Lindi. "Would you like me to come by and give you a ride home later, Miss MacTavish?"

"That won't be necessary," Lindi said coolly. "When my sister-in-law comes to the hospital, I'll take her car home."

Travis nodded. "Then I'll say good morning to both of you."

For a moment, his inscrutable dark gaze lingered on her. Why was he looking at her that way? she asked herself. As always with this upsetting man, she could find no answer.

After Travis left, Roy looked toward Lindi. "Sis, I've got something I need to talk with you about."

Lindi thought he was beginning to sound more like his normal self in spite of the discomfort he was obviously still feeling. She pulled her chair beside the bed. "Okay." She smiled. "I'm listening."

"Lindi, the doctor has told me I'm going to be laid up for a helluva long time. At this point, they're not even sure I'll ever be able to walk again—"

"Roy—"

He held up one hand. "Don't feel as if you have to give me the old pep talk routine. I know what I'm up against. That's my own private battle. I'm not giving up. I think I can lick this thing. Even if I wind up in a wheelchair permanently, I'll be able to run the newspaper again. But that could be six months or a year down the line. And I'm worried about what is going to happen in the meantime. Lindi, *The Clarion* has to keep going. It's the only way I can feed my family. But there's even more at stake than that. I'll explain why, but first I have to ask something of you. I want to know if you can stay on here and run the paper for us."

For a long second, Lindi was speechless. Then she gasped. "Roy, I don't know anything about running a newspaper!"

"Sure you do. You're a journalism major. You make your living from writing, don't you?"

"That's an entirely different field; you know that. I'm a free-lance magazine writer. I do some book editing on the side. It's a whole different world."

"But you'd pick it up quickly," he said, urging her. "I can tell you how the operation runs. I know you could do it, Lindi."

She shook her head, bewildered and stunned by Roy's surprising request. "But you have a managing editor—Travis Machado. Frances said he's an excellent newspaperman."

"Yes, he is. And Travis would continue as editor of the paper. I want you to take over the reins as publisher."

"Publisher? I—I just don't understand, Roy. What's the point in that when Travis Machado is perfectly capable of running the paper?"

"Lindi, Travis is a top-flight newspaperman, but he's not one of the family. We don't know a heck of a lot about Travis. And he has a disconcerting way of suddenly disappearing for days at a time. Oh, he always lets me know he's going out of town. But he never says why or where. He made it clear when he took the job that he might be called out of town from time to time. It was part of the deal when I gave him the job. I accepted his strange behavior because he's so good and I desperately needed an editor. And he's willing to work for the small amount the paper can afford to pay him. But you see, I need someone I can trust completely, someone in the family, to be down there, running things."

"In other words," Lindi said slowly, "Travis Machado would be taking orders from me."

"Yes. And he might resent that. Travis is an independent guy who wants to do things his own way. So you might have your hands full dealing with him. But I know you, Sis. You've got the MacTavish stubborn temper. I think you can deal with Travis on his own terms, okay."

"Roy, you said Travis came to the hospital and saw you that morning before he drove to Miami to pick me up. Did you say anything to him then about my taking over the running of *The Clarion* as its publisher?"

He frowned, searching his memory. "I was pretty groggy and full of sedatives that morning. But yes, I think I did tell him that I was glad you were coming and that I'd see if you'd be willing to take over the operation of the paper. Why?"

"Well, I think I know now why Travis Machado greeted me like I was the enemy who had just landed!"

# Chapter Four

Lindi moved from Roy's bedside to the window, staring at the hospital grounds below with unseeing eyes as she wrestled with Roy's startling proposition.

She had been totally unprepared for anything like this. Since Roy was now out of danger and growing stronger she had been contemplating a return to New York early the next week to resume her normal routine. And now Roy had dropped this bombshell, asking her to give up her career, her apartment—wanting her to change the entire direction of her life and move down here to run his newspaper. He was asking too much!

As if reading his twin sister's thoughts, Roy said, "I realize it's asking a great deal, Sis. More than I have a right to ask. I—I just thought there might be some way you could keep up your free-lance writing from down here; you wouldn't have to be in New York to do that. And you might even get some fresh ideas. You know, a new perspective. And you could combine that with overseeing the operation of *The Clarion*.''

Lindi turned and gazed at her brother with troubled eyes, understanding the worry and torment he was going through. His family depended on *The Clarion* for survival. She felt sure they had little in the way of savings. Frances had the job of raising the twins, and when Roy could be moved home from the hospital she'd have a handicapped husband to care for. No doubt Roy would need a lot of special physical therapy.

She thought that the poor guy must be at his wit's end. How could she turn her back on all that? After all, she was young and single. She did not have the responsibilities of a family. She liked Florida and she had always loved this quiet village. It had been a second home. Taking over the job of publishing the newspaper her grandfather had established might even be a stimulating challenge, an adventure.

At the same time, she thought of the changes she would have to make; they were staggering. It was true she could continue her free-lance magazine work from here. But other aspects of her career would have to be tossed overboard. She had worked hard to establish contacts with book publishers for the part-time editorial jobs she did. That would be lost. And she was building a clientele for her speech-writing jobs. She'd have to give that up. Her share of the apartment would have to be surrendered or subleased. Cimi couldn't afford the apartment on her own.

Then she thought of something else: Travis Machado. What would be the consequences of their daily confrontation? He was already angry at the thought of a New York woman coming down to tell him how to run the newspaper. Would she be up to the inevitable clash between their strong personalities? He was the most disturbing man she had ever encountered. Just the thought of being thrown together with him on a daily basis was upsetting and disconcerting. Her cheeks grew warm and her heart thudded uncomfortably at the prospect; thinking about it unnerved her.

Roy could see the struggle that was going on in her heart reflected in her troubled gaze. "Sis, I'm sorry to have laid something like this on you. Maybe I should have kept my big mouth shut about it—"

She shook her head. "No, Roy. It's something we have to talk about. We're family. In times like this, a family has to stick together. I know if the situation were reversed, you'd come to my rescue. It's—well, it would be a big change for me. I need to think about it. And I'm not sure I could cope with it. Operating a newspaper—I wouldn't know where to begin."

"You'd have plenty of help. Remember old Caleb Stoneman, the printer who worked with Grandad? He's still with us. Must be seventy-five at least and grouchier than ever. But the old coot has a heart of gold, and he knows the operation of *The Clarion* frontwards and backwards. Also, he knows all about the printing jobs we do. You know a small weekly newspaper can't survive on its own. We need the printing-business end, too. Caleb could fill you in on all that. He could be your teacher.

"As for Travis Machado, he's an excellent writer and newspaper editor, but I can't guarantee how much help you'd get from him. Travis is a strange guy. I have a lot of respect for him, but even after a year, I really don't know him that well. Like I said, he may resent your taking over. He probably thinks he should be the one to take over while I'm laid up. But that would be the least of the problems you'd have to deal with."

"What do you mean?"

"Well, I want you to know exactly what you'd be getting into, Lindi. There is something very unpleasant going on in this town and *The Clarion* is right in the middle of it."

"Frances mentioned something about out-of-town developers coming in with a lot of money and big ideas for changing Palmettoville. Is that what you're talking about?"

"Yes. And things are apt to become very rough around here before it's all over. About a year ago, a group of developers from another part of the state quietly infiltrated Palmettoville. They formed a coalition with local bankers, businessmen, and real estate people, selling them on the idea of starting a land boom here and making a killing in skyrocketing real estate values. It's hard to turn down that kind of money. Greed is a universal human weakness. They have a lot of influential local people on their side— people who are out to make a profit.

"The tactics they're using are scary. For example, they got into local politics. They succeeded in electing several of their supporters to the city council in order to get City Hall behind them. They are going around quietly buying up property. Their aim is to move the old-time natives out of town and then turn the town into a retirement resort that only millionaires can afford. They'll bring in dredges to cut boat canals and put up high-rise condominiums all along the beach.

They're planning the worst kind of uncontrolled growth, Lindi—the kind that wrecks the ecology and brings on all the problems of urban overcrowding, crime, and pollution. In my editorials the past year, I've been preaching restraint and caution, trying to open the town's eyes to what is happening, warning them that the quality of life here is at stake.

"The situation has split the town down the middle. Some citizens are as scared as I am, and they're behind me one hundred percent. But just as many think I'm a crackpot standing in the way of jobs and progress. I know I'm right; I've seen what this kind of unrestrained development can do. But there's big money involved. The out-of-town developers represent huge conglomerate corporations. One small newspaper fighting them is like a mouse nipping at the heels of a lion."

Lindi felt a mixture of anger and apprehension. "Frances is worried that the group you're fighting might have had you run over—"

"It's very possible. See what I mean? I'm a thorn in their side, that's for sure. They've gone so far as to buy the only local radio station just to combat my editorials with their own form of propaganda. But it's the subtle, undercover tactics that are scary. Our circulation has picked up since this fight began. You know, a conflict like this is good for local reader interest. But in spite of increased circulation, we've lost a number of advertisers, those who are on the other side of the fence. I know if the developers have their way it will mean the end of *The Clarion*. They're out to get me and out to get the paper, Lindi. They'd like nothing better than to run me out of town and put *The Clarion* out of business."

Roy paused. Then he smiled wryly. "Sounds like I'm trying to scare you off instead of talk you into staying here to run the paper."

But Lindi's green eyes were flashing. "You don't scare me, Roy. What you said just makes me mad. It reminds me of the times Grandad Eli would wade into a civic fight with his fire-and-brimstone editorials. I can hear him now, with that Scottish brogue rolling off his tongue, 'Lindi, me girrrl, no MacTavish ever ran from a fight!' "

For the first time since his accident, Lindi saw her brother laugh. "That sounds just like Grandad, all right. I've thought about him a lot, lately. Sometimes I feel as if the old man's ghost is standing behind my shoulder telling me what to say when I write one of my editorials. Maybe it's because I hung around him so much when I was growing up and later when I helped him run the paper, but the words seem more his than mine."

"You have his flair for words, that's for sure," Lindi exclaimed. "I've read some of your editorials."

"Runs in the family, I guess." Her twin brother smiled. "I've read your magazine articles."

"Thanks," Lindi said. Then she sighed. "Roy, I still can't get it through my head why you want me to take on the job of publisher of *The Clarion*. Okay, I can understand your reason for not picking Travis Machado because of his mysterious disappearances from time to time. You certainly need someone you can depend on. But don't you have someone else on your staff you could depend on—someone who would be better qualified than I?"

He gazed at her, his eyes filled with worry. "If it was just a matter of routinely getting the paper out and overseeing the printing jobs, I suppose my sports editor, Jake Tarson, could do it. Jake is an old hand at the business. Or there's Pat Horine, my advertising salesman, who knows enough to do an adequate job. But Lindi, we need more than that. The fact of the matter is, *The Clarion* has barely kept its head above water the past months. The trouble we've had with the group that opposes our stand on the development plans is partly to blame, and I can't seem to come up with any very good ideas for improving the business. You were always the one with the brains in the family, Lindi."

"Roy—"

"No, it's true. One reason I came back here to help Grandad with *The Clarion* is because I knew I just didn't have what it takes to hack it somewhere on a big daily. This was a quiet, sleepy town, and Grandad had been getting out *The Clarion* week after week the same way for years. It was a nice, safe rut for me to hide in. And after the old man passed away, I just went on doing things the way he'd been doing them. I guess that was okay until we ran into this fight with the people who want to destroy the town as we know it. I've been beating my head against a wall. I'm just not smart enough to cope with these new developments."

"What makes you think I am?"

"Because you got all the brains in the family! Even back in grade school and high school, you were always on the honor role, while I barely scraped by with C's and D's. After college you headed to New York, got a terrific job with one of the top advertising-public relations firms in the country, made a success out of that, then went on to do okay on your own. You're clever and sharp, Lindi. You've got big-city ideas. I know our methods and equipment are old-fashioned and out of date. You could breathe some new life into *The Clarion*."

"Roy, you're asking an awful lot of me—expecting a lot . . ."

A faint smile crossed his lips. "You're my big sister, aren't you? Mom always said you were born first. That makes you a couple of minutes older than I am!"

It was true that Lindi had always seemed older and more mature than Roy. She had been the responsible one. Growing up, Roy had been in one scrape after another. He had gotten through school by the skin of his teeth. Old memories flashed through Lindi's mind —their father in poor health for years, their mother trying to raise them and run the family insurance agency at the same time. Lindi had felt the heavy responsibility of shielding their parents from unnecessary worry. She could remember the many times she had helped Roy with his homework, sitting up half the night with him, cramming at the last minute to pass a test for which he hadn't been prepared. The night he and some high-school buddies got drunk on beer and drove through a neighbor's yard, it was Lindi who quietly paid for the damage to the lawn and fence out of her baby-sitting money to keep Roy from facing criminal charges.

Despite his shortcomings, Roy hadn't been a bad kid, just irresponsible and careless. He was one of the school's star athletes. And he had the ability to charm everyone he met. That winsome personality was one reason he hadn't worked harder. He knew he could get by on personality. He'd charmed most of his teachers into believing he was doing his work. And the whole time it had been Lindi behind him, seeing that he got to school on time, nagging him to get his homework done, coming to his rescue when he was in some kind of jam he couldn't charm his way out of. She became exasperated with him, but she never stopped loving him.

When they went their separate ways after school, Lindi worried a great deal about Roy. He flunked out of college in less than two years. She'd been enormously relieved when he'd moved down to Palmettoville and gone to work on their grandfather's newspaper. It had been a good move for him. He loved their grandfather and he liked newspaper work. It was the only job he'd stuck with. Marrying Frances had been another lucky break for Roy. She had been a stabilizing influence. She was a level-headed, practical young woman with a solid sense of values. And whatever other shortcomings Roy had, he had turned out to be a good husband and father.

But now Roy was in trouble again, the biggest trouble of his life. He was facing more than he could deal with. And he was turning again to his sister for help.

How could she turn her back on his cry for help?

Lindi sighed. "Roy, I have to do a lot of thinking about this matter. I can't give you an answer immediately. It means a drastic change in my life. Let me sleep on it, okay?"

"Sure, Sis. I didn't mean to put pressure on you, but I had to talk with you about it before you decided to hightail it back to New York."

"Of course; I understand. And I'll give it a lot of consideration. I promise."

She bent and kissed her brother fondly on the cheek. "Now you get some rest. Frances will be here this afternoon."

Lindi left the hospital, her head spinning, and drove home. Frances had lunch ready, a delicious salad filled with tropical fruits—papaya, kiwi, pineapple, mango, and bananas—and tall glasses of iced tea.

Once Lindi had relaxed, halfway through the meal she announced Roy's plan.

"Roy dropped a little bombshell on me this morning. He asked me to stay on and run *The Clarion* for him until he's able to work again."

"Well," Frances said, "I must admit that doesn't surprise me. You know, Roy has always looked up to you. He told me that your father's health was poor and your mother was wrapped up in running the family business, so you practically raised him, even though you were the same age. Lately, since he's been so worried about the business, I've heard him say several times that he wished you were here to give him some advice. You're so sharp, you'd know what to do. So I think he's had it on his mind. And then the accident—"

"Yes, he told me he mentioned his idea of having me take over publishing *The Clarion* to his editor the morning Travis drove to Miami to pick me up at the airport. Now I understand why he treated me like a tropical disease!"

Frances suppressed a smile. "Was it that bad?"

"Yes. At the time I sensed that he resented me, but I couldn't understand why."

"Oh, I wouldn't be too concerned about it. It takes a while to get to know Travis. He has a bit of a cold, aloof manner."

"I can just imagine how cold and aloof he'd be if I walked into his office Monday morning and announced that I was taking over the paper as the publisher and from now on he'd be taking orders from me!"

"Well, I don't suppose he'd react to that with a great deal of warmth," Frances admitted. "Travis doesn't like to take orders from anyone."

"Much less a young woman whom he probably considers a total greenhorn in the newspaper world," Lindi said grimly.

Frances was toying with her salad. "Then you . . . you've decided to turn down Roy's proposition and go back to New York?"

"No, I didn't say that. Travis Machado certainly wouldn't frighten me off."

"How about the people in town who are fighting Roy and the paper? The developers and businessmen behind them? I'm sure Roy warned you about them."

"Yes, he told me. And they frighten me least of all. They just make me mad."

They ate in silence for a few minutes as Lindi struggled with the decision that had been thrust upon her. Wherever her thoughts strayed, they had a way of returning to Travis Machado. The thought of facing him again both unnerved and excited her. She envisioned herself striding into his office to announce that she was taking over the role of publisher of *The Clarion*. A prickling sensation ran up her back as she pictured his black eyes locked in her direction, setting her emotions churning, his scowl draining the strength from her muscles. He had the ability to both infuriate and fascinate her. She wasn't at all sure how she felt about him, but whatever it was, it was not indifference.

"I don't know why I let that man upset me so," Lindi mused aloud.

"Travis?"

"Yes. He can be infuriating. I get angry every time I think about the way he let me ramble on about *The*

*Clarion* and didn't bother to tell me he was the editor. He did that deliberately to humiliate me. He must have been silently laughing at me the entire time."

Frances regarded Lindi with her large, dark eyes, her expression thoughtful. "Is it possible you are attracted to him?" she ventured.

"Certainly not!" Lindi replied indignantly, embarrassed by the flush she felt warming her cheeks.

"Well, you know, if you have strong feelings about someone, even if it's anger, that could mean the person has stirred your emotions. And Travis is the kind of man a woman would find hard to ignore."

"Well, I have no interest in Travis Machado other than his position on the newspaper. For heaven's sake, I hardly know the man! I haven't even been with him a half a dozen times. And I doubt that anyone would call him the communicative type." She hesitated, then sheepishly admitted, "Of course, you're right; he does have more than his share of masculine magnetism, or whatever you want to call it."

Frances nodded. "I think any woman would be intrigued by Travis. He has a lot of physical appeal." Then in a teasing manner she asked, "While we're on the subject of men, how is your love life, Lindi? Any marriage prospects back in New York?"

Lindi shook her head. "None at all. I guess I've been too wrapped up in my career since college. Most of the men I meet are married or not my type. There was Jeff Lansing back in college . . ."

"Yes, I remember him. You were pretty serious about him as I recall."

Lindi winced inwardly from the painful stab of an old memory. "We had an understanding. I guess you'd call it a kind of informal engagement. I really did care a lot. I suppose Jeff was the big romance of my life, at least up until now. But he was wrapped up in his studies of archeology. The summer he graduated he went off to South America on some kind of archeological dig. At first we exchanged letters regularly. I thought he'd be back in the fall and we'd be married by Christmas. But then his letters became less frequent and more impersonal. Finally there was the good old 'Dear Jane' letter. You know, '. . . perhaps we can still be friends' . . ."

Her voice trailed off. It was a painful subject, one she did not often care to talk about.

"I suppose a lot of women have a 'Jeff' somewhere in their memory chest," Frances said sympathetically. "There's something special about a first love. Fortunately I was spared that kind of heartbreak. Roy and I were sweethearts in high school. There never has been another man in my life. But getting back to Travis Machado, I'd be careful if I were you, Lindi, if you do stay on here and have to be around him a lot. He's devilishly attractive, that's for sure, in a wild, untamed sort of way. Don't let yourself in for another heartbreak. I think I'd better warn you that according to the town gossips, he's already involved with a woman, Shodra Nichols. Shodra is a businesswoman here in Palmettoville, a very sexy, glamorous widow. She owns several businesses, a used-car lot, a beauty shop, and a restaurant. Roy is leasing *The Clarion* building from her. She's a striking woman with long, blond hair and a figure that's unbelievable. Drives a big, flashy Lincoln."

Lindi felt a strange lurch in the pit of her stomach. She asked herself furiously what possible difference it could make to her that Travis was involved with that kind of woman.

Then she was seized with a daring impulse. Her green eyes sparkled and she raised her chin defiantly. She thought that she just might pay Mr. Travis Machado a visit on Monday morning. She'd beard the lion in his den, as the saying went. It would be interesting to see what his reaction would be if she told him she was seriously considering taking over the job of publishing *The Clarion*.

# Chapter Five

 Through the glass door of his office, Lindi could see Travis Machado. He was leaning back in his chair, boots crossed on his desk as he leafed through some pages of typewritten copy.

Lindi drew a deep breath. Her palms felt damp. There was a fluttering sensation in her stomach. Then she became irritated with herself. Why should a meeting with Travis Machado make her nervous?

She rapped on the glass sharply. Travis twisted in his chair, glancing in her direction over his shoulder. Seeing her, he scowled. He uncrossed his boots, swung around in his swivel chair, tossed the copy on his desk, and rose. Lindi had forgotten how tall and imposing he was. He seemed to fill the doorway like a menacing shadow. He nodded. "Good morning, Miss MacTavish. I've been expecting you."

"You have?" she asked with surprise.

"Yes. Come in, please."

She was disconcerted by his polite manner. She had been prepared for him to start breathing fire when he saw her. Of course, the politeness was all on the surface. His black-eyed gaze was glacial.

He indicated a chair on the other side of his desk. She sat down stiffly as he resumed his place behind the desk. He had a way of looking directly at her, without initiating any conversation, that she found unnerving. She also found his presence to be even more overwhelming than she had remembered. The very nature of his physical strength seemed to generate an electrical charge that could be felt in the air. Her gaze touched on a set of broad shoulders that tested the ability of his shirt seams to contain them, the wide silver belt buckle, ornate with turquoise, flat against a firm waist, and trousers that hugged his powerful thighs. She quickly looked away, disconcerted.

She glanced around the office. It was small and cluttered. The brown carpet was worn, the single window overlooking the main street was dusty. The furnishings consisted of one desk; an ancient manual typewriter; bookshelves containing a dog-eared dictionary, a thesaurus, and some reference books; and the chair on which she was seated. On the wall were framed vintage photographs of Palmettoville in its early days and several views of the construction work on the Tamiami Trail in the 1920s. She suspected the photographs had belonged to her grandfather.

One shelf held a bit of Seminole Indian handicraft, a doll made of palmetto and coconut fibers dressed in a traditional Seminole costume. It caught her eye, reminding her that her sister-in-law had spoken of the curious relationship Travis Machado had with the Indians of the Everglades. Before she had time to speculate about the significance of the Indian craft,

Travis's rich baritone brought her attention back to him.

"How is your brother today?"

"As well as we can expect, I suppose. He's still having pain and he goes through spells of depression. He's facing a long, uphill battle."

"Yes, I'm sure he is. I'm very sorry for him. Roy MacTavish is a fine man."

Lindi nodded. She drew a breath, raising her chin a fraction. "My brother had a long talk with me a few days ago. He's asked me to accept the position of publisher of *The Clarion.*"

Except for a momentary tightening of his jaw, Travis displayed no reaction to her announcement. "Roy mentioned that possibility to me the morning after his accident. And he's discussed it with me again when I visited him since then. That's why I said I've been expecting you." His gaze swung back to her, his black eyes smoldering. "Have you decided to accept his offer?"

"Yes. I think I must. He seems to feel he needs me, and I don't see how I can turn him down under the circumstances."

"Have you had any experience in newspaper work?"

Lindi's green eyes met his with a flashing challenge. "I majored in journalism."

A corner of his lip curled. "There's quite a bit more to the operation of a small-town weekly than they teach you in college."

"Yes, I am aware of that," was Lindi's chilly reply.

"A small-town newspaper can't survive on its publication alone. We also run a printing business here, everything from business letterheads to programs for the next Kiwanis Club meeting."

"Yes, I know that."

Travis was silent for a moment, withdrawn and contemplative. "And you think you can run an operation like this?"

"If I decide to take on the job, I expect to do just that."

"I'd give it a lot of thought. I doubt if you'd be happy here," Travis said bluntly. "Palmettoville isn't New York. And operating a newspaper is not a job for a young, inexperienced woman, especially with the fight going on between the developers and the conservative citizens who want to keep the town the way it is."

Lindi felt herself seething inwardly. His superior, condescending attitude infuriated her. If he hoped to discourage her, his approach was having the opposite effect. She was mad enough now to accept Roy's offer just to take Travis Machado down a few notches. "I wouldn't agree to the job if I didn't think I could handle it," she said sharply.

He shrugged. "Have it your own way."

She looked at him directly, trying to understand the man. This was a touchy situation she realized. She tried to see it through his eyes. His male pride and ego had been dealt a blow. For the past year, he'd been second in command. As editor of the paper, he would naturally expect to take over as publisher as well until Roy was well enough to operate the business again. It really must gall him to be told that a young woman, totally inexperienced in running a newspaper, was going to be his boss.

What if he quit? She wondered if Roy had considered that. Machado's kind of newspaper editorial skill did not come cheap. She had been impressed by the style and makeup of *The Clarion*. It had all the professionalism and polish of a big-city daily. And that was the work of a talented editor.

Still, no one was irreplaceable. If he got on his high horse and walked out, she'd just have to replace him or take over the job of editing the paper herself.

She decided to stop sparring with him. A direct confrontation was the best course. "Mr. Machado, I know you don't like me. I can understand your resentment. My concern is helping my brother and his family and seeing that *The Clarion* goes on despite Roy's injuries. You must be frank with me. If I do take over as publisher, are you going to quit?"

His black eyes met her green eyes with the force of a jousting knight riding head on. His jaw knotted as his heavy, dark brows scowled. "That thought had occurred to me."

Her eyes didn't waver. She was not going to show any weakness at this point.

Then he shrugged. "No, I guess not. I think too much of Roy MacTavish to walk out on him when he's flat on his back. On the other hand, if you're going to run things around here, you can fire me if you wish."

Lindi responded with mixed emotions. On the one hand she was relieved not to have the difficult task of replacing him. On the other, she did not relish the prospect of doing battle daily with a personality as strong as that of Travis Machado. "I have no plans to fire you, Mr. Machado. From what I've seen of the paper, you are doing an excellent job as editor. At the same time, I have some ideas for modernizing and building up *The Clarion*. I spent several years in one of New York's largest advertising and public relations firms. I think I have some fresh ideas to bring to this business. You may not always agree with me."

"And if I don't?"

"I'm the publisher."

"Yes, I suppose you'll be reminding me of that from time to time. Well, we'll just cross those bridges when we come to them. Meanwhile—" He rose, uncoiling his large frame from his chair with the lithe grace of the panther that stalked its prey in the Everglades. "If you're going to take over here, I guess you'd like to meet the staff."

"Yes, I would. I understand Caleb Stoneman is still with the paper. I knew him from the days when my grandfather published *The Clarion*, but the rest of the staff has all changed."

"Well, let's begin with the lady in the office next door, Rachel Douglas, my secretary and girl Friday. Rachel does everything from proofreading, to handling the distribution of the paper to out-of-town subscribers, to writing up job printing orders." A rare smile crossed his lips. "On occasion you might find her helping out in the composing room or writing some last-minute fillers."

As she rose, he opened the door to escort her out of his office. He touched her arm, sending a peculiar shock wave through her. "By the way, we're pretty informal around here," he said. "Everyone is on a first-name basis except for old Caleb Stoneman, who gets his hackles up if you call him anything except Mr. Stoneman. So, if we're going to be working together, why not call me Travis?"

"All—all right," she stammered, feeling disconcerted. Addressing him more formally by his last name had placed a distance between them, giving her a form of defense. A first-name basis made a subtle difference in their relationship that was hard to define, but it made her self-conscious.

"And I assume I may call you Lindi? Or is it unacceptable to address my boss by her first name?"

Was he being sarcastic? Her cheeks reddened. But she kept her temper in check. "Yes, you may call me Lindi," she replied, keeping her voice cool.

*The Clarion* was housed in a two-story building. The editorial and business offices were on the top floor. Below, on the first level, was, in newspaper parlance, "the back room," or the area where the printing presses were located.

When Travis Machado escorted Lindi from his office, they stepped into a large, open area occupied by numerous desks. The desks were separated only by waist-high partitions. The first of these "offices" was occupied by Travis's secretary, Rachel Douglas. She was a pleasant, round-faced young woman. Her desk appeared as neat and efficient as her practical dark blue blouse, tan skirt, and flat shoes. She wore her long hair in a bun and greeted Lindi with a warm smile, squinting a bit because she was slightly near-sighted.

"Miss MacTavish is going to take over as publisher until her brother is able to return to work," Travis told his secretary.

"How do you do," Rachel said. She wiped her hand somewhat nervously on her skirt and extended it to Lindi. "My, you certainly do look like Mr. MacTavish."

"Well, that's to be expected." Lindi smiled. "We're twins." She gave the plump girl's hand a warm squeeze, liking her immediately. She felt instinctively that she would have an ally in at least this member of the staff. "I'm glad to know you, Rachel. I'm sure we're going to get along famously." Which is more, she thought, than I can say for your editor.

Next Lindi met Jake Tarson, the sports editor. A cheerful, animated man in his mid-forties, Jake wore a striped shirt and sporty bow tie. He thrust a pencil behind one ear when he came to work in the morning and it stayed there until he left in the evening. Travis explained that in addition to covering all the sporting events in the area, Jake wrote a column called "Jake's Ramblings," which was extremely popular with the paper's readers. In addition to being a sports buff, Jake was an avid movie fan. His column often was devoted to motion-picture reviews as well as stories about stars, directors, and stunt people. He wrote on many other subjects as well, local history and character sketches of interesting people in the area as well. He also covered unusual hobbies, events, and people, such as an eighty-five year old man who made violins and some local youngsters who attempted to make the *Guiness World Book of Records* by staying on a seesaw day and night for two weeks.

Lindi liked Jake immediately. He had a childlike openness and a friendly grin that were appealing. He seemed totally devoid of hostility or hypocrisy. His enthusiasm was infectious.

She was amused by the society editor, Gladys Tindell, a thin, nervous, birdlike spinster who dressed as if she were prepared to dash off to an afternoon tea at a moment's notice. In addition to her society notes, Gladys also collected local news from nearby towns.

Lindi's first impression of the advertising salesman, Pat Horine, was not favorable. He exuded the smiling, glad-handing, extroverted personality one would expect in a salesman, but Lindi thought she detected a falseness in his smile and a calculating expression in his pale blue eyes. He wore a rumpled seersucker suit and smelled slightly of beer and cigars. She realized she had a habit of forming quick, intuitive opinions about people and that she should put off final judgment of the salesman until she got to know him better.

She reminded herself that his position was important to the success of the newspaper. He not only sold advertising space in *The Clarion* but also hustled printing jobs. When he was in the office, he worked up the advertising layouts, using various mat services to help illustrate his customers' ads.

These were the people who handled the editorial and business end of the publishing and printing company. Downstairs she met the other members of the staff, those concerned with the nuts and bolts of getting the printed words on paper.

There were two linotype operators, Mark Tremblay and Rudolf Garcia. Mark set straight editorial copy. Rudolf did advertising and printing jobs. The printer who made up the page layouts for the paper on big stone tables was Caleb Stoneman, who had worked on *The Clarion* since he was a boy. "Hello, Missy," he said gruffly. "Haven't seen you since you grew up and went off to college. Remember when you and your brother were little tykes, hanging around here getting in everybody's way. That was when your grandfather was still running things." He sent a squirt of tobacco juice into a tin can with deadly accuracy and muttered, "We put out a real paper in those days, when old Mr. MacTavish was alive."

Travis smiled as they left the composing room. "Caleb has never quite forgiven the younger generation that has taken over running your grandfather's newspaper."

In the press room where the big, old-fashioned presses were grinding out the current week's edition with a loud clanking, rattling din, Lindi met the three pressmen who ran the machinery. One day a week the presses were used to get the paper out. The rest of the week, they were busy with job printing.

When they left the noisy press room, Travis walked with Lindi toward the front door of the building, through the entrance hallway where a receptionist took incoming calls. A stairway to the left went up to the editorial and business area on the second floor. A door to the rear led to the composing and press rooms. The mingling odors of newsprint, ink, and dust permeated the building.

Lindi wrinkled her nose. "I'm surprised that Roy is still using Grandfather's ancient letterpress equipment. I expected that he surely would have installed offset printing methods by now."

"I suppose it's a matter of economics," Travis said. "Modern printing equipment costs a lot of money."

"True, but it's so much more efficient. And if the paper were printed on offset, it would be so much easier to use photographs instead of depending on engraving and mat services."

"Well, perhaps with a new publisher, we'll become prosperous enough to replace our old presses that are always breaking down at the wrong time."

She glanced at him sharply, trying to determine if he was being sarcastic. But as usual, his thoughts were hidden in the dark pools of his eyes.

"Good afternoon, Mr. Machado. Thank you for showing me around and introducing me to everyone. I'll be in Roy's office tomorrow morning."

He gave her a lingering, dark-eyed look that sent an involuntary shiver through her body. "I thought we had agreed on first names."

"Yes. All right . . . Travis."

Travis waited until she had stepped out of the front

entrance. Then he mounted the stairs in quick, angry strides and walked into his office, slamming the door behind him. "Damn!" he muttered aloud. Things weren't bad enough, with the developers about to rape the environment and destroy the town and Roy MacTavish getting run over. Now he had to contend with this New York City woman coming here to stick her nose where it didn't belong. "I majored in journalism," she'd said. A fat lot of good that was going to do her in the real world of newspaper publishing! She was probably going to throw her weight around with a bunch of kooky notions that would be the final blow to a newspaper that was barely hanging on by a thread now. What could be possessing Roy MacTavish to talk his inexperienced sister into taking over the reins as publisher? Had the accident scrambled his brains?

Travis stood at the window, glaring down at the scene below. Lindi was crossing the street to her brother's decrepit station wagon. She walked with clean-limbed strides, her light skirt snapping around shapely thighs, her back straight, her head at a jaunty angle. It was difficult not to notice how the skirt hugged her slender waist and trim hips. In the sunlight her hair gleamed like the copper of freshly minted pennies.

She was an attractive female, he had to admit, enjoying the view in spite of his anger. Her figure was smashing and was flattered by clothes worn in the style of a smart, successful city girl. Her pert nose, sprinkled with freckles, created an effect of wholesome freshness. But those snapping green eyes and that coppery red hair were warning signals. "Never tangle with a red-headed woman," a buddy had once warned him. This one obviously had a mind of her own. And that fighting MacTavish blood coursing through her veins could deal a man a lot of trouble.

He watched the skirt pull tight around her legs as she slipped behind the wheel of the station wagon. Physical arousal stirred in him. He toyed with the seductive fantasy of feeling her thighs pressed against his.

It was quite possible, he conceded, to resent a woman while at the same time finding her physically attractive. Nature had taken care of that paradox to keep the globe well populated.

Then he angrily took charge of his straying fantasies, reminding himself of the misery she was going to cause around *The Clarion*. Just how much was he going to take of her telling him how to do his job before he walked out? He debated that issue, trying to be objective. There was a lot at stake here. Roy MacTavish needed at least one person around here who knew how to get out a newspaper. He was indebted to Roy. Loyalty happened to be a quality that was of great importance to Travis Machado. And there was the other matter of his personal and economic situation. He couldn't afford to do anything impetuous or rash at this point in time. Too much depended on his keeping a cool head. As much as Lindi infuriated him, he might have to grit his teeth and bear it while trying to keep her from totally destroying *The Clarion*.

His glowering black eyes swept beyond the rooftops to the distant horizon beyond the city where the fringe of the Everglades began, leading to the mysteries of the Big Cypress swamp. A restlessness stirred in him as he temporarily forgot the petty conflicts of this civilized life that had been forced on him. . . .

# Chapter Six

"Well, Publisher, all ready to begin your newspaper career?"

"Hardly," Lindi said. "I think I must have been insane to agree to do this."

It was Monday morning. Lindi had spent a restless night and had risen early. She had dressed quietly, trying not to awaken Frances and the twins, and had tiptoed into the kitchen, planning to have a cup of coffee and walk to *The Clarion* building. She had been surprised to be greeted by the bubbling coffee pot and her sister-in-law waiting at the dinette table.

"I thought I was the early riser around here. Did you have a bad night too?" Lindi exclaimed.

"Sort of." Frances nodded soberly. "I stopped by the hospital last night. Roy is in a very depressed mood. I think it's really beginning to hit him that he might spend the rest of his life in a wheelchair."

Lindi realized that Frances looked drawn. Her eyes

were swollen as if she'd cried a lot during the night. Lindi's heart ached with sympathy for her sister-in-law and for her brother. "I—I hope Roy doesn't just give up."

Frances drew a deep breath, raising her chin. "He won't! The doctor said we can expect Roy to go through spells of depression. But I know Roy and I know he's going to fight this thing."

Lindi suspected that Frances was trying to reassure herself as much as she was her sister-in-law.

"You sit there while I make us some breakfast," Lindi ordered. "You'll feel better after you've had something to eat."

"No, please, let me. I feel better when I keep busy. That's why I got up early. I thought we could have breakfast together before I have to wake the twins for school."

Frances moved determinedly to the stove, so there was nothing for Lindi to do but take a seat at the table.

"After we have breakfast, I'll get the twins up and we'll drive you to *The Clarion*," Frances said, laying strips of bacon in a frying pan.

"Oh, I can walk. It's not that far—"

"No—it's warm, and with the humidity we have here, you'll feel uncomfortable by the time you get down there. You're going to need some transportation. *The Clarion* has a company car. It isn't much—a beat up old car—but it will get you around town. Ask Travis about it today."

"All right. And I need to start thinking about finding an apartment—"

"But you don't have to do that! You know you can stay with us."

"I know that," Lindi said gently. "But you'll be

moving Roy home from the hospital before long. If I'm actually going to take up residence here and run the newspaper for an indefinite length of time, I really do need a place of my own."

"Well, if you have your mind made up," Frances said reluctantly. "But it's not going to be easy. There's very little available in the way of apartments for rent."

Over a breakfast of bacon and scrambled eggs, they talked about *The Clarion* and the people who would be working for Lindi. "I liked Rachel Douglas right off. Same for Jake Tarson," Lindi said.

"Oh, yes, Jake's nice, isn't he? Everyone loves Jake. I don't think he has a mean bone in his body."

"That's the impression I got. I was kind of amused by the society editor."

"Gladys Tindell! Oh, she's something else. Was she wearing one of her outlandish hats?"

"Hats? No! I didn't think anyone wore hats any more!"

"Well, Gladys does. And they're really something to see."

"I can hardly wait."

"What did you think of Roy's advertising salesman?"

"Pat Horine?" Lindi frowned. "Perhaps I shouldn't let first impressions prejudice me, but . . ."

Frances nodded. "I think I know exactly what you mean. Do you have the impression that if you shake hands with Pat, you should count your fingers afterward?"

"That pretty well describes the feeling I had about him."

"Roy likes him." Frances sighed. "But it's pretty easy for someone to pull the wool over Roy's eyes. He likes everyone. And he wants everyone to like him. He's too trusting. Not that I think Pat's an out-and-out crook, but I wouldn't put it past him to pull something a bit shady if he thought there was a buck in it for him somewhere."

"Well, we could both be wrong about Mr. Horine, but I'll keep an eye on him. Old Caleb is still with the paper, I see. I can remember him from the time Roy and I were in kindergarten and our parents brought us down to Florida on vacation."

"Yes, he's about as ancient as those old presses that belonged to your grandfather. And he can still out-work any two other people down there. He never got married, you know."

"Typical crusty old bachelor." Lindi smiled fondly.

Frances nodded. "Lives alone with a cat and some chickens. Fishing and *The Clarion* are his sole interests in life."

"Well, I think he'll be a big help to me. He certainly knows the operation of *The Clarion* frontwards and backwards, though I'll probably have some trouble with him if I try to modernize the plant."

"Maybe not. He must get awfully tired, trying to keep those creaky old presses running." Frances sighed. "I think everyone down there would be overjoyed if we could put in some new equipment. Roy was just never able to swing it."

Frances sipped her coffee, then gave Lindi a quizzical look. "Haven't we missed someone?"

"Oh, yes. Our illustrious editor, the enigmatic Mr. Machado. Him, I think I'll have trouble with."

"I'm afraid you might. Two strong personalities clashing. Travis doesn't much like taking orders. He has his own way of doing things. Roy pretty much let him have his way."

"I was afraid he'd resent me so much he'd quit," Lindi said slowly. "So I came right out and asked him. He said he would stay. I think we have a kind of shaky peace treaty for the moment. I don't know how long it will last."

"Well, Travis thinks the world of Roy and he's very loyal. He probably feels obligated to stick with the paper until Roy can take over again."

"And I leave!"

"There may be other considerations. Apparently, Travis needs this job. He came down here for some reason. Why else would he be content to work for such a small salary? There's no future in a small paper like *The Clarion*. I know that, for one thing, Travis is working on a novel in his spare time. We suspect that is part of his reason for taking a job like this—to support himself while he gets his book finished."

Lindi was astounded. "Travis Machado, a novelist? He must be a more serious writer than I thought."

"I don't know if you can call him a novelist yet. It's his first attempt at that kind of writing."

"Have you any idea what his novel is about?"

"Oh, no. In case you hadn't noticed, Travis is a very private person. He simply never talks about his private life. But Roy put together little bits and pieces about him over the past year. Apparently he's led a pretty colorful life. He knocked around the world on tramp steamers for several years when he was barely out of his teens. Maybe he got the material for his novel from the adventures he had during that time."

Lindi fortified herself with generous helpings of bacon and eggs and several cups of coffee. Then she tackled the tough job of taking over her brother's business.

The first two days at *The Clarion* were spent getting

her new office in order. Roy had left it a mess. The ancient, battered roll-top desk brought a mist of nostalgic tears to her eyes. She could see her grandfather seated at this same desk, scowling fiercely at the paper on which he was writing the week's editorial. Framed on the wall above the desk were several awards for excellence in journalism.

Eli MacTavish might have been a small-town newspaperman, but he had won national recognition with his humorous and satirical editorials.

In a corner of the room was the ancient typewriter, a museum piece now, that her grandfather had used when he started the newspaper. Fondly, she touched the keys that the old gentleman would poke at in a furious two-finger assault that made the machine rattle like a machine gun. She wondered with a smile what he would think of the computer Lindi used to write on back in New York.

After Lindi brought some order to Roy's filing system, she poured over *The Clarion*'s books, familiarizing herself with the accounts they handled and the financial status of the business. As Roy had said, it wasn't good.

The fragile peace treaty between Lindi and Travis remained intact that week, largely because they kept out of each other's way. Travis ducked into his office, slamming the door behind him, whenever he saw Lindi. As for her, Lindi was satisfied to keep her distance. She had enough on her mind without dealing with the emotional turmoil of another clash with the managing editor.

One night after work, she had a long chat with Caleb Stoneman. They sat in her grandfather's office, after everyone else had gone home and the building was quiet and deserted, filled with ghosts of the past, and they reminisced about the days when Eli Mac-Tavish had been running *The Clarion*.

Lindi found a bottle of Jack Daniels whisky in a filing cabinet and poured them each a drink in paper cups.

"Cheers," Caleb said, and grinned when Lindi took hers straight. "You're Eli MacTavish's granddaughter, all right. Old Mr. Eli always set his bottle of Jack Daniels there beside his typewriter when he started batting out one of them fiery editorials of his. I admire a woman who can hold her liquor."

As they sipped the bourbon, they talked about the trouble that had come to the town, the bitterness developing between the land developers and the citizens like Roy who could see the town being destroyed along with the environment. And somehow the conversation got around to Travis Machado.

"That Travis is a strange one," old Caleb grumbled. "A good newspaperman—I give him that. But there's something eating at him. The way he showed up here in town, riding a motorcycle with all he owned in the world in one old suitcase tied onto the machine. You got to agree that's pretty strange, considering he'd had a good job on a big daily newspaper. Why would he take a job like this? A man running off from something like that, you figure it's got to be trouble with the law or trouble with a woman."

Lindi refilled her cup, uneasy about the direction the conversation had taken. She was torn between curiosity about Travis Machado and not knowing if she really wanted to hear the truth about him.

But Caleb was on a subject that interested him. "There are a lot of rumors about him—that he was raised by the Seminoles. Might even be related to members of a tribe who live in the Everglades not far from here."

"What makes you think that?"

"Why, he talks their lingo just like they do. I heard him once. Dan Cloudweather, he's a Seminole Indian who has a souvenir stand a few miles down the Tamiami Trail. Takes tourists on airboat rides. He was in town one day. I saw him and Travis in a bar. They were talking that Seminole ninety miles an hour just like blood brothers. Travis has one of those high-wheeled swamp buggies. On weekends, sometimes, he takes off into the 'Glades and disappears until Monday. Now, nobody but an Indian could go wandering off in that swamp without getting lost and winding up a meal for an alligator!

"Them Seminoles are strange, proud people, you know. The U.S. government fought the Seminole wars. Killed off the Indians by the hundreds until the tribes surrendered, signed a peace treaty in 1842 and were shipped out west. But some of them never surrendered. A few hundred of them, went back into the Everglades, hid in the big Cypress Swamp where the army couldn't get to them. To this day, they never signed a peace treaty with the U.S. They have their reservations, make their own laws. If one of them breaks a tribal law, their own council punishes them.

Caleb paused, wiping his lips with a forefinger. "Got any more of that Jack Daniels? Just a drop or so. That's fine." He swirled the liquor around in the paper cup, took a sip, and settled back in his chair, growing more garrulous as the level of whisky in his cup diminished.

"Sometimes Travis will disappear for a week at a

time. Never says where he's going or where he's been when he gets back. He lives on a houseboat, y'know."

"A houseboat?"

"Yeah, down on the waterfront. Bought it for a few bucks and fixed it up so it's livable. 'Course, he's got his old ace in the hole, like the song goes. His girlfriend is that widow, Shodra Nichols. And she's one sharp businesswoman. No telling how much property she owns around here. Got a beauty shop and a restaurant that I know about. Hell, she owns this building. I reckon any time ol' Travis gets hard up for money all he's got to do is drop a hint to his woman. . . ."

Lindi suddenly found the conversation becoming disagreeable. She interrupted the gossipy old man, making a determined effort to change the subject. "Mr. Stoneman, you know pretty well everything that's going on in this town. I want you to tell me everything you can about the people who are involved in this project to start a new development here. I want the names of the businessmen involved, especially those who are in city government, and the advertisers we used to do business with who have turned against us."

Caleb Stoneman gladly agreed. He spent the next hour talking about the subject as Lindi took notes.

It was dark by the time Caleb had exhausted the subject and drained the last of the Jack Daniels. He rose, bid Lindi a gracious good night, and walked with slow, dignified steps to the door, stumbling only slightly as he crossed the threshold.

After the conversation, Lindi felt inspired to write an editorial for that week's paper. She introduced herself as the new publisher of *The Clarion*, taking the place of her brother for awhile. She wrote about her grandfather and the kind of newspaper he had published, the kind of town he had loved, a town that was now threatened by an element that wanted to change it into something unrecognizable.

When the editorial was finished, she read it over and thought it was pretty good, but she wasn't sure if her judgment was reliable after the whisky she'd consumed with Caleb.

She gathered up the pages and went downstairs to the beat-up old red car, marked with *The Clarion*'s logo on the doors, which was parked in front of the building. A strange impulse seized her. She started the engine and drove the old heap down to the waterfront. At the local bar, she had another drink to reinforce her morale and asked the bartender if he knew where Travis Machado lived. Yes, indeed, the bartender told her and gave directions to one of the houseboats anchored not far away.

Still in the grip of the impulse, she followed the bartender's directions. As she approached the unusual floating dwelling, she saw a striking, blond-haired woman leave Travis's houseboat. The woman gave Lindi a curious, searching stare before getting into her sleek white Cadillac and driving off.

"Shodra Nichols," Lindi said aloud. Yes, that must be who it was. She felt a peculiar wave of mingled emotions that she couldn't define, emotions that triggered a lurching sensation in her stomach and brought a burning flush to her cheeks, causing her to clench her hands. The feeling passed, leaving her feeling foolish and angry with herself. What possible difference could it make to her who Travis Machado was entertaining on his houseboat? She couldn't care less if he had a whole harem there! All she wanted from him was his opinion of the editorial she had written tonight.

Lindi parked her car and walked across the rough planks of the dock. On the outside, the houseboat looked like a dilapidated barge. When Lindi stepped onto the deck, she was assailed by the pungent odors of the waterfront—the mingled smells of briny water, oil, tar, and fish. The sounds of the waterfront were there too—the lapping of water, the soft bumping of boats against their moorings, the call of a night bird. From a nearby tavern came the sound of voices and the music of a jukebox.

Lindi could see a light inside the dwelling. She heard the sound of a typewriter and recalled Frances's surprising bit of information about Travis writing a novel. Was he working on it tonight?

Clutching her own typewritten pages, she tapped on the door. The sound of the typewriter continued. She knocked again, this time more persistently. Inside the typing ceased. There was the sound of heavy footsteps. Then the door opened. Travis appeared as a dark shadow in the doorway, silhouetted by the light behind him. "What is it?" he asked impatiently. Then he recognized her, and the tone of his voice changed to one of surprise. "Well, if it isn't my boss!"

She felt sure he called her his boss just to irritate her. "May I come in?" she asked shortly.

"Of course." He stepped back, moving his hand in a gesture of welcome.

He was wearing a white turtleneck knit shirt, which hugged the muscular contours of his broad shoulders and deep chest, and a pair of deck-style slacks of a canvaslike material, tied at his waist with a piece of rope. On his bare feet were a pair of canvas shoes. All he needed, she thought, was a black patch over one eye, a ring in one ear, and a cutlass at his waist to look the part of a swarthy pirate striding across the deck of a frigate in another century.

She entered the houseboat. It was larger than she had expected and certainly in better shape on the inside than on the outside. The furnishings were comfortable: a rattan couch with a slipcover that bore a pattern of vines and reeds, a huge, red beanbag chair, a wicker chair suspended from the ceiling. The rough plank floor was covered with a woven reed mat. Shelves on one wall contained the speakers, amplifier, turntable, and tape deck of a stereo system. Shelves on other walls were filled with books. In one corner of the room was a desk that held a typewriter and stacks of paper. Off to the right was a small kitchen, or was it called a galley on a houseboat? A door to the left was partially open, revealing a water bed, unmade and rumpled. She remembered the blond woman who had just left. Had Travis and the woman shared the bed tonight?

Her cheeks stinging, she looked away from the open bedroom door. "I've never been in a houseboat before."

"Well, what do you think of it?"

She moved slowly around the room. We're sparring, she thought, like two warriors entering a ring, moving cautiously about, avoiding any direct confrontation, going through the motions of protocol as we test the situation. Was he as tensely aware of her presence as she was of his, she wondered.

"It seems quite comfortable," she murmured.

"It is."

"I've been told you arrived in Palmettoville a year ago with your worldly possessions on the back of your motorcycle."

A shadow of annoyance crossed his eyes. "You've been checking up on me?"

"Hardly," she said coldly. "Just a bit of gossip that was handed to me gratis. I only mentioned it because it appears to me that you've been able to acquire enough conveniences to make your living quarters very comfortable. Since I'm in the position of having to move down here and do somewhat the same, I was interested, is all."

He shrugged. "It isn't that difficult. What you see around you is early garage sale. You can pick up stuff like this for a song, especially if you work for a newspaper where you get to see the 'For Sale' ads before anyone else in town."

"Good point."

Her restless movements took her to the rows of books. "I read somewhere that one can tell a great deal about a person by his or her surroundings. I see a well-used dictionary, thesaurus, book of quotations, and a second-hand set of encyclopedias. Obviously the tools of a writer."

"Not a particularly acute deduction, considering the fact that you know I'm a newspaper editor. Incidentally, I suspect the set of encyclopedias is more third- or fourth-hand than second."

She continued down the row of books. "Biography, history, psychology, novels. Dickens, Victor Hugo, Flaubert, Dos Passos, Melville, Mickey Spillane. *Mickey Spillane?*"

He waved a hand. "Something light for bedtime."

She took down an anthology of English literature. "Ah, Sir Walter Scott. So this is how you knew about the *Lady of the Lake.* That really impressed me, you know."

He was watching her with a mixture of amusement and irritation. "Did you drop by to take inventory of my library?"

"Sorry. I didn't mean to appear nosy," she said, flushing. "Books happen to interest me. No, I had a very good reason for stopping by to see you tonight." She held out her pages of typewritten copy. "I had some ideas for my first editorial. I wanted to see what you thought of it before I send it to the composing room."

He raised an eyebrow. "You really want my opinion?"

"Yes, I do."

"But you're a professional writer. I understand you've been published in some of the largest national women's slick magazines. I'm just a country newspaper editor."

"That's why I want your opinion," she said testily. "I'm writing for a different kind of audience here. You know your readers better than I do. I want to know how you think they'll react to what I've written."

"Very well. Will you join me in a glass of wine while I read this? I happen to have in the refrigerator a bottle of fairly decent champagne that I opened just tonight."

Lindi thought about Shodra Nichols. An angry flush rose to her face. I can't believe this, she thought furiously.

"Oh, you had a party?" she asked coldly.

"Just a few friends who dropped by."

Make that singular, she thought grimly.

He stepped into the kitchen and reappeared shortly

with two full glasses of champagne. With cold fingers she accepted the glass he offered her, fighting down an impulse to fling the contents in his face. She thought she'd probably choke on it and considered putting it down untouched. On the other hand, the thought of another drink to calm her seething emotions was tempting. Probably Shodra had brought the champagne and, considering her affluence, it was no doubt an excellent vintage. Lindi thought she might, in fact, derive a certain enjoyment from having a drink at the glamorous widow's expense.

Then she gave herself a mental shaking. What was the matter with her, anyway? What possible difference did it make if Travis Machado had a party in the bedroom with Shodra Nichols? What was it to her? She must be losing her mind!

"Very good vintage," she murmured after her first sip.

"Yes," Travis said absently, settling his lithe frame on the couch as he prepared to read her copy.

While he read the piece, Lindi sipped the champagne and strolled around the room some more. In a small frame above Travis's desk was a typewritten copy of a quotation of the Roman philosopher, Cicero, composed 2,000 years ago, bearing the title, "The Six Mistakes of Man." The list of mankind's greatest mistakes included making advances by crushing others, worrying about things that can't be changed, becoming convinced that something can't be done just because we can't do it, spending too much energy on trivialities, neglecting improvement of the mind through reading and study, and trying to force our beliefs and lifestyle on others.

These six credos definitely gave an insight into the

character of Travis Machado. They must be important to him to have them displayed where he could see them daily.

She thought about the stories she had heard about his early life, how he had roamed about the globe on tramp steamers. That must not have given him the opportunity for much formal education. Yet he seemed well informed and well read. She thought about the many books on his shelves and decided he must be self-educated.

He had some knowledge of good music too, she realized, seeing the titles of a small stack of albums near his modest stereo system. They included some classics—Beethoven, Tchaikovsky, Grieg, and Prokofiev symphonies and concertos—along with a selection of classic jazz by artists like Bennie Goodman and Earl Hines.

Another wall held a display of framed color photographs taken in the depths of the Everglades, scenes of exquisite beauty depicting the flora and fauna of the region. One photograph displayed the stark symmetry of dwarf cypress trees, leafless in the dry season and festooned with clusters of stiff-leaved wild pine, an air plant related to the pineapple. Wild-life scenes included startling close-ups of a raccoon washing his meal in a puddle of water and an alligator displaying rows of deadly teeth in a gaping yawn. The most impressive, she thought, was a picture of a group of tree snails, each banded by colors that spanned the entire spectrum. Their beauty was breathtaking.

"Did you take these photographs?" she asked curiously.

"Yes."

The intimate knowledge of the hidden depths of the

Everglades that was required to obtain these photographs reminded her of the mysterious link between Travis Machado and that tropical wilderness.

Travis interrupted her train of thought. "This is quite good," he said, laying down her editorial.

She felt warmed. "You really think so?"

"Yes. The writing is very smooth, as I knew it would be. I think our readers will enjoy it and look forward to more with your by-line."

She was quite pleased. And wondered at the same time why his praise was so important to her.

"We should have another glass of champagne to celebrate your first contribution to *The Clarion*." He smiled as he refilled the glasses; then he raised his. "To the success of *The Clarion* under its new leadership."

For the first time his voice seemed to lack the undercurrent of irony; she thought his toast was sincere.

"Why, thank you," she said gratefully. She decided he could be quite pleasant if he chose to be.

He handed her the pages of copy. She accepted them and sat on the couch beside him.

"Perhaps you'd give me your opinion of something I've written sometime," he said hesitantly.

She wondered if he was referring to the novel he was working on. "Yes, I'd be pleased to. I don't know how much help I'd be."

"Probably a great deal. Roy told me of the editorial experience you've had with New York publishers."

He was looking directly at her. She was immersed in the swirling depths of his dark eyes; a magnetic force field seemed to surround them. She felt the chemistry boiling. What was the use in denying it?

She had been aware of this attraction from the first, fighting it, not wanting to admit it, yet undeniably aware of it. She had turned her back on it, smothered it with anger at times. Yet it persistently surfaced. What did this man have? Did all women react like this to him? Or was it something especially tuned to their biology?

With a supreme effort, she pulled her gaze away from his. "I—I really like your place here. I feel just a hint of gentle swaying from the water under us that is very soothing. I wish I could find something like this. I have to start apartment hunting, and Frances says it's hard to find a place here."

"Well, if you think you'd like living on a houseboat, it so happens one is available not far from here."

"Really?"

"Yes. It's in pretty bad shape. About like this one was when I got it. You'd have your work cut out, making it livable, but you could rent it for a song. I know the woman who owns it. She's been talking about junking it, but I think she'd rent it to someone who planned to do some repairs."

"I think I'd really like something like this! Living on the waterfront would be fun."

"It has its advantages. Sometimes you can catch supper from your back porch."

They both laughed. She realized it was the first time they had laughed together. In point of fact, it was the first time she had seen him laugh at all. He seemed unusually relaxed tonight. The air of dark, brooding introspection that usually haunted him had temporarily dissipated.

Perhaps it was the champagne. It was certainly having an effect on her. She had no business drinking any more after the Jack Daniels she had shared with Caleb Stoneman and the cocktail at the waterfront tavern, all on an empty stomach. She was beginning to feel dangerously reckless. An inner voice of caution warned her that her judgment was being impaired.

But the mood of the evening made her throw caution to the winds. It had turned into a pleasant evening. Travis Machado was the most fascinating man she had met in her entire life. When he wasn't in one of his dark moods, he could be extremely charming, as he was now. Tomorrow they would probably be at each other's throats again, but for the moment they had become relaxed with each other. Their defenses were down. Travis was treating her like a woman instead of a witch threatening to undermine his job.

Once again her eyes strayed in the direction of his face. She could keep her gaze away from his only a few moments at a time. Then, dangerously, like a moth drawn back to a deadly flame, she sank again into the power of his dark-eyed look. A languor stole through her muscles. She was aware of her heartbeat. She felt detached from reality. Was this what it was like to be hypnotized?

Her gaze trickled down the swarthy lines of his face to his throat, left bare by the knit shirt, and then roamed over the hard lines and hollows of his chest and shoulders. Her breath became thick in her throat.

With a struggle she made another bid for sanity. She swallowed hard. "Those photographs taken in the Everglades are fascinating," she murmured.

"You like them?"

"Indeed I do. I had no idea you were such a good photographer."

"Thank you."

"They especially interested me because I do a bit of photography, too. The colors are so brilliant. Were you using print film?"

"No. They were slides made into prints with the Cibachrome process."

"I think the pictures not only reflect photographic skill; they also show considerable artistic sensitivity, to say nothing of the first-hand knowledge you must have of the Everglades wilderness. What's it like, deep in the Big Cypress swamp? I've never been beyond the outer fringes."

"It's wild and desolate and forbidding," he said slowly. "Like a beautiful but dangerous woman, luring a man into a more intimate knowledge of her, still quite able to destroy him if he makes the wrong move."

With a feeling of panic, she realized his strong, sun-tanned hand had slipped down from the back of the couch to her bare arm. His fingers sent tingles of electrical sensation through her body as they slowly traced a line along the inner surface of her forearm, from the crook of her elbow to her wrist where a tiny pulse throbbed violently.

Her voice was thick as she asked, "Have you known many women like that?"

He shrugged, letting his answer remain a mystery.

"I—I think they are found more in fiction," she stammered.

"It's been my experience that people in fiction are only a pale reflection of those you meet in real life."

She tried to ask him to stop tracing the contours of her arm. He was driving her crazy. But the words wouldn't come. Her willpower had grown as weak as the muscles in her arms and legs. The tingling he had awakened was turning into smoldering coals deep within her.

"Tell me more about the Everglades," she asked softly, in a voice that seemed separated from her body.

"What do you want to know?"

"Are you ever afraid in that awful wilderness?"

"Of course not. The real danger is out here with civilized men."

"A moment ago you said it was women who were to be feared."

"Yes, but in a different way."

His fingers had moved tenderly from her arm to her throat, caressing the hollow there, dangerously close to the unfastened top button of her blouse. She could only stare at him in helpless fascination as he moved closer.

His gaze drilled into her eyes.

Then his arms slipped around her, pulling her against him. His body felt strong and hard and ruthless. Their lips were inches apart.

Her heart was pounding wildly now. "No . . . please—" she whispered.

He raised an eyebrow. "You find me repulsive?"

"Hardly," she said weakly.

He continued to hold her. She felt the warmth of his body burning through her light clothing.

God, this can't be happening, she thought. Her thoughts were spinning off in all directions. It was impossible to think clearly. Her entire body was a raging medley of sensations.

His mouth came down on hers savagely. Passion ripped through her in a blinding wave. Her arms were around him, her hands flat against the rippling muscles of his back. The taste of his mouth drove her wild. She worked her lips against his. She heard her own stifled moan. Her lips parted under the onslaught of his kiss.

Then his lips were elsewhere, nibbling at her earlobes, searching the hollow of her throat, the ridge along her collarbone to the hollow of her shoulder. She felt her blouse fall open as his fingers impatiently snapped the buttons.

Suddenly, looking past his shoulder, she saw the rumpled bed in the next room. Only then did some measure of sanity return to her ravaged mind. It was like a dash of icy water flung in her face.

"No!" she gasped. And this time she meant it.

She fought her way out of his arms. The passion of only moments ago vanished. With it went the intoxication from the drinks she'd had that night. She was suddenly cold sober and raging with fury.

He had planned to carry her to the very bed where, less than an hour ago, he had made love to his mistress! He was the worst kind of ruthless predator!

She was scorched with humiliation. What kind of temporary insanity had taken hold of her tonight? She had sat here, glamorizing him, idealizing him, turning him into some kind of exotic hero. Why, he was nothing but an oversexed, two-faced villain. He thought nothing of cheating on his mistress just to feed his male ego with a casual conquest!

How easy and cheap she must have seemed to him. She burned with shame and anger—anger at herself as much as at him. She had behaved like a giddy teenager swooning into the arms of the school football hero, ready to surrender on their first date!

He was glaring at her, his eyes dark with frustration and anger. "What suddenly bit you?" he demanded. "Isn't this what you came here for tonight?"

"Certainly not!" she gasped, white-faced. "Is that what you think?"

"It's pretty obvious, isn't it? You don't expect me to believe you actually came here just for me to read your editorial!"

"That's exactly what I came here for, you ego-ridden male animal."

"I didn't notice you complaining when I kissed you."

"I had too much to drink tonight," she spluttered. "You caught me off guard. You seemed pleasant and nice for a change and quite charming. I fell under the spell of the moment and let you kiss me. But I had no intention of going to bed with you. Certainly not in that bed!" She was clutching her open blouse with trembling fingers.

"What's wrong with that bed? It's very comfortable. Of course, if you'd prefer the floor—"

"Don't be insulting! I'm—I'm sorry if you think I led you on. I had no intention of being a tease. It—it was a mistake." She tried to keep her blouse together as she gathered up the scattered pages of her editorial.

"It sure was a mistake!" he said with quiet fury. "My friend was right: 'Never get mixed up with a red-headed woman!'"

"Not with *this* red-headed woman, anyhow," she retorted, raising her chin.

Their eyes were back to duelling again. Sparks flew as the steel blades of their glares clashed.

Then she turned and stumbled out, slamming the door behind her.

# Chapter Seven

"Travis, can we be friends?"

It was the next morning. After several attempts, Lindi had succeeded in finding the courage to walk into Travis's office. Now she stood before him making a supreme effort not to choke on the pride she was swallowing.

She had spent a sleepless night. After storming out of Travis's houseboat, she had driven back to Roy's house. She had been enormously relieved to find Frances and the twins in bed. It would have been excruciatingly embarrassing in her state of emotional turmoil to have to face anyone.

After a shower, she lay in bed staring at the ceiling as she tried to make some rational assessment of her behavior that night. She had to admit that she had been attracted to Travis Machado from the first time they met at the Miami airport. The man had more than his share of male sex appeal. She had felt the chemistry inside her bubbling every time she was around him. Even when he angered her, the attraction was still there.

But what did it mean?

Was she falling in love with Travis Machado? Her immediate reaction was to reject that idea. At this point in her life she wasn't sure what love was. She had thought she was in love with Jeff Lansing during her college days. For a while her life had centered around him. They would be married, share their lives, have children. It had seemed her destiny at the time. Jeff, she had thought, was so right for her. When he rejected her, the pain had been devastating. After that traumatic experience, she had shied away from men.

She mentally relived the night's events, trying to understand what had transpired to put her in Travis Machado's arms. Everything had worked against her: the setting, the drinks, the mood of the evening. She had been exposed to surprising new facets of Travis Machado, all of them making him more interesting. His colorful and romantic living quarters, the ingenuity he had shown in turning it into a comfortable abode, the depth of intellect revealed by his books and records, his sensitivity and skill as a photographer, his colorful past, his mysterious link with the Everglades—all had conspired to give him an aura of romantic charm that would intrigue any woman.

Added to that had been a relaxing of their feuding. The hostility between them had been put aside. They had been at ease with each other. She had found herself enjoying his company.

She should have left the minute she felt the physical attraction between them heating up. The instant he

touched her arm she should have sensed the consequences of that contact. Then she should have risen,
bid him a pleasant good evening, and fled. The ugly
scene and return of hostilities between them could
have been avoided.

She had been furious with him, and for good
reason. How intense his relationship with Shodra
Nichols was, she had no way of knowing. But he was
obviously involved with the woman. Their relationship was a topic of conversation in the small town.
They had been together that very evening. In fact,
Shodra was just leaving his place when Lindi drove
up. Lindi could feel nothing but scorn for a man who
would so readily cheat on his girlfriend. Thinking
about it now made her angry all over again. She felt
insulted and degraded. She had meant no more to him
than an easy conquest, a one-night fling, a boost to his
ego. Having satisfied his lust with such a casual
encounter, he would go back to his steady girlfriend,
probably bragging to his buddies at the tavern that the
red-headed lady publisher of *The Clarion* was an easy
mark. Pour a little champagne down her, turn on a bit
of male charm, and she was a pushover!

Lindi spent some time tormenting herself with that
line of thought and fuming with anger. But after
awhile her anger was spent, and she tried to get
another perspective on the situation. Grudgingly, she
had to admit that Travis was not entirely to blame.
Probably, by the infuriating double-standard male
code that his sex lived by, she was to blame for leading
him on and then not delivering. Perhaps she had given
him reason to believe she had come to his houseboat
with seduction in mind. His touching her arm had
been a tentative reaching out, a kind of questioning,
and her response had been affirmative. He had said

nothing about his feelings. He hadn't said he had discovered he was fond of her or cared for her even as a friend. He had simply touched her and she had melted in his arms, so overpowering had been the attraction she felt for him.

Looking at it from that viewpoint, she finally arrived at the conclusion that she had to share the blame for the night's emotional interlude. That didn't relieve Travis of culpability for two-timing his woman friend Shodra, but that was a matter for his conscience. Lindi admitted she had no right to judge other people's private lives.

The fact was that, like it or not, she had to work with Travis Machado on a daily basis. Their relationship had been strained enough. Now, unless they had an understanding about what had happened between them, the situation could be unbearable. She would be agonizingly self-conscious every time she faced him. The hostility that had existed between them before would be heightened. She couldn't go back to the office pretending nothing had happened. The only thing to do was to face him immediately and have it all out in the open.

It had not been an easy decision, and it was even harder to put into action. She had gone to work the following morning under a cloud of dread. For nearly an hour she had remained closed up in her office, fighting with herself, trying to work up her courage.

Finally, she had risen, raised her chin, squared her shoulders, and marched down to Travis's office before her courage deserted her.

Now she stood before his desk, somehow stammering out the speech she had rehearsed all morning. "We said some ugly things to each other last night.

I've thought it all over and I'm certainly willing to accept my share of the blame for the situation. I want to apologize for what I said. It was an enjoyable evening. You were a charming host. If—if things got out of hand, I was as much to blame as anybody," she said, her cheeks flushing. "If it's agreeable with you, I'd rather just forget about last night. We have to work together here every day, and it would be much more pleasant to be on friendly terms."

It was hard for her to analyze his response. Once again he had withdrawn into that strange, dark, introspective world of his. The icy walls around him had sealed shut. He was pleasant enough, accepting her apology, extending his own in return, agreeing to work with her on an amicable basis. But they were words. The whole time, those strange dark eyes were gazing at her in a contemplative way, revealing nothing of what he was thinking.

Well, she had done what she could to patch things up. She hoped they wouldn't feel too much strain in their daily contact. Then she went on to another subject. "I'm going to have to make a quick trip back to New York this week to wind up my affairs there. I have to see about helping my roommate find someone to take my share of our apartment. I need to box up my things and have them shipped down here and bring my little dog back with me. Can you take over and run things until I get back?"

"I'll see if we can survive," he said, giving her a steady look.

He was back to his sarcastic jabs. She made a great effort to hold onto her anger and swallowed a sharp response that sprang to her lips. Instead, she merely remarked, "I'll probably be gone a week."

He nodded. "All right."

"Before I leave, I'd like to see about renting that houseboat you mentioned last night. I need to have my apartment problem settled before I have my things shipped down here."

"Well, if you drive down to the docks past my place about a city block, you'll see it. You'd better check it out before you make a decision. I'm warning you, it's dilapidated. The owner is Mrs. Beatrice Simms. She owns a small shell souvenir shop on the waterfront. Anybody down there can tell you where Mrs. Simms's store is."

"That name is familiar," Lindi said slowly. "Is she the lady who writes a column for the paper now and then?"

"Yes. Mrs. Simms is a very smart lady. Some people regard her as something of a town character because she's a bit eccentric. But that lady has more scientific knowledge in her little finger than all the so-called brains of the development bunch combined. She has a degree in oceanography and has had several books published on the sea life in this region. She contributes some interesting articles on the area's bird and marine life to *The Clarion*."

"Hmm. Perhaps we could get her to write something about what this proposed development would do to the local ecology."

"I've been thinking along the same lines. You might suggest it to her if you see her this morning. I know for a fact she's hopping mad about the situation. She'd probably be delighted to give her views on the subject. She's pretty outspoken."

Lindi returned to her office, put her desk in order, and then drove to the waterfront. When she located the vacant houseboat Travis had described, her first reaction was dismay. It was in even worse shape than he'd implied. She went on board, stepping gingerly over loose boards and debris. The door to the living area hung open on one rusty hinge. Windows were knocked out. The interior was a cluttered mass of boxes, boards, and trash.

She began to picture the place cleaned up and painted and felt a bit more optimistic. It would take a major cleaning and repair job, but it could be a fun place to live.

Next she asked directions to Mrs. Simms' shop. The front of the small store was festooned with nets, barnacle-encrusted driftwood, conch shells, and a huge rusty anchor. A sign read SIMMS' SHELL SHOP.

Inside the store were shelves and display cases crammed with shells of every description. A frail, birdlike woman popped up from a desk at the rear of the place. "Good morning!" she said in a bright, cheery voice.

"Good morning. You're Mrs. Simms?"

"Sure am." Her glittering black eyes, inquisitive as a magpie's, flitted over Lindi in a swift appraisal. "Now don't tell me who you are. Let me speculate. That red hair, green eyes, sprinkling of freckles—if you're not Eli MacTavish's granddaughter, you can have your pick of any shell in my store."

Lindi smiled. "You knew my grandfather?"

"Well, I certainly did. Fine old gentleman. Stubborn and cantankerous at times, but a more honorable man never lived. I kept a scrapbook of every editorial he ever wrote. I know your brother Roy too, of course. He's a real sweet boy—running my silly little articles in *The Clarion*. Terrible thing about him getting run over," she added, her face growing solemn. "How is he getting along?"

"Some better, thank you, though he's understandably depressed at times."

Mrs. Simms nodded sympathetically. "I understand you're going to take over the paper until he gets back on his feet."

Lindi smiled. "Word gets around, doesn't it?"

"Well, my dear, this is still a small town and small towns love to gossip. Though it's not going to stay a small town if certain people have their way." Her beady eyes suddenly flashed angry sparks.

"That's one thing I wanted to talk to you about, Mrs. Simms. But there's something else too, and I suppose I'd better ask you about that first. Travis Machado told me about the houseboat you own. He said you might be willing to rent it."

"That old pile of junk?" Beatrice Simms laughed, an incredulous expression on her face. "What in the world would you want it for?"

"I thought of fixing it up and living in it. I need a place to stay. Apartments are scarce, I understand. I think it would be fun to live on a houseboat."

"Well, yes, but have you seen it?"

Lindi nodded. "I stopped by there on my way over here. It's in pretty bad shape I know, but I think I could get it cleaned up and painted . . ."

"Bad shape is an understatement," the frail shop-keeper exclaimed. "I don't know if my conscience would allow me to rent it to anyone, much less a nice young woman like yourself."

"I'd really like to see what I could do with it," Lindi said, persisting. "If the rent wouldn't be too high, I could afford to get some help cleaning it up . . ."

"The rent would be next to nothing." Mrs. Simms chuckled. "Right now it's nothing but a hangout for winos and derelicts. I've thought of scuttling it or junking it. The thing is an eyesore on the waterfront. Tell you what—if you're serious about fixing it up, I'll give you the thing rent-free for the first six months. How's that?"

"Why, that would be more than generous!" Lindi exclaimed.

"Generous, nothing. I'd be coming out ahead. Actually, the old tub is solid enough. Good, strong timbers. Fine bottom built of cypress. Needs to be put in dry dock and have the barnacles scraped off. A few years back, I took her in on a debt a man owed me. Always thought I'd get around to doing something with her but never did. If someone took on the job of restoring it, I'd be more than pleased."

"Then it's a deal?"

"Sure, if you think you really want to tackle a job like that."

Lindi was delighted; her mind was already busy with plans for remodeling the houseboat. She forced herself to put that aside for the moment. "There's something else I'd like to talk to you about, Mrs. Simms. As you know, my brother has been running some editorials about the development that is underway here in Palmettoville. *The Clarion* has taken a strong stand on this issue."

"I know all about it!" Beatrice Simms exclaimed, her black eyes snapping. "It's a dirty shame, the things those people are planning to do to this town."

"You've made a thorough study of the ecology of this region. Travis tells me you've written some books on the subject."

"That's right."

"We were wondering if you might do a series of articles for *The Clarion* about the impact of that kind of development on the waterfront."

"You bet I would! Do you realize the scope of their plans? Most of the people in this town are blind, deaf, and dumb about this thing. Either they don't know or they don't want to know. They're like a bunch of ostriches, burying their heads in the sand, believing everything the greedy politicians and businessmen are telling them—that it's progress, that it will bring jobs and money to the town."

"Maybe it's up to us to make them see the truth," Lindi suggested.

"We can try." The frail shopkeeper sighed. "Though it's sometimes hard to make people see the truth about things like this. The developers keep fooling people, keeping quiet about their long-range plans. Then one day the citizens are gonna wake up and find their town bulldozed out from under them. Do you know what they plan for this waterfront? They're going to wipe it out. Completely. Dredge in tons of fill and sand. Turn it into a millionaires' playground beach. If they have their way, they'll totally wreck the delicate ecology. They'll destroy the little islands that are nesting grounds for the coastal birds. The fill and dredging will wipe out the areas where fish spawn. They'll cut pleasure-boat canals that will fill up with pollution. On the other side of town are the fringes of the Everglades. Fortunately, some of that wilderness is now a national park. Still, turning this into an overcrowded resort area is bound to have some impact on that region too."

"I'm glad we have you on our side," Lindi said. "I'd very much like you to put all you've told me this morning in an article. I can promise we'll publish it."

"Glad to." The frail, elderly woman absently brushed strands of gray hair into place as she regarded Lindi with a worried expression. "I hope you realize what you're getting into, young lady. There are some huge, multimillion-dollar conglomerates behind this thing. They've got a bunch of local politicians, realtors, and businessmen on their side. They can throw a lot of money and a lot of weight around. They're already mad at *The Clarion*. There's not much telling what lengths they might go to in order to shut you up if you get to be too much of a thorn in their side."

Lindi remembered Frances's dark suspicion that Roy's hit-and-run injuries might not have been an accident. She felt a sudden strange chill in the air that made her shiver. With it came a flood of anger and resolve. "All I have to do is keep my grandfather in mind," she said. "I know how he would have felt about this situation and the stand he'd want Roy and me to take."

Early the next morning, Lindi drove to Fort Myers, parked *The Clarion*'s old Pinto and boarded a plane. When she landed in New York and rode a cab through the streets of Manhattan to her apartment, she was gripped by a sense of unreality. Ten days had passed since she had left here. It seemed a lifetime.

As she turned the key in her apartment door, she heard a joyous barking. She opened the door and a wriggling black-and-white streak came bounding into the room, tail wagging frantically. The little dog went into a dance of joy around her feet.

"Elmer!" Lindi cried, scooping the animal into her arms. "Gee, I missed you! Have you been a good boy while I've been away?"

Elmer whined a reply and tried to lick her face.

They were joined by Cimi Layne, who strode into the living room tying the sash of her robe around her waist. Even this time of the morning, with no makeup and her hair tousled, the raven-haired actress was beautiful. "Lindi!"

Lindi put her dog down and gave her roommate a hug. She had phoned Cimi the night before, giving her an approximate arrival time.

"I slept late this morning," Cimi exclaimed. "I was just heating up a pot of coffee, hoping you'd get here in time to have a cup with me."

"That sounds great."

"You must have had to get up before dawn this morning to make your plane connection," Cimi said, leading the way into the kitchen.

"Yes. It was murder. I did nap some on the plane."

The tiny kitchen was filled with the fragrance of Cimi's freshly ground coffee. The actress filled two cups with the steaming, dark beverage. "Now tell me first, how is your brother?" Cimi asked as they sat down at the table.

"Well, Roy is out of danger as far as his life is concerned, and we have that to be thankful for. But right now the doctors aren't sure if he'll ever walk again. He may spend the rest of his life in a wheelchair."

"Oh, Lindi! I'm so sorry to hear that," Cimi said, her luminous dark eyes filling with tears.

Lindi nodded sadly. "Roy is such an active guy. He was his high school's top athlete. You can imagine how depressed he's gotten over this."

"Of course. I want you to know I've been praying for him."

"Thank you, Cimi. I feel like a rat for not keeping you better informed. But so much was happening down there, I didn't know if I was coming or going half the time."

"You don't have to apologize. I know what a strain you were under."

"How have things been going here?"

"Oh, pretty much the usual routine. The show got its contract renewed, so it looks like I'll be working for the next year at least."

"That's great news! Congratulations."

"Thanks. You have a stack of mail. I put it on your desk. Also a list of phone calls a mile long. Elmer has been behaving himself. We've gotten to be real buddies, keeping each other company 'til you got back."

Lindi chewed on her lip. "Cimi, I have something to tell you. This isn't easy to say. We've gotten along so well together, sharing the apartment. But . . . well, Roy has asked me to move to Palmettoville and take over publishing *The Clarion.*"

Cimi's eyes widened. For a moment she didn't speak, appearing to fight back a sudden rush of tears. Then she said unsteadily, "Gee, that is a shocker. The way you're telling me sounds like you are going to do it."

"Yes. I just don't see how I can say no, Cimi. Things are really grim down there. I can't turn my back on my brother and his family."

Briefly, Lindi explained the situation in Palmettoville.

"Well it sounds as if you're taking on quite a challenge!" Cimi exclaimed.

"I am. And that includes a managing editor who has complicated my life considerably," Lindi said grimly, her cheeks flushing at the mere reference to Travis Machado.

"Oh? What is that supposed to mean?"

"Never mind. I'll tell you about him later. First, we need to talk about this problem of my moving out. Cimi, do you think you can find someone to share the expense of this apartment with you?"

"Finding someone to share the expense is no problem, as hard as it is to locate decent living space in Manhattan. Finding someone as compatible as we've been may not be that simple. But there's a girl on the show, Marge Davidson, who might work out okay. We've been good friends for a long time. She's in the process of getting a divorce and is looking for a place to live. I'll talk to her about it this afternoon."

"I hope you can find someone before I leave," Lindi said fervently. "I'd hate to go packing off to Florida and leave you in the lurch here."

"Don't worry about it. You have enough on your mind. The rent is paid until the end of the month. If Marge doesn't want the place, I'll find someone else, though I'm almost positive she'll jump at the chance. Have you rented a place down there or will you be staying at your brother's house?"

"I have a place." Lindi grinned. "Cimi, you won't believe this, but I'm going to be living on a house-boat."

Her roommate's eyes grew round. "A houseboat! Oh, Lindi, how glamorous!"

"'Glamorous' isn't exactly the right adjective, I'm afraid," Lindi admitted dryly. "At the moment, it's more like 'how decrepit'! But the owner is going to give it to me rent free for six months if I fix it up. I think it has all kinds of exciting possibilities."

"Oh, I'll bet it has. Listen, if you keep telling me about this place, I may quit my job and move down there with you! Imagine, no more fighting snow and slush. Palm trees waving in the breeze. Sitting on the deck of your houseboat in a bikini, sipping a mint julep while you get a gorgeous golden tan."

"Aren't mint juleps what you're supposed to sip on the veranda of a mansion on a Southern plantation?"

"Whatever. Make it a Singapore Sling. That has more of a South Seas nautical ring to it, doesn't it?"

They both laughed. Then Lindi exclaimed, "Why don't you move down there with me? I'd love to share my houseboat with you."

Cimi sighed. "What would I do for a living? Fish?"

"Maybe you could become a beachcomber," Lindi said, teasing her.

"It's tempting. But I guess I'm destined to keep on playing the femme fatale on the soaps for at least another year," she said resignedly.

"Well, maybe you can fly down for a visit after I get the houseboat repaired."

"Now that's an offer I can't refuse!"

When they finished their coffee, Lindi started the monumental task of moving. First she took care of her mail and telephone calls. Then she began packing her clothes and personal belongings in boxes. She had the dealer from whom she had bought her word processor come in and box up the computer and printer for shipment. At the end of three days, all her movable possessions were on a freight truck bound for Florida. What was left over she either gave to Cimi or donated to a charitable organization.

"Everyone should be required to move periodically," she philosophized when it was all over. "It's a catharsis—a way of purging yourself of unnecessary baggage. I had no idea I'd acquired so much junk!"

It was the last night she would be spending in her New York apartment with Cimi. In the morning, with a small bag in one hand and Elmer in his traveling case in the other, she would be going to the airport. She had wound up all her business affairs in the city. Cimi's actress friend, Marge Davidson, had agreed to take over Lindi's half of the lease, so that problem was out of the way. Now it was late at night and Lindi and Cimi were in the bedroom having their last heart-to-heart girl talk.

Lindi felt compelled to bring up the matter of Travis Machado. "I told you that one of my problems was with the managing editor of *The Clarion*. His name is Travis Machado. . . ." She launched into a subject that immediately had her emotions simmering. Thinking about those dark eyes that were like fathomless black pools sent a strange sensation coursing down Lindi's spine.

When she finished telling her roommate all about Travis, Cimi stared at her with a searching, speculative expression. "Y'know what? My radar is telling me, Lindi MacTavish, that for the first time since I've known you, you have run into a man who has got you turned on."

A warm flush spread over Lindi's cheeks.

Cimi continued: "Up to now, I've gotten the impression that you're strictly a career woman, all wrapped up in your job. You just haven't had time for men. If you go out with a guy it's only for a business lunch or maybe an occasional evening with a guy who means absolutely nothing to you. Where men are concerned, I thought of you as 'Cold Fish MacTavish.' I don't know if you realize it, but when you talk about this Machado guy, your eyes come alive and you get all flushed. Now come on. 'Fess up to your old buddy. Have you got a thing for Travis Machado?"

Lindi sighed. "Cimi, I don't know what I've got for Travis Machado. The man has me terribly confused. I have to admit I'm attracted to him. I suppose it's a physical thing. When he touches me, I feel an electric charge tingling all over me. I think about him a great deal. Sometimes it's hard to keep my hands from reaching out to touch him."

"I know the feeling." Cimi nodded. "I've had guys affect me the same way. It's kind of scary because I know if they got me in the right situation, I'd lose all control."

Lindi nodded soberly. "That pretty well describes the way I feel. It is just a physical attraction, isn't it? A matter of biology and chemistry?"

"That's what the 'Advice to the Lovelorn' columns say. I wouldn't knock it. It doesn't happen all that often. In fact, I suspect some women go through their whole lives without that kind of overwhelming passion."

"Yes, but there has to be more, doesn't there?"

"More for what? To live with the guy—to get married?"

"I'm certainly not planning to live with any guy. Maybe I'm old-fashioned, but I'd want more of a commitment than that."

"Yes; I always thought if you really fell for a guy, you'd be a one-man gal who would want it to be formal and permanent—a home, children, the whole bit."

"That's what I've always thought. But as you pointed out, when there's an overwhelming physical attraction, all your fine ideals may go out the window and you're swept overboard by the moment. I never thought anything like that could happen to me, but now I'm not so sure. I really don't trust myself around the guy. And that's what's got me so confused and miserable. I have the scary feeling I might be falling in love with Travis Machado, and that would be an absolute disaster."

"Why? Isn't there a possibility he could feel the same about you?"

"I doubt that very seriously. To begin with, he's involved with another woman, a young widow with smashing good looks who's a successful businesswoman in Palmettoville. From the local gossip I've heard, she's his mistress . . . has been for the past year."

"Are they living together?"

"No—they're not that open about it."

"Then maybe the gossips have blown the situation out of proportion. Maybe they're just friends."

"That I doubt. But it really doesn't matter." Lindi made a hopeless gesture. "Travis hasn't given the slightest indication that he cares anything for me as a person. All I am to him is an annoyance because he has to deal with me as his publisher. Being a robust male specimen, he probably wouldn't pass up the chance to get me into bed if I gave him the opportunity. All that would mean to him would be a conquest. I'd wind up brokenhearted and humiliated. And even if by some miracle he did start honestly caring about me, I have no idea what I'd be letting myself in for. I know nothing about his past. Roy told me that Travis has a disconcerting habit of pulling disappearing acts. He'll suddenly vanish for several days or a week at a time, and when he comes back he won't say where he's been. There's definitely some kind of problem in Travis's life that he's struggling with, something constantly eating at him. I just can't let myself fall in love with a man who has that kind of dark cloud shadowing his life."

Cimi gazed at her with thoughtful concern. "You

know," she murmured softly, "you might not have a great deal of choice in the matter, Lindi. If you're really falling in love with Travis Machado, there might not be a whole lot you can do about it."

Cimi's words were like an icy wind. Her friend had spelled out clearly exactly the kind of nameless fear that had been haunting Lindi ever since that night on Travis's houseboat. She had the helpless feeling that she was being drawn into an emotional whirlpool that was going to suck her down . . . and no matter how she struggled, she wasn't going to be able to escape. . . .

# Chapter Eight

𝒯his is going to be an exciting party!" Rachel Douglas exclaimed, her eyes sparkling.

Lindi smiled. "I hope so. Can you help me carry these things out to the deck?"

"Sure. What shall I take?"

"I think if you can handle the tray of sandwiches, I can manage the drinks."

The two women left the houseboat cabin with their trays. Lindi gazed around at the preparations with a feeling of anticipation. In the storeroom of *The Clarion* she had found several old strings of Christmas-tree lights left over from decorating the building during the Yuletide season. She had borrowed them and strung them around the cabin and deck of the houseboat, along with a few paper Japanese lanterns she had purchased at a variety store. The lights gave a festive mood to her housewarming.

It had taken a month of hard work to clean up the

ramshackle houseboat. Much still remained to be done, but already the transformation was dramatic. It was now livable. It had a bathroom that worked, a galley, a comfortable-sized room for a general living area, and a small bedroom. She had moved from her brother's home into her new living quarters that week. A celebration seemed in order, so she had invited the staff of *The Clarion* for a party that night.

The weather was perfect—a soft, warm, tropical night. Stars glittered in a cloudless sky. The water lapped at the sides of the boat. Lindi was wearing a beach outfit and sandals. Fastened to her waist was an ankle-length flowered sarong of clinging material. Beneath it, she was in a matching two-piece bathing suit. In her hair she wore a white orchid.

A soft breeze caressed her face and teased the sarong where it lapped over, giving glimpses of her smooth, bare thigh. The tropical climate, the excitement of the party, and the waterfront setting had conspired to put her in a daring, wicked mood. With very little effort, her imagination transported her to the South Seas and turned her into a Polynesian princess.

Rachel Douglas, the newspaper's secretary and girl Friday, had helped Lindi prepare for the party. During the past month, they had become good friends. Rachel was single, living alone. She had been through a teenage marriage that ended in divorce. All that had taken place several years earlier, and she appeared to have put it behind her. She was a bright, cheerful young woman, an indefatigable worker and totally devoted to *The Clarion*. Although slightly plump, she had pretty features and a beguiling, disarming smile. Lindi at first mistook Rachel's somewhat vague expression as an indication of childish innocence, but she eventually realized that Rachel was so nearsighted, she simply didn't focus very well on objects more than a foot away.

Now Rachel placed the tray of sandwiches on a deck table made out of a discarded hatch cover. "I just can't get over all you've done to this houseboat!" Rachel exclaimed, squinting slightly as she looked around. "When you told us at the office that you were going to live on this old houseboat of Beatrice Simms', I thought you had to be kidding. I used to drive past it and think it was going to sink any minute!"

Lindi smiled. "It's really a pretty solid old tub, I discovered. Fortunately, I ran into a waterfront character named Slinky Winston, who, I discovered, knows all about boats. He dry-docked it, cleaned the bottom, made the necessary structural repairs, and helped me find some laborers who were happy to get a few days' work cleaning and painting."

"I know you're going to have a lot of fun living here."

"I think so. I'm looking forward to it."

"Mr. Machado's houseboat is just a short distance down the dock. You'll be neighbors, won't you?"

Lindi's hand shook slightly as she arranged the drinks. Although she doubted Rachel could see well enough to notice her reaction, Lindi kept her face averted as she made a special effort to keep her voice casual. "Yes, he does live near me."

The preceding month had done nothing to decrease her awareness of Travis Machado or diminish the tension she felt when she was around him at the office. When she had invited the newspaper staff to her housewarming, she had been well aware that Travis would be coming. Was that the reason for the reckless, daring mood she was in? she wondered, feeling a rush of warm blood to her cheeks.

Soon the guests began arriving. Jake Tarson, bedecked in a short-sleeved Hawaiian sport shirt, came on board, wearing his usual happy, good-natured smile. With him was his wife Ethel, an attractive woman slightly taller than Jake. The society editor, Gladys Tindell, wore a print gown and a floppy-brimmed hat as colorful as Jake's sport shirt. *The Clarion*'s salesman, Pat Horine, also wearing a sport shirt, came in chewing on his ever-present cigar and exuding his air of phony warmth.

Lindi had invited her landlady, Beatrice Simms. Beatrice came appropriately attired in a flowing caftan. Like Rachel, she expressed pleased amazement at the renovation of the houseboat. "I just knew this old scow had possibilities if the right person got hold of her!" she exclaimed.

Lindi was kept busy playing the hostess, greeting her guests, arranging the deck chairs, seeing that everyone had refreshments. Suddenly, her concentration was splintered.

Travis Machado arrived.

The flimsy white knit shirt he wore hugged every rugged curve and bulge of his shoulders and biceps. His tan walking shorts left bare his muscular brown thighs, which rippled with strength as he stepped from the dock to the houseboat deck.

He was not alone.

Shodra Nichols was with him. Lindi gazed at the glamorous widow with mingled emotions. Shodra's blond hair was gathered at the nape of her neck. She wore cream-colored slacks that emphasized the length of her legs. The strap sandals on her bare feet called attention to the sexy effect of toenails painted scarlet red. Her blouse was wispy, clinging to the provocative curves of her proud bosom. How can a woman possibly be so fully dressed and still look totally naked? Lindi asked herself grimly.

Shodra wore makeup skillfully—just the right amount of eye shadow, cheek blush, lipstick. She used eyeliner to call attention to her deep, violet blue eyes and make them appear even larger. Her complexion was flawless except for faint lines around her eyes and lips that indexed her age at somewhere in the early thirties. That could be an age a man would find intriguing; it hinted at a sophistication and experience lacking in a younger woman.

Travis made the formal introduction. "Miss Lindi MacTavish, I'd like you to meet my friend, Mrs. Shodra Nichols."

Lindi caught the flash of diamond rings as Shodra extended a hand. "How do you do," Lindi said, hoping her emotional turmoil was sufficiently hidden.

"It's a pleasure to meet you, Miss MacTavish," Shodra said in a soft, pleasantly modulated voice.

Good Lord, she sounds as beautiful as she looks and smells, Lindi thought desperately as she caught a whiff of expensive, imported perfume.

She heard Shodra continue: "Travis has told me quite a bit about you. He says you have some revolutionary plans for *The Clarion.*"

Lindi felt inadequate and ill at ease with this older, more experienced woman. "I—I don't know how revolutionary they are," she said. "I just want to see if we can modernize the plant and improve the format of the newspaper. Most of the equipment is pretty badly out of date and in poor condition."

"Well, I want to wish you all the luck in the world. I know *The Clarion* has been having a struggle."

Lindi thought she sounded sincere. But why shouldn't she be? Her lover's job depended on the survival of the newspaper. Although with her money she could no doubt easily support Travis, he was not the kind of man who would go for that kind of arrangement.

Then Shodra slipped her hand through Travis's arm. "But we're here for a party, not to talk business and politics. Why don't we have a drink, darling?"

Steaming inwardly, Lindi watched them stroll together toward the refreshment table. Her emotions were mixed. The sight of Shodra and Travis together wrenched something inside her. At the same time, she had to admit grudgingly that Shodra wasn't just shallow looks and glamour. She was a sharp, intelligent businesswoman, in every way a match for a man like Travis.

Jake Tarson moved over to Lindi, temporarily distracting her attention from Travis and Shodra.

"You certainly are keeping things stirred up with your editorials and the series of articles by Mrs. Simms about the ecological impact of the proposed development." Jake grinned. "You have some businesspeople and realtors hopping mad."

Lindi shrugged. "We're not out just to make people mad. We want them to see the truth. I hope those articles of Mrs. Simms will make people in town realize what can happen to this area if the development goes through."

"I'm sure a lot of people do realize that. But if you want to see the way the tide is running, be at City Hall Monday night for the city council meeting. There's going to be an interesting fight over a zoning matter that can have far-reaching effects.''

Lindi shot him a questioning look.

Jake explained: "Some weeks ago, a realtor applied to the zoning commission to have the zoning ordinance changed to permit him to build a condominium in a residential area near the waterfront. The zoning commission turned him down. He has appealed to the city council. There's a neighborhood association in the area fighting this because it would mean the end of a fine old residential section. A lot of those people built homes there expecting to raise their children and spend the rest of their lives there. They can see their neighborhood going down the drain. The condominium is just the beginning. Next there will be shops and boutiques moving in. Want to bet on how the city council will decide?''

"I wouldn't give odds on that kind of bet," Lindi said grimly. "The developers have packed the city council with their people. They'll go along with any zoning changes the developers want.''

"Sure they will. This is going to be just the first of a whole series of zoning fights. See, what happens when the city council arbitrarily alters an existing zoning ordinance in this manner to accommodate some developers, it's what we call spot zoning. It's like the term 'block busting.' The neighborhood has A-1 zoning, which allowed single-family dwellings only. But now, suddenly, the city gives a developer a permit to build a condominium or a parking garage right in the middle of that A-1 zoning. Residents see their neighborhood becoming less desirable. Property values go down. Developers move in, grab up fine old residences for a song, then get more zoning concessions, and the neighborhood changes into a row of condominiums and a shopping center. In the end, our present zoning laws will mean nothing. It's all going to be changed to let developers bulldoze away the Palmettoville we know and replace it with a millionaires' resort."

"Maybe what this boils down to is a political battle for the control of the city council. There's a city election coming up soon. Maybe we need to back a slate of conservative people who will stand behind our zoning laws."

"Interesting possibility," Jake murmured. "I assume I'd be safe in guessing that *The Clarion* would back a conservative party."

"You'd better believe it!" Lindi said and added recklessly, "I might even run for a place on the council myself."

Jake's eyes widened behind his heavy horn-rimmed glasses. "Hey, now, that would stir up some excitement around town!"

"Well, don't go putting it in your column just yet," Lindi said, instantly backing down, shocked by her own rashness. "It was just a wild thought."

"But not a bad one. And maybe not as wild as you think," Jake observed thoughtfully.

But Lindi had other things on her mind that night. Once again she mingled with her guests, resuming her role as hostess. She was pleased that the party was going so well. Despite the differences in their personalities, the staff of *The Clarion* were a compatible bunch who enjoyed a party. She felt at ease with all of them except Travis.

Later in the evening, she found herself standing slightly apart from the others. She was leaning against a railing having a drink. By then the party was taking care of itself, and she was able to relax and enjoy the breeze and the setting. Then she became aware of Travis Machado walking toward her and immediately she stiffened, once again self-conscious.

"Nice party," Travis said.

"Thank you."

The ice tinkled softly in the glass he was holding as he swirled his drink. "So . . . looks like we're going to be neighbors."

"Yes," she said stiffly.

"You've done quite a job on this place," he observed, glancing around at the deck and roomy cabin, all freshly painted. "You should be comfortable here."

"I will be. Things inside are still a little bare. I need to get some more furniture."

"Do you have a bed?" he asked casually.

She felt a rush of blood to her cheeks. Why would he ask a question like that? "Yes, I have a place to sleep, if that's what you mean. It's not a water bed."

"I remember you have something against water beds," he said, giving her one of his inscrutable black-eyed looks.

Why had he chosen to bring up that humiliating episode on his houseboat? she wondered furiously. Was he deliberately trying to get her steamed up again?

"If you need furniture, don't forget the garage sales."

"I remembered what you said about that. I've been checking the classifieds before the paper hits the streets."

"If you need some cooking utensils, I have some I can lend you."

"Thank you," she said, nervously rubbing her hand

along the rail. Just standing close to this man made her feel uptight.

There was a moment of strained silence. Travis sipped his drink. His gaze took a lazy trip down the lines of her figure. She became burningly conscious of the brevity of her outfit. The top was no more than a bikini halter, leaving her shoulders and midriff bare above the sarong. She flushed, both angered and aroused by his bold stare. She couldn't seem to avoid a certain degree of female satisfaction in attracting his male interest. Running contrary to that feeling was a reaction of anger at his fickleness. Did Shodra Nichols realize what a philanderer her lover was?

She sought safer ground for their conversation by taking up a business matter. "Travis, I have a lead on a good buy on some modern printing equipment."

"Oh?"

"Yes. A large printshop in Fort Myers is going out of business. The owner has to sell out for health reasons. I understand he has just the kind of offset printing equipment I've had in mind for *The Clarion*."

"Are you going to buy it?"

"I'm very tempted. Yes, I think if I can swing a bank loan, I might do it! I want to give *The Clarion* a new format. Using the offset process, we can fill the paper much more easily with photographs of local events than we can with the old slow, costly process of photoengraving for the letterpress."

Travis nodded slowly. "But you might have to hire some additional people. The people we have in the pressroom aren't trained to handle offset work."

"I think it would be worth it. We'd have so much more flexibility both in publishing the paper and in our printing jobs."

"Well, that's true. There is no question that our outdated equipment is holding us back."

She nodded. "My mind is made up! Monday I'm going to call on the local bankers to see about floating a loan."

Travis took another sip of his drink. He was staring out across the water. He appeared to have lost interest in the topic. "Just look at that moon!"

Lindi followed his gaze. A full moon, huge and yellow, was appearing over the dark horizon, scattering a million golden coins over the gentle waves. Lindi thought desperately that even nature was conspiring to make her more romantically vulnerable tonight.

By ten o'clock, Lindi's guests had departed, leaving her alone and restless on the houseboat. She spent some time cleaning up the aftermath of the party and taking down the strings of lights.

Sleep was out of the question. She leaned on the railing, her arms crossed, gazing at the play of moonlight on the water. For no definable reason, she was overwhelmed with sadness.

The faint clicking of a typewriter reached her ears. She glanced in the direction of Travis's houseboat and saw that his lights were on. So he was burning the midnight oil, working on his novel. He wasn't spending the evening with his ladylove, Shodra Nichols. Lindi felt a measure of satisfaction at that thought. Then she asked herself what difference it made if Travis was with Shodra or not. Stop kidding yourself, was her own reply. It does make a difference! Without thinking, she'd struck the rail with her fist, angry with herself for her unreasonable feelings about Travis Machado.

A sudden impulse seized her. She unfastened her

sarong, allowing it to fall in a small heap, and stepped out of its circle. Now, in her brief two-piece bathing suit she was dressed for swimming, and that was precisely what she intended to do. Perhaps a midnight swim would cool off her overheated emotions.

She left the deck in a smooth dive, plunging into the water with a splash.

She was a good swimmer. The temperature of the water was perfect, just cool enough to be refreshing. In the moonlight her arms and shoulders gleamed phosphorescently as she split the water with smooth strokes.

She floated for a while, enjoying the relaxed sensation of drifting with the gentle swells. Then she swam slowly back to the houseboat hoping that now she would be able to go to sleep.

A rope ladder dangled into the water from the deck. She swam up to it, taking hold of the lowest rung. As she began her climb to the deck she glanced up and froze with a startled gasp.

Outlined against the starry sky loomed a dark figure, looking down at her.

For a moment Lindi was immobilized with fear. In her panic she was about to kick herself away from the boat and swim for dear life. Then the dark figure spoke. "I see you couldn't sleep either."

"Travis!" she cried. "You gave me a dreadful fright!"

"I'm sorry. I didn't mean to scare you. I was doing a little work tonight when I heard you splashing around out here in the bay. I decided a midnight swim might be a pretty good idea."

She could see him more clearly now. All he was wearing was a pair of swimming trunks. The sight of his bare torso and muscular legs gave her a peculiar shock. Obviously he had invited himself over to her boat to join her in a swim.

"I—I was just getting out," she stammered, filled with a new kind of panic.

He sat on the edge of the deck, swinging his legs. "Why not stay in a bit longer? There's a small sandbar out there just around the rim of the cove. I like to swim out there, catch my breath, then swim back. Think you're up to it?"

His dark eyes were flashing a challenge.

The daring, wicked mood she'd felt earlier in the evening suddenly swept over her again, brushing aside her caution. Impulsively she raised her chin. "All right!"

She kicked herself away from the boat and began swimming.

She heard a splash behind her. Afraid to look back, she continued to swim away from the houseboat. She soon found she couldn't outdistance Travis. With powerful strokes that roiled the water, he caught up with her.

"How did you learn to become such a good swimmer in the big city of New York?" he asked somewhat breathlessly as he overtook her.

She paused to tread water. "You seem to have forgotten that Roy and I spent all our vacations here when we were growing up. We practically lived on the beach and in the water when we weren't pestering Grandfather down at the newspaper."

She was aware of how close his body was to hers, and she nervously moved away from him.

"Have you caught your breath enough for that swim out to the sandbar?" he asked.

"Yes."

"Are you sure you can make it?" he asked, a slight taunting edge in his voice.

"Of course I can! In fact, I'll race you!"

Instantly she was off, burying her face in the water as her arms and legs became synchronized into the smooth movements of a skilled swimmer. Once she glanced back and saw the lights of her houseboat growing smaller in the distance.

They rounded the cove and reached the sandbar together, sprawling on the gleaming white sand of the tiny beach.

"I'd call it a tie," Travis said, when he'd recovered enough to sit up.

"You probably held back," Lindi said. "I'm sure you're a faster swimmer than I. You look like a man who's spent most of his life outdoors."

She sat up beside him, smoothing back her wet hair. Water was trickling down her body in tiny rivulets. She suddenly became aware of the moonlight swathing her bare skin in a luminous, golden glow. And she became burningly conscious of Travis's dark eyes taking in the view.

Self-consciously, she hugged her legs, resting her chin on her knees.

"Do you often have spells of insomnia?" Travis asked.

"No. I'm usually in dreamland minutes after my head touches the pillow."

"You're lucky," he said, his dark eyes brooding again. "Sleep and I are not good friends. I'm afflicted with the curse of insomnia. That's why I often swim out here late at night. A swim like this sometimes tires me enough so I can sleep."

"Perhaps you have a guilty conscience," she said and then bit her lip, wishing she could take the words back. She had put words to her own dark suspicions about him. What black secret lurked in his past that gave him those brooding eyes and kept him from sleeping at night?

Whatever it was, it would remain a secret. He simply looked at her without expression, as if he hadn't heard her remark.

"I heard your typewriter tonight. Sounds carry over the water. Do you like to write late at night?"

"Yes. Don't you think that late at night when we're alone, we are less able to escape the truth about ourselves? Our defenses are down. Late at night is when people are most afraid of death. Maybe that's when we're closer to the frightening question of human existence. It's when the remnants of the primitive regions of the mind come out of the shadows to haunt us. It's also when we're closer to the source of creativity."

She again felt the magnetic force between them. Her gaze was drawn to him in a moment of frightening intimacy. They were totally isolated out here: a man and woman alone, with all that implied. The rhythm of the sea around them was like the pulsing heartbeat of the universe. The full moon exerted its pull on the tides and on the subliminal rhythms of their bodies. The night was the breath of the life force throbbing within her. Time became one with the universe, mingling the dawn of creation in the sea with the dreadful force of destiny that had driven Travis's life like a silver wedge into hers.

She touched her tongue to her lips, which had suddenly gone dry. "Who are you, Travis Machado?" she whispered.

He raised an eyebrow. "Who am I?" He shrugged. "Who is anybody?"

He picked up a handful of sand, moodily watching as it trickled through his fingers. "Maybe I'm no more than this handful of sand, blowing in the wind for a brief while, then gone forever."

His dark-eyed gaze swung on her, his eyes glowing suddenly like coals that had been breathed upon. "Now, you know who you are. Lindi MacTavish, granddaughter of Eli MacTavish. You have your parents, your grandparents, perhaps generations beyond that. You have your roots. You have a place in the scheme of things."

"You sound bitter. I don't understand."

"I wouldn't expect you to."

Their words became silenced by the force of their eyes, locked now in a gaze that could not be broken, relentlessly searching the depths within each other. They were beyond conversation, logic, reason. There was this moment, this tiny isolated place, this warmth of their bodies. Some indefinable knowledge stirred deep within them both—an awareness, beyond comprehension, of the pure essence of each of them.

He reached for her hand. The touch of his fingers was electrifying. She sighed softly. Her fingers laced with his. It was a kind of joining, an unspoken union.

His gaze intensified. He moved closer. Gently his arm went about her, drawing her closer. She felt the contact of her damp bosom with the mat of curling black hair on his broad chest. His thigh, gritty with sand, brushed against hers; the touch made her quiver.

She looked up at him, her lips parting. With a soft murmur, his mouth touched hers. It was a gentle kiss that quivered with suppressed desire.

A weakness filled her body. She melted against him, her mouth responding hungrily to the taste of his.

It was a long, searching kiss. Time was blotted from her mind.

Then she ended the kiss, resting her forehead against the hollow of his shoulder, feeling strangely content for the moment. She knew nothing about this man, yet she knew everything. In the real world of daylight and offices and deadlines and printing machines, he was a disturbing mystery. She didn't know where he'd come from, what he was doing here, what he was running away from, or the reason for his baffling disappearances from time to time. Yet in this enchanted moment, those matters were unimportant. Their touching, their embracing, were ordained by the pattern of the stars, the timeless grains of sand, the eons of evolution reaching to this moment and bringing them together in this isolated spot.

She allowed him to lower her gently onto the sand and let herself enjoy briefly the feel of the hard, muscular contours of his body. She became aware of the night air on her breasts and his rain of kisses that sent pinpricks of sparkling fire cascading through her body.

Travis ran his tongue down the valley between her breasts to her navel. A delightful shudder coursed through her. A medley of sensations formed a heavenly rhapsody. All she could think about was the excitement of Travis's body touching hers, the fact that he wanted her . . . found her desirable.

He nibbled and tasted the delicate ridges and valleys of her body as she arched toward him, all her emotions clamoring for him to complete the sensations in an explosion of total fulfillment.

Travis explored her body with his hands, sending fresh shivers of sensual anticipation flashing through her. She felt at once totally relaxed but tightly coiled like a quivering spring. Her senses were both muted and finely tuned. She knew exactly what was happening and yet was only vaguely aware of what she was doing. It was a strange kind of intoxication, an unfamiliar level of consciousness in which both primitive passions and spiritual heights mingled. A blend of the distant past, the urgent present, and the shadowy future was hers to enjoy.

Travis's hands slid around her sides and pressed against her back, holding her while his mouth tasted the full delights of her body. His warm tongue on her flesh gave her goose bumps.

She slipped her arms around his neck, pressing ever tighter against him. Their lips met in a rapturous kiss that set off emotional skyrockets.

Her palms slid down his broad back, feeling the hard muscles. Great, pounding waves of desire for him washed over her. She nestled her face in the wiry hair of his chest, nibbling the ridges of his hard muscles, running the tip of her tongue over his collarbone, up his neck and then, again, hungrily finding his mouth. It was warm and moist, offering a prelude to the knowledge of him that her body so urgently longed for.

She thrilled to the pain of his intense kiss. She felt his tongue on her lips, exploring its contours. Then it thrust hungrily into her mouth and she accepted it, closing her lips and teeth over it, gently biting until she returned the favor, slipping her tongue into his mouth, exploring the deepest regions.

She listened to the pounding of her heart, heard the gasp of her own breath. It was a moment of delightful insanity. But though she drifted far out onto the sea of pure emotion and sensation, she did not entirely lose sight of her safe harbor.

Slowly, reluctantly, like a sleepwalker returning to the world of reality, she drew back from the final chasm of utter abandonment. A quiet voice of caution warned her that no matter what wild passions Travis could arouse in her, this was neither the time nor the place for total surrender.

She looked up at him, plunging her fingers into his luxurious black hair. "I'm sorry, my dear Travis," she whispered thickly, "but we have to draw the line here. I have too much at stake to gamble it all on a single night of passion, tempting though it is. Please try to understand."

He gave her a long, consuming gaze. The conflict of emotions in his eyes was frightening to see. In spite of the conflict, this time he did not appear angry or frustrated. She watched as the blazing heat of passion slowly cooled in his eyes and he withdrew again into his own private shadows.

She could almost sense a mutual agreement in his expression. Perhaps, she thought, he did not really want to become any more deeply involved than she. Like herself, he recognized they were playing with dynamite. Plunging into this kind of total relationship with her could carry consequences far beyond the pleasure of a few minutes' passion.

He sighed, his breathing returning to normal. "All right." He nodded slowly. "I didn't intend to lure you out here in an attempt to seduce you. I didn't even expect to kiss you. It was only supposed to be a friendly swim. I guess the moonlight got the best of us."

"Yes," she murmured, fighting back a sudden foolish rush of tears. "The full moon does bring out insanity doesn't it?"

For some reason she couldn't explain, the thought of Shodra Nichols had not entered her mind during the half hour she and Travis had been here together on this moon-drenched sandbar. Why, she didn't know. Probably she had subconsciously blocked the other woman from her thoughts. Now, as icy reality returned, sweeping away the dreamy glow, Lindi became very much aware of the beautiful widow in Travis's life.

Had his conscience suddenly awakened, and had he decided to be faithful to his mistress after all? Was that the reason he was so agreeable to their ending the kiss safely?

Lindi felt a stabbing pain of unreasoning jealousy.

"We'd better get back," she said briskly, jumping to her feet.

"Yes," Travis agreed.

They swam back to her houseboat in easy, measured strokes. When they clambered aboard, Travis picked up the towel he'd left on the deck, drew it around his shoulders, said "Good night" abruptly, and strode away into the darkness.

Lindi went into the boat's living quarters and peeled off her wet suit. She slipped into a terry cloth robe and paced around the room. She struggled with her thoughts, trying to gain some insight into the puzzle of Travis Machado. Twice now, a chance encounter had turned into a heated physical attraction between the two of them. What did it mean? Where was it leading her? Was Travis no more than a male predator, sensing her weakness and preying on it to satisfy his ego in a casual conquest? Or was he fighting the same kind of overwhelming attraction that had made her its victim?

If he would only talk to her! He kept his thoughts hidden. What did he feel for her—friendship, some measure of fondness? At first his reaction had been clear enough. It had been scorn and resentment. But had that changed as they became better acquainted? She dared to think so. It seemed to her that he had mellowed toward her. His words were less harsh, less tinged with the cutting edge she had first heard.

But what did that mean? And how did Shodra Nichols fit into the picture? Was she actually his mistress as the gossips implied? Or were they merely close friends? It was difficult to believe that no more than a platonic relationship could exist between a man as virile as Travis and an experienced woman as attractive as Shodra!

That thought galled her!

Then her thinking took another direction. She puzzled over Travis's reaction to her that night. He had obviously felt the same kind of powerful physical desire. Yet this time his kiss had been more tender than lustful. He had partially stripped her and his eyes had blazed with desire, drinking in the vision of her unclothed loveliness. And yet when she drew the line at their going any further, he had given her no argument—had, in fact, almost seemed relieved.

Those puzzling questions churned in her mind, making her temples pound.

"Now I really can't sleep!" she exclaimed bitterly.

# Chapter Nine

"What do you mean, Travis is gone?" Lindi demanded.

Rachel Douglas made a helpless gesture with the note in her hand and then laid it on Lindi's desk.

"I found it stuck in my typewriter when I came to work this morning," Rachel said.

Lindi had just arrived at her office, having overslept a bit. No sooner had she gotten seated than Rachel knocked at her door. Now, with a sinking sensation in the pit of her stomach, Lindi stared at Travis's hastily scrawled note.

Will be out of town a couple of days——

Travis

"I've heard about these mysterious trips our editor goes on," Lindi exclaimed. "Well, he sure picked a dandy time for this one! I'm going to try and get a big bank loan today so I can update our printing shop. They're moving my brother home from the hospital. Tonight the city council is going to decide on a zoning issue that may change the entire future of this town. And my managing editor chooses to take a two-day vacation! Rachel, do you have any idea where Travis has gone?"

*The Clarion*'s plump young secretary shook her head. "Travis keeps his private life strictly to himself. All of us have wondered about him. We do a lot of guessing, but nobody knows anything for certain about him."

Lindi sighed with frustration. "How long is he away when he takes off like this?"

"Usually no more than two or three days."

"Doesn't he ever give any notice ahead of time?"

"Not really, though I can see some signs."

"What do you mean?"

"I'm not sure if I can explain it exactly. Maybe it's partly intuition. It seems to me he becomes more uptight a few days before he leaves. He acts kind of strange, then he leaves as he did today. When he comes back, he's often in a black mood, more withdrawn than usual."

"How often does this happen, for heaven's sake?"

"Oh . . . not that often. Maybe four or five times since he's been editor of *The Clarion*."

Lindi shook her head in disbelief. "Well, I can't say I wasn't warned about him. My brother Roy told me this was something I could expect. Why Roy put up with it is more than I can understand."

Rachel shrugged. "Roy likes Travis and has a lot of respect for his ability as a newspaperman. They were really good friends. I guess your brother just accepted his strange behavior to keep him on the paper."

Lindi nodded. "That sounds like Roy."

"Your brother is easygoing, Lindi. He seldom got mad at anybody around here. The only times I've seen him really angry were over the development plans for the town."

"Well, I can understand why he didn't want to put the business completely in Travis Machado's hands, not knowing when Travis would pull one of these disappearing acts."

"You say Roy is coming home from the hospital? That's good news!"

Lindi nodded slowly. "Frances called me about it this morning. In fact, it was her call that woke me up. I'd overslept. I think the truth is, Rachel, they've done about all they can for Roy at the hospital. And it's so expensive, keeping him there. He's got a long convalescence and rehabilitation ahead of him. The physical therapist will be at his house three times a week to work with him."

"Is he in any better spirits?" Rachel asked, her large blue eyes showing genuine concern.

"Not a whole lot. He has his ups and downs, but Frances says he still sinks into depression. I'm going to stop by the house to see him after lunch."

Rachel smiled. "Give him my best wishes and tell him all of us here at the plant are praying for him. I'll get over to see him after he's settled." She started out of the office, then paused in the doorway. "I almost forgot to tell you again what a good time we all had at your party Saturday night. It was so much fun. I really envy you, getting to live on that houseboat."

Lindi smiled back a trifle weakly. "Glad you liked

the party," she said, but her thoughts were elsewhere, back on a lonely sandbar in the moonlight in the arms of a man whose kisses could ignite her entire body—a man who had totally upset the equilibrium of her life.

She thought about Rachel's observation. "It seems to me he becomes more uptight a few days before he leaves. He acts kind of strange . . ." Was that the reason for Travis's strange behavior on the sandbar Saturday night? Did he already have this mysterious trip on his mind even as he was kissing her?

With an effort, Lindi put Travis out of her mind. He was gone and there was nothing she could do about it for the time being.

She took care of some routine matters at her desk, then left for her appointment at the bank. She was dressed for her role as a young businesswoman in a suit of navy blue polyester woven to look like smooth gabardine. The contoured jacket had two flap pockets and a welt pocket. A snakeskin belt complemented the slender skirt, which had two pockets and back pleat. The skirt snapped smartly at her slender legs as she strode into the bank, her high heels clicking on the marble floor.

Nervously, she turned the pages of a banking magazine as she sat on a vinyl couch in the waiting area. Finally she was ushered into the office of the bank president.

Wallace Simmons was a rawboned man with sparse hair the color of Florida's sandy soil. His suit was dark gray, as conservative as his blue necktie. He leaned back in his chair, built a small temple with his fingers, and gazed at Lindi, his eyes like chips of ice behind steel-rimmed glasses. "I regret that we are not able to make the loan you have requested, Miss MacTavish."

For a moment Lindi was too stunned to reply. Then

she exclaimed, "But I don't understand. Surely the printing equipment would be more than enough collateral."

"Possibly. Let me be frank. We don't, at this point, consider *The Clarion* to be a very good business risk. The bank's board of directors feel that you may very well be out of business in six months to a year from now. And then we'd have the hassle of disposing of the printing machinery to recoup our loan. That's more of a burden than the board of directors thinks we should take on ourselves."

Lindi's green eyes flashed angry sparks. "I fail to see why your board of directors has such a pessimistic view of *The Clarion*'s future! It has been the town's only newspaper since the 1930s and we fully intend to stay in business for a long time in the future. How dare you suggest we'll be bankrupt inside of a year!"

"Please don't take this personally. It's simply a matter of business." He smiled with his lips, a physical reflex that did not reach his eyes. "Banks have to take a long, hard look at loans to small businesses these days."

Lindi's eyes narrowed. "By any chance could your decision have anything to do with the stand *The Clarion* has taken on the development plans for the city?"

"In a way, you could say that. I'm sure you are aware, Miss MacTavish, that your brother's editorials cost your paper the support of a large segment of the business community. You've lost advertisers as well as printing accounts. Apparently since you have taken over the role of publisher, there has been no change in the policy of *The Clarion*. A small-town newspaper cannot afford to be controversial, Miss MacTavish. When you make enemies of influential people, you

lose revenue. A bank has to take that into consideration.''

Lindi was fighting to keep her boiling anger from
erupting. ''Just where does the bank stand on this
matter of development, Mr. Simmons?''

''Well, naturally, we want to see the community
progress—''

''Mr. Simmons, you said we have made enemies of
influential people in Palmettoville. Do you consider
your bank one of our enemies?''

''Miss MacTavish—''

''Never mind. I think I know the answer. Good day,
Mr. Simmons.''

Walking out of his office, Lindi couldn't resist a
parting shot. She paused in the doorway, turned back
for a moment. ''You can tell the members of the
business community who are in your camp that you're
not going to get rid of *The Clarion* this easily. We're
going to be around for a long time, causing you a great
deal of irritation until we can get the town to see the
folly of this development plan!''

She left the bank and got into the newspaper's
battered car, feeling a lot less confident than she had
sounded. For a moment she sat slumped behind the
wheel, fighting back tears of frustration and disappointment. Then she drew a breath, squared her
shoulders, and started the engine.

Lindi drove to her brother's home where Frances
met her at the door. ''Roy's home!'' her sister-in-law
exclaimed, looking happier than Lindi had seen her in
weeks.

''I'm so glad. How is he?''

''Lindi, he seems in a much better frame of mind. I
think coming home has been good for his morale.''

''I'm sure it has!''

They went into Roy's bedroom, where Lindi was pleased to see her brother comfortably situated in his own bed and looking considerably more alert and cheerful than he had been at the hospital.

Lindi spent the next hour having a pleasant chat with Roy. "I've gotten a terrific bang out of that series on the ecology of the waterfront you had Beatrice Simms write," he said at one point. "I bet you've gotten some reaction on that!"

"Yes, we have," Lindi murmured, grimly thinking about the cold reception she'd had from the bank president that morning. Then she said, "Roy, I didn't want to bother you with business matters while you were in the hospital. But I think you're well enough for me to discuss some ideas I have for modernizing the plant. I want to install some up-to-date offset printing equipment."

Roy nodded slowly. "I know we need to do something about the worn-out old machinery we've been using. That's why I was so relieved when you said you'd take over the job of running the plant for awhile. You're a live wire, Lindi. If anybody can bring *The Clarion* up to date, you can."

Lindi almost wished her brother didn't have quite so much faith in her. Saving *The Clarion* might take more than her ability. It might take a miracle. "I heard about a large print shop in Fort Myers that's going out of business. We could get a really good buy on all their printing equipment."

"Sounds good."

"Yes—the hitch is how to finance it. It appears our local bank is not one of our supporters."

"No. Their greedy fingers are already counting the money they're going to handle for the developers. Have you thought about one of the banks in Fort

Myers? Maybe the guy who's going out of business could help you make the loan. He might even carry some of the note himself."

"That's a good idea. The bank there would be familiar with his plant. They'd know his equipment is worth a lot more than he's asking for it, so they ought to be willing to make a loan on it."

After lunch, Lindi drove to Fort Myers, her morale somewhat improved. She spent the afternoon talking with the printshop owner and his banker. The upshot was that she acquired all the printing equipment for *The Clarion* with the Fort Myers bank carrying eighty percent of the loan and the printer holding a second lien for the remaining twenty percent. She was delighted to swing the deal without having to come up with any capital, although she was less than happy with the terms of the note. The bank's interest was high, and they insisted on a substantial payment within six months. Could she have *The Clarion* showing a profit in such a short time?

Lindi had a quick snack for supper and then hurried to the City Hall, where the mayor and the city council were about to hear arguments on the zoning squabble.

The place was jammed. She threaded her way through the crowd and located Jake Tarson in an area reserved for the media. Present also were a cameraman from the local TV station and a newsman from the radio station.

"Hi." Jake grinned as she joined him. "You're just in time for the fireworks."

"Quite a crowd. Who are all these people?"

"Most of them are homeowners from The Clearwater Addition that's being threatened. Over there are the gentlemen who are trying to get the zoning

changed. The tall guy with the hooked nose is Lester
Martin, local real estate broker hotshot. Next to him,
that nice-looking gentleman in the gray suit that fits so
well is the developer C.C. Rothman. The nervous guy
sitting between them, leafing through a bundle of
papers, is their attorney.''

The mayor called the meeting to order. After some
minor opening matters were dispensed with, the city
manager brought up the zoning question.

The nervous-looking attorney spoke for the realtor
and developer. He presented the plans and architec-
tural sketch of the proposed condominium and described The Clearwater Addition as a residential
neighborhood that was old and deteriorating. He
urged the council to approve the zoning change on the
grounds that it would enhance and modernize the
neighborhood rather than detract from it. "Ladies
and gentlemen of the city council, don't stand in the
way of progress," was the theme of his argument.

Then the council heard the opposition to the zoning
change. The spokesman for the residents of The
Clearwater Addition was their neighborhood association president, Grady Alexander, a quiet-spoken man
in his mid-thirties, dressed in a dark blue knit shirt
and tan slacks. He was a tall, slender man with wavy
brown hair. Horn-rimmed glasses gave an added
element of strength to his features. Lindi was impressed by Alexander's demeanor. Although his voice
was calm, he made an eloquent plea for his neighborhood and painted an entirely different picture of the
situation. While this was one of the older residential
neighborhoods in the city, it was an area whose
homeowners maintained their property with loving
care. He stressed how changing the zoning ordinance

to allow the construction of a condominium would threaten the residential quality and property values of all the streets in the area.

Alexander was followed by a long line of homeowners who pleaded, some of them in tears, not to have their neighborhood destroyed. They showed pictures to illustrate how well the older homes were being kept up.

When all the property owners had been heard from, the mayor asked if anyone else wished to speak in opposition to the request for a zoning change. Lindi jumped to her feet and approached the council. "Your Honor, men and women of the council, my name is Lindi MacTavish. I am presently publisher of Palmettoville's newspaper, *The Clarion.* I'm sure many of you knew my grandfather, Eli MacTavish, founder of *The Clarion.* I know if he were here, he wouldn't sit quietly by when an issue like this was threatening the town he loved. The whole purpose of zoning laws is to give homeowners protection against this very kind of intrusion. These zoning ordinances were set up to maintain the integrity of certain neighborhoods. Real estate developers know if they can get one foot into a residential street with this kind of spot zoning, they can turn a quiet neighborhood of private residences into a commercial lane. It's been called block busting. What happens to this Clearwater Addition will happen to the rest of Palmettoville if you don't take a firm stand against this kind of encroachment."

Lindi's brief, angry speech was applauded by the homeowners. The mayor scowled and rapped his gavel for order.

Lindi went back to her seat in the press section. Jake Tarson was grinning from ear to ear. "Great speech," he said.

"Probably won't change things one way or the other," Lindi muttered, "but I feel better getting it off my chest."

She noticed that The Clearwater Neighborhood Association president, Grady Alexander, was looking in her direction. He smiled and nodded his appreciation.

The council conferred briefly and then voted. The zoning change passed easily as a majority voted to allow the condominium to be built.

There was a loud, distressed murmur from the bitter homeowners. Again the mayor rapped for order. Lindi's anger was rekindled, though she was not surprised by the council's decision. The real estate broker, Lester Martin, looked smug. The homeowners were angry and dejected, some of them in tears.

Lindi told Jake Tarson, "I'll see you at the office in the morning," and she threaded her way through the milling crowd. Outside, she took a deep breath of the tropical night air, catching the fragrance of magnolia mingling with the tangy smell of the waterfront. She suddenly felt weary; it had been a long day filled with stress, ending with a crushing disappointment.

She drove home, made herself a cup of hot tea, and turned down her bed. Before she could undress, there was a knock at her front door. Lindi was puzzled. Who could be calling on her this time of night? She switched on the deck light, looked through a window, and saw Jake Tarson and Grady Alexander.

She opened the door.

Jake spoke first. "Lindi, I was hoping we could catch you before you were in bed. Grady here was anxious to meet you and talk to you about something. You remember I told you at the city council meeting that Grady is the president of The Clearwater Neighborhood Association."

"How do you do, Miss MacTavish," Alexander said, his blue eyes warm and friendly behind the horn-rimmed glasses. "I tried to get over to talk to you at City Hall, but there was so much confusion when the meeting broke up, you got away before I could grab you. Hope you don't mind us coming by like this."

He was holding his hand out. Lindi extended hers and felt her fingers squeezed in a warm handshake. "Not at all. Please come in."

When they were inside the houseboat's main cabin, Lindi said, "I was just making some hot tea. Would you care for some? Or I have some cold beers in the refrigerator."

"The tea is fine," said the neighborhood association president.

Jake said, "If it's all the same to you I guess I'll have the beer."

The two men took seats on her couch while Lindi got the drinks. She brought them on a tray, which she placed on her coffee table before she sat in a comfortable old recliner that she'd bought for ten dollars at a garage sale.

"I really appreciate what you had to say to the council tonight, Miss MacTavish," Grady said.

"It was a futile gesture." Lindi sighed.

"I think all of us from The Clearwater Addition felt appealing to the city council was a futile gesture. Obviously their minds were made up on this zoning issue before the meeting was called to order. They were just going through the motions to satisfy legal requirements."

Lindi sighed. "This is just the beginning, you know.

The real estate people and the developers are getting into high gear. There's going to be a flood of these zoning changes in the coming months. The old residents are going to see their property values going down the drain as the commercial developers move in. The homeowners will panic and sell out at a loss. The developers will buy up those neighborhoods for a song. The town as we know it is in for a big change, and I'm afraid it's a change for the worse."

"We all agree on that," Grady Alexander said, his blue eyes grave. "We have to do something about it before it's too late. Appealing to the city council isn't going to help us. The majority on that council are totally controlled by the developers. There's only one way we can fight them—politically."

Lindi frowned. "What do you mean?"

"I mean a new mayor and a new city council. City elections are coming up in a few months. We want to put a slate together to fight this ruthless development. I'm throwing my hat in the ring for the mayor's job. And we want you to be one of the key people on our ticket in place one, running for a seat on the present city council."

"Me!" Lindi gasped. "Wait a minute. I'm not a politician!"

"Well, neither am I." Grady smiled wryly. "The last thing I ever had on my mind was running for some kind of public office. But I'm convinced we have to do something drastic if we're going to stop this flood of zoning changes."

"But why me? Whatever gave you the notion I'd get involved in a city election?"

Grady looked surprised. "Why, Jake told me. He said you were already thinking of running for city council."

Lindi remembered the impulsive remark she had made to Jake at her housewarming party. Obviously Jake had taken her at her word. "Now look, Mr. Alexander. That was just a spur-of-the-moment expression growing out of my anger and frustration. I'm sorry Jake took me seriously. I'm a newcomer to this town. Not many people here know me. I wouldn't have a chance of getting elected—"

"Don't be too sure of that! You're a lot better known than you think. In fact, you're a good spokesperson for all the small people in town who feel as we do. Folks read your editorials and all the things you've been printing about the threat to the ecology and the quality of life if this development goes through. They have a lot of respect for you. Why, if it wasn't for *The Clarion,* we'd have no public voice at all. No, I think you'd stand a darn good chance of being elected to a place on the council. Of course, we're going to be fighting a lot of power and big money."

"I know," Lindi agreed, looking at Jake and Grady with a worried expression. "From what I learned today, the business community is behind the developers and down on *The Clarion.*"

"Not all of the business community," Grady said, shaking his head. "I'd say the businessmen in town are divided down the middle about this thing. Some of them, of course, are only thinking of lining their pockets. But an equal number are as concerned as you and I about the long-range damage this is going to do."

There was a brief silence as Lindi pondered this new development. She had mixed feelings—flattered on the one hand that the people thought so highly of her and overwhelmed on the other by what was being asked of her.

"Why don't you give it some serious thought?" Grady suggested. "I realize we've sort of sprung this on you."

She nodded. "Yes. I'll have to give it a lot of thought. I've got my hands full with my brother's newspaper business, and this would put me under even more pressure. But I do thank you. I'm flattered that you'd ask me. It's tempting because it certainly would be a way of taking this fight directly to the voters of the city."

"Exactly." Grady's smile was friendly and encouraging. "I hope you'll keep that in mind when you're making your decision."

"Well, whatever I decide, you can count on *The Clarion* to be behind you one hundred percent," Lindi exclaimed. "I think it's a disgrace that we have a city council that will so blatantly alter zoning laws to satisfy greedy developers."

The grin that spread across Grady Alexander's face made him look boyish. His blue eyes framed by the dark rims of his glasses sparkled. "That's the spirit."

"Yeah, I'm already inspired to write my next editorial!"

They said good-night. Lindi found herself in bed at last, bone weary from the long day but unable to sleep. She listened to the soft lapping of the water outside her cabin window and wrestled with this new, overwhelming decision.

During the next two days, Lindi forgot about city politics as several truckloads of the printing machinery arrived. She faced a major reorganization of the plant to accommodate the new equipment. Temporary workers were hired to help with the task of moving and rearranging.

On the third morning, when she arrived for work, she saw Travis's battered pickup truck in *The Clarion*'s parking lot. "The prodigal son has returned," she muttered grimly.

She walked upstairs. Through the glass door of his office, Lindi saw Travis staring out of his window. She felt the usual lurch of her emotions at the sight of his broad-shouldered figure. Resolutely, she put a damper on her personal feelings, reminding herself of how angry she was at him for pulling his disappearing act.

She tapped at his door, then entered his office. Travis turned from the window. She was startled at how deeply lined and weary his face looked. His eyes held a hollow look of despair that shook her. But he drew a deep breath and squared his shoulders as he brushed his hand across his brow. Almost magically, the look in his eyes vanished as if a door to some private torment had been slammed. The change was so quick that afterward Lindi couldn't be certain of exactly what she had seen.

"Good morning," he said calmly.

"Good morning." For a long moment, Lindi could only look at him, hypnotized by the power of his gaze. Where had his sudden, mysterious trip taken him? Why did he look so tortured? Why the quickly veiled sorrow in his dark eyes? Why did he stubbornly refuse to share his secret with anyone else? Did his mistress, Shodra Nichols, know? What was the dark enigma in the life of Travis Machado that ate at him like a malignant illness, giving him no rest?

Her thoughts were a jumble of questions—questions that she knew would get no answers from him.

Then her anger, which had been churning below the surface, boiled up, taking the place of other thoughts.

"Nice to have you back," she said, a saw-toothed edge of resentment in her voice.

He nodded slowly. "Nice to be back."

"I don't suppose you'd care to explain why you decided to pull this disappearing act at this particular time?"

He simply stared at her, his silence giving her his answer.

She gritted her teeth, trying not to say something rash that she'd regret later. "We've been going through a crisis here. I managed to buy out that print plant in Fort Myers. Everybody on the staff has been working overtime, trying to make room for the new equipment."

"Sorry I wasn't here to help," he murmured.

Was she making him feel guilty? She hoped so. "There was an important city council meeting Monday night. I guess you could say the battle for the city is now in the open, with the majority of the city council siding with the developers."

"That's no surprise, is it?"

"No, I guess it isn't. It's just that it really hurt, seeing the life savings of those poor people—their homes in The Clearwater Addition—go down the drain. It's spot zoning, the cruelest kind of real estate maneuver—breaking into a quiet residential area block by block to turn it into a commercial development."

"Well, that's the name of the game," Travis said, his black eyes intense. "The kind of people we're fighting are without conscience."

"I want us to run a strong editorial this week, one that will singe the paper. I've made some notes. Jake Tarson was at the council meeting too, and he's written down his reactions to what happened there.

I'd like you to take our raw material and put it into an editorial. I'd do it, but you're a stronger editorial writer than I."

He raised an eyebrow in surprise. "Well, thank you."

Her eyes clashed with his. "I didn't say you were necessarily a better writer than I. It's just that you are more experienced in newspaper work."

A half-smile tugged at the corner of his lips. "Well . . . thank you anyway."

Her eyes narrowed. She couldn't resist another jab. "Too bad you couldn't have been at the meeting yourself. I think you'd be as angry at the city council as I am."

Again the enigmatic wry smile tugged at the left corner of his mouth. "I'm already angry at that bunch of greedy politicians."

"After the meeting, the president of The Clearwater Neighborhood Association, Grady Alexander, paid me a visit. He's working on a slate of candidates to run against the current council members in the upcoming city election. He—he asked me to run for a place on the city council."

Travis's dark eyebrows raised slightly. "Well . . . from lady newspaper publisher to city council-woman. You've cut a wide swath in the short time you've been here, Lindi MacTavish."

"Just what is that supposed to mean?"

He shrugged. "Nothing at all. Why?"

"I detect a certain undercurrent. Don't you think I should run?"

"I didn't say that. I was merely making an observation."

"I think you were doing more than that. But you

didn't answer my question. Do you think it would be a mistake for me to get involved in local politics?"

He rubbed his chin thoughtfully. "A local political race like this can become pretty nasty. Especially with the town split the way it is. There could be a lot of mudslinging. The fight might be shifted to a personal level. It could be a dirty business."

There was a silence that stretched into several long moments. Lindi frowned, thinking about what he'd said. Finally she sighed. "Well, I haven't given them a definite answer. I have a few days to decide."

Lindi moved on to her own office.

Later that morning, Jake Tarson knocked on her door and entered. "I'm working on a story about the city election. I was wondering if you'd decided whether you're going to run?"

"I don't know, Jake. I was talking with Travis about it earlier this morning. It's a hard decision to make. I know I'd be letting myself in for a lot of hard work and grief."

Jake nodded. "I guess you would. The town could use somebody like you on the city council, though. Grady Alexander thinks you'd have a good chance of being elected."

"He seems like a pretty intelligent, responsible person, but I really don't know a whole lot about him. Fill me in, Jake. If I'm going to go out on a political limb, I'd like to know whose tree I'm sitting in."

"Oh, heck, Grady is a real nice guy, Lindi. I've known him all my life. He's a widower, raising two kids on his own. He owns an insurance agency here in Palmettoville. He's a responsible businessman. Everyone likes him. I think he's got a good shot at the mayor's chair. The only thing, Grady is kind of naive about politics. He's the honest, trusting type. If the campaign gets dirty, the professional politicians are liable to cut him up into little pieces. He needs all the help we can give him."

Lindi nodded thoughtfully. "I guess I'll have another chat with him. Maybe he can help me make up my mind."

After work that evening, she and Jake Tarson stopped off at Grady Alexander's house. He lived in one of the rambling, old two-story homes in The Clearwater Addition. Like the other homes on the street, the grounds were attractively landscaped. The houses were carefully maintained.

"How dare those greedy developers claim this is a deteriorating neighborhood?" Lindi exclaimed, growing angry all over again.

"Oh, we know that's just a smoke screen. They have to say something so the city council will have an excuse to give them what they want," Jake said disgustedly.

Grady Alexander answered the doorbell. He was flanked by a pair of tow-headed boys. They stared at the visitors with curious blue eyes exactly the same shade as their dad's. Lindi guessed their ages at about eight and six.

"Well, this is a real pleasure," Alexander exclaimed, his voice warm and friendly. "Please come in."

The house was cool and quiet. The furnishings looked comfortably worn. "These are my two boys, Ted and Darin," Grady said, his hands on their shoulders. "Boys, this is Miss MacTavish and Mr. Tarson. They're from the newspaper. Now, why don't you two go out back and play for a while. We have some business to talk about."

They went into a cozy, book-lined den where they

were seated in comfortable easy chairs. On a piano, Lindi saw a framed photograph of an attractive young woman. Was she Grady's wife? She wondered what kind of sad tragedy had taken her from him.

"I'm still trying to twist Lindi's arm to get her to accept a place on the city council ticket you're putting together," Jake said, taking out his pipe.

"Yes," Lindi interposed, "I've been giving it a lot of thought, Grady. I have to admit it's tempting to plunge into this fight with both feet."

"You'd be a dynamic addition to the ticket, Lindi. I've been keeping my fingers crossed that you'd say yes."

"Who are your other candidates?"

"Well, I'm throwing my hat in the ring for the mayor's job. My council running mates will be Mel Sigler, who owns the Westside Pharmacy; Shirley Posten, housewife; Ray Ochoa, an architect; and Bill Harris, who works for a local construction company. They're all decent, honest people who are as dedicated to saving Palmettoville as we are. That leaves us short one seat on the council. And we're hoping you'll fill that spot, Lindi."

The fragrant aroma of Jake's pipe tobacco was filling the room. A breeze stirred the curtain at the window. From the yard, Lindi could hear the voices of Grady's two boys. She thought about the quality of life in this town, which she had loved since she was a child, about to go down the tubes. She drew a deep breath. "All right, Jake, you can go to work on that story. We'll make the announcement that I'm going to file for a place on the council. After the story breaks, we'll start the ball rolling with a big party and invite the whole town. We'll have the party at *The Clarion* building."

Jake smiled from ear to ear. Grady jumped up and shook Lindi's hand warmly. "This calls for a drink!" Then he grinned self-consciously. "Will root beer do? That's about the strongest thing we have in the house!"

The next morning's mail brought a letter that temporarily drove thoughts of local politics from Lindi's mind. She called Rachel into her office.

"Everyone is excited about your running for a place on the city council," Rachel began.

Lindi nodded. "I plan to throw a big announcement party soon to get the ball rolling. I need your help in planning it—a list of drinks and refreshments. Probably some musicians would liven things up. D'you think we can round up a Dixieland band complete with straw hats and striped jackets?"

Rachel nodded. "Our high school band director, Joe Rossett, is a terrific jazz musician. He has a group that plays for dances and parties on weekends. They can play anything."

"Great. Call them. If they don't have Dixieland uniforms, we'll get some for them. I want to hold the party here in the building. The band can march around playing 'When the Saints Go Marching In.' That should wake up the voters. I want balloons, clowns, kegs of beer, soft drinks for the kids—the works."

Rachel grinned. "I can see that your experience in public relations is going to pay off."

"Yes; when I was with the public relations firm in New York we handled a lot of promotions like grand openings and political rallies."

"I bet the opposition is going to faint when it dawns

on them they have a big-city public relations campaign fighting them."

"We'll see. At least we'll give them a run for their money! Now, Rachel, I want to invite the whole town. Let's run a half-page display ad in this week's issue to invite everybody. Also, please have handbills printed up and hire some schoolboys to spread them around town."

"Okay. Gee, I think running for office is going to be fun!"

"I hope you're right. I may regret I ever got myself involved. Travis thinks the race may become nasty before it's over. But first, something else has come up." She handed Rachel a letter. "Take a look at this."

The secretary quickly scanned the note. "It's from a New York publisher, giving you an assignment to do an article about the Everglades!" she said. "That's exciting, Lindi."

"Well, I queried them about it, and I guess they like the idea. It will mean some extra money, which I can use. But more important, it ties right in with something I've been wanting to do for *The Clarion*. We've completed running the series on the ecology of the waterfront that Beatrice Simms did such a great job on. That stirred up a lot of reader interest. Now I think we should write about the other great natural resource on the other side of Palmettoville, the Everglades, and emphasize how much damage unrestricted development could do there. I want to use a lot of photographs along with the text. We can do that more easily when we begin using the offset printing process. What it all adds up to is killing two birds with one stone. I'll make a trip into the Everglades and get the material and photographs for the magazine article and for the newspaper at the same time."

Rachel looked worried. "That sounds like a good idea except for one thing. A person doesn't just go wandering into the Everglades, Lindi. I took an airboat ride in there once. You get a few hundred yards into that wilderness and you lose all sense of direction. It's the most frightening, eerie swamp you can imagine. It's like something out of a scary movie . . . lanes of water winding through the saw grass, dead trees like skeletons, snakes, alligators, all kinds of weird birds. They even have a few bears and panthers left prowling around out there. Some amateurs who have tried wandering in there never came back. I guess their bones are somewhere, picked clean by the vultures." She shuddered.

Lindi smiled. "Don't worry. I'm not planning to venture in the 'Glades alone. I expect to have an expert guide—Travis Machado."

# Chapter Ten

"This is some wingding!" Grady Alexander exclaimed, raising his voice to be heard.

Lindi grinned, surveying the joyful bedlam taking place around them. Desks had been moved and the entire upper floor of *The Clarion* cleared for her opening political rally. A crowd milled around, filling the space. The ceiling was festooned with banners and balloons. Clowns were cavorting, handing out bumper stickers and campaign buttons. At one end of the upper floor, a Dixieland band was romping through a brassy version of "The Muskrat Ramble." Across the wall behind them, an enormous banner proclaimed, "Lindi MacTavish for City Council."

"Looks like every voter in town is here," Grady said.

"That's the whole idea." Lindi nodded.

"Including the opposition. The mayor is here, and

so are some of the people we're fighting—the real estate broker Lester Martin and the developer C.C. Rothman. Oh, oh . . . speak of the devil—"

Palmettoville's current mayor, William Dodd, approached them. With a great show of joviality, he removed his cigar from between his teeth and shook hands with Lindi and Grady. "I have to congratulate you, young lady, for putting on quite a show here. I can see we're going to have a spirited race ahead of us."

"I hope it's going to be a clean race, based only on the issues," Lindi said, eyeing him coolly.

"My sentiments exactly!" Dodd boomed. "And may the best man win, eh, Grady?" He winked and gave his opponent a friendly jab in the ribs with his elbow. "Y'see, Miss MacTavish, I've known Grady all my life. I have nothing but the utmost respect for him. 'Course, I think he really should stick to the thing he knows something about, which is selling insurance, but that will be up to the voters, now won't it?" He winked again, shoved his cigar back into his mouth, clapped Grady on the shoulder, and drifted off into the crowd. Almost at once, he was shaking hands with someone else.

"I don't believe it!" Lindi exclaimed. "He's busy electioneering at my rally!"

"Sure; it's second nature with him. Dodd is a consummate politician. Shaking hands and kissing babies is an automatic reflex with him, like breathing. He's not about to pass up the opportunity to glad-hand voters in a crowd like this."

"Why do I have the feeling something about him doesn't add up right?" Lindi muttered, giving the incumbent mayor a hostile look.

Grady laughed. "I don't think Bill Dodd is an out-and-out crook."

"You're entirely too trusting, Grady," Lindi retorted. "His exaggerated sincerity has the convincing ring of a used-car salesman's pitch to an unsuspecting customer."

Several people converged on them, engaging Grady in conversation. Lindi drifted through the crowd, smiling and greeting people. She saw her editor Travis, taller and more broad-shouldered than most others in the crowd. Close beside him was a blond head stylishly coifed. Shodra Nichols slipped her hand possessively inside the crook of Travis's elbow. An unpleasant sensation burned in Lindi. She tried to shake it off, aware that she had no one to blame but herself. She had invited this kind of pain by becoming emotionally involved with Travis.

She needed to talk with Travis, but she waited until later in the evening when he had become temporarily separated from Shodra. "Travis, could I have a few words with you?" she asked, touching his shoulder.

He turned, engulfing her with his gaze. "Yes, of course."

They threaded their way through the crowd to Travis's office, which he'd locked. He opened it with his key, then secured the door when they were inside to keep anyone from wandering in.

"What do you think of the rally?" Lindi began.

"Regular three-ring circus," Travis muttered.

Her eyes narrowed. "I take it you don't approve?"

He shrugged. "I'm sure it's the right thing to do. The town has never seen this kind of big-city promotion. You've no doubt gained some voters. I just don't like large crowds."

"I know. You prefer the solitude of the Everglades."

He gave her a searching look but did not respond vocally.

"That's what I wanted to talk to you about."

He raised an eyebrow. "What—the Everglades?"

"Yes. I know this is an unorthodox time to discuss business. I've tried to have a talk with you about this for the past several days, but we've both been so busy, I've barely seen you except to nod at a distance. This is the first opportunity I've had to get you off to the side for a few minutes."

"Well, you've been hustling around preparing for this rally, and I've been working overtime to get the new printing equipment into operation."

"I know, and I appreciate the hard work and extra hours you've put in, Travis. At this rate, we'll have the new presses in operation by the end of next week."

"They're long overdue. I have to compliment you. That was a shrewd business deal you pulled, acquiring all that up-to-date machinery. I've had a chance to look it over closely. It's first-class equipment."

Lindi felt a flush of pleasure at his praise. Coming from her editor, who had started out bitterly resenting her presence at *The Clarion,* his compliment carried extra weight. "Well, it still has to be paid for. So it's all a gamble."

He shrugged. "Business is always a gamble. But it's going to facilitate our operation tremendously. We'll be able to handle a larger variety of printing jobs. Might even be able to bring in business from neighboring towns. And *The Clarion* is going to have an entirely different look. With the offset process we can use a lot more photographs of local events and people—that'll add a new dimension and give the paper more reader appeal."

She nodded. "That brings us back to what I wanted to talk to you about. I've been in touch with a New York publisher for whom I've free-lanced a number of articles. I approached them on the idea of doing a photo essay on the Everglades. They liked the proposal and want me to do the piece. It will tie in perfectly with the newspaper. We can use some of the photographs and the material for a series of articles in *The Clarion* on the order of the stories Beatrice Simms did on the ecology of the waterfront."

There was a moment's silence as Travis gave her a searching look.

Lindi pressed on. "I want you to act as my guide on a trip into the Everglades. I understand you have a four-wheel-drive swamp buggy that will take you anywhere in the Big Cypress swamp. I want you to take me into the regions that tourists never see, where I can get some photographs of the wildlife and vegetation."

His expression became withdrawn, and in his eyes she saw dark, hidden depths much like those of the mysterious wilderness they were discussing. "Why me?" he asked in a guarded tone. "There are a lot of Seminole guides along the Tamiami Trail who have airboats. They'll take you where you want to go."

"Maybe. But more likely they'll follow the usual tourist routes—make a circle of a few miles in the saw grass and then back to the highway. I want to go miles into the swamp with someone I can communicate with."

His eyes remained aloof, his thoughts hidden. "You may not like what you see. It's a tropical jungle swamp back there—no place for a city girl. There are swarms of mosquitoes, snakes that may drop on you from a tree limb you pass under, alligators that could snap off a leg."

"Are you trying to scare me off?" she asked, her gaze challenging his.

"Well, I want you to know what you're letting yourself in for. It's not like going to the city park for a Sunday afternoon picnic."

"I know that. My grandfather warned us never to go wandering into the 'Glades by ourselves. That's why I want you to be my guide. Everybody tells me you know every inch of the Big Cypress Swamp like you know the main street of Palmettoville."

"That's a slight exaggeration. Nobody really knows the Everglades except perhaps the Seminoles—the Mikasuki and Muskogee tribes. And a lot of the younger generation don't know the swamps like their fathers and grandfathers."

"But from what I've heard you know it as well as the Indians do. I've been told you were raised by the Mikasukis."

It was a daring chance, but she took it, disregarding the consequences. Perhaps the shock of such a direct approach might open a crack in his defenses, giving her a glimpse into that secret past he guarded so jealously.

His eyes flared momentarily. "And just who told you that fairy story?"

"Is it a fairy story?" she challenged.

He gave her a long, steady look. "Perhaps it isn't. But that's beside the point. All right, Lindi. I'll give you a guided tour of the Big Cypress Swamp. When do you want to go?"

"As soon as possible. Before I get bogged down with this city election thing."

"Well, then, how about day after tomorrow? I need to do some work on my swamp buggy, but I can have it gassed up and ready to leave early Monday morning."

"All right. That's fine."

"We should leave before dawn. You may see some interesting sights as dawn spreads through the wilderness."

"Yes, that would be good."

He gave her a steady look. "We may not get back that night."

There was a sudden, heavy silence in the room, a silence filled with undefined implications. His gaze trailed down her body. She felt a hot flush rise to her cheeks. Her tongue felt thick as she asked, "Well . . . where would we sleep?"

He smiled. "Oh, I suppose you might curl up on a seat in the swamp buggy. Or we might find an abandoned Indian *chikee* hut on one of the hammocks. I'll take cots and bedrolls along."

Her heart beat with a strong, pulsing rhythm. The thought of spending a night in the wilderness alone with Travis Machado poured adrenaline into her veins. She was irritated at herself for the seductive emotions that had been so instantly stirred. She also felt a measure of fear. What was she letting herself in for? The cautious side of her nature warned her that it was insanity to place herself in that kind of vulnerable situation with a man who held such an overpowering attraction for her. Running counter to the caution was a bolder, more reckless impulse that gave her the courage to think she was quite capable of coping with any situation.

She raised her chin, challenging his bold look with an expression that let him know she was still the boss, both of the paper and of any personal situation that might arise between them. "Early Monday will be fine. You can pick me up at my houseboat."

He grinned, his teeth flashing white against his swarthy complexion. "Bring along plenty of mosquito repellent."

Again their eyes met in a way that made her knees tremble. She drew a shaky breath. "We'd better get back to the party."

Travis unlocked the door. Then Lindi was again immersed in the bedlam of the rally. She welcomed the noise and confusion; it dispelled the upsetting emotions that Travis stirred in her.

For the next half hour she was occupied with her role as hostess and political candidate, answering questions, meeting people, soliciting votes.

Suddenly she found herself face to face with the glamorous widow, Shodra Nichols. "This is an impressive event," Shodra said in her smoothly modulated voice. "I can see the touch of big-city public relations know-how." Her large, violet eyes were surveying Lindi, analyzing her in an acutely female fashion. "At this rate, you may stand a very good chance of being our next councilwoman."

"I hope so," Lindi said evenly. "I really don't have any political aspirations. In fact, a political career is the last thing I really want. But I don't see any way of keeping this town out of the hands of the developers except to get some responsible people in the city government who will stand by our zoning laws."

Shodra nodded slowly. "You may be right. You'll have some powerful opposition. I'm sure you know C.C. Rothman is not going to stand idly by and see you get elected."

"Yes, I'm sure Mr. Rothman and Lester Martin and

the other real estate people will be fighting us tooth and nail."

Shodra made a gesture as if brushing a fly aside. "Lester Martin is just a yes man, a very small person greedily trying to line his pockets. The real power behind the whole development move is Rothman."

Why do I have the feeling we're only sparring around with all this political talk? Lindi thought. What is it she really has on her mind?

Lindi got the answer to that in the very next words Shodra spoke. "Travis tells me the two of you are going on an expedition into the Everglades."

The widow's gaze was penetrating. So this is what our little talk has been leading up to, Lindi thought. "Yes. I want to do an article on the area. Travis knows it so well, I thought he would be the ideal guide."

Lindi thought that Shodra's beautiful violet eyes could be luminous and inviting when she looked at Travis. But they could also become bright and speculative. She was an experienced, clever woman, apparently wise in the way of romantic involvements. "You're an attractive young woman," the glamorous widow said slowly, her eyes continuing their analytical appraisal of Lindi. "And Travis is a virile hunk of man. Do you find him attractive?"

Lindi was disconcerted by the woman's direct question. She stammered, "My interest in Travis Machado is strictly business, Mrs. Nichols."

That wasn't entirely true. She knew it. And the wise look in Shodra Nichols's eyes told her the other woman knew it too.

Shodra said, "Whatever your business relationship, you are only human, Lindi. You're young and vulnerable. Travis is an experienced man of the world. Thrown together in such a wild, romantic setting, perhaps spending the night together in the wilderness, I'm sure your emotions could get the best of you."

Lindi felt her cheeks redden with anger. "This conversation is becoming pretty personal, don't you think?"

"Yes, indeed I do. I intended it to. I don't want us to be enemies, Lindi MacTavish. But I have the distinct feeling that we are becoming rivals. I gave up my childish naiveté a long time ago. I'm quite aware that Travis finds you attractive. It's only normal. You're young, vital, quite different from the run-of-the-mill small-town girls around here. You have a good education. Obviously you're smart and energetic, a go-getter. You're a good writer. Travis admires all that in you. Needless to say, you have the physical endowments to attract a man. You have a firm, shapely young body, a slim waist, nice legs, all the curves in the right places. The freckles and pert nose give you a wholesome appeal that an older man of the world might find quite charming. Your personality is warm. At first Travis resented you like the dickens because you were taking over the paper when he thought he should have had the job. But he's come to admire and respect your achievements. So, the situation has changed quite a bit since you first arrived."

Lindi was speechless with embarrassment and anger. She didn't know how to respond to this situation. "Why are you telling me all this?" she demanded.

"Oh, I like to be direct. Cards on the table—all that old stuff. I'm a realist, Lindi. I see things as they are. Perhaps it would be to your advantage to be a realist too. At your age, one tends to romanticize these situations. I know, because I've been there. But if you have cast a romantic mist around Travis Machado, I think I should warn you that Travis is not going to get serious over anyone right now. He might very well decide to seduce you if he has the opportunity, but that's all it would amount to. Travis is struggling with his own personal devils right now. I don't know what they are, and if I did I wouldn't tell you. All I can tell you is that Travis and I have an understanding. I'm good for Travis, because I don't expect anything at all from him. But a young, idealistic woman like yourself would expect more than a fling . . . more than one night of passion. And Travis is not in a position to give you or anyone else more than that. So, do yourself a big favor, Lindi MacTavish. Don't let yourself become involved with Travis Machado."

With that, Shodra Nichols walked away, leaving Lindi stranded in an emotional earthquake.

# Chapter Eleven

Lindi was engulfed by smothering blackness as they left the dirt road and plunged headlong into the swamp. Dawn was still an hour away. The giant wheels of Travis's swamp buggy churned through the marsh with a sucking noise. They rode high above the grass that whipped at the vehicle with its saw-toothed blades.

Civilization had suddenly become remote and unreal. They had entered a time warp, stepping into a dripping prehistoric age. It was the way Lindi had dreamed the world was before humans arrived, a tropical garden awaiting the appearance of Adam and Eve. Around them, skeletal limbs of dead trees wore shrouds of moss. They drove through tangled masses of palmettos past floating mangrove islands. Palm trees formed tropical silhouettes against the night's dying stars. Lindi half expected a dinosaur to suddenly appear in the vehicle's dancing headlights.

Travis was silent as he drove, occupied with the task of guiding his machine through the treacherous terrain. The swamp buggy itself resembled a mechanical prehistoric monster as it lumbered through the muck and marsh on wheels nearly as tall as Lindi.

The stars gradually faded from the canopy of black velvet above them. Soon the first blush of dawn could be seen along the distant horizon, far across the vast ocean of grass. Lindi watched the rosy shafts of light begin to touch the clouds.

Travis drove a while longer, then parked on a hammock, a small area of solid ground surrounded by marsh and dwarf pond cypress trees.

"Coffee?" Travis offered, taking a thermos from the storage area behind the seat.

"Yes, thank you," Lindi said gratefully. Travis had come to pick her up at three-thirty in the morning, and she felt groggy. Travis poured the steaming black liquid into a Styrofoam cup and handed it to her. She sipped the beverage, becoming more alert as the caffeine stimulated her nervous system.

The spreading rosy light gradually drew the curtain of darkness from the wild beauty that surrounded her. She began to make out the clusters of air plants, bromeliads, and wild orchids that created splashes of delicate color in the cypress and hammock trees.

As they sat in breathless silence, wildlife began to appear. A great white heron was a motionless carved figure in the top branches of a leafless hammock tree silhouetted against the golden sunrise. A brown pelican left its perch and flew past them. Travis touched her arm and pointed in the direction of a mangrove thicket. There she caught sight of a nesting wood stork.

As the sun rose and more light shone on the

Everglades, Lindi assembled her camera equipment. Using a powerful telescopic lens, she took photographs of the animal and plant life surrounding them.

After a while, Travis started the engine and they moved on, deeper into the wilderness.

At noon he stopped near a grassy hammock on which stood a deserted Indian *chikee* shelter. "Hungry?"

"Yes. Bouncing around on this thing has given me quite an appetite."

Lindi had brought along a basket packed with a picnic lunch that she'd prepared the night before. They clambered down from the vehicle.

As Lindi spread a cloth on the ground, Travis gazed around at the distant horizon. She was impressed by how naturally he had become a part of these surroundings. A mile into the swampland and she had been hopelessly lost. Yet he had driven all morning, over terrain that blurred into an endless panorama of sandy islands, tree hammocks of slash pine and mixed hardwoods, wet prairies, marshes, dry prairies, and estuarine mangrove forest, and he appeared always to know where he was and where he was going. She realized how utterly dependent she was on him out here. If he disappeared, she would surely die, and her bones would be picked bare by the birds and animals.

"Are the mosquitoes eating you up?" he asked.

"No. I've been using repellent in liberal doses."

He grinned. "Some call the Big Cypress the most primitive, wildest swamp in North America, with a bigger mosquito population than anywhere else in the world."

"How did the Indians ever survive here?" she wondered.

They sat down to a lunch of fried chicken, potato

salad, various cheeses, and a bottle of wine. Lindi felt a comfortable companionship with Travis. She warmed happily when he complimented her cooking.

When he finished eating, he relaxed, leaning against a tree and munching a chocolate chip cookie for dessert. "You asked how the Indians survived here. They got their strength from their Beings of Power, the earth and the sun and the grass and the water. There was an ancient people here long before Columbus, the Calusas. They probably lived in the 'Glades a thousand years ago. They first built the *chikees,* thatched huts open all around in the summer to catch the cool summer breezes and draped with hides to act as windbreakers in the winter. The Everglades gave them plenty of food—fish, turtles, fat young deer, ibis, wild turkeys. They raised beans and squash and corn and ate palm cabbage. They had ground coontie, or comptie root, that they made into cakes or sofkee—a soft gruel."

"You know so much about all this, you should be writing the article," Lindi said.

"Well, perhaps I can help some on your research. What do you want to know?"

"Why did the Seminoles choose to live in such a harsh environment?"

"It has its advantages. Game and plant life are abundant. The climate is almost tropical." He paused to reach for another cookie. "As European settlers moved into Alabama and Georgia, the Creek Indians migrated down into Florida. The Creek tribes spoke Muskogee and Hitchiti. Those various tribes eventually were lumped together under the name 'Seminoles.'"

"I remember reading about the Seminole wars in high school history class."

"Yes." Travis nodded soberly, his eyes growing dark with an inner pain. "As white settlers began to populate Florida, they decided there were too many Indians around. Andrew Jackson, the first territorial governor of Florida, decided the solution was to pack up all the Seminoles and ship them off to some barren reservations out west. That's what happened to a lot of them. But others refused to leave their homes. The government in those days had a way of making treaties with Indians and breaking them when convenient. There were bloody Indian wars in Florida as the army tried to force the Seminoles out of their homeland. Men, women, and children were slaughtered. Stories about the hardships their ancestors suffered have been handed down from generation to generation for a hundred years and more. When they fled back into the Everglades to escape the soldiers, Indian mothers dug holes in the ground and hid their children in them, covering the holes with palmetto leaves. They say many infants were killed to keep them from crying and giving away the hiding places."

Lindi's heart was wrenched. "How horrible!" she gasped.

"Yes. When you know those things, it's understandable that it has taken a long time for the Seminoles to trust the white man. Those bitter old memories are still strong. The remnants of the tribes who weren't killed retreated into the Everglades where the army couldn't reach them. They never surrendered. To this day, they have remained an unconquered people. Their chiefs and councils make their own laws and punish their own criminals according to tribal laws."

"Do they still live back here in the wilderness?" Lindi asked.

"There are about seven hundred Mikasukis in the Big Cypress region. Most of them are in settlements close to modern civilization along the Tamiami Trail. The younger members of the tribe are slowly drifting away from the older ways of Indian life. They go to school, learn English, drive cars, watch television. But they still have their green corn dance, a time when the tribes gather again back in the 'Glades, where the white man doesn't go."

"What is the corn dance ceremony like?"

"The event lasts four days, maybe a week. Members of the tribes come from all around. There are feasts and purification ceremonies. The younger people are instructed in the ancient traditions by the elders of the tribe. It was at these times that the tribal elders passed judgment on members of the tribe who had broken tribal laws. Murderers were put to death. Others might be punished by whipping or by having their ears cut off."

Lindi shuddered. "Do they still do that?"

"No. They're more inclined now to hand miscreants over to the civil authorities, although the federal government is very careful not to interfere in tribal courts."

Travis suddenly rose, dusting loose blades of grass from his jeans. "White people are seldom allowed to witness a corn dance ceremony. You can consider yourself privileged."

Lindi stared at him. "I don't understand."

Travis gazed at her in an enigmatic manner. "It so happens you picked an opportune time to make your trip into the Everglades. The Mikasukis are holding their corn dance this week. We're on our way there now."

Lindi jumped to her feet, her eyes wide with excitement. "Do you mean we are actually going to see an authentic Seminole corn dance?"

"Since you're with me, yes."

"Then what I've heard about you is true! You're a member of their tribe. Otherwise you wouldn't dare intrude on their ceremony. Are you part Mikasuki?"

He did not answer her question. Instead he said, "There is one thing you must promise. I want your word of honor that you will not use your camera."

She cocked her head to one side and gazed at him mischievously. "Would they cut our ears off?"

He scowled. "It's nothing to joke about. If I'm going to take you with me, I expect you to respect their dignity and their customs."

"Oh, all right. What a scoop it would be, though, if I could bring back pictures of their ceremonies."

"Word of honor?"

"Yes. Cross my heart and anything else you want."

He glared at her. "This is no joking matter. If you get any smart ideas, I might not take you before the tribe council. I might hand out the punishment myself."

She glared back. "You wouldn't dare, Travis Machado!"

"If you cause too much trouble, I might let you walk back!"

She turned pale. "You know I'd be lost before I walked a hundred yards in this godforsaken swamp."

"Then you'd better do as I say! Now come on, get back in the swamp buggy."

Once again they prowled through the vast, watery wilderness. Lindi gasped with pleasure and wonder at the lush tropical vegetation and the wildlife. She caught sight of birds with red plumage stalking through the marsh on pipestem legs; she remembered they were roseate spoonbills. There was a splash in the water near their wheels, and she gasped as the snout of the huge, armored creature that had existed since the mists of prehistoric time slid silently by. "Look, a crocodile," she exclaimed.

"Alligator," Travis said, correcting her. "There are crocodiles in the 'Glades, too. But that's an alligator."

"How can you tell the difference?"

He grinned. "I suppose it wouldn't matter much if it took your leg off. But crocodiles have narrower snouts and are more of a greenish grey. You rarely see them, especially in this area."

They caught sight of stately wading birds—herons, egrets, and wood storks. A rare bald eagle settled in a tree within range of Lindi's camera.

Travis astounded her with his knowledge of the vegetation. He identified plants, trees, and bushes for her as her camera shutter clicked. She photographed tiny wildflowers almost lost in the wiry grass—the scarlet brilliance of tiny wild poinsettias, the yellow tea bush, and pale blue chicory.

When they stopped and shut off the engine from time to time, they were surrounded by the sounds of the tropical jungle. She heard the rat-ta-ta-tat of red-headed woodpeckers riveting away at tree trunks, the caw and screech of other birds, and the sudden chilling, bellowing roar of a male alligator.

Once Travis grabbed her arm and pointed. She just caught sight of a tuft-eared wildcat bounding on high back legs into the brush.

Of all the trees, she thought the cypress was the most impressive, especially the giant river cypress. They squatted in the muddy water on huge bases, their root clusters, called cypress knees, looking like dead stumps in the stagnant water. Their trunks were great silver-grey columns reaching up to the heavens; their short branches were draped with Spanish moss and festooned with colorful air plants. Some were more than a hundred feet tall.

"They're magnificent," Lindi cried.

"Yes, the few that are left. Some of the giants you see were here before Columbus came. They could withstand the rains and the hurricanes and the lightning. But they couldn't stand against the lumbermen's saws. Now there are only a few of these magnificent specimens left."

Then they encountered the deadly side of the swamp. Travis pointed to a huge diamondback rattlesnake slithering across a sandy hammock between palmettos. "You must always be careful where you walk. There are four kinds of snakes you need to watch out for. Their bite can be fatal. They are coral snakes, water moccasins, diamondbacks, and pigmy rattlers."

Lindi shuddered. "How would I know which ones are poisonous?"

"Just stay away from anything that looks like a snake."

"With pleasure."

Travis also pointed out some plants to avoid. "See the vine with the clusters of three pointed leaves growing up the trunk of that tree? That's poison ivy. Over there, the smooth shrub with greenish-white berries is the poison sumac. It has an oil that's very poisonous to touch. The other thing to stay away from is the manchineel tree. There's one over there. It has an apple-shaped fruit."

"The forbidden fruit," Lindi murmured. "I'll remember."

Travis gave her a searching look. "Make you feel like Eve?"

His gaze held hers. She felt her breath catch in her throat. She did feel like Eve, here in this tropical Garden of Eden alone with the man whom God created as her mate.

It was a dangerous thought, one that brought a flush to her face and made her heart pound.

Then it was late afternoon and they were approaching the gathering place of the Mikasukis. Travis stopped the swamp buggy. He stripped off his short-sleeved sport shirt. For a moment the rippling muscles of his broad shoulders and deep chest were bared. Her gaze was pulled magnetically to his smooth skin, the curling mat of hair, the trim waist above his belt buckle. He unfastened the belt buckle, revealing the soft line of hair that ran from his navel downward. Lindi felt her breath grow thick in her throat and she forced her eyes in another direction.

Had he done that deliberately? she wondered, half angry, half aroused. Was he testing her, making an attempt to discover the extent of her desire? Could he feel the chemistry at work between them? She could see the male hunger in his eyes. She sensed with a female knowledge that made her pulse race that he wanted her . . . wanted her with a desire as primitive and basic as the wild jungle that surrounded them. Did she want him to make love to her on those terms? It was a question she knew she would probably have to answer before this journey ended.

When she looked back, he had donned another shirt, a colorful, loose-fitting garment with intricate designs, the traditional garb of the Mikasukis. Tied loosely around his neck was a bandanna. With his dark hair and swarthy complexion, he looked more than ever like an Indian come back to his home in the Everglades.

They drove on. Near sunset, they approached a break in the marshy wetland, an expanse of dry land like a great sandy island in the swamp. Among the trees on the great hammock were numerous *chikee* shelters. Smoke rose from campfires. Dozens of four-wheel-drive vehicles were parked under the trees. The land teemed with people. Lindi's pulse beat more quickly. This was the secret gathering place of the Mikasukis, far back in Big Cypress Swamp. Here the clans and families gathered for their traditional sacred ceremonies, which few outsiders had ever seen.

As they drew closer, Lindi exclaimed at the colorful dress of the Indians. Women wore floor-length skirts sewn with intricate designs and full capes around their shoulders. Some had row upon row of beads circling their necks. A few of the older men had donned traditional one-piece kiltlike dresses, which were decorated with rows of designs in various colors. But most of the men, like Travis, wore blue jeans and colorful shirts or blouses with bandannas tied around their necks.

Travis pulled into the clearing. He was instantly recognized and greeted. Lindi felt herself the object of curious and not entirely friendly stares. Travis spoke quickly in soft, guttural language of the Mikasukis. Lindi assumed he had explained her presence in a satisfactory manner, because the cold stares changed to shy smiles and nods.

Travis led her to one of the *chikees*, where he was greeted with obvious joy. Was he a part of this family? Lindi wondered. She had no way of knowing, and he offered no explanation. He motioned her to sit beside him at a table, where they were served steaming bowls of food—wild game, vegetables, and sofkee. Lindi wasn't always sure of what she was eating, but she was ravenous and the food was delicious.

After the meal, they moved outside. By then dusk had settled over the wilderness. There was singing and dancing. The music made by gourds, coconut shells, tortoise shells, rattles, and flutes carved from hollow reeds sounded strange to Lindi.

She saw a group of men assembled in a loose circle. An individual she assumed was a medicine man approached them carrying a stick to which was fastened a pair of steel needles like snake fangs. The medicine man raked the instrument over the arms and bared chests of the men, drawing blood.

"Why is he doing that?" Lindi gasped.

"It's part of the purification process," Travis explained. "According to traditional beliefs, the bleeding purifies their bodies. It's part of the ritual before the feather dance. Another part of the traditional purification rites is the black drink. It's an emetic concocted from herbs—also a means of cleansing the body and the soul."

Lindi wondered if Travis would participate in the age-old rituals. For the moment, he seemed satisfied to watch and explain to her what was taking place.

As the evening wore on, Lindi heard the muttering of thunder and saw distant flashes of lightning on the horizon. Clouds began moving across the sky, hiding the stars. Uneasily, she thought about the torrential rains that sometimes struck the region that time of the year and wondered if the rituals might be cut short.

The rhythm of the instruments, the chanting of the dancers, the exotic setting—all were having a hypnotic effect on her. She felt her emotions blend with her surroundings. She was in a dream state. The reality of

her civilized life had faded. Time had become mean-
ingless. Her identity had somehow been altered. She
had been transported to a primitive age where she was
much closer to the breath and rhythm of nature and
the universe. She could sense the blending of man and
the jungle wildlife, the pattern of the stars, the
heartbeat of eternity with her own. The ageless
knowledge of her subconscious was close to the
surface.

She didn't resist when Travis took her hand and led
her to a circle of the tribe's elders. It was all a dream,
wasn't it? She heard soft, throaty words that had no
meaning. But she recognized the wisdom in the eyes
of the old men.

A cup was handed to Travis. He sipped from it;
then, facing her, he gave her the drink. She understood without his telling her that she, too, was to
drink from the cup.

When she handed it back, she saw the kindly smiles
of the men of the council.

Travis led her away from the circle. Raindrops were
beginning to splatter in the leaves and make little
hissing sounds in the campfires. "Have to get you to a
shelter," he said urgently.

They paused at his swamp buggy only long enough
for him to grab the bedrolls; then he ran into the
darkness, pulling her after him. "Hurry," he commanded. "The sky is going to open any minute."

They came to a *chikee* hidden in a grove of trees.
Travis pulled her into the shelter just as the cloudburst
struck. Amid claps of thunder, torrents of rain fell in
blinding sheets, but the thatched roof kept them dry
just as it had kept the Seminoles of the Everglades
and the Calusas before them dry for many centuries.

The *chikee* had the traditional small platform in the

center, set several feet above the ground. Travis had explained that it was used as a table during the day and as a place to sleep at night, keeping the people safe from the dampness and possible danger of snakes on the ground. Now he spread the bedrolls there.

Lindi asked, "Travis, what did that ceremony mean, when you and I drank from the cup together?"

Travis looked at her, his eyes filled with a dark fire that consumed her. "That was the traditional Seminole wedding ritual. We just got married."

# Chapter Twelve

The violent weather that raged about them was nothing compared to the storm that exploded inside Lindi. She stared at Travis, at first too stunned to speak. Finally she gasped, "What do you mean, we're married?"

His face was illuminated by flashes of lightning, but she could not define his expression. She thought he might be laughing at her. His voice, however, was serious. "Just what I said. We were just married."

"No, we weren't!" she cried. "Nobody said anything to me about getting married. Travis Machado, how dare you pull a stunt like this? I wouldn't marry you if you were the last man on earth!"

He raised an eyebrow, his gaze raking her body boldly. "Sure of that?"

She flushed, raising her chin. "Certainly," she said frigidly, although inwardly she was less than sure.

"Nevertheless, we are married," he insisted.

"But that's only according to Indian custom."

"Well, at the moment, we are on an Indian reservation in an Indian nation," he pointed out.

"That's not fair! I didn't even know what was being said. What gave you the crazy notion of getting us involved in an Indian marriage ceremony anyway?"

"It seemed like the practical thing to do."

"Practical!" she gasped. "What is that supposed to mean?"

"Well, the chiefs weren't too happy about my bringing a stranger, and a white woman at that, to their ceremony. So when we arrived I told them that you were my woman, that we were going to be married during the corn dance according to the old Seminole tradition."

"I remember now—you said something to them when we got here, and suddenly they stopped glaring at me. Some of the women giggled. Travis, that was pretty high-handed of you! Did it occur to you that you should have talked to me about it?"

"Well, you didn't want to get scalped, did you?"

"Don't be ridiculous! You know your people wouldn't do anything like that. This is the twentieth century—not the old West."

There was a violent crash of thunder that shook the earth. Lindi was almost blinded by a bluish-white flash. Lightning struck a nearby tree. The air became so charged with electricity that the hair on the back her neck rose. With a cry of terror, Lindi flung herself against Travis. His strong arms went around her protectively. She buried her face against his shoulder. Her body was quivering from head to toe. Tears of fright ran down her cheeks.

Travis stroked her hair. "It's all right. Just lightning hitting an old cypress tree. You're safe here."

"Are you sure?" she asked as she looked up, her face streaked with tears.

His eyes were as dark and violent as the storm. She felt the burning pressure of his hard, masculine body against hers. Suddenly she realized that although she might be safe from the storm here, there was a different kind of danger threatening her.

She tried to drag her gaze from his, but she lacked the willpower. His eyes burned into her very depths, igniting flames that licked through her body. The strength of his arms around her sent a throbbing current through her beating heart.

His lips drew nearer. The strength drained from her legs. She melted against him, wanting to be closer . . . closer. A soft moan tore from her throat as his lips claimed hers. Her mouth was on fire, then her entire body.

The kiss was as violent and primitive as the storm. His tongue thrust deeply into her mouth. His hands moved over her, slipping inside her blouse and under restraining garments, to cup the delicate flesh of her throbbing breasts.

"Travis . . ." she whispered hoarsely.

He carried her to the platform bed where the bedroll provided a soft mattress.

The storm raged around them. Rain pounded on the palm fronds and fell in sheets around the *chikee*, but under its shelter they were dry and snug.

Tenderly, Travis undressed her. Her thoughts were a jumbled chaos.

She was vaguely aware of his fumbling with his own clothes. She heard a zipper open. Then a fresh gasp tore from her lips as his bare flesh pressed against hers.

"Travis . . . Travis . . . no . . ."

It was a weak protest.

"Yes," he said hoarsely. "We have to . . ."

"Oh, Travis, it's—it's—"

"I know. You want me too. You can't say you don't—"

"I don't know what I'm saying," she gasped. "Travis . . . we shouldn't . . . not here . . . not like this."

"Can you think of a better place?"

His mouth and hands were exploring all her body's secret places and fanned the flames of passion into a raging inferno. She dug her fingers into his hair.

"Travis . . . oh . . ."

Her head thrashed from side to side as her body arched against him.

"I've wanted you for weeks," he said roughly.

"Yes . . . I know," she panted. Silence. "Oh, Travis, that's so good. . . ."

There was a longer silence except for the rustling of their bodies on the bedrolls, their strained breathing and exclamations of ecstasy. He carried her to the heights of fulfillment, beyond anything she had dreamed possible. She wanted to cry out that she loved him, for now she had to face the truth.

Yes, she was in love with him, had been in love with him perhaps from that first moment in the Miami airport. She had tried not to admit it, but now in the throes of blinding passion, she had to face the stark truth. Yes, she was glad they had been married tonight in the custom of Travis's people. This was her wedding night. She was a willing bride, giving herself

joyfully to her husband. They made love with abandon in that primitive setting with the elements raging
about them, the thunder shaking the earth, lightning
crashing into the trees, rain beating down in torrents.
But all that fury combined couldn't match the savage
fury of their primitive passion. It swept them along in
a raging maelstrom.

If any rational thought remained that she might
regain her reason in the morning and regret this
insanity, she was not aware of it.

The boiling tide of their passion crashed on rocky
cliffs in one explosive climax after another and then,
at last, toward morning, subsided into the slumber
like that of a peaceful, spent sea after a violent storm.

When Lindi awoke in Travis's arms, the other storm
outside their shelter had ended too. Morning sunlight
was glittering on wet leaves. Birds were singing. The
rainwater had quickly been absorbed by the sandy soil
or had drained into the swamp. From the direction of
the Indian camp, she heard voices as the people
continued their celebration.

She gazed at the man beside her—the man who had
joined their lives in the marriage ceremony of his
people. In repose, Travis's face looked calm and at
peace. The lines of bitterness and anger around his
mouth had smoothed out. She couldn't resist running
her fingers tenderly through his tousled black hair.
When she did, he stirred.

What manner of man was he? Who was he? With a
sudden wave of panic, she had to face the truth that
she knew almost nothing about this man she had
fallen in love with, the man she now considered her
husband. He appeared to fit in so naturally with the
Mikasukis. They had greeted him like a family mem-

ber. Yet looking closely at his features, she couldn't be sure if he truly was an Indian. His dark hair and swarthy features gave that impression, but on closer inspection, he did not have Indian characteristics. Then how was it he spoke their language so fluently, knew their customs so intimately, was accepted by them so readily like a blood brother?

What was the cause of the restless brooding in his eyes, his strange disappearances? He was constantly brooding on some dark secret that never stopped tormenting him.

What part did Shodra Nichols play in his life?

That thought came crashing into the serenity of the morning. Suddenly, the previous night's romantic dream turned into the morning's harsh reality. In the madness of passion, she had not allowed the thought of Shodra Nichols to come between her and the man she loved. But that did not eliminate the other woman from Travis's life. What part did Shodra play in that life?

A cold, unpleasant suspicion began to intrude on her fragile happiness. Was it possible that Shodra was still very much part of Travis's life . . . that Shodra had not lost Travis at all . . . that nothing would be changed when they returned to Palmettoville?

Lindi blinked back a sudden rush of tears. With a determined effort, she put those dark thoughts aside. Travis was coming awake. She smiled tremulously, greeting him with a kiss.

"Storm's over," she said softly.

"So it is."

She sat up, but he pulled her back down beside him. She realized they were still both naked. The touch of his flesh against hers awoke a thousand sensations.

"Time for breakfast," she whispered shakily.

"Is it?"

"Yes—"

"Are you all that hungry?"

Yes, my darling, hungry for you all over again. . . .

She might as well have spoken the words aloud. He read the need clearly in her eyes, felt the fever in her flesh. His hands roved over her, caressing all the secret places that now were his, scalding her nerve endings with renewed heat.

"It was good . . . very good. . . ." he murmured, his lips against her hair.

"Yes," she whispered thickly.

"Want more?"

Her cheeks burned. "Yes."

He tilted her chin and gazed into her eyes until she thought she would swoon.

He began kissing her all over again, gently at first, his lips tender and soft against her hair, her eyelids, her cheeks, her ears, her mouth, her throat, moving over every inch of her body and, not satisfied, turning her over to kiss her back, trailing down, down over every curve. Her heart was hammering wildly. Blood pounded through her arteries like molten lava, igniting a raging furnace deep within her.

"Oh, Travis," she gasped.

Then they were locked in each other's arms. She pressed avidly against him, molding her soft, yielding curves to the hard, masculine outlines, moving her legs, lifting herself to him, welcoming him with frantic eagerness. She was his bride. He was her husband . . . her man . . . her lover for this moment and all moments to come.

"Yes . . . yes . . . oh, that's so good," she cried.

His exclamations were hoarse in her ears.

He demanded and she gave willingly in total surrender.

Anything you want, my darling, her heart cried. Just ask and I'll give. Tell me and I'll do it. . . .

"Oh . . . mmm . . ."

She was barely aware of her own moans.

Expertly, he led her to the mountaintops where ecstasy exploded over and over. Behind her closed eyelids she saw a burst of fireworks. There was no earth, no worldy existence, only a state of pure feeling.

Like a detached leaf slowly fluttering to earth, she returned to consciousness. She felt dazed, out of touch with reality. They remained quietly in each other's arms for long, lazy minutes.

Then an unexpected thing happened. She was jerked back to reality with a rude shock. Travis smacked her bare bottom smartly with his broad palm.

She jerked upright with a gasp. "What the—!"

"Mosquito," he explained blandly. "If you continue to lie around here like Eve, they'll turn you into hamburger."

He reached in his camping bag for a can of insect repellent and sprayed her from head to foot.

"What a mundane way to end a romantic interlude!" she spluttered.

"True," he admitted, "but that's life in the swamp."

They dressed and had breakfast with Travis's people, then spent the morning watching the activities in the Indian camp. Lindi saw the wildcat dance, the deer dance, and the colorful feather dance, in which the dancers used sticks decorated with white egret plumes. The performers stomped the ground to the hypnotic pounding of drums, the buzzing of rattles attached to their ankles, and the wailing squeal of hollowed-reed flutes.

Lindi sat close to her bridegroom, stealing glances at him from time to time to reassure herself that she was not dreaming.

A cleared area formed the "square ground." On logs sat the men of the tribe—the priests, the elders of the tribe, and men in their prime. Twelve-year-old boys had been fasting and praying, preparing for the ceremony that would initiate them into manhood. They would bear stoically, without flinching, the ordeal of splinters stuck under the skin of their arms, to prove their manhood.

For the tribes in the Everglades, it was a time of starting over, of quenching the old fire of the past year and starting the new tribal fire. It was a time of forgiving past sins, of cleansing and renewal.

Some were punished by having a long deep scratch inflicted down the back from the neck to the heel. Others held out their arms for the medicine man to give them a less severe scratch that would let out the evil blood so they would be cleansed and purified.

Travis explained the rituals that were taking place; without his help, Lindi would have understood none of it.

The elders of the tribe recounted the stories and traditions of generations past so that the ways of the Seminoles would be preserved for the young.

Lindi watched the pageantry through the eyes of a woman in love. She seemed to be seeing everything through a romantic haze. All the sounds that reached her ears were like music. The air she breathed was sweet. As often as she could, she touched her bridegroom, her enjoyment of the morning increased ten-fold because she was with Travis.

Later, the Indians played the traditional stickball game, fast and furious, accompanied by much shouting, excitement, and laughter. The competing teams hit a stuffed ball with looped wooden rackets, trying to strike a mat on top of a tall post that represented the type of post victims of warring tribes had once been tied to, Travis explained.

"Seminole games aren't competitive in the same way as the white man's games like football or baseball. The competing players encourage each other, and honor, skill, and sportsmanship—rather than the satisfaction of winning—are what's important."

That afternoon, Travis and Lindi started for home. She felt reluctant to return to civilization. Out there in the wilderness, life had an entirely different dimension. She understood more clearly the harmony between the Seminoles and the Everglades. What had transpired between herself and Travis had been simple, direct, and uncomplicated. With their return to the complexities of twentieth-century life, nothing seemed as simple as the love between a man and a woman that blossomed under the shelter of a Seminole *chikee* during a thunderstorm. When they left the Everglades, would the romantic dream of the night before turn into dust?

Lindi suddenly felt frightened. She had a premonition that a different kind of storm awaited her after they left Big Cypress Swamp.

Travis wasn't much help in dispelling her fears. He had fallen back into one of his taciturn moods. He said less than a dozen words all the way home.

It was night when they arrived at her houseboat.

"I'm starved," she said, "and I'm sure you must be too. I'll make us something to eat."

Travis followed her into her floating home. He settled on the couch with a book while she busied herself in the kitchen. It was a domestic scene. She thought with an ache that it would be lovely to live with Travis like this, to come home with him at night and share their meals. But he had said nothing about their future together, and she was afraid to ask.

They had a meal of cold roast beef, cheese, tossed salad, and wine. Travis helped her clean up the dishes, then pulled her down on his lap on the couch. They listened to records for awhile. He seemed reluctant to have the evening end—she wanted it to go on forever.

"Let's go out on the deck," he said suddenly.

They held hands as they walked outside. The sky was clear and cloudless as if washed clean by the previous night's storm. Travis pointed up at the Milky Way. "The Seminoles believe the Milky Way is a path that the spirits of the dead follow when they go to heaven."

"That's a lovely idea."

She looked up at his strong profile in the starlight. She was so much in love her throat ached from the fullness in her heart.

Restlessly, he asked, "D'you want to go swimming?"

"All right. Let me change into a bathing suit."

He drew her into his arms. His gaze was soft, lingering on her features in a manner that made her heart throb. A smile tugged at the corner of his lips. A mischievous gleam twinkled in his eye. "Ever go skinny dipping when you were a kid?"

She blushed. "Not exactly."

"It's a perfect night for it. Nobody around. I'd have

to go all the way back to my place to get a suit. Why bother?"

He was giving her a challenging look, and she felt reckless. "All right," she stammered.

"We'll swim out to the island."

"You first," she said, feeling her cheeks growing warmer. "I'll turn my back."

He chuckled. "Modest, eh?"

"Humor me, okay? It's going to take a little while before I get used to walking around naked in front of you."

"Okay."

She turned. She heard the rustle of his clothes falling on the deck. Then there was a splash and a shout from the water. She turned and saw him waving at her. "Come on." He grinned.

"You promised not to look."

"All right," he agreed. He turned and began swimming away in slow, lazy strokes.

Lindi quickly shed her garments. The cool night air washed over her body. She felt a sense of freedom, of abandon. She left the deck in a smooth dive. The water closed around her, invigorating and refreshing. Tiny bubbles tickled her. When she broke the surface, she laughed with the pure joy of being young and alive.

She caught up with Travis. Their bodies glistened with the pale sparkle of phosphorescence in the starlight. They swam close together. The rhythm of their strokes made her think of the rhythm of their lovemaking. It was as if the life pulse of their bodies beat to the same tempo.

They reached their private island, the tiny sandbar just big enough for the two of them. She no longer felt self-conscious as Travis's hungry gaze drank in the vision of her glistening curves. Instead, she gloried in the fire the sight of her ignited in his eyes. Right now he looked at her as if she were the only woman in the entire world. He seemed oblivious of the sea, the sky, the entire universe around them. His vision had but one focus—her.

How exciting it was, she thought, to be so utterly the center of a man's attention, to be totally absorbed by his gaze, his emotions, his desire.

He drew her close to him. Her bare flesh clung to his. Flash fires ignited all through her body. His lips claimed hers. She surrendered willingly, eagerly.

The waves lapped around them with a gentle, undulating rhythm. The night breeze carried the intimate whispers of their lovemaking across the sea where they dissolved with the mists. A night bird flew overhead. The sand, still warm from the day's sun, was a soft bed. Her senses reeled. There was no room for conscious thought . . . only the soaring heights of ecstasy in the arms of the man she loved.

The stars had moved across the heavens in a slow, stately procession when Travis sat up beside Lindi. She gazed up at him, seeing the dark, troubled shadows in his eyes again. It was devastating to be so close to him, to be one with him, and then to have the curtain suddenly drawn and to feel shut out from the private world into which he had withdrawn.

"Travis—"

Lost in his brooding thoughts, he didn't reply.

She suddenly felt chilled and shivered. "I want to go back," she said shortly.

"All right."

Again they swam. But this time, she felt isolated from him. The joyous abandon that had thrilled her so on the swim out was gone. The adventurous mood of the evening had evaporated. She didn't know what had gone wrong, only that she felt terribly alone. Not knowing, not understanding—that was what troubled her the most.

When they reached the houseboat, Lindi gathered up her clothes and went inside to shower and change into clean shorts and a blouse.

Later, she found Travis still on deck. He had dried himself with a towel she'd given him and was dressed in his blue jeans and shirt. Still barefoot, he stood leaning against the rail, staring over the water at— what? She couldn't begin to know.

He turned to look at her. There was nothing in his eyes to give her a clue to his inner thoughts. She joined him at the rail. Until now she had lacked the courage to put her doubts and fears into words. She hadn't wanted to risk destroying the delicate fabric of the romantic dream she had lived the past twenty-four hours. But sooner or later she had to face reality.

She could no longer hide from the knowledge that not once during the past twenty-four hours had Travis said he loved her. He had desired her, needed her, wanted her desperately, yes. But there had been no word of love spoken. And during the peaceful moments between the storms of passion there had been nothing from him about a permanent commitment.

Where do we go from here? she wondered with an ache. The night before, they had been married in an ancient Seminole ritual, but as Travis had pointed out, they'd been on a Seminole reservation where the laws and customs were not those of the white man. Now they were back in their own society where there were different laws. The ancient marriage rites of the Seminoles were not recognized here. She had no claim on Travis Machado.

He would have been totally insensitive not to be aware of her troubled thoughts. Couldn't he read them clearly in her eyes?

He seemed on the verge of blurting out something. There was a moment of brittle silence. He appeared to be involved in a bitter inner struggle. Then the struggle, whatever it was, became too great; he drew back, and once again the shadows in his eyes closed in, shutting her out.

His voice was abrupt. "It's late. I'd better get back to my place. Good night, Lindi." He kissed her, and then he was gone.

She stood alone at the rail for a long time, knowing she had never felt so alone in her life. Her throat ached, and the burning tears trickled silently down her cheeks. She had no one to blame but herself; she had invited heartbreak by her rash, impulsive, head-long plunge into Travis Machado's arms. How naive she had been to believe that the Indian marriage ceremony had meant anything to him! Had she been childish enough to think he would want to make it a permanent commitment by going through a civil ceremony with her once they were back in civilization?

That night her tear-soaked pillow was her only consolation. The next morning when she got to work, Travis was not in his office. On her desk, she found a sealed note from him. She tore it open with trembling fingers and read the words through a blur of tears. Gradually her heartbreak turned to anger.

Lindi,
I wish I could explain more fully. There are some personal matters I have to work out. It's very difficult for me to put it into words at this point. I will be away for a few days.

Travis

She read the few lines over several times as the anger inside her grew until it blotted out all other emotion. "Well, you've done it again, Travis Machado!" she cried. She crumpled his note into a tight ball and flung it into her wastebasket. "At least this time I think I'm cured! For good! I hope you never come back!"

# Chapter Thirteen

$\mathscr{I}$ must talk with you about something rather important," Shodra Nichols said. "Could we have dinner together this evening?"

Lindi was momentarily at a loss to know how to answer. That morning had been frantic. First she had come to work to find Travis's note informing her that he was pulling one of his disappearing acts again. The result had been fresh emotional wreckage. She was furious with him and even more angry with herself for ever becoming involved with Travis Machado. She was upset and distraught. Then she was faced with a new onslaught of stress when problems rose over the new printing equipment that was to be put into operation that week. She had spent most of the morning in the pressroom, wrestling with these matters. By the time they were under control she felt like an emotional basket case. She returned to her office with a splitting headache. Close to tears, she sat down and tried to make some sense of her notes for the Everglades article. At that point the phone rang. It was Shodra Nichols, inviting her to dinner that evening.

Lindi's mind was in shambles. She pressed her fingers against her throbbing temples, trying to deal with this startling development. What possible motive had prompted Shodra to call her? What "rather important" subject could Shodra want to talk with her about? Travis Machado, no doubt. Lindi doubted if she could deal with any more conflict over Travis.

An excuse to avoid the meeting was on her lips when, as if divining her thoughts, Shodra said, "It's a business matter."

"A business matter?" Lindi struggled to shift mental gears. What possible business matter could Shodra have in mind? Then an icy thought crossed Lindi's mind. Shodra owned this building. Her heart took a sudden plunge. Was Shodra going to use the lease as a weapon because of her jealousy over Travis's interest in Lindi? *The Clarion* was walking a thin financial tightrope. An unexpected expense like an increase in rent could break the rope. "Is—is it about the lease?" Lindi asked, her throat constricting.

"Oh, nothing like that. It's really too complicated to discuss on the phone, and it's rather confidential. Could I pick you up at your place about seven-thirty?"

Lindi touched her tongue to dry lips. "Y-yes . . . that will be fine."

"Good. See you then."

Lindi struggled with this new development for awhile and finally gave up trying to make any sense of it. She spent several hours working up a rough draft of her Everglades article. Then she left her office early, pausing at Rachel Douglas's desk on the way out. "Rachel, I'm going to take some film to the photo lab. I won't be back this afternoon."

"Okay, Boss. Those the pictures you took in the Everglades?"

"Yes."

"Get some good ones?"

"I think so."

Rachel was giving her an envious look. "I'll bet it was an exciting experience, seeing the Big Cypress Swamp with Travis."

Lindi felt a rush of blood warm her cheeks. She mumbled, "Yes, Travis is a competent guide. He knows that area quite thoroughly."

"See lots of wild animals?"

Lindi nodded. "Quite a few. I'll show you the pictures when they're processed."

She left the building. After dropping off the film, she went home, took two aspirin, and lay down with a cold compress on her forehead. She tried to nap, but her thoughts were too feverish. All the events of the past weeks paraded through her mind like flashes from a vivid movie. What a drastic turn her life had taken with that phone call from Frances telling her of her brother's accident! At that point fate had seized her destiny. She had been carried along on a tide of events over which she seemed to have no control. The thought was frightening.

She relived her first meeting with Travis Machado at the Miami airport. The first impression he had made was as fresh and vivid as the moment it happened. She could never forget how his dark-eyed gaze had sent a hot flush all over her body, how his touch had made her tremble. Whatever it was that stirred a violent physical attraction between a man and a woman—electricity, body chemistry—it had existed for them in an overwhelming quantity. There had been more, though, as she came to know Travis as a person. She had felt a spiritual response to his inner being, a kind of cosmic destiny that bound her to him, made her his woman. The things she had learned about him had awakened respect and admiration. He was intelligent and sensitive. He was very much a man. In the wilderness of the Everglades, she had felt totally safe with him. She had known that whatever happened in that desolate, frightening swamp, he would take care of her.

And yet there was the dark, brooding side of him, the frustrating wall she could not penetrate, the mystery she could not solve.

As she thought about how she had surrendered to Travis, how she'd let her emotions rule her mind, she was totally humiliated. What a naive idiot she had been to believe the Indian wedding ceremony had the same meaning for Travis that it had for her! Thinking about that awakened her anger afresh. It should have meant something to him—after all, the Seminoles were his people. He had obviously grown up in their tradition. How could he use their sacred ceremony just to satisfy his male ego with another conquest? He was despicable!

Then another thought assailed her. Maybe he had lied to her! Maybe there hadn't been a wedding ritual at all! She didn't understand their language. All she knew was that they'd stood before the council of elders; words were spoken; she and Travis drank some kind of herb potion. Travis told her it had been a wedding ceremony. He could have deceived her about that to make her more vulnerable. Then, having satisfied his macho ego, he wanted to wash his hands of her. Conveniently leaving town was a neat way to do it!

In a frenzy of frustrated anger and humiliation, she pounded her pillow, wishing it was Travis Machado she was hitting.

The worst part of her emotional turmoil was the ambivalence she felt toward Travis. She would catch herself reliving the thrill of his kisses, the ecstasy of his lovemaking, and she would be swept into a beautiful, misty realm of fantasy. Her body would tingle, a flush would warm her all over. And then the fantasy would come crashing down into a pile of bitter wreckage and Travis would be the dark monster who had destroyed her young dream. How she hated him for that!

Was she going to be cursed for the rest of her life with this conflict—torn between tender memories and bitter anger toward this man who had turned her life upside-down?

She wished she had never come to Palmettoville . . . had never laid eyes on Travis Machado!

She glanced at her watch and thrust the painful subject of Travis Machado from her mind. It was time to get dressed. She didn't feel any more rested, but at least her headache was gone.

From her wardrobe, she selected a pale yellow blazer and skirt. She knew that no matter what she wore, Shodra was going to appear in something infinitely more stylish. But the yellow of the suit did flatter Lindi's red hair and green eyes. The front-pleated A-line skirt emphasized her slender waist. The floral print blouse that went with the outfit had a stand-up ruffled collar with a self-fabric bow whose ends fluttered down necktie style. 'It made her feel very feminine.

The horn of Shodra's cream-colored Cadillac convertible sounded out front at precisely seven-thirty. Lindi wasn't surprised. The glamorous widow had impressed her as the kind of sharp businesswoman who kept appointments on the dot.

Lindi stepped from the deck of her houseboat to the dock and slid into the passenger side of the expensive car. As Lindi expected, Shodra looked exquisite in a simple white sheath that was molded to her glamorous figure. Her shoulders were bare. A rounded neckline dipped just enough to give teasing glimpses of her lush bosom and called attention to a string of costly pearls at her throat. Her golden hair was caught up in a bun at the nape of her neck, with not a single strand out of place, despite the fact that the top of the convertible was down. Her high-heeled shoes moved efficiently from the brake to the accelerator. The overall impression was that of cool sophistication. Beside her, Lindi felt self-conscious and inexperienced.

"Hello, Lindi," Shodra said coolly. She swung the long, sleek car around, driving as skillfully as Lindi thought she probably did everything. "I thought we'd have dinner at the country club, if that's all right with you. We have a seafood buffet tonight that's usually quite good."

"That's all right." Lindi nodded.

There were enough wealthy people living in Palmettoville to support an attractive country club. The main building was nestled in a grove of royal palms. Scarlet bougainvillea grew around it in profusion. The grounds were immaculately tended—the hedges were trimmed and the flower beds were lush with tropical plants. The club had a splendid eighteen-hole golf course and an Olympic-sized swimming pool. The building housed a ballroom, a lounge, and a restaurant with a wall of glass overlooking a small lake.

The buffet offered a variety of shrimp, fish, and oyster dishes along with salads and vegetables. "We have a new chef," Shodra said. "He's excellent."

As delicious as the food looked, Lindi had little appetite.

They were seated at a quiet table near the expansive picture windows. Shodra ordered cocktails from the bar as Lindi gazed out at the lake, watching a pair of swans glide majestically between the water lilies.

When the drinks came, Shodra sipped her martini, her violet eyes gazing at Lindi with a long, steady look. "Was your trip into the Everglades productive?"

Lindi flushed. Was she always going to do that every time someone brought up the subject? "Yes," she said shortly. "I think I got some interesting photographs."

"Yes, I should think you would. Travis is an excellent guide."

Lindi shrugged. "He should be, since he is a Seminole."

Shodra smiled coolly. "Did he tell you that?"

"Not exactly. He speaks their language. They treat him like one of the tribe. I assumed—"

"He was raised by the Mikasuki Seminoles," Shodra explained, "though he isn't Indian himself."

Lindi gave Shodra a close look. What other carefully guarded secrets about Travis Machado did Shodra know? Lindi wondered if Shodra knew why Travis disappeared from time to time on his mysterious trips out of town. Perhaps she even knew where he was right now. She wished she knew the extent of Shodra's information about the mysteries of Travis Machado, but she lacked the courage to ask. Besides, she doubted if Shodra would tell her.

Shodra had said this meeting was about a business matter. Yet here they were starting right off on the subject of Travis Machado. Lindi didn't like it. She knew Shodra must be seething with jealousy over the trip Lindi had taken alone with Travis, staying together overnight in the wilderness with all that implied. It was understandable that Shodra would feel compelled to do some poking and prying. But Lindi had no intention of playing that game. "You said you had a business matter to discuss?"

"Yes. It has to do with *The Clarion*. Do you want to talk about it now or after we eat?"

Lindi looked at the other woman sharply. "I doubt if I could eat anything after that statement until I find out what it means."

Shodra smiled. "I can hardly blame you. But please don't feel threatened. It's nothing like that at all. To get right to the point, would you be interested in selling *The Clarion?*"

For a moment Lindi was speechless. She had anticipated a number of things that might be behind this meeting and had rehearsed a response to each of them. This caught her totally unprepared. "Sell *The Clarion?*" she echoed, her mind temporarily blank. Then she recovered to some degree and stammered, "Why would you want to buy the newspaper?"

Shodra laughed softly. "I don't want to buy it. I have my hands full keeping up with the businesses I already own. The last thing I'd want to take on is a newspaper that is operating in the red."

"We're not operating in the red," Lindi exclaimed, her eyes flashing.

"Perhaps not," Shodra said, an amused smile playing around her lips. "But you must be darn close to it. You don't have to get your hackles up, Lindi. I've been around this town all my life, and I pretty well know the profit-and-loss condition of most of the operations here. I keep a close feel of the business pulse of the community. I know that your brother Roy was just barely getting by. Then he launched his editorial campaign against the development movement and lost a bunch of advertisers overnight. Now you've taken over, and you've gone way out on a limb to modernize your printing plant. You're up to your neck in debt. If you can't turn things around in a few months, *The Clarion* will go under. Let's face facts, unpleasant as they may be."

Lindi tried to keep her anger under control. Everything Shodra said was true. However, Lindi didn't appreciate having it laid out in such a cold-blooded, heartless manner.

"If all that is true, why on earth would you want to buy the business?" she asked coldly.

Shodra raised an eyebrow. "I already told you, I don't want to buy it."

"Who, then?" Lindi asked, growing confused.

"Let's say I was approached this week by an interested party. This gentleman asked me to act as a kind of go-between—a business representative, if you want to call it that. He is serious about wanting to buy your business, Lindi. He is in a position to put up a sizable piece of earnest money immediately. And the offer he has made is extremely generous."

Shodra paused, reached into her handbag for one of her business cards, and wrote on the back of it with a small gold pen. She pushed the card across the table. "How does that figure strike you?"

Lindi stared at the figure the other woman had written. She blinked, thinking she must have read it wrong, but a second look confirmed the amount. "Yes," she said, nodding slowly. "It certainly is a good offer!"

Seconds ticked by as Lindi pondered this surprising development. Shodra sipped her martini, apparently content to be silent for the moment.

As Lindi recovered from the first wave of surprise, she sorted it all out and came up with an obvious answer. She directed a narrowed look at Shodra. "The person offering this kind of money for a small-town newspaper and printing firm that is hanging on by a thread is not doing it for sound business reasons unless he's a complete and total moron."

Shodra nodded. "I would say that is a valid observation."

"So it must be someone who is willing to part with a lot of money just to shut us up."

"Another good observation."

"The people behind this development scheme. They want *The Clarion* out of the way and are willing to pay big bucks to do it. We must be more of a thorn in their side than I'd suspected!" Lindi cried triumphantly.

Shodra simply smiled, but her blond head tilted forward.

"Let me see. There's the real estate broker, Lester Martin. He's trying to swing that condominium deal that The Clearwater Neighborhood Association has been fighting."

Shodra made a flicking motion as if brushing away a fly. "Lester is small peanuts. He's the local real estate hotshot, but he doesn't have this kind of money."

"Then it must be the developer, C.C. Rothman."

"Now," Shodra said, "you're getting warm."

Lindi looked across the table with a narrowed, hostile gaze. "And you're on his side."

"No, I'm not."

"Well, you're acting as his agent in this business offer, aren't you?"

"That doesn't necessarily mean I'm in his camp. He came to me because I'm a well-known, established businesswoman in town. He knew that with feelings running high the way they are, you probably wouldn't even listen to his proposition. He thought you might consider the offer in a more rational manner if I brought it to you."

Lindi mulled over this surprising new development. Finally she sighed. "Well, if it were up to me I'd tell him where he could put his offer, but the final decision really isn't mine. The business still belongs to my brother."

"Yes. I knew you'd want to talk it over with Roy. It is a good offer."

Lindi glanced at the other woman. "You think we should accept it, don't you?"

"That's not for me to decide."

"It would mean security for Roy and Frances," Lindi admitted reluctantly. "It would gall me to turn the paper over to that man. I'd feel as if we were selling out this town. He'd immediately turn it into a propaganda machine for his development scheme. The people who care about this town would have no public voice any more. Still, Roy has to make the decision."

Shodra slipped a slender gold case from her bag, placed a cigarette between her carmine lips, and touched a flame to the tip with a lighter. She inhaled, then pursed her lips thoughtfully. "For what it's worth, I can tell you that I'm on your side in this development thing. This has nothing to do with you and me personally, Lindi MacTavish. I've lived in Palmettoville since I was a child, and I like the quality of life we have here. Unless we are careful and make long-range growth plans, developers like C.C. Rothman will step in and turn our town into an urban sprawl with all the ugly things that go with it—traffic problems, crime, and deteriorating neighborhoods. Profit is his only motive. I'm glad you're running for city council. I hope you win the election."

Shodra's endorsement came as a surprise. As jealous as she was about Travis, Lindi thought Shodra would try to sabotage her chances in the election out of spite. She was relieved that the businesswoman could be this objective. Lindi would much rather have Shodra on her side during the election campaign.

After her meeting with Shodra Nichols that night Lindi drove to her brother's house. She described the offer that had been made for the newspaper.

Roy was propped up in bed. "Boy, that's a lot of money," he said, his eyes wide with surprise.

"Yes, it is. *The Clarion* must be a real thorn in their side."

"Of course it is. Especially with the election coming up. The influence of the town's only newspaper could go a long way toward swinging the election."

There was a lengthy silence as Roy stared at the figures Lindi had given him.

Lindi said, "Shodra thinks it's a heck of a good offer. You're sure not likely to get another one like it."

"What do you think, Sis?"

"Well, it would mean security for you and Frances

and the kids. You could stop worrying about whether *The Clarion* is going to keep its head above water from month to month."

"That didn't exactly answer my question."

"Roy, I can't answer that question for you. It's not my decision to make."

He grinned crookedly. "You're my big sister. I never was any good at making decisions. What do you honestly think about *The Clarion*'s chances of surviving if we don't sell out?"

"I honestly don't know," Lindi admitted candidly. "I have hopes that with this new printing equipment we can increase the business. I've already been approached by the publisher of the *Coastal News*, over in Key Winslow, to print their weekly edition on our offset presses. We've picked up some other job-printing work. But Roy, the next six months are going to be nip and tuck. The way the election turns out may have a lot to do with the paper's future. If we win, it will mean that most of the voters in town are on our side. We can stand behind the zoning laws, maybe even make them stronger. That will put an end to this whole corrupt development scheme. I suspect C.C. Rothman and his backers will quietly fold their tents and slither out of town. On the other hand, if we lose—well, the developers will take over the town, and the way they despise *The Clarion*, they'll make certain we bite the dust."

"So, it's pretty much of a crap shoot, right?" Roy sighed.

Lindi nodded. "That's the way it looks now."

Roy chewed his lip. "Boy, I hate to make decisions." He glanced across the room. On his dresser was a framed picture of their grandfather. The old man glared out of the photo from under his craggy eyebrows. Roy chuckled. "Look at the expression on the old man's face. I'd swear he's been listening to every word we've said."

Lindi followed Roy's gaze. "I wouldn't be surprised if he had." She smiled fondly.

"You know what he'd say. Damn the offer. Print the truth."

"I guess he would."

Roy sighed. "If I sell the paper now, I'd turn my back on everything he taught me. He'd come back to haunt me, I know he would. After all, I started this whole thing with the editorials I wrote against this development plan from the very beginning. I've been proud of the stand I took. It's the one grown-up thing I've done in my entire life. How can I turn chicken now, when so much depends on *The Clarion*?" He slowly crumpled the paper containing the figures C.C. Rothman had offered. "Let's tell them to shove their offer, Lindi. We'll keep the paper going, sink or swim. If the town drowns, we'll go down with it!"

Lindi spent the next day writing and polishing her article about the Everglades. The photo lab delivered the processed film. She studied the contact prints, selecting the ones she would send to the New York publisher and those she would use in the feature article that would appear in *The Clarion*.

It was after dark when she got home that night. As she was preparing a sandwich and salad for supper, she heard the familiar sound of a typewriter from across the water. Her fingers trembled and her breath caught in her throat. Travis was back. He was in his houseboat, apparently working feverishly on his novel. Why hadn't he shown up at the office today? Had he just gotten back?

Lindi ate very little. Her appetite had vanished. She moved restlessly around the main cabin. The clicking of the typewriter made her nervous. She selected some records and turned on her stereo to drown out the sound of the typing from Travis's houseboat. She tried to read and realized she had scanned the same page twice without having the slightest grasp of its meaning.

Too many questions were churning through her mind. Why was Travis treating her like this? How could he be so cruel? He had vanished into thin air. Then, when he came back, he hadn't made any effort to talk to her. He'd gone to work on his book. Didn't he realize how she had missed him, how upset she was? She couldn't believe he was that insensitive.

She struggled with possible explanations for his actions. Was this his way of cold-bloodedly ending their affair, of washing his hands of her?

Finally, she threw her book down. She couldn't go on like this. She had to confront Travis . . . settle once and for all where she stood with him.

She walked out of the cabin and started down the dock. She was mentally rehearsing what she would say to him. Should she be casual?

"Hi. I thought I heard your typewriter. When did you get back?"

Or should she be honest about her feelings, cut out the pretense—let him know immediately how she felt?

"Travis, what's the big idea, anyway? How could you just go dashing off with no more explanation than that short note? And why didn't you come see me the minute you got home?"

Suddenly, she froze in her tracks. She could see Travis's houseboat moored a block away. Pulled up at the dock was a cream-colored Cadillac convertible. She didn't have to see the registration slip to know it was Shodra's flashy car. Travis's typewriter was silent now.

A rush of tears burned her eyes. Bitterly, she said aloud, "Well, I think I just got my answer."

# Chapter Fourteen

Travis knocked on her office door the next morning. She had dreaded facing him after what she had seen. She hoped her eyes were no longer puffy from the flood of tears that had soaked her pillow last night. All she had left now was her pride.

"Travis, I'm very busy today," she said shortly.

He stood in the doorway, his dark eyes solemn and thoughtful. Slowly, he moved into the office, closing the door behind him. "I know you're angry with me for taking off those few days."

"Oh, it really doesn't matter," she said tonelessly. "You can take off whenever you wish. We seem to manage quite well without you."

He leaned against the wall, crossing his arms. "Does that mean you'd just as soon I didn't come back at all?"

"You can take it to mean anything you wish," she said bitterly.

There was a moment of brittle silence. Lindi desperately wanted him to leave her office. His presence was tearing her apart. Right now she wished he and his mistress would get in Shodra's flashy car and drive out of her life forever. He would leave behind an emptiness no other man could ever fill, but at least there wouldn't be this agony every time he came near her.

"I finished the last chapter of my book last night," he said.

"Oh? When did you have time?"

"What do you mean by that?"

I mean, she thought, how could you be writing when you and Shodra were busy making love? Perhaps she inspired him to write the final love scene in his book!

The thought of Shodra in his arms tore into Lindi's heart with agonizing pain. How could he do that after Lindi had given him all of her love? Then she thought the answer to a man like Travis was—easily. Hadn't he betrayed Shodra when he went off into the swamp with Lindi, married her in the Indian ceremony, and made love to her that stormy night? Lindi should have known better than to trust his motives when the whole town knew of his affair with Shodra. She supposed that she had naively believed his romance with Shodra had ended, that Lindi had won him for herself. What a blind little fool she had been! How she despised herself for being so dumb. How she hated him!

"Once you said you'd take a look at the book I was working on," he reminded her.

"Yes," she said woodenly. That seemed a century ago.

"Well, I brought it along this morning. Of course, I

didn't know you were going to be in such a vile mood."

Lindi glared at him. He had a lot of nerve, making a nasty crack like that when he was responsible for the emotional state she was in. Of course, he wasn't aware that she had seen Shodra's car parked at his doorstep so late. He probably thought he was very cleverly hiding his duplicity from her, that she was angry with him only because he'd taken two days off from his job.

"Bring your manuscript in here," she said icily. "I'll look it over as soon as I have time."

"Don't strain yourself." He was responding to her mood by growing angry in return. His eyes reminded her of that night in the swamp when lightning flashed in the black sky. He walked out of her office.

Good riddance, she thought, and promptly felt the flood of tears returning. She fled to the washroom, where she cried in private and then bathed her face with a wet towel until she could face the world again.

When she returned to her office, Rachel told her she'd had a call from Grady Alexander. She returned the call and heard Grady's warm, cheerful voice. "Thanks for calling back, Lindi. I know you're busy, but I was wondering if we could get together for dinner tonight? I'd really like a chance to talk over some plans for the election campaign."

Lindi welcomed a break from the emotional turmoil she'd been going through. Plunging into the council race with all her energy might be good therapy, under the circumstances. "All right, Grady. I'd like that."

"Great! Can I pick you up around seven?"

"Yes . . . seven would be fine."

"See you then."

For the remainder of the day, Travis stayed in his

own office. He made no further offer to talk to her or
to bring her the manuscript.

That night she dressed for her dinner appointment
with Grady in a casual, sleeveless, one-piece dress and
high-heeled sandals. She didn't think of it as a date,
though she would welcome an evening of companionship with a man as nice and uncomplicated as Grady
Alexander. What had ever possessed her to become
involved with someone as complex as Travis Machado
was more than she would ever be able to understand.
He was like the swamp he loved, wild and untamed,
filled with complicated trails, mysterious dark backwaters, unfathomable depths, stormy moods.

Grady called for her promptly at seven. "My, you
sure look pretty." He smiled awkwardly.

"And you look very nice," she returned. He did,
indeed, look pleasantly neat and relaxed in a pair of
sharply creased grey slacks and a short-sleeved blue
sport shirt.

She sensed that he was a bit shy. It was a welcome
change not to be in the company of a man whose very
presence kept her insides churning.

Grady's small foreign car was parked at the dock
near her houseboat. He opened the car door for Lindi
and then went around and slid behind the wheel. As
they drove away, they passed Travis's houseboat. He
had just stepped out of his cabin door. He stood on
the deck, staring at them, a strange expression in his
eyes. Lindi looked away, pretending she hadn't seen
him.

Grady took her to a quiet Italian restaurant on the
fringe of town. It was not as glamorous as the country
club where she had dined with Shodra Nichols a few
nights earlier, but it had a pleasant atmosphere and
the food was good.

"That's an unusual home you have," Grady said. "What's it like, living on a houseboat?"

"Very nice," Lindi said and added in a mutter, "though I don't care much for my neighbors."

"I beg your pardon?"

"Nothing. Just thinking out loud. Tell me how the campaign is going."

"Very well, I think. D'you know, we've gotten a surprising number of contributions. I don't think money is going to be a problem. That's one of the things I wanted to talk with you about—how to spend our campaign funds in the most effective way. I know you're experienced in this sort of public relations work. That kick-off rally of yours was really something. It set the town back on its heels. People are still talking about it. I want to see what other ideas you have. The election is only a couple of weeks away," Grady said. "We need to get busy."

"Yes, we do," Lindi agreed. "I've been planning some full-page ads. We'll start them this week. By the way, you'll be interested in this: it looks as if we've got them running scared. Would you believe that C. C. Rothman has offered us a big chunk of money to buy out *The Clarion*? That can only mean that our newspaper campaign is getting results." She told him about her meeting with Shodra Nichols. "Incidentally," she added, "we told him what he could do with his offer!"

Grady was all smiles. "That's terrific news, Lindi! But we can't let up on our efforts. The next important thing is to meet the public, make a lot of speeches. In a small town, the voters want to see and hear you and shake your hand." He drew a paper from his pocket. "I've made a list of possible forums. The Lions, the Rotary, women's clubs, veterans' organizations, a knife-and-fork luncheon club . . ."

Lindi examined the list. "You expect me to appear at all these places?" she gasped.

He nodded. "To be frank, Lindi, I don't consider myself much of a speechmaker. I was very impressed by the way you handled yourself that night at the city council meeting when you jumped up and spoke against the high-handed way the present council ignores zoning laws just to toady up to the developers. You get some real fire and brimstone into your talk. You've got a lot of spunk. People admire you for that."

Lindi laughed self-consciously. "I was angry that night."

"Well, you ought to get angry more often. Your eyes flash and your voice is firm. It's—it's very becoming."

He was looking at her as he spoke, but then he reddened slightly and dropped his gaze. She smiled. "Thank you, Grady. You're a nice man. I guess it's just the MacTavish Scottish temper coming out." She looked at the list again and sighed. "Well, it looks as if I have my work cut out for me. In addition to talking to these groups, I think we should hold another campaign rally on the eve of the election—maybe have a fish fry at the city park and invite the whole town."

"That's a great idea." Grady nodded enthusiastically.

"Another thing," Lindi said thoughtfully, "is that we need to meet with the sheriff to see if he's made any progress in finding the hit-and-run driver who struck Roy. Y'know, Roy's wife has thought from the beginning that the developers could have been behind that."

Grady stared at her with shocked surprise. "You

mean she thinks it wasn't an accident—that Rothman and his people hired a hit man to deliberately run Roy down?"

"Well, it's only a suspicion, but I wouldn't put it past that bunch to do something like that."

"I find it hard to believe they'd resort to violence," Grady said slowly, "but I guess it is possible. If it could be proven, that would certainly guarantee us the election."

"Grady, you find it hard to believe because you're such a fine person, you can't conceive of people stooping that low. I find it kind of hard to accept too, but greed can make men do ruthless things."

Grady nodded. "Of course you're right. We'll make it a point to pay a visit to the sheriff's department."

Over dinner, they outlined the speeches she would make, planning how best to present the issues. Afterward, Grady took her home. He saw her to her door, giving her hand a squeeze as they said good-night. "Lindi, this was a very nice evening. I think we've accomplished a lot and . . . well, I just enjoyed being with you."

"Thank you, Grady. I enjoyed it too."

Lindi sensed more than a friendly interest in Grady's manner. He was a very eligible widower, nice looking, stable, kind, and considerate. If she had never become involved with Travis Machado, she might have wanted to give a friendship with Grady a chance to develop. But after the heartbreak Travis had dealt her, it was going to be a long, long time before she'd think about getting involved with another man.

"Hello," Grady suddenly said, bending down. "Were you expecting some mail?" He handed her the thick Manila envelope that had been propped against her door.

She frowned. Then she thought she knew what it was. "Just some material from the office," she mumbled. "Good night, Grady."

Inside her cabin, she stared at the Manila envelope. She knew it was Travis's novel. There was no note attached. That was typical of him, she thought angrily. Just dump the manuscript on her doorstep as if it were an orphan child, leaving it up to her to either read it or take it back to him. Well, she had no intention of having a confrontation with Travis, nor was she going to read the bulky manuscript. At least not that night. She tossed it on her desk.

The days passed swiftly. She was on a hectic schedule, trying to do her job at the newspaper between appearances at an endless number of civic organizations to make campaign speeches. Travis said nothing to her about the manuscript. At the office, they made a point of avoiding each other.

Every time she came home, her eyes were drawn to the Manila envelope on her desk. She thought that what she ought to do was simply give it back to Travis and tell him she didn't have the time to read it.

Still, the manuscript had an intriguing fascination. She knew that many first novels were semiautobiographical. What if the book held the key to the mystery of Travis Machado? What if it answered the baffling questions about his strange behavior, his secret past?

The temptation to read the story was hard to fight, but with the campaign heating up and going into its final round, she simply did not have the time.

As planned, she and Grady had a private conference with Sheriff Billings about the matter of the hit-and-run driver who had struck her brother. If Lindi hoped for a break in the case, she was disappointed.

"I'm sorry, Miss MacTavish," Billings said. "It's beginning to look as if we'll never know who ran your brother down. All we have to go on is that one person who saw the car speeding away said it had an out-of-state license, but the witness didn't get a number. It's awfully hard to solve a hit-and-run crime when there are so few witnesses to the actual act. Without a license number or a clear description of the car and driver, we have so little to go on. By the time we started looking for the driver, he was in the next county and probably out of the state by that night."

"My brother's wife thinks Roy's editorials could have had something to do with it. He was making some very powerful people angry. After what I've seen of these developers, I think she could be right."

"Yes, ma'am, she talked with me about that, and I agree that is a possibility. But if it was a professional who ran down your brother, it would be doubly hard to find him. A professional at that kind of thing would have duplicate license plates, maybe even another car waiting. On the other hand it could have been an out-of-state tourist who blundered down that side street just as Roy stepped off the curb, hit him, then panicked and drove away. He might have been drinking. You can't imagine how many people get killed or hurt by drivers who had one drink too many."

When Lindi and Grady left the sheriff's office, Lindi was grim. "I don't care what Billings says, I'll always believe C.C. Rothman and his bunch had Roy run over." Then she sighed. "But I might as well become resigned that we'll never be able to prove it. The important thing, I guess, is for Roy to put this tragedy behind him and get on with his life."

"Yes," Grady agreed, "and the best way to punish Rothman is for us to win this election and get him and his greedy crowd out of town!"

Election day arrived. That night a throng of the Neighborhood Association supporters and campaign workers gathered in the offices of *The Clarion.* Lindi's stomach was in knots. Would this turn into a victory party or would the night end in defeat?

They had gambled everything on the issue of strict zoning laws and careful long-range growth planning. In her speeches, Lindi had hammered away at the unscrupulous way the present mayor and city council had favored the big-money developers by caving in on zoning issues. She emphasized the disaster this kind of development would have on the quality of life in Palmettoville.

That night, the mood in the upper floor of *The Clarion* that had served as campaign headquarters was brittle with tension. The early election returns did not look promising for The Association. There were sober expressions on most faces.

Lindi looked around the crowd, at the people who had worked so hard, at the staff of *The Clarion,* who were busy on the phone gathering results from the various precincts. Not until this race began had she realized she had so many friends and supporters in this town.

In the room, she saw Travis with Shodra Nichols close at his side, just as she had been the night of the kick-off campaign party. Lindi felt the same pain, except now it was intensified a thousand times because of all that had happened between her and Travis since that night. She had loved Travis, had become his bride for a short while, and now had lost him forever.

As the precincts totaled their votes, they were posted on a huge board across one side of the room. It was close to nine o'clock when the tabulated votes took a sudden turn in favor of The Neighborhood Association's party. At ten o'clock the outcome of the election was declared. Grady Alexander was the new mayor. All the council candidates running with him on the party ticket had won.

Pandemonium broke loose in the campaign headquarters. Suddenly confetti and streamers appeared. Champagne corks popped. People were shaking hands and pounding one another on the back hysterically. The noise was deafening. Out in the streets, automobile horns were honking. An exuberant Grady Alexander forgot his shyness and gave Lindi a big hug and kiss.

In the furor, Lindi saw Shodra kiss Travis. The joyful mood of the moment turned to ashes for her. Somehow she kept up a smiling front as she acknowledged congratulations. The crowd called for a speech.

Grady Alexander stood on a desk, holding up his hands for silence. It took several minutes before he could be heard. "All I want to say is that you can count on me and the people of your new city council to stand behind our campaign pledges. We are going to treat this matter of Palmettoville's growth sanely. We are not going to let a few opportunists destroy the homes and quality of life we love!"

There was a roar of applause. Horns and whistles blew. Streamers sailed over the crowd.

Again Grady held up his hands. When he could make himself heard, he said, "I want us to hear a few words from a young woman who was the real fireball behind our campaign. Without her energy and promotional ideas, I don't think we would have succeeded. I give you Lindi MacTavish, your hostess at this party, publisher of *The Clarion*, and now city councilwoman!"

Lindi wished she could have escaped this. But Grady extended a hand to help her up on the desk beside him. She was greeted by fresh applause. "I think I've about speeched myself out these past couple of weeks. All that's left for me to say now is thanks to all of you good people who worked so hard to support us. Tonight's victory really belongs to you."

When she was able to get to a phone, she called her brother to share the good news. Frances answered. She was tearful with joy. "Roy is sitting in front of the TV set. Lindi, the therapist was working with him today and Roy took his first step! The doctors are very optimistic now."

"That's the best news tonight!" Lindi cried into the phone over the din around her. She swallowed hard and brushed tears from her eyes.

She knew that this night was a turning point for them all. *The Clarion*, with its modern printing plant, was going to prosper now. The advertisers they had lost would return. The whole corrupt development movement would fold like a punctured balloon. The town would return to normal.

It was a happy ending for everyone except Lindi. Shodra Nichols appeared before her looking flushed and bright-eyed. "Congratulations, Lindi. You won the race. But I won the man." With a smile of victory, she moved back into the crowd and then Lindi saw her at Travis's side, hugging his arm possessively.

Lindi suddenly felt very tired and lonely. She was close to tears and she didn't want to cry here. After a while she was able to slip away unnoticed. She went home.

Wearily, she unlocked the front door of her houseboat and entered the main cabin. She switched on the light. Again her gaze was drawn to the manuscript of Travis's novel on her desk. It was inexcusable of her to have kept it so long. She must return it to him soon, she thought, with an apology.

But as she stared at it, she again was intrigued with its contents. She decided she could no longer resist the temptation to read it. This might be her last chance to settle the questions about Travis Machado that had frustrated and bedeviled her from the first day she met him.

What better time than this to read it? She was through with the pressures of the political campaign. She was too keyed up to sleep.

She made a pot of coffee and settled down with the manuscript and an editing pencil. At five o'clock the next morning, she turned the final page. Her neck was stiff. Her body felt numb with fatigue. Her eyes burned.

She stared at the bundle of typed papers. The title of the novel was *Tomorrow's Dawn*. It was good—far better than anything she had expected. Travis was a born novelist. As a former free-lance editor, she felt excited and thrilled by the possibilities of this work. It could become a best seller. But there was more to it than that. If it was autobiographical as she suspected, then it had revealed to her at last the mystery of Travis Machado.

# Chapter Fifteen

Lindi slept away most of the next day. She didn't go to the office at all. She kept the phone off the hook, knowing she wouldn't have a moment's peace otherwise. Late in the afternoon, she treated herself to a long, leisurely bath, soaking in a sea of bubbles as she read the newspaper. Then she dried herself, rubbing her skin into a healthy glow with a rough towel. She dressed in a cool blouse, shorts, and sandals and prepared a steak and salad. She put a tape on her stereo and ate by candlelight. Her houseboat was rocked gently by the waves. After the turmoil of the past days, she needed this respite of peace and quiet.

Then she glanced out of a window and saw lights on in Travis's houseboat, and her sense of peace evaporated. She had to get his manuscript back to him. It was not a task she faced with much courage.

Mustering all her resources, she bundled up the

manuscript and walked to his place. No matter how she felt about him personally, it wasn't fair to keep his material any longer.

He came to the door when she knocked. His dark-eyed gaze swept over her, sending an icy chill racing up her spine. She chastised herself furiously. Why did she allow herself to react to him this way?

He raised an eyebrow. "Hello, neighbor. Come to borrow a cup of sugar?"

"Don't be sarcastic. I came to return your manuscript and to apologize for not reading it sooner."

"That's okay. It's pretty bad, huh?"

She shook her head slowly. "No, Travis. As a matter of fact, it's excellent."

"Really?" He looked surprised. "I couldn't tell, myself. Are you sure you're not just being polite?"

"Of course not! I earned part of my living in New York by reading and editing manuscripts. I know a darn good piece of writing when I see it. You shouldn't have a bit of trouble getting this book published."

"Well, come on in and tell me how to do it! I'm a newspaperman. I don't know the first thing about getting a book published."

He opened the door wider, stepping back so she could enter his cabin. She hesitated. A thousand warning signals went off inside her. She didn't want to set foot in his houseboat. It contained too many painful memories. She remembered that first night she had come here, that first time she had melted in his arms. She had made a vow never to be alone with Travis Machado again. He had hurt her enough for a lifetime. She simply didn't think she could be trusted not to fall into another trap if he got her alone.

She felt foolish, just standing on his threshold. With

the feeling of a moth circling dangerously near a flame, she stepped cautiously into his cabin.

"Well, I'd say this calls for a celebration," Travis exclaimed. He grinned. "The second one in two nights!" He was in a strange mood. The brooding, dark shadows she was so accustomed to seeing in his eyes were not there tonight. He appeared to be in a lighthearted mood. Was Shodra making him this happy? The thought stabbed Lindi painfully.

He stepped into the kitchen and returned with a bottle of chilled wine and two glasses. He filled them, handed her one, and raised his. "Shall we drink to the success of *Tomorrow's Dawn?*"

She nodded. "All right."

They touched glasses. She looked into his dark eyes and felt as if she were drowning in their swirling depths. Her fingers shook as she raised her glass to her lips and swallowed the wine.

"Now," Travis said, placing the manuscript on his desk and sinking comfortably down onto his couch. "Tell me how to go about approaching a publisher with the book."

Lindi placed her empty glass on the coffee table. She remained standing, planning to flee to the safety of her own home at the earliest opportunity. "I have a friend in New York, a literary agent. He has a very good reputation. I could give him a call, and then you could send him the manuscript. I'm sure he'd be happy to handle it for you."

"That would be very kind of you," Travis said gratefully, his gaze trapping her eyes hypnotically.

Lindi nervously wiped her palms on her slacks. "I want to ask you something, if I may. You don't have to answer, of course."

"Well, I'll try if I can."

"It's about the story in *Tomorrow's Dawn*. It begins with a young boy who was in an airplane that crashed somewhere in the Everglades. The boy was the only survivor. A family of Seminole Indians found him sick and feverish, wandering alone in the swamp. They took him in, nursed him back to health, and raised him. He had been too young at the time of the crash to remember much about it except that he had been traveling somewhere with his parents. It was a small, private plane. His father was the pilot. The boy and his mother were the only other two people in the plane. The wreckage was never found. One of those violent grass fires that sometimes engulfs the Everglades in dry seasons swept through the region. It might have been started by the burning plane. Later, the boy decided the fire had destroyed the plane's remnants, and his parents' bodies had disappeared somewhere back in that swamp wilderness where few people ever go.

"The boy grew up like an Indian, but he was haunted by the uncertainty of who he was. What kind of family did he come from? The question became an obsession with him as he grew older, and he spent his time and energy trying to find some link with his missing past."

Travis listened quietly. For a moment the dark shadows again clouded his eyes. He nodded slowly. "Yes, that's a pretty good summary of the story. What is your question?"

Lindi hesitated. It took a lot of courage to ask her question. Did she even have the right to become this personal? She was afraid of what his reaction might be. Yet she had her own obsession to know the truth. She touched her tongue to her dry lips. Her knees felt weak, and she sank into a convenient chair. Her hands were tightly clenched in her lap. "Many first novels have an element of the author's own life in them. They may even be semiautobiographical." She looked directly at him. "Travis, are you that lost boy in your novel?"

There was a lengthy silence. She could hear the soft creaking of the boat's hull, the muffled slap of waves outside. Travis's face was solemn. He appeared lost in thought. Then he sighed and nodded. "Yes."

Lindi wasn't sure she could define everything she was feeling at that moment. It was as if at last a door had opened and she was coming face to face with the real Travis Machado for the first time.

"That explains those strange disappearances of yours! You'd vanish without warning for several days at a time. You got some kind of clue about your background and took off to investigate, right?"

Again he nodded. "I've spent a lot of time and money on the search. At first it wasn't all that important. I was curious, but I considered the Seminoles my people. For a few years, I worked as a merchant seaman. I was young and adventurous. Wanted to see the world. But in the back of my mind, this thing kept chewing at me. The older I got, the more important it became. I wondered if I might have a brother or sister somewhere. What kind of genes did I carry around with me? Maybe there was a streak of insanity in my family, or some other kind of genetic weakness that I'd pass on to my kids if I ever got married. Questions like that kept haunting me. I don't guess you could understand what it's like, not to have the faintest idea who you are or where you came from, Lindi. You are very much the product of your family. You know all about your lineage, all the way back to Scotland, and you're proud of your people. It was one of the first things you talked with me about when I picked you up at the airport in Miami that day."

Lindi sighed, feeling an unexpected wave of compassion and sympathy for him. "You must have hated me for that."

"Oh, nothing that drastic. But I guess I did envy you, and I was more than a little bitter about it."

"But Travis, I can't understand why you were so secretive about all this. Why didn't you tell Roy or me or somebody why you had to go off on those trips from time to time?"

Travis shrugged. "I don't know if I can explain it exactly. I had some kind of psychological hang-up about it. In a way, I suppose I was ashamed of not knowing who I was. It must be basically important to a person's ego to know at least something about one's roots, I suppose."

"And all this explains why you gave up a good editorial job on a big city newspaper to come down here and settle for a modest job on the staff of a small-town weekly?"

"Well, it all started here. The plane crashed somewhere in the Big Cypress Swamp. It was like going back to start looking from square one. And I wanted to be closer to the only family I'd known, the Seminoles. Also, I had more free time this way to follow up on any leads I could uncover about my identity. That job I had on the big daily kept me strapped down six days a week. I told your brother Roy, when I asked him for this job, that I might have to be out of town from time to time on personal business, and he hired me on that basis."

"How did you ever start looking?"

He smiled wryly. "All I had to go on was my name. I was so young when the plane crashed, I had only the vaguest childhood memories of my parents. I could remember nothing about where we came from. All I could tell my Indian family was that my name was Travis Machado. At first I began researching telephone directories all over the country for the Machado name. It was like hunting a needle in a haystack. Nothing came of it. Then one night I awoke from a sound sleep with a kind of revelation. I don't know if it was a message from my dead parents or if it was just a solution welling up from my subconscious. Maybe, I thought, I had the last name wrong. After all, I was only a toddler when they found me. And the Seminoles had trouble with English pronunciation. I grew up calling myself 'Machado.' I decided to try other sounds that were close: 'Mersado,' 'Meshado,' 'Mikado.' Again I was hunting a needle in a haystack. I spent a fortune on phone calls. I paid a private investigating firm. When we'd get a lead, I'd drop everything and fly to interview people who thought they knew something about a family by that name. We also searched all the old airport flight records and newspaper files for information about the disappearance of a private plane. The trouble was, it happened so long ago—over thirty years ago. It's not easy to find records going that far back."

Lindi had forgotten everything else for the moment. She was completely absorbed in this human drama. "The book leaves the reader guessing about whether the hero ever finds his identity. Is that how the story really ends, Travis?"

He smiled, again with the look of happiness that was so different from the brooding darkness that had characterized him. "I guess I'll have to revise the ending, Lindi. The long search finally paid off. That last time I went out of town, a couple of weeks ago, I got my answer. It was the spelling of my name that had thrown me off for so many years. The family name is Mersada, not Machado. We found a family by that name in Georgia. They did have relatives who disappeared while flying a private plane down to Key West. My father was a doctor. His hobby was flying; he'd been a pilot in World War II. They were on a vacation trip. I didn't have any sisters or brothers, but I have living relatives, some aunts and uncles and cousins. You can imagine their reaction when I told them my story. It was like having a ghost return to their midst. They had long ago considered me dead along with my mother and father. One of my aunts even had a photo album of my family, with pictures of me when I was very little. I brought it back with me. Now I not only know who my real parents were, I know what they look like."

Lindi shook her head in amazement. "That has to be the most remarkable story I've ever heard. Why on earth didn't you tell us about it when you came back? Think what a powerful feature story it would have made for *The Clarion*. 'After Years of Searching, *Clarion* Editor Finds His Long-Lost Family!' "

Travis shrugged. "You were up to your neck in the election campaign. The whole town has had nothing else but the election on its mind. It wasn't the proper time to bother people with my family story. Wait until the city's problems calm down. We can always run a story like this, if you think anyone would be interested."

Lindi thought, I'm certainly interested—more interested than you'll ever know.

She had been so engrossed with Travis's words that

she had forgotten the reality of their situation. Now it all came back to her in a wave of sadness. With an effort, she shook off the spell she had fallen under while listening to Travis's incredible life story. She understood so many things about him now. But it was all too late where they were concerned.

She rose from her chair. Her voice was impersonal now. "Travis, your book should be very successful. I wish you all the luck in the world with it." Then she said, "I have to leave—"

"Is that the only reason you're being so helpful?"

"Wh—what do you mean?"

"The book," he said, nodding toward the manuscript. "Did you take all this time to read it and offer help in getting it published just because you like the book?"

"Yes. . . . Why else would I?"

He stared at her in a way that awoke a fluttering sensation in her stomach. "Well, considering all that happened between us, I was hoping there was some personal interest involved."

"That's all in the past," she said through stiff lips.

His gaze darkened. A shadow crossed his face. She felt as if the temperature in the room had dropped several degrees. "I never thought you were the fickle type," he said slowly, shaking his head.

She gasped. "Me, the fickle type?"

"Well, it's pretty obvious, isn't it? Ever since I came back from that last trip, you've been cold and distant, as if I had some kind of disease. You washed your hands of me. Then you started running around with Grady Alexander."

"I'm not 'running around' with Grady Alexander!" she exclaimed. "We went out to dinner one evening to discuss campaign strategy." Then she thought furiously, Why am I defending myself? How dare he put me on the defensive!

Travis's eyes drilled into her. "Oh? Was his 'campaign' successful?"

She turned white with anger. "You have the gall of a dozen male chauvinists! After the way you cheated on me with Shodra!"

His eyes widened. "What are you talking about?"

"You know good and well what I'm talking about, Travis Machado!" Suddenly all the heartbreak he had dealt her welled up and poured out in a tearful flood. "You used your phony strategy of that trumped-up Indian wedding to make me believe you were serious about our relationship. Then you pull one of your disappearing stunts without any explanation. Two days later, you come sneaking back without a word to me. But you sure let your mistress, Shodra Nichols, know you were back. I saw her car parked at your dock that night. I'm not entirely the trusting, naive little pushover you think I am, Travis!"

With that, she whirled and ran blindly to the door. But Travis stood and with lightning speed intercepted her. She tried to get around him. He caught hold of her waist. Furiously, she beat at him with both fists, venting all the pent-up anger and frustration he had caused her.

Ignoring her blows, he carried her bodily to the couch and held her trapped in his powerful arms until she had exhausted herself.

"You've got a nasty left hook," he said, rubbing a bruise on his cheekbone.

Breathing hard from her violent exertions, she glared at him through burning tears, wishing she had something more lethal than her fists to hit him with.

"Are you through beating up on me?" he asked.

"Good. Then maybe you'll stop acting like a child and listen to me."

She tried to put her hands over her ears, but he caught her wrists and held them in an iron grip, forcing her to listen. "First of all, Shodra Nichols is not, nor ever has been, my mistress. We were friends; that's all. Lately, she's become too possessive. It's true she stopped by my place that night, but I certainly didn't invite her. I could see the way things were going, and I told her we had to stop seeing each other."

Lindi stared at him, hearing what he said but not believing a word.

He went on. "The reason I didn't call you as soon as I got back that evening is because I was so near the end of my book I wanted to wrap it up. I planned to finish it and surprise you with it that night. But after Shodra interrupted me, it took me 'til past midnight to get it finished, and I thought by then it was too late."

"I don't believe you," Lindi said coldly. "Now will you let me up so I can go home?"

"Why don't you believe me? I'm telling you the truth."

"I don't believe you," she said tearfully, "because you've been stringing me along since the very first. That Indian wedding meant nothing to you—if it was a wedding at all. You probably just made up that whole thing . . . a line to get me into bed with you. And I was dumb enough to fall for it!"

He scowled so angrily that some of her own anger was dissipated in a wave of uneasiness. She had the feeling that Travis could be a violent man. Had she pushed him too far?

"I don't lie about something as important and

sacred as a Seminole ceremony," he said, his words like cold, sharp knives.

"Then why did Shodra tell me only last night at the victory celebration that I might have won the election, but she had won you?"

"I don't know why she said that. Female strategy, I guess. I told you she was possessive. Shodra knew from the very beginning that you were a threat. She could see how much I cared for you. She was fighting tooth and nail to hold onto me. But it's you I love, Lindi. I wanted us to have a real wedding ceremony that would make it all legal. But first I wanted to clear up this thing about my own life. I didn't know if it would be fair to you to marry me and start a family not knowing what kind of genetic problems I might have in my past. But it's all right! I come from good, old healthy stock. Part Italian, but I think that will mix with Scottish genes okay . . . at least it will be interesting to see what happens!" He grinned.

Lindi stared at him. A small wisp of incredible happiness was beginning to form deep within her, but it was as fragile as a child's soap bubble. She didn't know whether she could believe him or trust what she was hearing, though she wanted desperately to do so. "Why—why didn't you tell me all this before . . . after you found your family?"

"Because I couldn't get close to you!" he exclaimed. "I told you, you were treating me like a leper. I thought maybe if you read my novel, it would be a way of reaching you, but you'd apparently tossed it into a closet and forgotten about it. Then I saw you with Grady . . . I'll admit I was jealous." He chuckled. "I even considered punching Grady in the jaw."

"I—I wish I could believe all this," she said, on the

verge of tears. She couldn't bear it if he was stringing her along again.

"Maybe this will help convince you."

He went to a cabinet and took out a small box. "When I located my relatives I found they had some family memorabilia and some jewelry that had belonged to my mother. It was rightfully mine, and they were nice enough to turn it over to me with no argument. One of the items is this diamond ring that had been my grandmother's engagement ring. I brought it back to put on your finger if you'll wear it, Lindi."

He slipped the beautiful flashing gem on her finger. "A little big, but we can have it sized," he said.

Then he took both her hands in his and gazed deep into her eyes. "Lindi, there's a wedding ring that goes with it. I love you with all my heart, and I want you to be my wife. As far as I am concerned, we have been married since we went through the ceremony of my Indian family. But perhaps we should make it legal in the eyes of the state. Will you marry me—again?"

Happy tears of joy trickled down her cheeks. "Yes, Travis," she whispered. "Yes, my husband . . . I will marry you again. . . ."

# Silhouette Special Edition

## $2.25 each

| | | | |
|---|---|---|---|
| 111 ☐ Thorne | 128 ☐ Macomber | 145 ☐ Wallace | 162 ☐ Roberts |
| 112 ☐ Belmont | 129 ☐ Rowe | 146 ☐ Thornton | 163 ☐ Halston |
| 113 ☐ Camp | 130 ☐ Carr | 147 ☐ Dalton | 164 ☐ Ripy |
| 114 ☐ Ripy | 131 ☐ Lee | 148 ☐ Gordon | 165 ☐ Lee |
| 115 ☐ Halston | 132 ☐ Dailey | 149 ☐ Claire | 166 ☐ John |
| 116 ☐ Roberts | 133 ☐ Douglass | 150 ☐ Dailey | 167 ☐ Hurley |
| 117 ☐ Converse | 134 ☐ Ripy | 151 ☐ Shaw | 168 ☐ Thornton |
| 118 ☐ Jackson | 135 ☐ Seger | 152 ☐ Adams | 169 ☐ Beckman |
| 119 ☐ Langan | 136 ☐ Scott | 153 ☐ Sinclair | 170 ☐ Paige |
| 120 ☐ Dixon | 137 ☐ Parker | 154 ☐ Malek | 171 ☐ Gray |
| 121 ☐ Shaw | 138 ☐ Thornton | 155 ☐ Lacey | 172 ☐ Hamilton |
| 122 ☐ Walker | 139 ☐ Halston | 156 ☐ Hastings | 173 ☐ Belmont |
| 123 ☐ Douglass | 140 ☐ Sinclair | 157 ☐ Taylor | 174 ☐ Dixon |
| 124 ☐ Mikels | 141 ☐ Saxon | 158 ☐ Charles | |
| 125 ☐ Cates | 142 ☐ Bergen | 159 ☐ Camp | |
| 126 ☐ Wildman | 143 ☐ Bright | 160 ☐ Wisdom | |
| 127 ☐ Taylor | 144 ☐ Meriwether | 161 ☐ Stanford | |

-------------------------------------------------

## Silhouette Special Edition

## Coming Next Month

### The Law Is A Lady by Nora Roberts
When Phillip Kincaid was scouting locations for his movie, he didn't expect the long arm of the law to point him in the right direction. But Victoria Ashton, town sheriff, was just the woman he'd been waiting for.

### That Other Woman by Elizabeth Neff Walker
Courtney certainly seemed to fit the stereotype of the "other woman." But when Eric Collins pursued her, she was swept off her feet like a young girl—right into a storybook romance.

### Come Lie With Me by Linda Howard
Therapist Dione Kelley helped Blake Remington to walk again. So how could she believe his words of love when she knew they were only spoken out of gratitude?

### Saturday's Child by Natalie Bishop
What was Jarrod doing on the set of the soap opera Brynne starred in? He *couldn't* want her back again—not when he had made it brutally clear that he didn't need an actress complicating his life.

### Strictly Business by Kate Meriwether
When her father announced a contest, there was a mad scramble for Roxie's hand by the VP's of his company. Moody Todd McKendrick was the front runner, but why couldn't he be a bit more enthusiastic about winning her?

### The Shadow Of Time by Lisa Jackson
Mara had believed that Shane Kennedy was dead, killed in Northern Ireland. Now he was back—and his bitterness at her apparent desertion vied with the passion still raging between them.